Acknowledge

Writing a novel often is a team effort. A writer draws from the many relationships and experiences of his or her life. I often talk to friends and relatives about plot possibilities and various characters who inhabit the world of my books. There are several people, though, I would like to mention by name. Gretchen Snodgrass has edited all five of my novels. Gretchen loves the written word and is very meticulous when it comes to finding my many mistakes. Gee Gee Rosell, a true Hatteras gal, has been a great help over the last few years, offering her insights and ideas, which have added to the authenticity of my Outer Banks stories. Gee Gee introduced me to Tony Zoccola, a great resource person for technical questions about law enforcement and federal crime agencies. Carolyn Sakowski, president of John F. Blair Publisher, has been very gracious, offering her time and skill as an editor and providing a means through Blair's distribution channels to get the books into brick and mortar and online stores. Thanks Gretchen, Gee Gee, Tony, and Carolyn. I appreciate all of your contributions.

Of course, I must thank my lovely wife, Judy. She has adjusted to living with a writer over the years. We started going to the Outer Banks back in the mid-nineties with our three kids, Rebekah, Sarah, and Joseph. Now we look forward to many more years on those same beaches with our new grandsons—Max, Matthew, and Noah.

I would also like to thank Outer Banks Bookstore owners who have been selling my novels for the last five years. Because of them, *Murder at Whalehead* and *Murder at Hatteras* have become regional bestsellers. Hopefully, *Murder on the Outer Banks* will follow suit.

A Note to Readers

If you enjoyed *Murder on the Outer Banks*, please email all of your friends and tell them about it. Also, I would like to hear from you. Email me with any comments or questions at joecellis@comcast.net and visit my website at www.joecellis.com.

For those of you interested in reading my other novels, they can be ordered from your local bookstore or from the internet at many of the popular online sites. They are also available on Kindle and Nook.

Thanks for checking out my books,

Joe C. Ellis

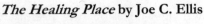

The Healing Place by Joe C. Ellis

ISBN-13: 978-0979665516

The rural community of Scotch Ridge on the outskirts of Martins Ferry, Ohio is a safe haven from the dangers and corruption of the world until the day Nathan Kyler arrives. He has envisioned a diabolic plan—an obsession to sacrifice another human being. His target is Christine Butler, the preacher's daughter. Soon after Christine disappears, the community rallies to find her. A mile from the Scotch Ridge Church deep in the Appalachian woods is a spot known as the Healing Place. Here something incredible happens.

Murder at Whalehead by Joe C. Ellis

ISBN-13: 978-0979665509

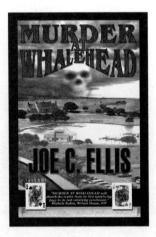

On the northern Outer Banks looms an old hunting lodge known as the Whalehead Club. During the roaring twenties Edward and Marie Knight entertained prominent guests at this isolated Mansion by the Sea. Now it has become one of North Carolina's leading tourist attractions. Less than a quarter mile away deep in the marsh along the Currituck Sound lies the body of a young woman. Someone has killed and craves to kill again. The Butler family never expected to cross paths with a homicidal maniac while

The First Shall Be Last by Joe C. Ellis

ISBN-13: 978-0979665523

Two young lovers separated by war cling to hope and sanity by exchanging passionate letters. As Howard heads for his first battle on the Pacific island of Peleliu, Helen fulfills her call of duty by working at a local factory. They discover they have more to worry about than the Japanese forces deeply entrenched on the island. A platoon member, Judd Stone, seeks revenge against a black Marine named Josiah Jackson. Howard fears Stone may go to any length to get what he wants, even murder.

Murder at Hatteras by Joe C. Ellis

ISBN-13: 978-0979665530

Gabe and Marla Easton move to Hatteras Island on North Carolina's Outer Banks to escape from a stress-filled world in hopes of conceiving their first child. Shortly after their arrival, a brutal rape and murder occurs on the island. As the investigation proceeds, the Eastons are drawn into the search for the killer. Soon, everybody seems to exhibit suspicious behavior. They have no idea of the terror that awaits as they move closer to identifying the killer.

1

Sheriff Dugan Walton didn't mind leading 5K foot races in the Chevy Impala the department had recently purchased. Today, however, his new deputy made it difficult to focus on the race route. Her name was Marla Easton. She was a thirty-four-year-old widow with wavy dark brown hair that reached the middle of her back. Her deep blue eyes occasionally short circuited his mental wiring, making it challenging to put together a coherent sentence. But he tried not to waste time dwelling on it. Realistically, he had a better chance of seeing Elvis beam down from a UFO than romancing Marla Easton. Growing up together in a small Ohio town, they had known each other most of their lives. They were good friends and, now, fellow officers serving the citizens of Dare County, North Carolina.

"You're not going to believe this," Marla said. Her hand rested on the top of his seat, brushing his shoulder as she twisted her slim waist to peer out the back window.

"What's happening?" Dugan glanced at the rearview mirror to check on the lead pack of runners but quickly refocused in front of him in anticipation of the turn onto Sir Walter Raleigh Avenue. They were approaching the two-mile point, and Dugan knew he needed to be cognizant of the aide station workers handing out cups of water.

"Doctor Hopkins just took over the lead."

"Doc Hopkins? He's got to be sixty-five years old." Dugan knew the retired doctor was fit but no way should he be banging elbows with young studs in a 5K race. "What's his two-mile time?"

Marla checked her watch. "11:20. Does that sound right?"

"Impossible. He's on pace to break eighteen minutes. Maybe 17:30." How could that be? Dugan, in his mid-thirties, ran regularly to keep in shape for any physical challenge that confronted him in the line of duty. His best time for a 5K was in the low nineteens.

Marla gripped Dugan's shoulder. "He's pulling away."

Dugan took a deep breath, trying to ignore the tingling that surged through him at her touch. He could see Hopkins clearly in the rearview mirror, his long gray hair bouncing with each stride, his legs tanned and muscular for an older man. He ran loosely, effortlessly. Manteo High's top distance runner, Eric Morrison, struggled to hang on but faded with every stride. "There's something wrong with this snapshot."

"He's good. That's all."

"No. He's in his sixties. Gotta be taking something."

"C'mon, Dugan."

"Seriously. Steroids. Testosterone. Amphetamines. Something. I beat him in a race two years ago. Ran 19:30. He's on something."

"You're just jealous." Marla leaned against him to get a better view out of the rearview window. "Wow. He's really pulling away now."

Dugan drew in her familiar fragrance—a combination of vanilla and wildflowers. He fought the temptation to savor it. *Don't go down that dead end—rejection alley.* "A man that old shouldn't be experimenting with his body. Not good for the heart. Wouldn't be surprised if he keeled over at the finish line. A doctor should know better."

"Did you know that Doctor Hopkins was a medical researcher?"

"No. What kind of research?"

"I'm not sure, but he wasn't a regular doctor." Marla turned around in her seat and faced the windshield. "Mee Mee Roberts goes out with him occasionally. He belongs to our Buxton Book Club. I like him a lot, and she thinks he's a fascinating guy."

Dugan glanced in the mirror again. With only about 500 yards to go, Hopkins showed no signs of letting up. Dugan passed a crowd of spectators in front of the Pizza Hut and then slowed to turn left onto Queen Elizabeth Avenue. Not far now—a few hundred yards.

Dugan believed Marla would make a great deputy, but she had a lot to learn about people. In his thirteen years of law enforcement on the Outer Banks he'd seen it all: rapes, robberies, murders, child molestations. Nothing surprised him anymore. When something out of the ordinary occurred, there was always a good explanation.

Dugan peered up to see the skull and crossbones on the sign hanging from Poor Richard's Sandwich Shop. The symbol of death. A chill surged through him. Doc Hopkins was on something. Runners crossing ethical lines for fast times wasn't anything new but was definitely more deadly with age.

Dugan made the final turn onto Festival Park Road. Now it was a straight shot across the bridge and onto the small island where the race would finish. The arch of the bridge made for the only hill on the course. Dugan kept glancing into the rearview mirror anticipating Doc Hopkins's sudden collapse. To his surprise, the old guy kept up his stride and even smiled. Shouldn't he be in great pain at this point in the race? Must have popped painkillers. No one challenged him; his lead had stretched to forty yards.

Dugan pulled off to the side as they neared the path that led to the outdoor amphitheater, put the car in park, and turned off the engine. Marla threw open her door, bolted into the October sunshine, and, pumping her fists in the air, cheered for Doc Hopkins. She hurried down the asphalt path to watch him finish in front of the stage. Dugan followed. Her exuberance irked him. Was he a bit jealous? If that doctor was taking his own designer drugs, it didn't make sense to cheer for him.

Hopkins crossed the line at 17:35. Two minutes faster than he'd run two years ago. *That's got to be a world class time for his age group.* Hopkins walked steadily through the narrowing chute. Eric Morrison finished second in 17:50, stumbling, almost falling until a race volunteer helped stabilize him. Dugan then observed Hopkins as he exited the chute and leaned on his knees, catching his breath.

Marla approached the doctor and placed her hand on his back. "Great race, Doctor Hopkins. Are you okay?"

"Fine. Fine, Marla." He peered up at her and smiled. "I mean, Deputy Easton. Just a little winded." He straightened and placed his hand around her waist. They walked toward Dugan. "By the way, congratulations. Mee Mee told me you were the newest member of our county's fine law enforcement team."

Marla smiled that beautiful smile. Dugan didn't want her to notice how that smile enchanted him, so he turned to watch the other runners finish. Roger Stern, a member of the county's forensic investigation unit, crossed the line next, managing to break nineteen minutes. Stern was a big-headed jackass. Dugan knew he would have to endure Stern's bragging about posting a 5K time faster than anyone else on the force this year. Somehow Stern would throw in a mixed metaphor or two—*I'm sweating like a bullet. Ran a helluva time, though, like a rabbit in a windstorm.* Worse than his self-absorbed ramblings was the fact that he was a good-looking man: six-two, light blond hair, chiseled jaw, well built. Women drooled over him. Dugan's Richie Cunningham looks didn't draw much attention from the ladies, although he did manage a date now and again.

Dugan turned to face Marla and Doc Hopkins. It was warm for a mid-October morning, mid-sixties, and sweat dripped from the doctor's face, but Dugan didn't notice any signs of extreme stress: no twitching or shaking, no bloodshot eyes or impaired coordination. In fact, the doctor appeared quite healthy.

"Nice race, Doc," Dugan said.

"Thanks, Sheriff Walton. Beautiful day to run."

"How do you feel?"

"Excellent. Never felt better."

Dugan noticed his face glowed, his skin very smooth for an old man. "You've improved over the last two years."

Hopkins nodded.

"When I raced against you two years ago, I beat you. No way could I keep up today."

"You never know. You might have pulled it off."

"No, Doc. You were two minutes faster today than you were two years ago."

"That's amazing," Marla said.

Hopkins, his hand still around her waist, smiled at her. "I don't put limits on myself."

"Do you mean to tell me old age doesn't affect you?" Dugan asked.

"I'm in a battle against aging."

Marla patted his back. "You seem to be winning."

"I am, indeed."

Roger Stern stepped up to them. "Hey Marla, did you catch my finish?"

Marla placed her hand lightly on Stern's bare shoulder. "I'm sorry, Roger. I missed it. I was talking to Doctor Hopkins. Did you know he won?"

Stern eyed the doctor. "You beat the Morrison boy?"

Hopkins nodded. "Felt pretty good today."

"You ran like a horse on fire. Congratulations." Stern stuck out his hand, and the doctor shook it. "Guess it's true. Some old dogs improve with age."

Dugan bit his tongue. If Stern let out another nonsensical saying he might slap him. And how much longer was Marla going to rest her hand on Stern's arm? Dugan took a deep breath to collect himself. He needed to let go of these petty irritations. "So tell me, Doc, how'd you get so fast lately? Are you on something?"

"Dugan!" Marla dropped her hand from Stern's shoulder. "How could you ask that?"

"I meant vitamins or some nutritional concoction." Dugan couldn't help smiling. His question had made her unhand Fabio.

Hopkins cleared his throat. "Good question. I've always been a health conscious person. Good diet. Plenty of vitamins. Early to bed, early to rise. But lately I've been on a new program."

"What kind of program?" Dugan asked.

"It's incredibly unique. I can't say much now, but in time the world will know. Anyway, I need to run a couple cool-down miles. You want to join me, Roger."

"Sure," Stern said. "Why not? Can't let grass grow under a rolling stone."

Stern and Hopkins headed toward the bridge at an easy gait. Dugan glanced at Marla. She watched them depart, probably focusing on Stern's butt.

"Did you hear what he said," Marla asked. "In time the world will know."

"I heard him."

"I bet he's writing a book on the secret of staying fit in your golden years."

Dugan chuckled. "I'm sure that's it. He'll probably end up with his own show on the Oprah network."

Marla glared at him, eyes narrowing. "He didn't look like he was hyped up on drugs to me."

Dugan had to admit she was right. Hopkins appeared healthier than ever, clear minded, and a lot younger than sixty-five. But still, two minutes faster? "You don't realize how fast 17:35 is for a guy his age."

"Maybe you don't realize how determined and dedicated that man is. Add to that his knowledge of the human body. I bet he doesn't touch red meat or sweets or anything with caffeine."

"Maybe." *But I doubt it.* Dugan peered over his shoulder at one of the park's food stands. "Want a hamburger, doughnut, and a coffee? I'll buy."

Marla smiled sheepishly. "Yeah. I'm starved."

Marla gulped down her last bite of hamburger and swigged her coffee. That hit the spot. She still couldn't get over Doctor Hopkins's amazing race. To Marla, he definitely didn't look sixty-five. Maybe forty-five. She and Dugan decided to stroll around the park and chat with the locals. At the docks they checked out the small crowd walking the decks of the *Elizabeth II*, a replica of an old English merchant vessel. In the distance they heard the clang of the blacksmith's hammer shaping hot iron at the first English settlement site. Dugan wanted to walk in that direction.

Marla guessed Dugan still had a crush on her. Ever since grade school he had often sneaked a peek at her with those lovelorn green eyes. Whenever she'd meet his gaze, he'd quickly look away. Back in high school he had few friends, but she and Gabriel always liked him. She guessed his loyalty to Gabriel kept him from ever letting his feelings be known. Now that she was thirty-four years old and widowed, she wondered if she could fall in love with him. Physically, she preferred someone like Roger Stern. But there was something about Dugan, an indefinable quality.

They entered the settlement site to the sound of "Greensleeves" being played on a lute and the smell of a wood fire. An older man sat on a stool under a magnolia tree and plucked the instrument. He wore loose trousers that came to mid-calf and a linen coat belted at the waist with a cord. A group of tourists had gathered before the blacksmith's shop to watch the muscular man stoke the fire and pound red-hot iron bars into useful implements.

"See that young couple standing by the lute player?" Marla asked.

Dugan shifted his attention from the blacksmith to the couple. "What about them?

"The girl's talking about their upcoming wedding. She wants to have it someplace on the Outer Banks—the Whalehead Club in Corolla or here in Manteo amid the Elizabethan Gardens."

"You can read lips?"

Marla nodded. "I have a deaf cousin, Audra Stevens."

"I remember Audra."

"We hung out a lot when we were kids. Her skill fascinated me. She taught me the basics—mouth shapes and facial expressions. I'd stare at myself in the mirror and say the alphabet or sing songs. Got pretty good at it."

Dugan raised his eyebrows. "Do you have any other hidden talents I don't know about?"

Marla grinned. "Plenty."

Above the music and crowd noise Marla heard the public address system in the distance calling the 5K participants to gather for the awards ceremony. Dugan wanted to head back in that direction. He'd check with the race officials to make sure everything went smoothly, and then they would head out in the cruiser and take a loop around town before heading back to the office to catch up on some paper work.

As they approached the large group of runners crowding the amphitheater stage near the finish line, Doctor Hopkins mounted the few steps to receive his trophy. The crowd cheered and applauded loudly. Hopkins held up his hand and took the microphone from the race director. "Thank you, fellow runners and all of you who came out to support us today. I know you clapped extra enthusiastically because this first place trophy was handed to a guy who's been around the block a few more times than most of you." Another round of applause rippled through the crowd. "They say that good advice is something a man gives when he's too old to set a bad example. I hope I'm not that old, but I would like to give you some advice. Don't let your age put limitations on your life. I'm running faster now than I did twenty years ago. Why? Because I refuse to let age dictate the level of my aspirations."

Marla scanned the audience and noticed how intently they listened. Most understood his victory today was quite spectacular. He earned their attention.

"Do you want to live to be one hundred?" Doctor Hopkins asked. "How about this? Would you like to run six miles on your one hundredth birthday? I plan on it. Believe me, it's possible. I know what I'm talking about. But it will never happen if you give up the fight. I'm talking about battling against the ravages of age. Eat healthy. Exercise daily. Keep your mind agile. It's got to be more than some five-step program you follow. To make it stick, it has to become your lifestyle. I've done a lot of research over the years in the causes of aging and age-related diseases. Let me just say that recently I've made great strides."

"Today's race proves that!" Roger Stern hollered. He was standing about ten feet in front of Marla, much taller than the people who surrounded him. Marla couldn't help but admire his wide shoulders.

"Thanks, Roger," Doctor Hopkins said. "It is true. I've made great strides physically and medically. Soon you'll find out more about what I've learned. For now, though, I encourage all of you to run the race! Fight the battle! Don't let age limit your life!"

The crowd exploded with applause again as the doctor descended the stage. Dugan shook his head. Marla didn't understand why he was so skeptical. Perhaps years of law enforcement had jaded him, caused him to assume the worst about people. Would that happen to her eventually?

"Let's get out of here. I've heard enough of this bull," Dugan said.

"It makes sense to me. Fitness can't be a chore. It has to be a part of your lifestyle."

"Mark my words, Marla. Hopkins won't live much longer if he's experimenting with performance enhancing drugs. A sixty-five-year-old body can only take so much."

The drive from Manteo to Rodanthe took about half an hour, miles and miles of sand dunes and water. Marla loved this section of the Outer Banks with its unspoiled beaches and raw beauty. By late afternoon, though, she struggled to keep her eyes open. Her first five days on the job after months of training was exciting but exhausting. She looked forward to getting home, spending time with Gabe, and hitting the sack early. She turned right off Route 12 onto Island Pine Drive and then drove a couple hundred yards down a narrow asphalt road lined with tall pines and live oaks. Her blue beach house was on the right. Home sweet home. They had moved there six months ago from Buxton where she used to work at the bookstore in town. Rodanthe seemed to be the perfect place for Gabe and her—halfway between her good friends in Buxton and her new job in Manteo.

Her three-bedroom home sat on pilings, eight by eight posts, between a patch of woods on the right and a rental house on the left. The yard on both sides of the wide, cement driveway consisted mostly of sea oats. It really didn't need much maintenance. From her front deck in the morning she could look to the left and see the sun rising above the Atlantic Ocean or in the evening to the right she could view a beautiful sunset over the Pamlico Sound. Their first few months in Rodanthe felt precarious, especially when thunderstorms blew in off the ocean. But the spectacular sunrises and sunsets, and the unbelievable beauty of the raw surroundings more than made up for the perilous sensation of living on the edge of nature's wrath.

Gabe and his best friend Ryan sat on the top step, waiting for her. Ryan's mom, Shelly Bottoms, watched Gabe after school every day for an hour until Marla got home and all day on Saturdays when Marla worked. The Bottoms lived only two doors down. Marla insisted on paying her, but she refused to accept any money. Our sons hang out 24/7 anyway, Shelly always said. It was true. The boys were inseparable, two rough and tumble first graders who delighted in the outdoors, video games, and boyhood shenanigans.

Gabe stood up, brown eyes wide and lips tight—that I'm-about-to-ask-an important-question look on his face. His black hair was disheveled and left sneaker untied. "Mom, could I stay at Ryan's house tonight? Please, please, please, please, please."

"What!" Marla's heart sank. She had hoped to spend some quality time with him that evening, but then again, she was dead tired.

Ryan stood up. Blond and wiry, he smiled revealing a gap in his front teeth. "My mom rented the *Transformer* movies for us. We wanted to stay up and watch all of them."

"Yeah, Mom. All three of them."

"But don't you miss me?"

Gabe rushed down the steps and wrapped his arms around her waist, pressing the side of his face against her stomach. "Yeah, I miss you, but we'll have time tomorrow." He raised his head, his eyes like big brown marbles.

Tomorrow was Sunday. They could go out to breakfast and then to church. Besides, how could she compete with the *Transformer* movies? "Okay. If you really and truly missed me, you can stay at Ryan's."

He nodded. "Really and truly."

"But we're going to eat dinner together." Marla peered up at Ryan. "Tell your mom Gabe will be over in about an hour."

Ryan leapt and shouted, "All right! Optimus Prime-time tonight!"

Marla cooked up hamburgers and macaroni and cheese for dinner. Gabe gobbled his food, but Marla made him sit still and tell her all about his day before she would give him his favorite dessert, a Klondike Bar.

After polishing off his ice cream, Gabe asked, "Did you arrest any criminals today?"

"No. But we did drive the sheriff's car through Manteo, leading a 5K race. Oh . . . and we caught a couple teenage boys lighting firecrackers."

"Did you arrest them?"

"No. Just gave them a warning. They were tourists' kids."

Gabe tilted his head. "Do you think you'll ever catch a murderer?"

"Maybe." But I'm in no hurry to do that, Marla thought.

"That would be cool!"

It didn't take long to gather up the few necessities for Gabe's overnighter—an extra pair of underwear, pajamas, a toothbrush. Marla walked him down the street to Ryan's house, not more than fifty yards away. Ryan opened the door as they approached the front porch, and Gabe charged up the steps and into the house. The door shut with a loud thud behind him.

"Goodbye, Sport," she said to a walnut door with frosted glass. As she walked back home she realized this was the beginning of a long letting-go process. She wanted to cry but held back the tears. She needed a hot bath and a good night's sleep.

After a thirty-minute soaking in the tub Marla stepped into comfortable sweatpants, funneled into a long-sleeve t-shirt, and planted herself on the La-Z-Boy recliner in front of the television. Halfway through an episode of *Cold Case Files*, she dozed off.

She peered at the red and white target. It seemed so far away. The odd ringing threw off her focus on taking the safety off her Magnum. Where was the safety? Now the ringing became an alarm. Someone's robbing the bank? The shooting range turned into downtown Manteo. Where's that safety? She fumbled with the gun and dropped it onto the sidewalk. The robber rushed out of the bank and faced her. She tried to reach her gun but the robber stepped on it. The ringing increased in volume. She glanced up to see the barrel of the thief's handgun. Rinnnnnnggggggg. *It's the phone! I'm dreaming.* She forced her eyes open and reached for the phone on the stand next to the recliner.

"Hello."

"Marla?" It was Dugan's voice on the other end. "You awake?"

"Now I am."

"Bad news."

A thousand thoughts rushed through her head but none seemed logical. "What happened?"

"Doc Hopkins."

"What about him?"

"He's . . . he's . . . dead."

"Dead?" A cold wave flowed over her. "How could he be dead?"

"Just got the call. Thought you'd want to know."

"Was it . . . like you said—a drug problem?"

"Not directly."

"What do you mean?"

"He died of a gunshot to the head. Possible suicide."

Impossible, Marla thought. He was too full of life today. "I don't understand."

"I'm heading over there in a few minutes."

"I'm coming with you."

"What about Gabe?"

"He's at Ryan's for the night. Pick me up."

"Be there in ten minutes."

2

Doctor Hopkins lived on Weir Point Drive just off Route 64 near the Fort Raleigh National Historical Site. The one-story brick home sat on the back of a double lot among tall cedars, loblolly pines, and live oaks. Two deputies had secured the scene after receiving a call from a neighbor. Dugan drove cautiously up the driveway, the tires rumbling on the circular pattern of bricks. He parked beside the other department vehicle, another white Chevy Impala. In the middle of the yard he saw a dark figure standing eerily still. On closer inspection, he realized it was a statue.

Dugan opened his door and the interior light came on. He eyed Marla. "Are you all right with this? Gunshot to the head. I guarantee you it won't be pretty."

Marla opened her door. "I'll manage."

"It's harder when you know the person."

"Either I'm cut out for this or not. Better to find out sooner than later."

We'll find out. That's for sure, Dugan thought.

A spotlight beamed down from the apex of a gable on the right side of the house. It illuminated the sidewalk that crossed the yard and then turned right toward the front porch.

Dugan kept eyeing the statue and noticed it had wings. For some inexplicable reason he felt drawn to it. "Mind if we take a closer look at that angel standing there?" Dugan asked.

"Odd, isn't it?"

"Definitely caught my attention."

The figure stood about twenty yards from the sidewalk. Dugan led the way through the grass. The statue, nearly six feet tall, had been cast in bronze. The folds of its robe and feather texture of its wings were highly detailed. It gazed heavenward and leaned on a long sword, the tip between its feet. The green patina blotching its forehead and cheeks and severe shadows cast by the spotlight gave its face an uncanny aspect.

"Now that's . . . otherworldly," Marla said as they walked around it.

"Do you believe in angels?"

"Yeah, but I hope mine does a better job of watching over me."

"Won't get much information out of this one. She's not talking" Dugan said. "Let's head to the house."

They crossed the yard and headed up the sidewalk. Three steps led up to a wide front porch. Lantern-style lights on each side of a mahogany door brightened the entryway. The door swung open, and Deputy Horace Wilford appeared and motioned them inside.

"Shuuuuweee, Sheriff. We've got a mess in there. The body's in the kitchen," Wilford said. He was young, around twenty-three, husky, and baby-faced.

"See anything unusual?" Dugan asked.

"No sir. Not for a suicide. He's facedown on the table with a pistol in his hand. Guess my only question is why would a guy like Doc Hopkins kill himself?"

"I don't believe he did," Marla said.

Wilford shrugged.

"We won't jump to conclusions," Dugan said.

The foyer led into a large family room with mahogany floors, dark leather couch and chairs, and a massive stone fireplace. A large oil painting of a lush garden with fruit trees hung above the couch, and the mounted head of an impressive buck stared down from above the fireplace. Deputy Wilford pointed to a wide doorway on the left. "The kitchen's in there."

When they turned the corner, Marla gasped. Hopkins sat in a wooden chair bent over the table, the back of his skull blown off. Blood soaked his long gray hair. His hand rested on a pistol. Blood and brain matter were splattered on the wall behind him.

Deputy John Reeves stood next to the stainless steel refrigerator, poking information into his iPhone. "Checking to see if Hopkins owned the gun," Reeves said. Reeves was tall and thin with close-set eyes. His black ball cap made him appear crane-like.

Dugan walked around the table and leaned over to inspect the pistol. It was a Smith and Wesson revolver with the words *.44 Magnum Hunter* etched into the barrel. From that side of the table Hopkins faced him. The bullet had entered the middle of his forehead.

"That's a long barrel on that handgun," Dugan said.

Marla circled the table and joined Dugan. Her eyes watered, but she swallowed and blinked back tears. She pointed at the gun, her voice unsteady. "Wouldn't it be easier for someone committing suicide to shoot himself in the temple?"

Deputy Wilford stepped closer. "That's how I'd do it."

Dugan nodded. "To shoot yourself in the forehead with a barrel that long, you'd have to pull the trigger with your thumb."

"He might have done it that way," Reeves said. He held up his iPhone. "According to the records, he bought the revolver two years ago in Powell's Point at the Outer Banks Gun and Ammunition Shop."

"Wouldn't be the first time someone shot themselves in the forehead," Dugan said.

"That doesn't make sense," Marla said. "If he shot himself in the forehead, wouldn't he be thrust backward instead of forward? Would he even be able to hold onto the gun?"

Dugan rubbed his chin. "Hard to say. His body might have recoiled and landed on the table. You don't know what kind of grip reflex may have kicked in once the bullet tore through his brain."

Reeves cleared his throat. "If Hopkins didn't pull the trigger, then this is a murder scene." He held up his iPhone. "Do you want me to call Stern and get forensics over here? The coroner and ambulance are already on their way."

"Have you seen any signs of an intruder?" Dugan asked.

"Haven't looked that hard yet," Reeves said.

Dugan peered at Marla. She met his gaze with determined eyes. He had to admit, her comment reflected logical reasoning. "Yeah. Go ahead. Call Stern and get them over here as soon as possible."

Reeves strolled to the other side of the kitchen, sliding his finger across the face of his iPhone.

"What about the neighbor?" Marla asked. "How'd he find the body?"

Wilford coughed once into his hand. "Well, he lives in the next house down, the one on the right. Name's Fergusson. Said he heard a gunshot and that's unusual for these parts. He and Hopkins are hunting buddies. Came over and rang the front doorbell. No one answered so he went around back. He knocked, but no one answered." Wilford pointed to a window next to the back door. "So he looked through that back window. Saw everything pretty clear from there. That's when he called the sheriff's department."

"How'd you guys get in?" Dugan asked.

"Back door was unlocked."

Reeves crossed the kitchen, slipping his iPhone into his shirt pocket. "Stern says he'll have his unit here in about twenty minutes."

"You boys wait here," Dugan said. "Deputy Easton and I will be over at the neighbor's house. Tell the emergency crew not to touch anything yet."

"Will do, Sheriff," Wilford said.

Marla and Dugan departed through the front door. As they passed the statue, Marla couldn't help staring at it. A chill shot through her, one of disquietude more than fear. "That thing gives me the weirdest feeling, the way it gazes into heaven."

"I know what you mean, like it has some kind of spiritual connection. When I first saw it, I had to get a closer look. Guess I shouldn't let supernatural inklings get to me."

"I don't know about that," Marla said. "Maybe the angel does have something to say. Right now we can't hear her."

They walked across the yard and onto the street. As they approached the next house, the red and white whirling lights of an emergency vehicle appeared down the road. "Hope those EMTs keep their hands off things for now," Dugan said.

"Then you believe it's a murder scene too?"

"No. But it could be. It's important to be open-minded."

"Of course," Marla said. Was he trying to gently admonish her for being adamant about refusing to believe Doctor Hopkins committed suicide? He was probably right, but Marla kept remembering the doctor's wide smile and unusual youthful vigor for a senior citizen. Suicide didn't make sense.

Mr. Fergusson lived in the next house on the right. Solar-powered lights lined the long driveway and sidewalk. Like the other houses in the neighborhood, it did not sit on the familiar posts used to support most of the homes on the Outer Banks. Instead it had a traditional brick foundation with a wood-framed top designed with lots of gables. It only took four steps to get to the porch. Dugan hit the doorbell, and the door swung open almost immediately.

"Mr. Fergusson?" Dugan asked.

"Yes, Gary Fergusson. I've been waiting for you." A man in his late fifties or early sixties stepped onto the porch. He had a severely receded hairline, carried a noticeable paunch, and wore a North Carolina Tar Heels sweatshirt. "I'm a little shaken up. Sylvester was one of my best friends. We've gone hunting together for several years, ever since he moved here." His face was pale, bags under his eyes.

"Sorry about what happened to Doc Hopkins. Must have been difficult finding him like that," Dugan said.

"Extremely."

"What made you decide to check on him?" Dugan asked.

"Like I told the other officer, I heard a gunshot. That's a rarity around here. At first I didn't think much about it. I was watching a fishing show on T.V. The more I sat there, the more it bothered me."

"How long did you wait before you went over to check on Doctor Hopkins?" Marla asked. As soon as the question left her mouth, she wondered if she should have kept quiet and let Dugan conduct the interview.

"'Bout ten minutes. Like I said, a gunshot's a rare thing in this neighborhood. I know Sylvester keeps quite a few pistols and rifles in his house. He'd never fire one round here. He's very safety oriented. Finally, it occurred to me that one might have gone off accidentally. He could've been cleaning it. Then I decided I better check on him."

Dugan nodded. "Tell us everything that happened once you left here."

"Well . . . I went to his front door and rang the doorbell several times. Waited at least two minutes. I didn't want to go around back unless I had to. Sylvester's a private man like me. I wouldn't want people snooping around the back of my house at night."

"Did you see any strange vehicles parked out front?" Marla asked. Dugan glanced at her but didn't look perturbed by the interjection of her question. She thought it was a good question.

"No. Nothing unusual out front."

"What happened next?" Dugan asked.

Fergusson took a deep breath and blinked several times. "Went around back and knocked on the door. No answer again. I decided to look in the window." Fergusson swallowed and took another deep breath. "That's when I saw him. I ran back over here and called the sheriff's department."

"You didn't go inside to check and see if he was alive?" Dugan asked.

Fergusson shook his head. "No sir. I could see his brains were blown out. I didn't need a closer look."

"Did you see anything unusual at the back of the house?" Marla asked.

Fergusson laid his hand on his cheek, eyes searching the darkness of his front yard. "Yes. I did see something out of the ordinary back there—the lights."

"What lights?" Dugan asked.

"In the research lab. When Doc moved here five years ago, he converted the unattached garage in the back into a research lab."

"So the lights in the lab were on?" Marla asked.

Fergusson nodded.

"What's so unusual about that?" Dugan asked.

"I can see the lab from my back porch. He rarely works out there this late at night. But even if he did, wouldn't he turn the lights out before he went back to the house?"

Dugan shrugged. "Hard to say. It's easy to forget to turn out lights."

"Maybe we should head back there and check out the lab," Marla said.

"Definitely. Thanks for your time, Mr. Fergusson. We may come back later if we have any more questions."

"That's fine. I'll do what I can to help."

"Mr. Fergusson?" Marla said.

He lifted his head to look at her, eyes bleary.

"You were good friends with Doctor Hopkins. Do you think he committed suicide?"

Fergusson shook his head. "He loved living. He'd be the last person I know, who would take his own life."

"That brings up another question," Dugan said. "Did he have any enemies?"

"Not that I know of. Not around here anyways."

On the way back to the Hopkins house Marla apologized for interjecting her questions.

"No need to apologize," Dugan said. "They were good questions."

"But I'm a rookie. I should probably keep my mouth shut and let you handle the interviews."

"Not necessarily. You have a different perspective than I do. Maybe you'll notice something no one else sees."

Dugan's encouragement made her feel better. Did he see potential in her? Dr. Hopkins's grisly death had sickened her but didn't quash her desire to pursue this career. In fact, she sensed a flame flicker and grow within—a desire to uncover the truth and seek justice.

They walked back to Hopkins's house and saw the ambulance parked in the driveway. Two attendants sat on the back bumper, one smoking a cigarette.

"What's the story, Sheriff?" the smoker asked. He was short and squat with a thin mustache and a shaved head. "Wilford told us to wait out here for now."

"We haven't decided if this is a crime scene yet or not, gentlemen. Be patient."

"Looked like a suicide to me, Sheriff," the other EMT said. "'Course I didn't get a good look."

"Just hang out for a while. We'll let you know what's going on in a bit," Dugan said.

They walked around the vehicle into the back yard and saw the three-car garage that had been converted into a lab. No lights.

"Fergusson said the lights were on, right?" Marla asked.

"Right."

"That means someone turned them off, and it wasn't Dr. Hopkins."

"Possibly," Dugan said. "Could be on a timer or some kind of motion detector. Better take a closer look."

Each of the three garage doors had a section of windows. The entry door on the left side of the building also had a window. All were black.

They crossed the yard to the entry door, and Dugan pulled a handkerchief out of his shirt pocket. He carefully gripped the doorknob with the handkerchief, turned it, and nudged the door open.

"Still no lights," Marla said. "Must not have a motion sensor."

With the handkerchief wrapped around his hand Dugan entered and searched for the light switch. The strong odor of a pet shop assaulted Marla's nose. After a few seconds a row of florescent lights flickered on. Cupboard doors hung open; boxes had been tumbled out of them onto the floor. Notebooks and papers were scattered everywhere. Bottles, beakers, test tubes, and chemicals crowded the countertops. Animal cages and aquariums lined the shelves.

Marla took a couple of steps into the lab, her eyes growing wide. "Looks like a whirlwind came through this place."

3

Dugan laid his hand on Marla's shoulder. "Be careful. Watch where you step. Look, but don't touch."

"Right." Marla panned the lab. "Somebody went wacko in here. What do you think? Robbery?"

"Maybe. Then again, Hopkins could have done this—roid rage. He may've been taking something that caused drastic mood swings. An experiment went badly, and he lost it."

"Maybe so, Dugan, but dead men don't turn out lights. Someone besides Dr. Hopkins was in here." She stepped around the end of a long island counter supported by oak cabinets. Most of the cabinet drawers were opened. Notebooks were scattered on the counter top between various size bottles of chemicals, glass beakers, microscopes, and scientific meters. On the other side the file cabinet drawers were opened, half of their contents scattered on the black-and-white tile floor. "Somebody ransacked the place. They were looking for something specific."

"How do you figure that?" Dugan asked.

Marla waved her hand at the mess in front of her. "Why would Doctor Hopkins dump the contents of his files on the floor? I could see knocking over the equipment and breaking glass beakers in a fit of rage, but this looks more methodical."

Dugan circled the island counter, studying the clutter before him, and joined Marla on the other side. "I see what you mean. Whoever did this pulled files out, checked them, and tossed aside whatever wasn't relevant."

"Looks like he rummaged through everything until he found what he wanted then turned the lights out and left."

Dugan rubbed his chin. "But that doesn't make sense either. Why would the killer stage a suicide and then come in here and leave the place looking like an obvious robbery?"

"Perhaps something went wrong. Let's say he kept one eye on the window and saw Mr. Fergusson come to the back porch. Then he knew he didn't have time to keep things neat. He tore through everything until he found what he was looking for and then took off."

"That's a strong possibility. I'll have forensics do a thorough investigation in the house and here. Hopefully, they'll come up with something to shed more light on what happened." Dugan crossed to the other side and examined several shelves loaded with animal cages and aquariums. "Interesting. Doc Hopkins must have been testing animals. What an odd assortment. Mice, turtles, fish. Look, there's even a few lobsters over here."

Marla crossed the room, making sure to step in the open spaces. She pointed at a rodent cage. "This one has a name—Jasper." A label had been placed at the base of the cage with the name and the date—May 15, 2007. "Wonder what this date represents?"

A white mouse popped up, sticking its nose between the bars, and Marla whipped her finger away. "Yikes. Wasn't expecting that greeting."

"What's the matter? Little mouse scare ya?" Dugan asked.

"Not really. It just surprised me. This must be Jasper."

Dugan tapped the cage, his hand wrapped with his handkerchief, and the mouse reacted by sitting on its hind legs as if it were begging. "Must be hungry."

"Someone needs to be notified about these animals. By tomorrow they'll all be hungry." She knelt and examined a large glass tank on the shelf below the mouse. It contained a turtle that looked to be a nearly a foot long. "This one has a name too."

Dugan knelt beside her. "What is it?"

Marla pointed to a label at the base of the tank. "Methuselah."

Dugan grinned. "Who was the oldest man in the Bible? I'll take Old Testament for one thousand, Alex."

"Very funny," Marla said flatly. She pointed to the turtle. "Look. Someone carved numbers into its shell."

Dugan leaned to get a better view. "I think it's a date—1895. Way back when some kid probably found it in the woods and carved the date on its shell."

"1895? Is that possible? That would make it more than 115 years old."

"What do you expect with a name like Methuselah?"

Marla stood and offered her hand to Dugan. "You need help getting up, old man?"

Dugan grasped her hand and waited for her to tug him to his feet. "I must not have the same longevity genes as Methuselah here." He forced himself to let go but the feel of her hand lingered in his mind.

Marla scanned the cages and tanks along the rest of the shelves. "Whoever tore this place apart didn't bother the animals."

"No." Dugan eyed the papers at their feet. "If it *was* a thief, he wanted information or drugs."

"Or both."

Dugan and Marla left the lab and headed to the back porch. Deputy Wilford stood at the top of the steps, hands on his wide hips. Dugan peered up at him. "I want crime scene tape around the lab." He thumbed over his shoulder.

"That big ol' garage is a lab?" Wilford asked.

"Yeah. The place is a mess. It's possible that someone shot Hopkins and then went out to the lab to steal drugs or even information. Don't know if the perpetrator found what he was looking for or not. Keep your eye on the place just in case he comes back."

Wilford straightened, chest expanding. "Will do, Sheriff."

"While you got the tape out, string some on the front porch and back porch."

"I'm on it." Wilford thudded down the steps and strode toward the driveway in the direction of the vehicles.

Dugan gazed into the night sky, the canopy of stars like glitter on black velvet. The temperature had dropped, probably into the low fifties. He rubbed his arms. "Left my jacket in the car. You cold?"

"I'm fine." Marla had donned her gray Dare County Sheriff Department hoodie before she left the house. "I hear a vehicle coming."

Dugan tilted his head. "Probably Stern and the crime tech team."

They walked around the corner of the house to see headlights approaching. A white Chevy Tahoe pulled in behind the other vehicles and several people got out.

"Is that you, Stern?" Dugan shouted.

"Yeah. Be with you in a minute, Sheriff."

The forensic team, four of them, went to the back of the SUV. Stern often rubbed Dugan the wrong way, but he had to admit, the man excelled in crime scene analysis. His team was very knowledgeable and had served Dare County for many years. Good people.

Dugan and Marla walked up the driveway to the front of the house where the vehicles were parked. "Have you met the CSI folks yet?" Dugan asked.

"Not formally, but I think I know who they are. 'Course, everybody knows Roger," Marla said.

Yeah, Dugan thought, all the women, anyway.

Roger Stern stepped out from behind the Chevy Tahoe. He carried two black cases that resembled large fishing tackle boxes. Jessie Lou Winters, a short, muscular blonde in her late forties, followed him, carrying a clipboard and a black briefcase. Behind her Big Jim Thomas, six feet four inches tall and nearly three hundred pounds, looked like an old grizzly bear with his unkempt beard and scraggly gray hair. The photographer and video guy, Perry Lane, came next, hauling his cameras.

"Hey, Marla," Stern said. "Didn't expect to see you out here tonight."

"When I heard the victim was Doctor Hopkins, I wanted to come."

Stern shook his head. "Hard to believe, isn't it? So full of vitality this morning. I guess if life was fair, John Lennon would still be alive and Lee Harvey Oswald would be dead."

Dugan tried to bite his tongue but couldn't. "Lee Harvey Oswald is dead, Roger. Mark David Chapman shot Lennon."

Stern waved his hand. "You know what I mean."

The muscular blonde placed her briefcase on the ground, stepped forward and extended her hand toward Marla. "I'm Jessie Lou Winters."

Marla shook her hand. "Marla Easton. I've seen you around."

Jessie Lou motioned to the big bearded man. "This mountain here is Big Jim Thomas and the guy with the cameras is Perry Lane.

Marla nodded toward the two men. "Nice to meet you."

With a gravely voice, Big Jim said, "Howdy, Marla. Hope yer enjoyin' yer new job. We'll be crossin' paths now and again."

The photographer smiled then quickly averted his eyes.

"We think this might be a homicide, but we're not sure," Dugan said. "The body's in the kitchen. Take plenty of pictures and video. Dust everything for prints and whatever else you can do to help us make that determination." Dugan turned and waved toward the back where Deputy Wilford was draping crime scene tape around the lab. "You might find something in that garage. Doc Hopkins converted it into a laboratory. Someone ransacked the place."

Stern blew out a long breath, a half-whistle. "Sounds like an all-nighter."

"No doubt about that," Dugan said. "Follow me." He led the way along the sidewalk, up the steps, onto the front porch, and into the house. They stopped in the family room in front of the fireplace. "The body's around that corner in the kitchen. You've got a lot of work to do in there. Marla and I will walk through the house and check things out. If we find anything suspicious, we'll let you know. You can do a tour later, but right now I want you to focus on the kitchen and garage out back."

"That'll be plenty for now." Stern motioned toward the kitchen like an army scout giving the troops the okay to move forward. The three forensic specialists passed through the wide doorway, but Stern lingered. "Marla, I wanted to check with you. Are we still on for tomorrow night?"

Dugan eyed Marla. Her face reddened. Here we go, he thought. Big date night with Stern the Stud.

"Well . . . uh . . ." She nervously smoothed her hair on the side of her head, tucking it behind her ear. "I'm having a difficult time finding a sitter. Shelly, my neighbor, is busy tomorrow night."

Dugan raised his hand. "I'm off tomorrow night. I promised Gabe a fishing trip to the Rodanthe Pier." Suddenly, Dugan felt very noble. His offer proved his magnanimity and lack of jealousy. *Go ahead. Go out with Roger Stern. I'll even facilitate the romance by watching your son.* Perhaps this was the best way to rid himself of this silly crush—face the fact Marla wasn't attracted to him. Let her go. Maybe she and Stern were meant for each other. Anyway, Dugan enjoyed spending time with Gabe. They hit it off well together.

Stern spread his hands as if preparing to receive a gift. "There you go. We can kill two birds in the bush with one hand."

Dugan cringed. Maybe he shouldn't expedite a relationship between his new deputy and a guy who can't keep his metaphors straight.

"I guess that would be all right," Marla said. "Dugan, are you sure about this?"

Dugan put his best face on. "No problem. Gabe and me'll have a great time. You better make room in your freezer for all the fish we'll bring home."

"Okay, then," Marla said.

"Pick you up about seven?" Stern asked.

"Seven is good."

Stern saluted like a boy scout, about-faced, and walked into the kitchen.

Marla turned to Dugan. "Very nice of you to watch Gabe for me. He likes you a lot, you know."

"The feeling's mutual. If I ever had a son, I'd want him to be just like Gabe." Dugan noticed Marla's blue eyes fixed on him, as if she were looking into him rather than at him. That was rare. It froze his train of thought.

Finally the silence became uncomfortable and she glanced around the room. "Well, what's next?"

"I noticed in the foyer a door on the left. I think it's an office. Let's check it out first."

They walked toward the front of the house and Dugan tried the door. It was unlocked. He reached around the wall and flipped on the light to reveal an office, probably about ten by twelve feet. A large mahogany computer desk and companion printer station took up most of the space in the back of the room. On the wall to the left hung a large landscape painting, a river valley winding through mountains. Dugan guessed it to be a scene from the western part of North Carolina, the Blue Ridge Mountains. A recliner sat next to a window that looked out onto the front of the property, and a bookshelf took up most of the opposite wall.

In general the office appeared undisturbed, not overly neat but nothing out of place. Dugan walked to the computer desk and, using his handkerchief, moved the mouse. The wide, flat screen monitor lit up. Access required a password.

Marla stepped up beside him and bent over to get a better look. "Try 'jasper'."

Dugan wrapped the handkerchief around his index finger, poked in the letters and hit the enter key. The wrong-password error message popped up. "No luck."

"How about 'methuselah'?"

Dugan typed in the letters and hit the enter key. Hopkins's desktop appeared. "Voila! I'm impressed. Good guess."

Marla straightened and took a deep breath; a smile lit up her face. "Most people pick passwords they can remember, things important to them like names or dates."

Dugan studied the desktop. Immediately, he noticed four folders with similar names in the upper right corner—training 2009, training 2010, training 2011, and training 2012. Training for what? Distance running? He double-clicked the 2009 folder. The window contained twelve folders, the months of the year. He double-clicked January.

Each day was documented with distances and times. Below those numbers the weather was described with brief statements: cold and sunny—40 degrees, windy but unusually warm—55 degrees, downright cold and snowy—15 degrees. Then Dr. Hopkins wrote a few sentences about how he felt physically: *Really tired today. Don't know how much longer these old joints can pound away on these roads. May have to cut back on mileage tomorrow.*

Dugan closed that window. "I wonder if . . ." He double-clicked the 2010 folder and then opened the October folder. "He recorded the race we ran together two years ago."

"Was it on the same course as today's race?" Marla asked.

"Yes. The Colony Lost and Found 5K. Here it is, exactly as I remembered. He ran a 19:55 that day. I ran 19:35. Look at his comment—*My time was good for a sixty-three-year-old man, but I don't plan on racing again until I'm a lot faster.*"

"And today he finally raced again," Marla said.

"And he was definitely a lot faster. Doc Hopkins knew this day would come." Dugan slapped his thigh. "He had to be on something to cut two and a half minutes off his time."

"But we don't know that for sure yet."

"We will once the autopsy results are completed. I'm guessing they'll find illegal substances. Maybe several in-demand drugs, the kind people ransack labs to steal."

"Do you think that's what this is all about? A lab full of designer performance-enhancing drugs?"

"I'd bet my next pay on it." Dugan closed the two windows and opened the 2011 folder. Then he double-clicked the October folder. "All right, let's see where his training was one year ago." He hit the page down button until October 23 appeared. "Ran eight miles in about sixty minutes today. Cloudy and mid-fifties. Felt incredible. This is the first day of the rest of my life. What will I feel like one year from now? Fifty years from now? Time will tell."

"He couldn't have been serious," Marla said. "Fifty years from now? That would make him one hundred and fifteen years old."

"Just like Methuselah, the turtle." Dugan felt a weird buzz go down his spine as his and Marla's eyes met. "My guess is that he's been testing chemical compounds on animals and himself, ones that increase physical endurance. He came up with a drug that genetically reprograms muscle fibers to use energy more efficiently. He made a breakthrough."

"And someone found out about it," Marla said. "A drug like that would be in high demand."

"No doubt. It would be worth millions of dollars both legally and on the black market. Doc's time in the race today tipped someone off. The thief knew Hopkins was on to something."

Marla knotted her eyebrows. "Then it's possible the killer was at the race."

"Possibly. Or else he saw the results online. Nowadays road race results are posted on the net within two hours after the finish. A sixty-five-year-old man running 17:35 would definitely grab the attention of anyone knowledgeable about 5K times."

"Especially someone who pushes performance-enhancing drugs."

"It's a good hypothesis, anyway. We'll wait and see what the CSI crew comes up with. In the meantime let's check out the rest of the house."

Marla led the way out the door but stopped at the bookcase. "Look at some of these titles: *The Science of Life Extension, Anti-Aging Strategies, Ageless Animals, Engineered Negligible Senescence*."

"Negligible what?"

"Senescence. Not sure what that means. Check this one out." She pointed to the next book, a thick black one that was not completely pushed back into place. "He must have been reading this one today. It's sticking out almost halfway. Let me see your handkerchief."

Dugan handed Marla the white handkerchief, and she covered her hand with it and gripped the wide spine of the tome. She carefully slid it out and lowered it.

"What do ya know?" Marla said. "It's a family Bible."

"I didn't know Doc Hopkins was a religious man."

Marla thumbed through the pages and almost dropped the book when her thumb reached the cover. "Did you see that?"

"Some kind of cutout?"

Marla opened the cover and flipped through the first few pages. At page thirty-five with the heading GENESIS 3, a rectangular section had been cut out of the pages, and a small book rested in the space.

"It's some kind of diary." Marla extended the Bible toward Dugan. "Here. Hold the Bible and I'll remove the book."

Dugan took the weight of the Bible into his hands, and Marla delicately pried the smaller book from its slot. It had a light gray cover with the words "Methuselah Journal" handwritten on it in script. She opened it to the first entry, October 15, 2011, and read the first sentence: "Today I injected myself with the Methuselah serum."

4

"Keep reading," Dugan said.

Marla cleared her throat. "It's nine o' clock in the evening. This is my first entry into the Methuselah Journal documenting my journey into negligible senescence. It's been over twelve hours. I feel fantastic. I don't know if it's an emotional high or if the serum has already begun the transformation process. On this evening's seven-mile run I posted my best time of the year.

"My colleagues from the old days would say I've gone mad, but they haven't seen what I've seen. I've been doing the research on my own now for five years. I appreciate what we had accomplished together, but no one agreed with the direction I wanted to go. In hindsight it was the right decision. Perhaps luck had a lot to do with it. I tried so many combinations before I came up with a formula that worked. A one in a million chance? More like one in ten million. You could say I hit the medical research lottery. My serum is definitely working—on the test animals, anyway. Time will tell if it works on me.

"Besides, I wasn't willing to wait any longer. Time is slipping away and I'm sixty-four years old. At this stage in life I'm willing to be a human guinea pig. If my body has a fatal reaction to the serum in the near future, I will have no regrets. I've lived a great life. Considering I've been battling prostate cancer for a year now, I had extra incentive to take the plunge. Not only could my self experimentation lead to great strides in the realm of longevity, but it will also be interesting to see the serum's effect on cancer cells.

"I haven't been this excited for almost fifty years, the day I ran my best high school mile. I remember every detail as if it were yesterday. May 4th, 1965. The Oak Valley League Championship. Sunny and 65 degrees. I broke away from the pack in the last lap, crossed the finish line, and leapt into Coach Thomas's arms. He lifted me, spun around once, then set me down and showed me his stopwatch. 4:29.7—a new school record. Today I feel like a kid again."

"Let me see the book," Dugan said. He placed the Bible on the seat of the recliner, and Marla handed it to him. Dugan thumbed through the pages. "This could be extremely important."

"It should give us a better idea of the drugs involved. I'm sure he'll mention more about this serum—what compounds or chemicals he used."

"Any names recorded within these pages are possible leads. Who knows? He may have mentioned the killer—someone from his past."

"Could I look at it again?" Marla took the journal and turned to the last page. "There must be nearly two-hundred entries. The last one is October 23, 2012—today."

"Read it."

"Today was an incredible day. The best ever." Marla paused and glanced up, her eyes a glistening blue. Dugan sensed the irony in the words and the grief in her expression. She read on. "It started when I examined my face in the mirror this morning. I noticed very few wrinkles. I look much younger than a year ago. My hair is still gray but it has been gray for twenty years. I don't know if it will return to the dark brown shade of my mid-thirties. It's definitely much thicker.

"The biggest highlight of the day?—the Colony Lost and Found 5K. It's been two years since I've run a road race. I knew I would post a good time, but 17:35 is over ten seconds faster than any of my recent time trials. The adrenalin generated by running against competition helped. I haven't run that fast for twenty-five years. I'm living proof the Methuselah serum works. I'm flying sky-high right now. Life has begun anew for me. It's time to take the next step in my plan—traveling around the world and running in the most highly recognized races. I've been obsessed with research for so many years, ever since Anna died. But there is a more important focus now. I need to take responsibility for what I have created. Each step of the way is incredibly important in the process of presenting my work to . . ." Marla looked up.

"That's it? He stopped mid-sentence?"

Marla nodded. "I wonder if he was writing this last entry when he heard someone at the door or possibly breaking into the house. Then he slipped the book back into its slot in the Bible and placed the Bible on the shelf, not taking the time to push it all the way back."

"Sounds reasonable," Dugan said. "Then he went out to answer the door or check on the noise. He might have been ambushed."

"Or else he knew the visitor. There really weren't any signs of struggle in the house. He may have recognized the killer and welcomed him, not knowing what was about to happen."

"Good point. To be sure we better take a closer look in every room. We may have missed something—a vase knocked over or a piece of furniture broken or out of place."

Marla held up the diary. "Could I take this home and read it tonight?"

"Well . . ." Dugan rubbed the shadow of whiskers on his jowl. "Yeah, but I want to read it too."

"Maybe we can get together sometime tomorrow and talk."

That sounded good to Dugan. He had to admit he enjoyed these long hours with Marla. It seemed like they made a good team, professionally anyway. "Let's meet somewhere for lunch."

"I'll have Gabe with me. How about Lisa's Pizzeria at one o'clock?"

"I never say no to pizza." Dugan picked up the Bible and slid it into the empty space on the bookshelf. "Take care of that journal. We might find the break we need within those pages."

Marla held the book up to the pouch on her sweatshirt. "It'll fit in here." She carefully lifted the edge of the pocket and angled the book into the pouch, then patted her belly where the journal rested. "It's safe."

Dugan led the way back into the family room. He could hear the muffled tones of the forensic crew working in the kitchen. He and Marla took a couple minutes to inspect the family room, closely examining the

Joe C. Ellis

tops of the two lampstand tables, coffee table, and the fireplace mantel for any signs of a disturbance. Everything looked to be in its place.

Dugan pointed to a short hallway on the right. "I'm guessing we'll find a couple bedrooms in that direction."

"I'll follow you."

They checked out what appeared to be two guest bedrooms and their accompanying bathrooms but didn't see anything unusual. Dugan figured the master bedroom must be on the other side of the kitchen. They crossed back through the family room and stopped in the kitchen to watch Stern and Jessie Lou dusting for prints on the table. Standing behind the seat that Hopkins's body still occupied, Perry Lane prepared to photograph the blood and brain matter splattered on the wall. Big Jim loomed in background and jotted notes onto a small pad.

"Any luck?" Dugan asked.

Stern looked up. "Can't see the forest on the wall yet. You?"

Forest on the wall? Dugan shook his head. "Found a journal in Hopkins's office that may be helpful. Other than that, nothing unusual." Dugan pointed to a doorway in the far left corner. "We're heading in that direction to check out the master bedroom."

The third bedroom was quite large with a king size bed, a crimson comforter neatly spread over the mattress with a stack of golden pillows at the head. A wide oak dresser and mirror stood against the right wall next to an open door that led to a bathroom. On the wall opposite the bed hung a flat panel television, at least fifty inches wide.

Marla immediately walked to an immense framed painting of a beautiful woman on the wall next to the walk-in closet. The subject appeared to be in her late thirties wearing a silky blue robe half unbuttoned. She stood in a shadowy garden. The sun's glow through the boughs of loosely painted trees lit the long tresses of her sandy blonde hair. With her head slightly turned to the right, she gazed at the viewer with beckoning green eyes.

"This must be Anna," Marla said. "He mentioned her on the last page of the diary."

"I remember. Doc became obsessed with his work after she died."

Marla shook her head. "I don't see how he lived this way."

Dugan stepped up beside her. "What way?"

"How could he wake up every morning and be greeted by this beautiful portrait? It would be a daily reminder of the pain of loss."

Dugan nodded. "Yeah. She's frozen in time. Always young. Always alluring. And he wakes up every morning a day older, a day farther away from those prime years."

Marla reached and gripped Dugan's arm. "Maybe that's why he was so driven. The most precious thing in life was taken from him."

"Yeah, but hard work could never bring her back."

"But maybe it wasn't about bringing her back to life."

"What do you mean?"

Marla released Dugan's arm. "Perhaps he wanted to strike a blow to Death, somehow gain a measure of retribution."

Dugan shrugged. "Or maybe get even with God."

"With God?"

"Think about it. God ordained death. It's sacred. God has scheduled a day for each of us to die. If that serum adds ten or twenty years to a person's life, then that day is delayed. God is forced to wait."

"But can you really force God to do anything?"

Dugan glanced out the bedroom door toward the kitchen. "Apparently not."

They spent about ten more minutes inspecting the master bedroom but didn't find anything suspicious. Dugan wanted to check with Roger Stern one more time before calling it a night. It had been a long day, and he felt guilty keeping Marla out any later. She had put in long hours during her first week on the job. Not much more could be done anyway until the CSI people finished their work.

Dugan had to admit he had enjoyed the week with Marla. He had woken up looking forward to each day. Was it possible he was developing some kind of addiction to her? The thought bothered him. He didn't like the idea of having a yearning that only time with another human being could satisfy. It wouldn't be so bad if she felt the same way, but he knew she didn't. That made him vulnerable or even pathetic. He was the elected sheriff of Dare County, North Carolina. No way would he allow himself to become a love-sick mass of gelatin over a woman who viewed him as only a good friend. *Get a hold of yourself, Walton. Toughen up.*

The crime scene team barely noticed him when he re-entered the kitchen, each of them intent on the task at hand. Finally Stern looked up and acknowledged him but had nothing new to report. Dugan reminded them to do a thorough job in the lab and to take some time to check out the rest of the house—the more eyes examining the place the better.

When Dugan turned to leave, he noticed Marla hadn't followed him into the kitchen. He entered the family room to see her standing by a lamp reading the journal. "Anything interesting?" Dugan asked.

"I opened it randomly about halfway through. It's dated May 15, 2012. Listen to this: Today is Jasper's birthday. He's five years old today. That is truly a reason to celebrate. You could say he's officially the million-dollar mouse. He has reached more than twice the age of the normal lab mouse, breaking the current longevity record. However the Methuselah Foundation doesn't want to examine him until he's dead. I might never cash in on that award. Jasper could live indefinitely. This is much bigger than the money they're offering anyway.

"According to Hans Metzger, a million dollars is small fish compared to what a secret group of pharmaceutical kingpins is offering. I received an email from Hans this morning. I can tell he's worried that I have made a significant advance. We worked for ten years side by side. I had to break away from him. He was unwilling to think outside the box. We could have spent another thirty years plodding along, turning over every stone to make sure each step of the scientific method was followed so that no detail would be left undocumented. I knew there had to be a better way. He may be a more meticulous researcher than I, but I'd rather be lucky than good. He wasn't willing to take chances. But now he's worried that my risky methods paid off.

"Too bad. Once I tell the world what I've accomplished, I hope he doesn't expect compensation for the years we researched together. He doesn't deserve it. If I would have stuck with him I'd still be growing old with very few positive results to show for it. I didn't tell him much, although I hinted that I'm on to something. I guess I get a kick out of making him squirm. There were so many teams working on this project. Every year the Methuselah Foundation has been handing out their cash awards for minor advancements and lab mouse longevity records. But I've hit a grand slam. Now I'm curious. Just how much money is this mysterious organization putting on the table for a successful serum and formula? Ten million? It still wouldn't be worth it." Marla glanced up. "That's all he wrote that day. What do you think?"

Dugan pointed at the journal. "I'd say you just revealed the motive."

"Right out of the Bible—the love of money."

Dugan raised his left eyebrow. "The root of all evil."

5

Methuselah Journal Entry: October 24, 2011

Like my many colleagues, I've always believed the key to negligible senescence in the human animal can be achieved only at the cellular level. I am convinced I have accomplished this through experimentation on ageless animals, the study of their cell structures and mitochondrial DNA, and the transference of the dynamic processes contained within these cells through a serum to animals with much shorter life spans. I admit my efforts were sometimes haphazard. When I felt I reached a dead end I didn't waste time trying to find out why. I moved on to the next potential path of success.

*Every day I felt like I was playing the lottery and hoping to hit it big. The animals in the lab on which I focused my cellular analysis all exhibited the classic characteristics of agelessness: the rougheye rockfish (*aleutianus), *the eastern box turtle (*terrapene Carolina), *the ocean quahog species of clam (*artica islandica), *the European clawed lobster (*homarus gammarus). *All of them have been known to show little signs of aging, even when well over one hundred years old. Methuselah,* *my turtle (approximately 120 years old), was one of my favorite subjects, although he was not nearly as old as Clara the clam (350 years old). All played important roles in my research.*

Within these negligible senescent animals can be found amazing cellular characteristics which profoundly contrast with all other species. Mutations to their mitochondrial DNA occur at a much lesser frequency, thus avoiding the acceleration of aging experienced by other animals. Their cells contain enzymes which have the ability to digest lipofuscin granules or intra cellular junk caused by the breakdown of proteins and other molecules. Their cell loss and atrophy is at an incredibly slower rate than, let's say, a human being, whose cells are replaced very slowly, more slowly than the cells die. These ageless animals have very few senescent cells which have reached the point where they can no longer divide. These cellular characteristics have made possible indefinite life spans for these animals. Methuselah is much more likely to become the victim of a careless driver who crushes his shell than to die of old age.

Early on the goal was to develop a serum which would transfer these cellular properties to a lab mouse. After thousands of variations and attempts, I finally succeeded with Jasper. I believe he is well on his way to a new longevity record. He has lived well beyond the normal lifespan of two and a half years for a lab mouse. In eight months he will break the current longevity record as recorded by the Methuselah Foundation. Once I determined that Jasper was healthy and successfully living beyond the normal life span, I injected myself with the serum. It's been nine days and I feel great.

Methuselah Journal Entry: December 24, 2011

I woke up today missing Anna dearly. It's been nearly seventeen years since I lost her, but some days the pain is as acute as the day she died. The holiday season doesn't help. The Christmas lights all over town bring back memories. It was our favorite time of year, the only time I would attend church with her. Of course, I went because she insisted. At times I was drawn to the idea of a loving Creator, probably because of her love for God and for me. Her death extinguished any spiritual flame that may have been flickering. Why would a loving God cut someone like Anna down in the prime of life? If God wanted to draw me closer, why would he rip my heart out? It didn't make sense. I haven't darkened the doorway of a church since.

I still believe in a Creator. The universe is too ordered to doubt that an intelligent force is behind it. But this Cosmic Designer isn't interested in me or anyone else on a personal level. He set things in motion and then stood back to watch indifferently, maybe even apathetically. He gave life, and, for most species, appointed death. That was his mistake, though. There are a few animals who defy death, and I have tapped into their secrets. I have plucked eternal fruit from the Tree of Life. I plan on missing my appointment with the Grim Reaper. Will God be angry? I doubt it. He's probably not even paying attention.

Tonight I will spend Christmas Eve alone. I will get through it. The pain of loss now motivates me. I am mapping out my strategy for a new world—one in which I hold the key to life. There is so much to consider. This serum is miraculous and dangerous. God appointed Death for a reason. To upset the natural order of things has its consequences. Who deserves a drink from the Fountain of Youth? Everyone? Or a select few?

Lately I've been spending a lot of time with Mee Mee Roberts, the owner of the bookstore in Buxton. She is several years younger than I and has a youthful spirit. We have a lot in common. Like me, she is athletic and loves to read. My feelings for her are growing. I don't know yet if it's mutual. Time will tell. If she does have a strong attraction to me, I'm tempted to offer her a drink from the Fountain. We could grow young together. We have a date on New Year's Eve, the big dinner and dance at the Hatteras Civic Center. Maybe I'll mention the "L" word at the stroke of midnight after welcoming in the New Year with an affectionate hug and a kiss. If she is receptive, I could bring her home and reveal my discovery.

Of course, no one could ever replace Anna. It was on New Year's Eve I lost her. We were dancing at a ball in Washington, D.C. A lot of my research colleagues were there. Halfway through "Unchained Melody" she became dizzy and said she needed to sit down. On our way back to the table she collapsed. A brain aneurism took her life almost instantly. That night I felt Death's sting. This morning, like so many mornings since, it struck again. But the pain brought to mind the words of Shakespeare: "So shall thou feed on Death, that feeds on men, And Death once dead, there's no more dying then."

Joe C. Ellis

Methuselah Journal Entry: January 15, 2012

It's been three months since I injected myself with the Methuselah serum. My personal physician, Dr. Stanley Milburn, has been pressuring me for the last six months to begin prostate cancer treatments. I put him off, knowing I was on the verge of a breakthrough. I wanted to see what would happen if I came up with an accurate formula and effective serum. Could the reversal of aging in my cells combat cancer?

I am very hopeful. For months my symptoms increased: the constant sensation of the need to urinate, having to get up to take a leak three or four times during the night, interrupted flow, blood in the urine, discomfort in my back and hips. Ever since the injection my symptoms have been gradually decreasing. Last night I got up once to pee. I've never been so excited about draining my dragon in my life—just one time! Best night of sleep I've gotten in years.

Next month I have an appointment with Stanley. He wants to set up surgery to begin seed implant therapy. I'll insist on another PSA test and rectal exam before I agree to anything, although the "gloved" finger isn't one of my favorite exams. I'm confident that Stanley will discover things have softened up in there. I could be wrong. Maybe it's wishful thinking. If the PSA test comes back positive, then I'll have to go through with the procedure. I know I'm getting younger, but I don't want to take chances. Cancer has no preference. It kills both young and old. Still, I have great hope.

It's hard to keep all this to myself. Hans Metzger, my former research partner, called me today. He knows about my prostate cancer and asked me how it's going. I couldn't keep my mouth shut. I told him the symptoms seem to be decreasing. He became suspicious and asked about my research. Of course, I didn't tell him I injected myself with a serum that worked on a lab mouse. Basically, I said I've been stepping up to the plate, closing my eyes, and swinging for the fences. He laughed and told me I'll never succeed with that approach. I wanted to say you're wrong. I've already knocked it out of the park. Instead, I said, "We'll see. Time will tell." He must have noticed something in the tone of my voice. He asked if I was holding something back from him. I guess I got a little impertinent with him. I said if my methods are doomed to fail, why are you even worried? He tried to say he wasn't worried. Right. Poor Hans. He'll be so jealous when I break the news to the world.

Methuselah Journal Entry: February 2, 2012

Lately my mind has been burdened about the potential consequences of unveiling my discovery to the world. The more I think about it, the more I wonder if I should set a match to the formula and dump the serum down the drain. Or perhaps offer the injection to a limited few—only to those I completely trust.

At other times I become more profit minded. I guess it's my natural human tendency toward greed. Recently, I talked to a former research colleague. Rumor has it there's an underground organization that wants to get their hands on a formula and serum that could increase an average person's lifespan, even if only by a mere ten years. Its members, probably pharmaceutical bigwigs, have pooled their resources. What would they be willing to pay for a serum that doubles the human lifespan? Or triples it? I could become a very rich man if I wanted to be.

Think about it. If the serum is sold to the wealthy, then those same people would have longer lives to amass more riches. They would have more opportunity to gain control of the monetary pie, to corner the market on industry and technology. The disparity between the rich and the poor would continue to widen. They would also have the advantage in the political arena, which would increase their influence on culture in general. Those few would become god-like—immortal and powerful.

On the other hand, if the serum is produced in mass quantities and made available to the public in general, think of the repercussions. Our world can support only so many people. Without death, earth would become overpopulated. Food supplies would eventually run out. Wars would erupt over resources. Generational euthanasia may be instituted to ensure there is regular turnover. Older segments of society would be exterminated so that the younger people have their opportunity to live in a world free of severe shortages.

Decisions, decisions. Then there are the serum's healing properties to consider. If it can cure cancer and other age-related diseases, then it would be cruel to withhold it from those who are suffering. Think of the financial burden from medical expenses shouldered by society that could be eliminated if the aged could be restored to a mid-adult state.

But that outcome would rock two of our major industries—caring for the elderly and the funeral business. It's almost as if we need death to maintain a balance in this world.

It's getting late. I don't think I'll solve these future problems tonight. I might be counting my eggs too soon, anyway. The serum may yet fail. However, I'm feeling younger every day. When I'm sure of my success, I will definitely need an effective plan before I present my discovery to the world.

Methuselah Journal Entry: February 25, 2012

I got a call from Dr. Stanley Milburn today about my PSA results. He couldn't believe it. They were normal. At my appointment last week he knew something unusual was going on. He couldn't find anything atypical during the rectal exam. He checked me twice, which I didn't appreciate, and then told me he could no longer feel anything suspicious in the area. Now he wants to run another PSA test. It would be a waste of time. Obviously, the serum has succeeded in not only reversing aging in my cells but has also stopped the growth of cancer cells, slow-growing prostate cancer cells anyway. Perhaps it has even eliminated them. For the most part, prostate cancer is a disease of old men. That could be the reason the serum worked—my rejuvenated cells and renewed body somehow recognized the destructive presence of the cancer cells and eliminated them.

Cancer is not my area of expertise. I am only speculating. The serum may not be as effective on fast-growing cancers. I should offer myself as a case study to experts in the field. I'll have plenty of time to do it at some point in my future. But not now. I am not ready to surprise the world. It's been only five months since the injection. I will wait at least a year to see if there are any adverse effects. If I had to estimate, I'd say I'm about fifteen years younger, very comparable to a fifty year old. My hair is slightly thicker. I still have wrinkles, but my skin is not nearly as thin as it was back in October. It doesn't bruise or bleed as easily as it did before. I'm thinking more clearly, remembering names and places more easily.

I believe my most accurate assessment for my current age-state is my running times. I've always kept a running journal. When I was fifty, my best 5K time was 18:40. Today I went to Manteo High School's track and timed myself for 5000 meters. I hit 18:37. I definitely pushed myself to the limit. I don't think I could have run much harder, even if I had the benefit of competition pushing me. That kind of time for a sixty-five-year old puts me at the national-class level. I'm one of the elite in the United States. If I could drop one more minute, I could be the best in the world. Wouldn't that be fun—being the number one sixty-five-year old distance runner in the world? I would be tempted to travel to the big races on every continent and compete with the best. What a frivolous way to spend a few years. I'd love it. We'll see what happens. In the next six months I will keep timing myself and monitoring my age-state progress. If I am able to run a world-class time for my age group in practice, I'll enter a local race and see what happens. Posting that kind of time publicly will definitely raise some eyebrows.

Methuselah Journal Entry: April 3, 2012

I think I'm becoming obsessed with timing myself at the track. I set another personal age-group record today for 5000 meters: 18:13. I looked in my running journal from twenty years ago and found similar times when I was forty-five years old. How much younger will I get? With today's time I am currently the top sixty-five-year-old 5000 meter runner in the country. Nobody knows this but me. I haven't entered a road race for a year and a half. It's very tempting to show off, but I want to wait and see how much faster I can get.

Methuselah Journal Entry: July 21, 2012

I can tell the rate of rejuvenation has slowed over the last couple of months. My 5K times continue to improve but by lesser increments. In May I dropped down to 18: 03, in June 17:54, and today's time was 17: 49. According to my running journals, I could run in the mid-17s when I was thirty-five years old. That's all the faster I expect to get. I estimate sometime in October I will reach that state. Hopefully, I will remain there indefinitely. I will be thirty-five forever.

Someone might argue that my intense focus on physical conditioning has skewed the results. That is a reasonable observation. Perhaps I have become obsessive about getting in the best shape possible to prove my serum works. Even if that is the case, you cannot dispute that I am now posting world-class times for my age. I may not have been in this good of shape a year ago before I injected myself with the serum, but I was training at a high level every day and not even within two minutes of being world class. Breaking the age-group world record for 5000 meters will be proof positive.

Methuselah Journal Entry: September 15, 2012

I have come to an important decision. I'm not going to base my strategies for presenting my research to the world on greed. That would be wrong. I don't care how much this so called Medical Mafia is offering for a successful formula, I refuse to place the most important discovery of the twenty-first century into the hands of those who will exploit it, causing the gap between the haves and the have nots to further widen. Providing the serum to the masses at a low cost would also be a mistake. The world is not ready for it. It would upset the delicate balance between life and death.

With time it will become evident that my research has succeeded. My running will be the means by which I make the world aware of my success. I plan on traveling the world and running in the most prestigious races. As the months pass, those who understand the significance of my times and are able to put one and one together will conclude I have injected myself with a successful Methuselah serum. At that point I hope to make connections on every continent with the wisest and most trustworthy people, ones who will help me put together an effective, long-term plan for the successful introduction of human agelessness. It will take the combined effort of intellects from many fields to accomplish this: social, political, medical, philosophical. There is no hurry. Time is on my side now. My first race will be local, about a month from now at the Colony Lost and Found 5K. It will be the first stepping stone in the journey of offering hope to the world. From there I will begin my mission.

After coming to this conclusion this morning, I received a call from Hans Metzger. He said he was concerned about me, knowing several months had passed since we last talked. He asked if I started seed implant therapy yet for my prostate cancer. I told him the cancer was gone. He assumed I had some kind of radical surgery. I told him that wasn't the case. Then he began questioning me about my research. I told him at this point I wasn't ready to divulge any details, but that I had been making progress. He said he could be a great connection for me to a clandestine organization which was paying a huge sum of money for a successful Methuselah formula. I said I wasn't interested. Then he became irritated with me and reminded me of all the years we worked together forming the basis of research upon which I have built my current findings. I assured him I had gone a completely different direction from what we had compiled in our partnership. Then, point blank, he asked me if I had injected myself with a successful serum. I told him it was none of his business. He hung up on me. I had to laugh. Poor Hans is burning up with envy.

6

The old man examined his face in the bathroom mirror. He smoothed his neatly trimmed white mustache and beard. Repositioning his wire-rimmed glasses on the bridge of his bulbous nose, he noticed the bags under his eyes, the deep lines in his brow, and his sallow cheeks. He had plenty of hair on the sides of his head but not much on top. Would it grow back? He lifted his crimson pajama sleeve and examined the pinpoint of blood on his age-spotted forearm where he had injected himself with the serum. A strange energy surged through him. Was it his imagination or was it working already? Leaning closer to the mirror, he noticed a stray hair dangling from his nostril. With his thumb and forefinger he pinched it and yanked, wincing. He held the white strand up to his mouth and blew it into the air.

"Gone with the wind," he said and smiled. *White nose hairs, baldness, age spots, wrinkles, and farsightedness, all gone with the wind.* He glanced around the hotel bathroom. It was bright and clean as expected, plenty of white towels hanging on the racks and an inviting whirlpool tub he'd enjoy later. Nothing special but more than adequate. He'd pay off Pugach and send him on his way. He didn't trust that thug. The sooner Pugach left, the better. He'd hang out for a day at the hotel and enjoy a walk along the beach. He didn't want to rush out of there and stir up any suspicion. He was just a vacationer, that's all, enjoying a day on the Outer Banks. Then he'd drive up to Washington D.C. and make the delivery according to schedule.

His green Stanley coffee thermos sat on the counter next to the coffee maker. He picked it up and made sure the lid was on tight. At his feet sat the black briefcase. He leaned over and grabbed the handle and lifted it. In his hand he held the Fountain of Youth, the fruit of the Tree of Life. He would exchange it for a billion dollar payday. One billion dollars. Unbelievable. He was set for life, a long, long, long life.

The old man entered the spacious hotel room. Two queen-size beds sat against the wall to the right with a nightstand in between them. Pugach lay stretched out on the far bed, smoking a cigarette. The colorful painting of a vase of summer flowers on the wall above him contrasted with his menacing demeanor. The black stubble on his jaws matched his head, which he must have shaved a couple days ago. He had thick, black eyebrows, not quite a uni-brow but close. A white scar zigzagged down his cheek to his chin. A souvenir from a knife fight? He was a muscular man of medium height and weight, his cut body well defined by the tight jeans and navy blue t-shirt he wore. Tattoos covered his arms. He hadn't bothered to remove his pointy-toed cowboy boots, which were still muddy from cutting through the woods at the back of Hopkins's house.

The old man walked between the beds and placed the thermos on the night stand next to the lamp. He pivoted and stared at the mud soiling the blue-and-red-striped bedspread at Pugach's feet.

Pugach blew out a stream of smoke. "Any coffee left in that damn thermos?"

"No. It's empty."

"Shit."

"I can brew more. There's a complimentary coffee maker on the counter by the sink."

Pugach flicked ashes onto the bedspread. "Don't bother. I'm not stickin' round here much longer."

Good, the old man thought. You're not my idea of pleasant company. "You know this is a non-smoking room."

"Screw this room."

The old man walked to the other side of the room and placed the briefcase on top of a dresser next to the television. He glanced over his shoulder and noticed Pugach staring at the briefcase.

Pugach nodded toward the briefcase. "So that's it. The Fountain of Youth?"

"Yeah."

"Must be worth a shitload of cash."

The old man shrugged.

"You're paying me a hundred thousand bucks—most I've ever made for offing a guy."

"It had to be done. I'll get your money, and you can head out of here." The old man turned toward the coat-and-clothes rack beneath which he had placed his suitcase.

"Don't bother." Pugach grinned.

The old man halted and faced Pugach. "What?"

Pugach pulled a manilla envelope from under his leg and waved it in front of his chest. "I found this in your suitcase."

"You opened my suitcase?"

"Don't worry. I counted the dough. It's all there."

The old man felt his cheeks burning. "I know it's all there. I'm a man of my word. If I said I'd pay you a hundred thousand dollars, I meant it."

"How much are you making on this deal?"

"That's none of your concern."

Pugach reached into his t-shirt pocket and pulled out a folded piece of paper. He shook it a couple times to release the folds and smoothed it on his lap. "I found this in your suitcase too. Detailed delivery instructions from an organization who call themselves the Methuselah Triumvirate, otherwise known as the Medical Mafia."

"I don't appreciate you rummaging through my personal belongings."

"I'm sure Dr. Sylvester Hopkins didn't appreciate you rummaging through his personal belongings either."

The old man couldn't argue that point.

Pugach folded the paper and inserted it back into his t-shirt pocket. "What do you think? Will the cops call it a suicide?"

"I don't know. I doubt it. I wish you wouldn't have shot him so quickly."

"He was useless. I could tell he wasn't going to talk."

"So what if he didn't talk? We could have taken our time in the lab. Kept things neat. Instead, we had to hurry and tear it apart to find what we wanted."

Pugach moved to the edge of the bed and planted his boots on the floor. "We found it, didn't we?"

"Yeah, but now I'm afraid a good investigator will figure out what happened."

Pugach put his cigarette out on the corner of the lamp stand, the smoke curling and dissipating. "You worry too much, old man."

The old man stood straight and put his hands on his hips. "I won't be old for long."

"You injected yourself with the serum?"

"That'sright."

"Isn't that risky?"

"What do I got to lose? I'm seventy-one years old. If it works, by this time next year I'll be as young and strong as you. Now, could I please have my instruction sheet back?"

Pugach patted his t-shirt pocket. "You're not going to need it."

"What do you mean?"

Pugach grinned, revealing a chipped front tooth. "Don't count on becoming Peter Pan either."

"Peter Pan? What are you talking about?" Fear, like a cold glass of water shot through him.

"Peter Pan—forever young. Don't count on it." Pugach arose from the bed and ambled to the desk next to where the old man stood. He lifted a leather jacket from the back of the chair and funneled his arms into it.

Good. He's leaving, the old man thought.

Pugach zipped the jacket, walked to the dresser and lifted the briefcase.

"You can't take that."

Pugach put his hand into his jacket pocket and pulled out a pistol. "The Methuselah Triumvirate just got a new delivery boy."

The old man raised his hands. "D-d-don't do this. W-w-we can work out a deal. There's lots of money involved here. A billion dollars. More than you or I could ever spend in a lifetime."

"One billion dollars? Now that *is* a lot of money. But like you, I plan on living forever. And I just don't know what inflation will be like one hundred years from now."

The old man closed his eyes and lowered his head.

"You know the difference between my plans and your plans?" Pugach asked.

The old man opened his eyes and stared at the barrel of the gun.

"I plan on living forever, and so far so I've been right. But . . ."

The barrel flashed, and the old man felt a searing jolt in the middle of his chest. He fell backwards onto the floor.

"Your days are done."

The old man could barely breathe. In his agony he glanced up to see Pugach stepping over him. He heard a door open and close. He was alone. He placed his hand on his chest. His shirt was wet and warm. He lifted his hand and saw his palm covered with blood. Above him he could make out the edge of the desk. He reached up and gripped the corner of the desk. He tried to pull himself up but didn't have the strength.

His finger nudged something on top of the desk. A pen? He extended his hand as far as he could on the desktop until he felt the object under his fingertips. He dragged it off the edge. The pen landed and bounced away from him. The room was swirling, his vision blurry. Somehow he managed to turn onto his belly and reach the pen. The pain was unbearable. Unsteadily, he wrote one word on the back of his hand before everything went black.

7

Dugan sat in a booth at Lisa's Pizzeria in Rodanthe, waiting for Marla and Gabe to arrive. He usually took Sundays off, but with the ongoing murder investigation, he figured he might end up putting in a few extra hours. His stomach rumbled, reminding him how hungry he was, and the sumptuous smell of good Italian cuisine didn't help. The restaurant was small but popular. For an afternoon in October the place was hopping, only one empty table and three waitresses, a blonde and two brunettes, scurrying to and fro in an effort to keep the customers happy.

Dugan sipped his coffee and glanced at his watch—1:05. Marla wanted to meet at one. If she didn't get there soon, he'd order an appetizer to hold him over, maybe fried mushrooms. Two tables away a hefty man with a butch haircut held up today's edition of the *Outer Banks Sentinel*, showing the front page to a redheaded lady who sat across from him. The headline read: MURDER AT MANTEO? Dugan guessed a reporter arrived shortly after he and Marla had left the crime scene last night. The crime tech guys couldn't give a definite answer concerning Hopkins's death so the reporter added a question mark.

"Can you believe it?" the big man said. With his free hand he held up the sports page which featured a photograph of Doc Hopkins breaking the tape at the finish line of yesterday's race. "The guy makes the front page of the news and the sports page on the same day. Not the way I'd want to make the front page, though."

Me neither, Dugan thought. He wondered if Marla discovered anything new in the pages of the diary. Stern and his crew came up empty handed but were heading back later that afternoon for another go round. Sometimes a second look with fresh eyes helped. The best chance was in Hopkins's lab. Just one slip up—a fingerprint, a shoeprint, a scrap of paper, a cigarette butt, something out of place, mud or blood or some kind of crud—something that would prove someone besides Hopkins had entered the lab that evening. Dugan trusted the CSI team's talents. If it could be found, they would find it. Dugan would head back to the crime scene after meeting with Marla and see if his fresh eyes could detect some missing piece to the puzzle.

Dugan peered over the big man's shoulder to see Marla enter the restaurant with little Gabe leading the way and another person, a slender woman, right behind her. As they drew closer Dugan recognized the woman, Mee Mee Roberts, the bookstore owner and Marla's former employer. Mee Mee walked with a spry step, quite fit for a gal in her late fifties. She had sandy blonde hair, about shoulder length, and a cute nose upon which was perched wire-rimmed glasses. Marla had mentioned how well Mee Mee knew Doc Hopkins, and Dugan guessed she invited Mee Mee along to fill them in on any pertinent information that might shed light on the case.

Dugan waved, and Gabe jumped, hopped, and skipped over to his table, leaving the two women behind.

"Hey, Dugan!" Gabe shouted.

Dugan raised his hand, and Gabe leapt to slap it. "What's up, Sport?"

"Mom says you and me are going fishing tonight."

"That's right. Taking you to the Rodanthe Pier."

"Awesome!"

"Hope you been doing your exercises. You might hook a big one, and I don't want it to pull you into the ocean."

Gabe laughed and flexed his biceps. "Don't worry about me. I can reel in a shark with these muscles."

Marla tousled Gabe's hair and slid into the seat across from Dugan.

"Can I sit next to Dugan?" Gabe asked.

"I guess so," Marla grumbled, the mock look of disappointment in her eyes.

"How you doing, Mee Mee?" Dugan asked.

Mee Mee smiled, a sad smile. "Happy to be alive, I guess." She sat next to Marla as Gabe plopped down by Dugan.

"Sorry," Dugan said. "I hear you and Doc Hopkins were good friends."

"Pretty close." Mee Mee glanced at Marla, and they seemed to connect on some wavelength to which Dugan didn't have access.

The waitress, a tall brunette with a pixie-style haircut, arrived and took their drink orders. Dugan raised his coffee cup to remind her he needed a refill. They quickly agreed to split an extra large pepperoni pizza, and the waitress assured them she'd deliver it to their table in about fifteen minutes.

Marla yawned, stretched her arms, and arched her back.

"Get much sleep last night?" Dugan asked.

Marla shook her head. "Stayed up 'til four reading that diary. But I finished it."

"Run across anything relevant to the case?"

"Definitely. I'm convinced Dr. Hopkins succeeded in producing a Fountain of Youth serum. He somehow discovered how to reverse aging in human cells."

"Did you bookmark the important parts?"

"Of course." Marla lifted her purse from the seat, unzipped it, and pulled out the journal. Pieces of note paper had been inserted between the pages. She flipped through to the first marker and placed the open book on the table. "Do you remember Jasper?"

"The lab mouse?"

"Yes."

"Was it a pet mouse?" Gabe asked.

"No," Marla said. "But I'm sure Dr. Hopkins thought the mouse was special."

"Oh," Gabe said, his brown, questioning eyes focused on his mom as she prepared to read.

"Listen to this. *Early on the goal was to develop a serum which would transfer these cellular properties to a lab mouse. After thousands of variations and attempts, I finally succeeded with Jasper. I believe he is well on his way to a new longevity record. He has lived well beyond the normal lifespan of two and a half years for a lab mouse. In eight months he will break the current longevity record as recorded by the Methuselah Foundation. Once I determined that Jasper was healthy and successfully living well beyond the normal life span, I injected myself with the serum. It's been nine days and I feel great."*

Dugan said, "I remember the journal entry you read to me last night—something about the mouse being worth a million dollars. How long ago was that entry you just read written?"

"October 24th, 2011."

"Almost a year ago?"

"Yes. Jasper is now the oldest living lab mouse on earth. And I checked on the Methuselah Foundation. They've got a website." Marla extracted her iPhone from her purse and poked her finger at an app icon. About twenty seconds later she read: "Our Mission: significantly extend the healthy lifespan of humanity." Marla glanced up. "They are serious about this." She navigated to another link. "Their strategy involves the development of revolutionary new life extension therapies through the experimentation of research teams whose common goal is to extend the life of lab mice. There are two categories of cash prizes. Longevity—a one million dollar cash prize awarded to the team who breaks the world record for the oldest-ever mouse. Rejuvenation—a one million dollar cash prize awarded to the team that develops the most successful late onset-rejuvenation that extends the life of the mice."

"Let me see that." Dugan reached across the table, and Marla handed him the phone. He skimmed down the webpage, gleaning the key points to the organization's mission. "This million dollar prize might have something to do with the murder. Someone else wanted to collect it—a competing researcher."

Mee Mee leaned forward. "But Sylvester could have cared less about collecting that prize money."

"Are you serious?" Dugan asked.

"Yes. He told me so himself."

"Why not?"

"He knew he was onto something bigger than extending the lifespan of a mouse. He thought he'd made the greatest discovery of the twenty-first century."

"How much did he tell you about it?" Dugan asked.

"Not much about the technical aspects of the Methuselah serum. I don't think he told anyone that he injected himself. But he liked to talk about his strategy of presenting his discovery to the world. I figured he came up with a new vitamin or chemical compound that helped to combat age-related diseases, maybe add a few years to the average person's lifespan. I didn't know he discovered a way to reverse aging in human cells."

Marla placed her hand on Mee Mee's shoulder. "Did you know he considered offering you the opportunity to be injected with the serum?"

Mee Mee whirled toward Marla, eyes wide. "What?"

Marla flipped through the journal. "Look here." She pointed at the page. *"Lately I've been spending a lot of time with Mee Mee Roberts, the owner of the bookstore in Buxton. She is several years younger than I and has a youthful spirit. We have a lot in common. Like me, she is athletic and loves to read. My feelings for her are growing. I don't know yet if it's mutual. Time will tell. If she does have a strong attraction to me, I'm tempted to offer her a drink from the Fountain. We could grow young together. We have a date on New Year's Eve, the big dinner and dance at the Hatteras Civic Center. Maybe I'll mention the "L" word at the stroke of midnight after welcoming in the New Year with an affectionate hug and a kiss. If she is receptive, I could bring her home and reveal my discovery."*

Mee Mee looked from Marla to Dugan, her face blanching. "He told me he loved me that night, but I didn't repeat the words back to him. I could tell he was hurt, but I didn't love him. We were good friends, that's all. After that night he didn't call as often." She shook her head. "Do you mean to tell me I could be thirty-five again right now?" Mee Mee eyed Dugan and then shifted her gaze to Marla.

Marla nodded slowly. "I have no doubt about it. If you would have gone home with him that night, he would have offered to inject you with the Methuselah serum."

"Hmmmmmph." Mee Mee sat back, crossed her arms, and stared at the ceiling.

"Are you okay?" Dugan asked.

Mee Mee blinked. "Just imagining myself out on the Pamlico Sound windsurfing again like I did twenty years ago."

"Wind surfing?" Dugan asked. "That's dangerous. Were you good at it?"

Mee Mee peered over her wire-rimmed glasses. "Got a couple shelves full of trophies at home to prove it."

Dugan held up his hands. "I believe you."

"Once you turn forty, the sport really beats you up. As much as I loved windsurfing, I gave it up when the other local windsurfers switched over to kiteboarding. By then the store demanded more and more of my time. But, boy, I really do miss being out on the sound—just letting it fly—wherever the wind took me."

Dugan scratched his cheek. "I didn't know our local bookstore owner had such a wild streak."

Mee Mee smiled wistfully. "I got an incredible sense of euphoria out on the water, as if the laws of this world didn't apply to me."

Gabe sat up straight. "Mee Mee, could you teach me to windsurf?"

Mee Mee chuckled. "Maybe one of these days, Sport, when you're a little older."

"Would you have accepted Dr. Hopkins's offer?" Marla asked.

Mee Mee shrugged. "It would have been tempting. I'm guessing Sylvester felt very alone in Eden. I could have been his Eve."

"Then again," Marla said, "things weren't quite perfect in Paradise."

"That's true," Dugan said. "What else did you find in the journal?"

"Dr. Hopkins wrestled with the ethical questions of offering the serum to others. He figured the rich would exploit this kind of opportunity to gain an even greater advantage in the world. Making the serum available to the masses would upset the balance between life and death—lack of resources, overpopulation—that sort of thing. Like the rest of us, he was tempted to make a buck. Let me rephrase that—mucho, mucho dinaro, but he felt very responsible. He wanted to do the right thing."

"With that kind of serum, what is the right thing?" Mee Mee asked.

"Well . . ." Marla flipped through the journal. "This was one of his later entries: *I have come to an important decision. I'm not going to base my strategies for presenting my research to the world on greed. That would be wrong. I don't care how much this so called Medical Mafia is offering for a successful formula, I refuse to place the most important discovery of the twenty-first century into the hands of those who will exploit it . . .*"

"Medical Mafia?" Dugan leaned on his elbows.

"Yes. One of his former colleagues told him about an organization known as the Methuselah Triumvirate. From what I gather they were rich pharmaceutical executives who wanted to get their hands on a new drug that could increase human lifespan. For some reason they were also known as the Medical Mafia."

"That makes sense to me," Mee Mee said. "The bigwigs at the drug companies aren't any better than Al Capone and Bugsy Siegel. They've got their hands so deep in our pockets—three hundred dollars for a bottle of antibiotics. A thousand bucks for chemotherapy drugs. Come on. How much profit do they need to make?"

"Apparently," Marla continued, "this Methuselah Triumvirate was willing to do anything to acquire a successful Fountain of Youth drug, even if it only extended the average lifespan a few years."

Dugan asked, "We need to make a list of any names from the journal of people who might know anything about this organization."

"There are a few names but no addresses or phone numbers."

"Nevertheless, names are good leads. I'm sure we could track them down."

"There is a name that comes up several times—a former research partner, Hans Metzger."

Mee Mee sat up. "Hans Metzger?"

"Do you know him?" Dugan asked.

Mee Mee nodded. "Met him once when he came to town to visit Sylvester. Didn't like the guy at all."

"Why not?" Marla asked.

"He seemed disingenuous to me. Supposedly they were old friends, and Metzger made the trip down from Washington, D.C. just to reconnect with Sylvester, talk about the good old days. But I could tell he had an ulterior motive. He kept trying to get Sylvester to open up about his current research."

"How long ago was this?" Dugan asked.

Mee Mee tilted her head. "Bout six months ago. Believe me, Metzger wasn't interested in reviving the friendship."

The waitress arrived with the pizza and pitcher of Coke, and Dugan cleared the middle of the table to make room. For the time being while Dugan poured the drinks and Marla divvied up the pizza, they tabled the discussion about the contents of the journal. The pizza hit the spot. Dugan gobbled three large slices down within ten minutes. He noticed Gabe almost kept pace with him.

"Take it easy there, Sport," Marla said. "You'll get a stomach ache."

With his mouth half full, Gabe said, "No way. I loooooooove pizza!"

As Dugan watched the boy smiling and chewing, he pictured himself as Dugan's father—tossing a baseball to the boy, fishing, camping, wrestling around on the floor—things Dugan's father rarely did with him. He loved the kid. Did he love the boy's mom too? He had to admit, lately he caught himself daydreaming often about her. Whenever she inadvertently touched him, his heart soared. But fantasies didn't qualify as love. And schoolboy emotional sensations didn't register as love either. He was a realist. He didn't want a one-sided relationship. His mother and father had had that, and it made for a miserable home life until his father finally left. Then at least he didn't have to listen to their arguments. He'd rather stay single and wait for a woman who truly loved him. Marla was beyond his reach. Every once in a while, though, she looked at him with appraising eyes, as if she were sizing him up. Was it possible she actually wondered if he would make a good husband? Dugan doubted it, but he kept the door of that possibility open just enough to allow a sliver of light through.

Dugan glanced up and noticed Mee Mee eyeing him.

"You know, Dugan," Mee Mee said, "you'd make a great father."

He shifted his gaze to Marla and noticed Mee Mee's words got her attention. His face suddenly felt hot. Mee Mee glanced at Marla and they connected again on that wavelength Dugan couldn't tune in to. Had they talked about this before? Dugan tried to discern from Marla's expression whether or not she was surprised by Mee Mee's statement.

"Don't you think so, Marla?" Mee Mee asked.

Marla's eyes widened slightly, and her mouth dropped open for a few seconds. "Of course. Dugan's a good man. Known him most my life. He'll make a great daddy some day."

To Dugan, Marla's words seemed patronizing. "Please, ladies, you don't have to proclaim the merits of my future fatherhood. I may never get married."

Marla slapped her hand on the table. "I don't believe that. Seriously, you'd make a wonderful dad."

Now she feels guilty, Dugan thought.

Gabe gulped his soda and set the plastic cup on the table. "I'd like you to be my dad, Dugan."

All three adults turned towards Gabe. Dugan felt a lump in his throat and swallowed. As he studied the seven year old he recognized something in the boy—himself at that age and the gnawing need for the love of a father. Dugan picked up a napkin and wiped his mouth. In the uncomfortable silence his mind raced to fill the void. Back to the case. "So you think this Hans Metzger guy could be a person of interest, eh Mee Mee?"

"For sure. Call it a woman's intuition, but I could tell he wasn't on the up and up. Sylvester might have trusted him, but I didn't"

"I don't think Dr. Hopkins trusted him either," Marla said. "When he mentions Metzger in the journal, it's not in a favorable light."

"What do you mean?" Dugan asked.

Marla paged through the journal. "Like this entry: *I can tell he's worried that I have made a significant advance. We worked for ten years side by side. I had to break away from him. He was unwilling to think outside the box. We could have spent another thirty years plodding along, turning over every stone to make sure each step of the scientific method was followed so that no detail would be left undocumented. I knew there had to be a better way. He may be a more meticulous researcher than I, but I'd rather be lucky than good. He wasn't willing to take chances. But now he's worried that my risky methods paid off.*"

"My, my," Mee Mee said, "Sylvester *could* see past Metzger's masquerade."

"Here's another one: *Hans Metzger, my former research partner, called me today. He knows about my prostate cancer and asked me how it's going. I couldn't keep my mouth shut. I told him the symptoms seem to be decreasing. He became suspicious and asked about my research. Of course, I didn't tell him I injected myself with a serum that worked on a lab mouse.*"

"His cancer symptoms decreased?" Dugan asked.

Marla nodded. "Later in the journal he talks about a PSA test that came back negative. The serum completely healed him of prostate cancer. Metzger kept contacting him, inquiring about his illness, and eventually Dr. Hopkins told Metzger he was cancer free."

"Hmmmm." Dugan sat back and rubbed his chin. "Metzger might have been looking for the race results online—a final proof that Doc Hopkins succeeded."

"Then what?" Marla asked. "Do you think he drove down from Washington, D.C. on the pretense of a friendly visit, shot Dr. Hopkins, and then ransacked the lab to find the serum?"

"It's a possibility. At least we have another name for the list of people to question. We'll plan on a drive up north to look up Hines and Metzger." A Lady Antebellum tune, "Need You Now," erupted from below Dugan's side of the table. He sat back, dug his hand into his pocket, pulled out his iPhone, and touched the answer icon. "Sheriff Walton." His eyes locked on to Marla's. "Yes . . . Are you sure? . . . Okay . . . Nags Head . . . Comfort Inn. Is anyone on the scene yet? Not yet? I'll get there as fast as I can. Send a couple deputies as soon as they can be freed up." Dugan ended the call.

Marla placed both hands on the table and leaned forward. "What's going on?"

"There's been another murder."

8

Dugan stood, his chair tottering backwards. He pulled out his wallet and threw a twenty on the table. "I've got to take off. There's no one at the scene yet. The hotel manager is waiting."

Dugan's urgency sent a jolt of adrenaline through Marla. "Where? What happened" She placed her hands on the table, leaning forward to rise.

"At the Comfort Inn in Nags Head."

"Someone got killed?" Gabe asked.

Marla shooshed him, stood, and faced Dugan. "Can I come with you?"

Dugan pointed to the boy. "What about Gabe?"

Marla shifted her eyes to Mee Mee.

Mee Mee waved her hand. "No problem. I'll take Sport with me."

"Aw, Mom. I want to go to the murder scene with you and Dugan."

"You go with Mee Mee. A crime scene is no place for a boy."

"Please, Mom."

Mee Mee patted Gabe's shoulder. "Come with me, Sport. I've got a new book for you at the store."

Gabe turned to Mee Mee, the disappointment in his face fading. "What kind of book?"

"A shark book."

"A book about fishing for sharks?"

"How did you know?"

"Thanks, Mee Mee," Marla said. "Shall we pick him up at the store?"

"Yeah. There's always plenty for me to do there, even on Sunday."

"We've gotta move," Dugan insisted as he turned and headed for the door.

Marla grabbed her purse and quickly kissed Gabe. "Love ya, Sport."

"Love you too, Mom."

Hurrying toward the exit, eyeing Dugan's backside, she couldn't help thinking how dashing he seemed when duty called.

The drive from Rodanthe to Nags Head was about twenty-five miles. At normal speeds Marla usually covered the distance in a half hour, but Dugan kept the pedal down, zooming along Cape Hatteras National Park Road at 80 to 90 miles per hour. The lights and, when needed, the siren on the Impala cleared the way along the two-lane road. Drivers hastily pulled off to the side when they heard or saw them coming. The speed felt exhilarating to Marla, although at times a natural fear arose, buzzing in her chest and lodging in her throat. She tried to stifle the feeling by focusing on the beauty of the dunes, thickets, and salt marshes, but the scenery flew by so fast her stomach became queasy. She pressed the button on the door's arm rest to lower the window slightly. Fresh air would help. Better keep my eyes straight ahead, Marla thought, before I lose my lunch.

"Are you sure this is a murder?" Marla asked.

"The hotel manager thinks so, but it's better not to count victims before they're tagged."

"Sounds like a good policy. The murder rate is fairly low in Dare County."

"Yeah, last year we had one, the year before, none, and this week, possibly two."

"Do you think they could be related?"

Dugan shot her a quick glance. "The possibility crossed my mind, but I really can't base the hunch on sound reasoning."

"Intuition?"

Dugan chuckled. "Maybe it's ESP."

Marla gazed at Dugan's profile. His freckles had faded since junior high. She never considered him to be attractive as a kid, but his looks definitely improved as he aged. He had become uniquely handsome with his orangish-brown sideburns and strong jaw line. He had a good body. Most women probably wouldn't consider him "hot." He didn't get Marla's blood boiling, that's for sure, but the more time she spent with him, the more his looks grew on her. Most importantly, she felt comfortable around him. She knew she could be herself and didn't worry about putting up a front to impress the "boss." She liked him a lot and wondered how fine the line was between like and love. Did love have to sweep her off her feet?

"ESP huh?" Marla asked.

Dugan smiled. "That's right."

"Can you tell me what I was just thinking?"

Dugan's lips tightened before he said, "I've always had trouble reading a woman's mind."

That's probably best, Marla thought. She wasn't quite sure where those thoughts were leading anyway. At thirty-four maybe she had become too old to fall hard for anyone. She'd already fallen head over heels for one man, the love of her life—Gabriel. And he had been murdered seven years ago. Gabe was the product of that love. Her child was far more important than any future romance that may ever develop between her and another man. Perhaps her view of love was changing.

Once in Nags Head, Dugan turned off Cape Hatteras National Park Road onto Gulfstream Street. He went only a few hundred feet before making a right turn onto Old Oregon Inlet Road. The Comfort Inn was a six-story, bright-white hotel with aqua-trimmed windows perched on the edge of the ocean. As they pulled into the parking lot Marla could hear the surf pounding on the beach. Dugan navigated to the closest open space, one not far from the covered entrance. When Marla opened the car door, the strong breeze slammed it against her. Although it startled her, she knew she should have expected it. The breeze always blew with greater force near the ocean, but the sudden impact against her shoulder and leg gave her an eerie sensation, a foreboding chill. Now she wondered if it had been a good idea to accompany Dugan on this call. What awaited them in this hotel room? She didn't have time to dwell on it. Dugan already had launched out his side of the car and was hurrying toward the entrance.

"Wait up," Marla called. Dugan stopped at the glass door and held it open for her. She entered and blinked, adjusting to the transition from harsh sunlight into the darker interior. Earth tones enveloped the room, brown tiled floor, viridian walls, a medium oak front desk, and splashes of yellow-green from the ferns placed around on various tables.

A man with a round face, wide eyes, and an obvious comb-over greeted them. He wore beige pants and a striped blue shirt. "I'm Orson Fellows, the hotel manager. You must be law officers. I saw you get out of the sheriff's vehicle."

Dugan glanced down at his flannel shirt and jeans. "Sorry, I'm not dressed for the occasion, but I got the call. I'm Sheriff Walton," he motioned to Marla, ". . . and this is Deputy Easton. More deputies and an emergency vehicle will be here shortly."

Marla nodded. "Nice to meet you."

The hotel manager wrung his hands. "They t-told you about the b-body?"

"Yes," Dugan said. "Are you the one who discovered it?"

He shook his head no. "Maria Burgos, one of our maids, found it about forty-five minutes ago when she entered the room to clean it."

"Is she here?" Dugan asked. "I'd like to talk to her."

"She's a little shook up. I told her to sit down back in the workers' lounge. I'll send for her."

"No hurry. I'd like to see the body first."

The manager nodded. "Follow me."

They walked a short distance down a green carpeted hallway with pale yellow walls. The manager stopped in front of stainless steel elevator doors and pressed the "up" button. The doors separated instantly.

They entered the elevator. With his head bowed slightly, eyes hooded by his bushy brown eyebrows, the manager said, "The room's on the sixth floor. It was occupied by a man named Vernon Gray."

Marla felt her weight slightly increase and her stomach become queasy as the elevator shot up and then slowed down. *Get your mind off the nausea. Think of a question.* "Did . . . did the man have an ID?"

"Of course. You must have a credit card to secure a room. Our staff also will ask to see a driver license if they notice anything suspicious about the person. Lots of identity theft going around nowadays."

The elevator doors opened and the man led them to the left and down a long hallway with doors on both sides and an occasional painting of an ocean scene hanging in the space between the rooms.

"Did the man have a guest with him?" Dugan asked.

"As far as we know, he was alone. That's what he indicated on the form anyway."

They stopped in front of room 620 near the end of the hall. "How did the maid know he was dead?" Dugan asked.

The manager pulled the plastic key card out of his shirt pocket. "She shook him and discovered he was stiff. Then she turned him over to make sure and saw the blood all over his chest and carpet. It rattled her pretty badly." He inserted the card into the slot on the door handle and removed it rapidly. The small indicator light flashed green, and he turned the handle and opened the door slightly.

Dugan placed his hand on the door to keep it open. "Do you mind if I keep the key for now?"

"Certainly not." He handed Dugan the plastic card. "Would you like me to bring Maria up here to talk to you?"

"Please do. Tell her not to worry. We'll come out into the hallway to interview her. She doesn't have to look at that body again."

The manager nodded, lowered his head, and marched quickly down the corridor.

Dugan met Marla's gaze and said, "You all right?"

"I'm fine. Why?"

"You look a little pale."

"Must have been the ride here." She rubbed her belly. "A little queasy, but I'll be fine. Lead the way."

Dugan pushed the door all the way open, and Marla instantly whiffed a coppery odor, similar to the smell at Dr. Hopkins's house but stronger.

"Whew," Dugan said. "The victim lost a lot of blood in here."

"That's what smells?"

"That and decomposition."

Dugan entered the room and Marla followed. The lights had been left on by the maid. The room was fairly long with two queen beds, both covered by somewhat disheveled blue-and-red-striped bedspreads. To the right sat a long dresser, a flat-screen television atop of it. Next to the dresser was a wooden chair and desk. The corpse lay on its back between the desk and the far bed. Beyond the body Marla could see a white countertop and mirror and a door to the left that she assumed led to the bathroom.

The victim was old, probably in his seventies. His eyes had rolled up into the back of his head with only the bottoms of his irises showing, his mouth frozen into a grimace. He had a large nose on which wire-rimmed glasses sat askew. His crimson pajamas made it difficult to detect the bloodstain, but upon closer inspection Marla could see the darker red surrounding a hole in the pajama top on the left side of his chest.

Dugan pointed. "The manager said the maid shook him and turned him over. See the blood on the carpet?"

Marla inspected the floor between the victim's arm and the side of his body. A large section appeared dark brown against the green hue of the rug. "He bled a lot."

"Did you notice what was in his hand?"

Marla shifted her eyes to the victim's left hand and saw nothing.

"Not that one. Over here."

Dugan stepped out of the way and Marla scooted to her left and leaned to get a look. The right hand gripped a pen. Was he shot in the act of writing something? Maybe signing his name to a document? A check? "I don't see any paper or notepad he could have written on."

"Could be underneath him," Dugan said.

"Or the killer might have taken it."

"Assuming he didn't shoot himself."

Marla examined the floor around the body. Then she looked at the desk, dresser and night table. "I don't see a gun. If he was alone and shot himself, it would still be here."

"Let's lift him up and look underneath him to make sure. The maid already disturbed the body. It was face down when she entered the room. Maybe she rolled him on top of the gun."

The thought of touching a dead body didn't help ease the nervous tension in Marla's stomach. She swallowed and tried to relax. "Where do you want me?"

Dugan stepped between the bed and the body. "Stand beside me. I'll grab his arm, and you grab his pant leg. We'll just lift him up enough to make sure a gun's not under him or a piece of paper he might have written on. Then we'll set him back in the same position."

Marla took a deep breath, blew it out, and said, "If you insist." She carefully moved into the small space next to Dugan, reached down and clasped the silky crimson material near the victim's knee.

Dugan counted to three, and they lifted and peered under the body. Nothing. Slowly, they lowered the corpse to the floor.

Dugan brushed his hands together several times and then pointed to the night stand. "Look there." On the corner of the nightstand in the glow of the lamp next to a green thermos lay a cigarette butt.

"This is a non-smoking room," Marla said. "I saw the sign on the door. Why would he reserve a non-smoking room if he smoked?"

"Doesn't make sense . . . unless Mr. Gray had a visitor who smoked. We might be able to get some DNA evidence from that cigarette butt. Did you notice when we entered the room that both bedspreads were slightly mussed?"

Marla nodded. "You think the visitor murdered him?" Marla asked.

"That'd be my guess."

"And the motive?"

Dugan rubbed his chin and looked around the room. "Robbery. Let's see if we can find his wallet. The thief would have taken money and credit cards."

Marla walked toward the entry door where the coat rack was located. She had spotted a suitcase below a black windbreaker hanging on the rack. The suitcase, about two feet long and composed of blue polyester, had two zipped compartments on top. She glanced at Dugan. "Here's his luggage. Should we disturb it?"

"Don't grab the handle. There might be prints." Dugan stepped beside her.

"It's unzipped."

Dugan knelt and carefully lifted the top, touching only the fabric.

Marla crouched beside him. "There's the wallet tucked right beside that t-shirt."

Dugan pulled a handkerchief from his front shirt pocket and used it to extract the brown leather wallet. He carefully spread the two sides to reveal a number of fifties and twenties. "That doesn't make sense."

"Got to be three or four hundred dollars there. Robbery must not have been the motive."

Using his forefinger and thumb, Dugan pinched the corners of the plastic cards inserted in the slot on one of the side sections and jiggled them out. He laid them on the floor. "There's his license. Vernon Gray. Born 5/7/1938. That makes him . . . uh . . ."

"Seventy-four years old."

"Right. Math wasn't one of my stronger subjects." With his fingertip he flipped the card over to look at the next one. "Mastercard. Vernon Gray." He flipped the credit card off the pile. "Whoa. Another driver license."

Marla leaned closer. "Two driver licenses?"

"Check out the name."

Marla gasped. "Hans Metzger."

When their eyes met, Dugan raised an eyebrow. "Like I told you, I've got E.S.P." He flipped the driver license off the pile. "Discover Card. Hans Metzger."

A surge of pin-prickly energy rushed up Marla's back. "He must have . . . he must have been involved in the murder. The journal mentions him several times. Somehow he knew Dr. Hopkins formulated a successful serum."

"Plus Metzger may have seen Doc Hopkins's 5K time from Saturday's race. He knew all right. But I don't think he pulled the trigger."

"He hired a killer?"

"That's right—someone to do the dirty work."

"And the hit man double-crossed him."

Dugan collected the cards and inserted them back into the wallet. Then he tucked the wallet into the same position in the suitcase next to the t-shirt. He stood, placed his hands on his hips, and panned the room.

Marla rose beside him. "Dugan, what are you looking for?"

"The killer was interested in something much more valuable than the contents of Metzger's wallet."

Marla laid her hand on Dugan's arm. "The serum?"

Dugan nodded. "My guess is Metzger revealed too much information about what was taken from the lab."

"And the killer wanted more than what his contract offered."

"Exactly." Dugan strode across the room toward the far bed and stood next to the body. He turned and faced Marla. "I'm going to check his arm."

"For what?"

"A needle mark." He crouched, leaning over the body. "There it is."

Marla hurried over and noticed the victim's arms rested beside his body palms up. Near the middle of the left forearm she spotted a small red dot. "He injected himself with the serum."

"No doubt. And the killer figured out Metzger stood to cash in major bucks on the magic formula they'd stolen from the lab."

"Makes sense," Marla said. "If he had no qualms about killing Dr. Hopkins in cold blood, why would he hesitate to knock off Metzger?"

"It's all about the money—the root of all evil. This Medical Mafia wants the Fountain of Youth serum desperately. They don't care who hands it over. Metzger's assassin must have tied all the loose ends together and realized his payoff was pocket change compared to what Metzger would make."

"So you think he shot Metzger and took off with the serum?"

"Maybe." Dugan crossed his arms.

Marla noticed Dugan's eyes, that faraway look he got whenever he ruminated over an issue or a problem. "What are you thinking?"

"That serum," he said. "It's like . . . it *really is* like the forbidden fruit from the Garden of Eden. It just hangs there in front of your face, tempting you."

"Without a moral compass it's easy to pluck it from the tree and take a bite."

Dugan shook his head. "I don't care how moral your compass is, if you're human, you want to take a bite. Don't you want to be well off and live a long, healthy life?"

Marla shrugged. "Yes, but not if it meant killing someone."

"Leave murder out of the equation. Wouldn't you pick the fruit and take a bite if it meant wealth and longevity?"

"I don't know. It would be tempting. But didn't God tell Adam and Eve not to eat the fruit of that tree?"

Dugan scratched his cheek. "Seems like there were two trees in that garden that were off limits. 'Course, I'm not a Bible scholar. I sure would like to know one thing, though."

"What's that?"

"Is the fruit still in this room, or did the hit man find it and take off?"

A loud knock rattled the door, and a muffled voice said, "Sheriff Walton, I brought Maria up here to talk to you."

Marla and Dugan's eyes met, and then Dugan led the way across the room and out the door. In the hallway a middle-aged lady in a white uniform stood next to Orson Fellows. About five feet tall, she had dark, shoulder-length hair and very pretty brown eyes. Marla guessed she was Hispanic. With all of the tourist industry jobs available, the Outer Banks had become a multi-cultural region.

After introducing himself and Marla, Dugan asked, "Did you notice anyone in the hallway before you entered the room?"

Maria shook her head no. Her eyes shifted from Dugan to Marla and back to Dugan.

"Have you seen anyone who looked suspicious to you? Not just on this floor. Anywhere in the hotel?"

"I don't think so," she said. "I'm very busy. Much work to do."

Dugan nodded. "When you found the body, the man was lying on his stomach, right?"

"Yes."

"And you turned him over?"

"Yes, to see if he was alive. But he was very stiff."

Marla asked, "Did you notice he was holding a pen?"

Maria bobbed her head. "Oh, yes."

Marla continued, "But you didn't see any scraps of paper he could have written on?"

"No paper." Maria pointed to the back of her hand. "Here."

"On his hand?" Dugan asked. "He wrote on his hand?"

Dugan and Marla's eyes met. Marla said, "We missed it. Metzger's palms were up."

"And when we lifted him, we didn't examine the backs of his hands," Dugan said. He turned to Maria. "Do you remember what he wrote?"

Maria shook her head. "I don't know. 'The something.' I'm not sure."

"*The something*? Okay. Well . . . I guess that's all for now, Maria," Dugan said. "Thank you very much"

Maria nodded. Dugan asked Fellows for his cell phone number and told him he'd call if he needed anything else. Together, the maid and the manager retreated down the hallway.

Dugan thumbed toward the door. "Let's check out the back of Metzger's hand."

They entered the room and Marla said, "It's got to be on the back of his left hand."

"Why's that?"

"Because the pen's in his right hand, and he injected himself into his left arm."

Dugan tapped his finger on his temple. "I knew that."

They circled the body and knelt at the head. Marla decided to let Dugan do the honors. He carefully lifted the arm. Because of the onset of rigor mortis, the whole body seemed to resist the attempt. Finally, Dugan managed to lift it enough for Marla to get a peek.

Marla read, "T-H-E . . . R-M-O-S"

"That's it? 'The Rmos?'" Dugan lowered the arm. "What does that mean? Is it a name?"

"Maybe he didn't live long enough to finish what he wanted to write."

"The Ramos? The Rumors? The Rooms?"

Marla raised her head and stared at the object in the glow of the reading lamp on the stand between the beds. She reached and grabbed Dugan's wrist. "Look there."

Dugan peered in that direction. "Thermos!"

9

The thermos appeared to be an older model, the kind Dugan's grandpa had carried to work into the West Virginia coal mines. As Dugan approached it, a strange sensation danced down his spine, through his legs to the tips of his toes—a feeling he had only experienced in church a few times. He picked up the thermos and slowly moved it in a circular motion to see if he could feel any coffee swirling on the inside. It definitely wasn't filled with liquid, but something rocked back and forth. Marla walked between the beds toward him. He spun off the plastic black cup to reveal a white round cap. He set the cup on the nightstand.

Marla said, "Do you think it could be . . ."

"We'll see." Dugan tried to turn the cap with his left hand. It was on tight, forcing him to clasp the cylinder against his body in order to get better leverage. The cap released, and Dugan twisted it off. He stared into the hole. "Can't see anything." He tilted the thermos, feeling the contents sliding toward the opening. A black cap appeared at the ledge of the opening. With his thumb and index finger Dugan lifted the cap slightly and threaded it through the opening. A narrow glass bottle filled with yellow-green liquid slid from the mouth of the thermos into Dugan's hand.

"That's got to be the serum," Marla gasped.

Dugan nodded. "That'd be my guess." He lowered it into the lamplight. "So this is the fruit of the Tree of Life."

Marla stepped closer. "It looks toxic."

"Hold this." He handed Marla the bottle.

She stared at it, her hand shaking slightly. "I don't want to drop it."

Dugan lowered the thermos into the glow of the lamp to illuminate the inside. He tilted his head to get a better view. "There's something else inside here. Looks like a rolled up piece of notebook paper." He inserted two fingers into the opening, his hand pivoting at different angles in an attempt to latch onto to the paper. "I can't get it."

"Let me try. I've got long, skinny fingers."

They traded objects, and Marla shook the thermos in an attempt to get the rolled up paper closer to the opening. She crossed her index and middle fingers before sticking them into the opening. After a few seconds she extracted her fingers, the paper, rolled up like a scroll, pinched between the tips. "Got it."

"Careful. Don't pull it out too fast. You might tear it."

Marla inched the paper through the opening using her thumb to help ease it forward until the end finally came out. She set the thermos on the nightstand and placed the scroll of paper on the bed, spread it, and flattened it with the palm of her hand. Printed in block lettering at the top were the words METHUSELAH FORMULA. Below the heading a multitude of numbers, letters, plus signs, parentheses, and other symbols filled the page. Marla had no idea what they could mean. Dr. Hopkins had carefully written each character by hand. In the margins he had scribbled a few notes which were harder to read.

Dugan lifted the paper from the bed. "This formula is more important than what's in the bottle. This is how it's made. "

Marla nodded. "The chemical combination for agelessness."

Dugan turned the paper over. "Look here." He pointed to a heading at the bottom of the page. "INSTRUCTIONS ON HOW TO INJECT THE SERUM. With a hypodermic needle withdraw 10 ml of serum from the bottle. The needle should be inserted into the subcutaneous fat layer just below the skin. Squeeze a couple of inches of skin on the forearm between the thumb and fingers. Insert needle into the fold but not into the muscle. Press plunger. Release the grip on the skin fold and remove needle."

"Sounds simple enough."

Dugan shook the paper. "This formula is what the Medical Mafia wants. Who knows what they're willing to pay for it."

"What are we going to do with it?"

Music erupted from Dugan's pants pocket, Lady Antebellum's "Need You Now." "My phone. Hold these."

Marla took the serum and formula.

Dugan fished his phone out of his pocket. "Sheriff Walton . . . yeah . . . okay. We're on the sixth floor. 620." Dugan listened, his eyes darting back and forth across the room. "We think it's a murder. We'll need the forensic team here as soon as possible. They're still down at the Manteo crime scene . . . Sounds good. We'll see you in a few minutes."

"Who was it?"

"Wilford and Reeves. They're in the parking lot." Dugan slid the phone back into his pants pocket and lifted the thermos from the nightstand. "Slide the bottle back into the thermos."

"Why?"

"No one needs to know about this yet but you and me."

"Are you serious?"

Dugan knew he shouldn't confiscate an important piece of evidence from a crime scene without following standard procedure, documentation, and proper explanation to all who may participate in the investigation, but he was the sheriff, and this was an exception—more than exception, like finding the Holy Grail or a golden idol from a cursed Pharaoh's tomb. The fewer people who knew about it the better. "I know what I'm doing. Hurry." Dugan leaned the thermos toward her.

Marla funneled the bottle back into the opening and let go. "The formula too?"

"Yes. We're taking the thermos with us. We need time to process this. Figure out a plan."

Marla rolled the notebook paper into a tube and slid it into the thermos. Dugan replaced the white cap and screwed on the plastic cup.

Dugan handed Marla the thermos. "When Wilford and Reeves get here, I'll send you down to the car to get some latex gloves and crime tape. Take the thermos with you. Try to keep it out of sight. Hide it under the front seat. The tape and gloves are in the equipment bag in the trunk. Just bring the whole bag back up."

"I'll do whatever you say, but I don't feel quite right about this."

"Trust me. I've got this feeling. Call it spiritual intuition. We got here first and found the serum and formula for a reason."

"Are you saying . . ." Marla glanced at the ceiling and then met Dugan's gaze,

". . . God appointed us to guard the contents of this thermos?"

Dugan's head wobbled and then bobbled. "Yes . . . that's what I'm saying."

Someone knocked twice on the door. "Sheriff Walton, you in there?"

"They're here," Dugan whispered. "Stand by the door and hold the thermos behind your back. Here's the keys to the car."

Marla took the keys and stuffed them into her pocket. She walked toward the door and stood against the wall, the thermos in her right hand tucked behind her.

Dugan opened the door. "Come on in, boys."

Wilford, the big deputy with a baby face, and Reeves, tall and crane-like, entered the room. Both wore black ball caps with the sheriff's department emblem, golden letters on a blue patch with the Cape Hatteras Lighthouse in the middle.

"Shuuuuweee, Sheriff," Wilford said. "Another murder?"

"Looks that way."

Reeves nodded at Marla. "Deputy Easton, how's it going?"

Marla shrugged. "It's going."

Dugan motioned into the room. "The body's next to the far bed. Take a look and tell me what you think."

Both deputies craned their necks. Dugan backed out of their way and they approached the body.

"Deputy Easton," Dugan said, "could you go down to the vehicle and bring up the equipment bag?"

"Sure thing, Sheriff."

Marla slipped out the door and headed to the elevator. As she waited in front of the stainless steel doors, she examined her reflection in the metal. She was still slim and shapely in her tight jeans and pink v-neck top, but she looked older. She noticed several new wrinkles and slight shadows under her eyes. Was it the stress of the last week? A new job and two murder investigations? She lifted the thermos and stared at the black cup on top. *Wonder if this would help?* She imagined herself injecting the serum into her arm.

When she glanced up at her reflection, the doors parted, splitting her face in half. She entered the elevator thinking how vain she had become, not wanting to graciously accept the natural process of aging. *You can't stop the sands of time.* Then again, she thought, sensing the weight of the thermos in her hand, maybe you can.

It felt good to step outside into the light. The breeze whipped her hair across her face as she strode toward the patrol car. She felt self-conscious about carrying the thermos but knew that was silly. People carry thermoses all the time. Still, she panned the parking lot to see if anyone was watching her. She noticed a man sitting in the driver's seat of a black sports car parked next to the sheriff's vehicle. Was he staring at her? Yes. But that's normal. She was walking in his direction. Why shouldn't he stare at her? When she got a better view of him, she noticed how intimidating he looked. He had short black hair, a few days growth of beard and a uni-brow. A white scar zigzagged down his cheek to his chin. To Marla he resembled a terrorist. His heavily tattooed arm—which included a skull wearing a crown and smoking a cigar—hung out the window.

Marla turned her back to the man as she hit the button on the keyless remote to unlock the car doors. Knowing he could reach out and touch her, she moved quickly. She opened the passenger's side and slipped the thermos under the seat. Then she closed the door and hit the button to lock the vehicle. She glanced over her shoulder to see the man still eyeing her. Now she wished she would have been in uniform with her pistol strapped to her side. She walked to the back of the car and pressed the button on the keyless remote to pop the trunk. She spied the black equipment bag but hesitated.

Something didn't feel right about Mr. Scar. Leaving the thermos under the front seat while she carried the equipment bag up to the hotel room seemed unwise. She dug her iPhone out of her jeans pocket, activated it, and hit her contacts button. She scrolled to Dugan's name. Scanning the parking lot, she decided it would be better to call Dugan from inside the vehicle, doors locked. To keep her distance from Mr. Scar, she walked to the driver's side and hit the unlock button. Quickly, she opened the door, slipped into the vehicle, and slammed the door shut. She glanced to her right to see the man staring at her through the passenger-side window. He had an odd expression on his face, as if he were trying to decide what to do.

Marla tapped Dugan's name on her phone's contact list. The sound of the ring confirmed the call had been initiated. "Come on, Dugan, pick up."

It rang three and a half times before he answered. "Sheriff Walton here."

"It's me. I'm in the patrol car."

"Is there a problem?"

"I don't want to leave you-know-what down here."

"Why not?"

"There is a suspicious man parked next to the sheriff's car. You need to get down here now."

"I'm on my way."

As soon as Marla ended the call she heard the engine of the black sports car start. She glanced out the passenger side window to see it take off, turn toward the exit, and make a right onto the street. She noticed the patrol car's passenger-side window was lowered about an inch. Then she remembered on the ride to Nags Head she'd cracked it open a bit because she needed fresh air after becoming nauseated. She'd forgotten to close the window. Did the man hear her conversation with Dugan? Damn. She should have gotten the license plate number. What a rookie mistake. She didn't even identify the make of the car. Was it a Cougar? A Mustang? The keys trembled in her hand. Maybe she should go after him, at least try to get the license number. No. Dugan will be here any second.

A long minute passed as she waited for Dugan. When he appeared at the hotel entrance, she unlocked the door and stepped out of the car, leaving the door open.

Dugan trotted toward her, arms raised. "Where is he?"

"He took off as soon as I made the call." Marla threw him the keys.

"Which way did he go?"

"Made a right out of the parking lot." Marla circled the car, swung open the passenger door, and jumped in.

Dugan leapt into the driver's seat, pulling the door shut behind him. In an instant he had the key in the ignition and the car started. He peeled out, squealed around the turn to the exit, and turned right onto the main road without stopping. No sign of the black sports car.

"Did you get the license plate number?"

Marla felt her heart sink into her stomach. "It happened so fast. I didn't get it."

"Any letters or numbers at all?"

"No. I'm sorry." She noticed Dugan's jaw tensing, facial muscles tightening, the way they did whenever he became frustrated.

"What was the make of the car?"

"It was a black sports car."

"A Stingray? A Jaguar? . . . " He turned left onto Gulfstream Street.

"I'm not sure. I'm not good with car types."

"Marla, these kinds of details are important."

A knot formed in her throat. She sought for words to defend herself. "The man freaked me out. I almost panicked." Everything had happened too fast. She glanced at Dugan. He squinted at the road and bit his lower lip. She knew he wasn't happy with her.

At the stop sign Dugan lifted his hands from the wheel. "Which way should I go?"

"I don't know."

He turned left onto Route 12. "Marla, you realize that getting the license plate and the make of the car is standard procedure."

Marla took a deep breath and let it out slowly, trying to control her emotions. Now he's harping on following procedure, she thought. What about five minutes ago in the hotel room? Taking yet-to-be-catalogued evidence from a crime scene isn't standard procedure.

At the stoplight Dugan shot a glance her way. "Didn't you learn that in training?"

"I learned all about standard procedure. I've already said I'm sorry." As Dugan turned right onto Route 158, she gazed out her window, mumbling, "You don't seem to be too worried about following protocol."

"What?"

"Nothing."

"I'm going to drive around this area for about ten minutes. Keep your eyes open. Maybe you'll spot the vehicle."

"Yes sir," she said tersely.

"Do you remember what the guy looks like?"

Marla gritted her teeth. *Now he thinks I'm a total incompetent.* "Of course I know what he looks like. I'll never forget that face."

"Good. Of course, this guy could be completely innocent. We don't anything about him."

"Yeah . . . but . . ." Marla knew she had to confess.

"But what?"

"I think he heard me make the phone call to you."

"How could he? Weren't you inside the vehicle?"

"I didn't realize the passenger-side window was down about an inch. He could have heard me tell you that I thought he looked suspicious."

Dugan made a right onto Grey Eagle Street and pulled into the parking lot of the Whalebone Seafood Market. "Well, in that case he is definitely a person of interest. I need to let Wilford and Reeves know where we are."

As Dugan made the call to Reeves, Marla scanned the neighborhood for any sign of the car or the man. Across the street she noticed a white house with blue awnings. Farther down she saw what looked to be a hotel. A couple typical three-story beach houses lined the street with their thick posts suspending the structures above the ground. Nothing unusual. No black cars.

Dugan concluded his call to Reeves and proceeded east on Grey Eagle Street then made a left back onto Route 12. He slowed when they passed the Owens Motel, and Marla peered out the widow into the parking lot. "Don't see the car," Marla said.

They moved on and turned left onto Gull Street. At the stop light Dugan said, "We'll check out this shopping plaza straight ahead. Lots of cars. He may have ducked into one of the stores."

They crossed Route 158 into the plaza and circled the lot. On the far side near the Gap Outlet, Marla spotted a black sports car that resembled the one at the Comfort Inn. "Hold up. I think that's it."

Dugan stopped the car in front of the vehicle. It had been backed into its parking space. "That's a Dodge Viper. You sure that's the one?"

"I don't know. It looks exactly like it."

Dugan drove to the back of the lot and backed into a spot where they were somewhat hidden but still able to keep an eye on the Viper. "We'll sit here awhile and see what happens."

"We forgot to get the license plate number, and I can't see it from here. Want me to go check it out?"

Dugan's phone rang—"Need You Now." "Wait a second." He dug his phone out of his pocket and answered, "Sheriff Walton here." He listened for what seemed almost a minute. "You're kidding me." After another long pause he said, "Okay. We'll be there in twenty minutes. Tell them to keep their pants on." Dugan started the car. "We've got to go."

"What about the suspect?"

Dugan shrugged. "I'd like to question him, but this Viper might not even be his car. It might belong to some lady shopping at the Gap."

"What's the hurry? Who called?"

"Roger Stern down at the Manteo Crime scene. You're not going to believe this."

"Another murder?"

"No. The FBI showed up at Doc Hopkins's house. They're taking over. They want me on the scene pronto with any evidence I've taken from the scene. Where'd you put the journal?"

Marla lifted her purse from the floor of the car. "It's in here."

"We better turn that over to the Feds." Dugan sped around the parking lot to the exit.

"What about the thermos?"

He turned right onto Route 158, engaged the siren and lights, and accelerated. "As far as I'm concerned," he shouted over the siren, "that thermos is from a different crime scene. We're keeping it."

Pugach stood next to a rack of shirts in the Tommy Hilfiger store. He positioned himself far enough from the window to make sure no one could see him clearly from the parking lot. However, he had no problem keeping tabs on the squad car. He had donned a straw beach hat with a wide brim and had removed his sunglasses. He wondered why they didn't hang around for very long. The girl had gotten a good look at him. Perhaps something more important had come up. He noticed they had turned right out of the parking lot. He headed out the door, not bothering to pay for the hat.

He snagged his sunglasses out of his shirt pocket, positioned them on his face, and headed to the Viper. He assumed they had found the formula and serum in the hotel room. He felt ninety-nine percent sure of it. Perhaps it was in the thermos the girl had placed under the front seat. Metzger, the bastard, had made the switch on him in the bathroom last night. He hadn't discovered it until he arrived at his apartment in Washington, D.C. Then he drove right back down to Nags Head. The lawman and hot brunette had no idea what they had gotten themselves into. He unlocked the car, got in, and revved the engine. Now it was his turn to follow them. Sooner or later, he'd catch up. In all likelihood he'd have to kill both of them.

10

Dugan didn't like the idea of the FBI taking over the Manteo investigation. It sounded like they didn't want any help from local law enforcement—only the evidence that had been collected. There had to be a reason. Some element in the organization had an interest in negligible senescence. The news of Hopkins's death registered as a blip on their radar. Maybe they had heard about the Medical Mafia and the money they were putting on the table to acquire a successful serum. Maybe it was the formula itself.

When Dugan was a kid, he revered G-men and rarely missed *America's Most Wanted*. Back then he had hoped to one day become a federal agent. After many years of training and experience, he no longer held them in as high esteem. They were human just like him. He knew the FBI had a tarnished history. He had read several books that examined corruption in the agency since its inception in 1924. From the beginning they wielded great power and exercised advantages not available to local law authorities. With today's technologies their capabilities bordered on omniscience. Dugan hadn't worked with them often, but the few times they did collaborate didn't rank as his favorite investigative experiences. He felt the particular agents with whom he worked were arrogant and condescending. Could it have been his own feelings of inferiority?

As they sailed along Cape Hatteras National Park Road, Dugan noticed Marla had clammed up. Had he been too hard on her? She needed to learn to accept constructive criticism if she wanted to be an effective officer. Then again, it had been a tough week—two major investigations and lots of overtime. He stole a glance at her. Those beautiful blue eyes stared at the highway. Probably shouldn't take those quick peeks at her, he thought. *Makes me weak inside. Get a hold of yourself, Sheriff. Don't lose your edge.*

He cleared his throat. "I didn't mean . . . to be so . . . critical back there."

"You're the sheriff," she said sharply. "If I don't meet your standards, it's your job to tell me."

Dugan took another quick peek. He could see her eyes were watering. "No, no. I'm very happy with your progress. You're learning a lot. It takes time." He reached out and clasped her forearm. "I'm actually very impressed with you. You've done a good job this week."

She took a deep, steadying breath and swiped her hand across her cheek. "Thanks. That helps."

"I think you could become one of the best."

He felt her hand rest on top of his. "Really?"

"Sure." He couldn't think of much else to say because his hand, sandwiched between her hand and forearm, felt wonderful. He let the pleasure linger a few seconds before he snapped out of it and eased his hand away and back onto the steering wheel. He closed his eyes for a second or two. *Don't let yourself get chopped up into some lovesick stew. You'll end up like forgotten leftovers in the back of the fridge.*

"Do you think it's wise not to tell the FBI about the murder in Nags Head?"

"I'll tell them if they ask, but I'm not turning over more cards than necessary."

"You make it sound like a game."

Dugan chuckled. "It is in a way. This is *our* turf. If they want us to cooperate at the scene, fine. If they tell us to take a hike, then I'm going to try to keep one step ahead."

"Why don't you trust them?"

Dugan stole another quick glance at her. "Maybe I'm jealous. Don't you remember when we were kids I always bragged that someday I'd be a G-man."

"Yeah, but so what?"

"I'm just a local sheriff. Maybe I don't have the right stuff."

"Nonsense. Surely, you don't believe that."

Dugan couldn't help smiling. "Right now I'm not worried about meeting their standards. I have *my* job to do. That includes investigating crimes committed in Dare County. The truth is they are good at what they do, but they're far from perfect."

"What do you mean?"

"Power corrupts people."

"You think they have too much power?"

"With an organization like the FBI it's a necessary hazard. To combat serious crimes and outsmart the most devious criminals you need the freedom, authority, and equipment to get the job done. Some people within the organization don't possess the character to responsibly manage those kinds of advantages."

"Every organization has a few bad apples."

"True. But we're not talking about the local Rotary Club or the community theater. These people have a long leash. A corrupt agent can do a lot of damage."

"Dugan, you sound a little paranoid."

Dugan considered Marla's comment. Maybe she was right. He thought about the thermos under the front seat. Possessing the discovery of the twenty-first century definitely contributed to his uneasiness. Then he recalled all of the documented examples of corruption he'd read about. "A little paranoia isn't a bad thing. Do you know much about J. Edgar Hoover?"

"He was the first director of the FBI."

"Correct. That's one man who abused the power of the organization."

Marla shifted in her seat and faced Dugan. "For example?"

"There're many. Early in his career Hoover became jealous of popular agents like Melvin Purvis, the guy who got Dillinger. He simply maneuvered Purvis out of the organization. He overstepped his bounds when investigating people he considered radical or subversive. In the mid-fifties he initiated a program called Cointelpro. They went after Martin Luther King, Junior's civil rights organization and other groups similar to them."

"What do you mean 'went after'?"

"They planted forged documents, used illegal wiretapping, burglarized their premises, and spread false rumors to ruin their reputations. He would use the organization's manpower and technology to collect damaging information about people he didn't like."

"Why didn't the president fire him?"

"You mean presidents. Hoover ran the FBI from 1924 to 1972. Truman, Kennedy, and Johnson all wanted to get rid of him."

"Why didn't they?"

"Too risky. He knew too much. Like I said, power corrupts. He used all of the organization's means to find every skeleton in every closet of every politician who could threaten him."

"Hmmmph." Marla shifted in her seat to face the road again. "That's unconscionable. But he was only one man."

"But don't you see? The same kind of nature is in all of us." Dugan tapped his chest. "The battle's in here. Some people resist the temptation to abuse power. Others give in to it. But all of us are vulnerable."

"I agree, but that doesn't mean the agents at the Manteo crime scene are corrupt. They might be good guys."

Dugan shrugged. "You're probably right, but you never know. We'll play it by ear. Wait and see what happens when we get there."

Marla fell quiet again for about a minute, and then she said, "Dugan, by hanging on to the Methuselah serum and formula, aren't we unnecessarily taking the path of temptation?"

Dugan kept thinking about the bronze angel in Doc Hopkins's front yard and the weird sensation it gave him. Finally, he said, "Yeah. No doubt about it, we are. But sometimes you walk through that valley for a reason. Maybe God trusts us. That's why it ended up in our hands. Maybe God wants us to guard it from those who would use it for selfish gain. But you're right. We're human. Does the possibility of selling the formula for millions of dollars tempt you?"

"No. Not really, . . . but I wouldn't mind being thirty forever. I hate wrinkles."

Dugan laughed. "I know what you mean. My youth left town and forgot to tell me."

For the next ten minutes the tension in the car eased. Marla confessed the week had been stressful but exciting. She looked forward to next week. Dugan admitted he enjoyed working with her. After he said it, though, he wondered if he should have kept his mouth shut. He didn't want her to get the wrong idea. Sure, he had a crush on her but his professionalism came before personal feelings. No way would he compromise his standards just because he liked someone. And he'd never let her take advantage of him if she figured out how he felt. She wouldn't do that anyway, would she? He hoped not. Before he knew it they had turned onto Weir Point Drive, heading for the Hopkins place.

As they neared the driveway, Roger Stern and his crew were packing up. Parked to the right of their Tahoe was a black Crown Vic. Had to be the Feds. Dugan pulled behind the Crown Vic. He stepped out of the car and motioned to Stern to come over. He wanted to talk to him privately.

"Be with you in a sec, Sheriff." Stern, holding a large black tackle box and a briefcase, waited for Jessie Lou Winters to finish placing plastic containers into the back of the vehicle. He carefully positioned his cases into the remaining space, said something to Big Jim, and walked over to the sheriff's car where Dugan and Marla waited.

"Hey, Marla, how ya doing?" Stern called out.

"I'm good," Marla said.

"Sheriff, I guess you want us to head up to Nags Head, huh?" Stern asked.

Dugan raised his finger to his lips, a sign for Stern to keep his voice down.

"Something wrong?" Stern asked.

"Where are the Feds?"

"'Round back, probably still in the kitchen."

"What happened? They just show up?"

"Yeah. Kind of strange. They wanted us out of there faster than Moses."

"And they wanted all the evidence you uncovered?"

"Everything."

"Find anything interesting today?"

Stern nodded. "In the lab—couple sets of latent footprints that didn't belong to Doc Hopkins. I believe one set was made by boots, like cowboy boots—very smooth on the bottom with a heel and a pointed toe. The other I'd guess to be penny loafers."

"That makes sense." The scene from the hotel room passed through Dugan's mind, the cigarette butt on the nightstand in a non-smoking room and both bedspreads slightly mussed. Dugan guessed Metzger wore the loafers and the boots belonged to the killer. "Did you say anything to them about the crime scene in Nags Head?"

"Not a word. Didn't get the chance to really. Why? The two connected?"

Dugan eyed the back of the property, glimpsing the corner of the garage-lab. "Yeah, but I'm not anxious to lose that crime scene too. Keep quiet about Nags Head. I'll let them know when I'm ready."

"Don't worry. I'll turn blind lips to them."

"I'm pretty sure the victim up in Nags Head was a friend of Doc Hopkins. He may have plotted Doc's murder."

Stern straightened, eyes widening. "Friends like that got a closet full of sheep's clothing."

Dugan shook his head. He wanted to tell Stern to cut the screwball sayings, but when he thought about the last one, it actually made sense. Instead, he said, "Well . . . get your crew together and head up to Nags Head. It's a pretty basic crime scene, a hotel room. Probably a couple hours work."

"Good. We've been putting in a lot of overtime." Stern faced Marla. "We still on for tonight?"

Marla shrugged. "I don't know." Her eyes met Dugan's. "Do you plan on taking Gabe fishing tonight?"

"Of course." Dugan had almost forgotten about his offer to watch Gabe. Remembering the sensation of Marla's hand upon his, he regretted his good heartedness. On the ride down he had sensed a flicker of romantic hope. Now his accommodating ways served to douse that flame and throw gasoline on Stern's passion pyrotechnics. "Let It Be"—the words of an old Beatle's song played through his mind. Managing his inner conflicts about his attraction to Marla would get a whole lot easier if he'd just apply those words. *Don't push it. Don't try to control it or manipulate it—just let it be. Whatever happens, happens.* "I'm counting on that fishing trip. After these last two days I need to sit and listen to the old Atlantic lap the shore."

"Great," Stern said. He turned to Marla. "Pick you up about seven?"

Marla glanced at her watch. "It's two-thirty now."

Dugan said, "I'll have you home by four. I have a feeling the Feds don't want us hanging around."

Stern laid his hand on Marla's shoulder. "Sounds good. If anything changes, just call my cell."

Marla rested her hand on his. "Will do."

Let it be, let it be, Dugan kept telling himself.

Walking to the back of the house, Marla felt slightly confused. She had to confess her affection for Dugan had grown over the last week. Working side by side with him definitely gave her a deeper insight into his character. He was a good man, smart, compassionate, dedicated, and determined. Perhaps a little insecure. Maybe a little insensitive, but what man wasn't? He did make a good recovery once he knew she was upset. Yes, Dugan seemed like the kind of guy who would make a good husband for her and great stepfather to Gabe. But Roger Stern was so darn good looking. Six-two, blond hair, broad chest, and nice biceps. She imagined him without his shirt on, cut like a Michelangelo statue with great abs. She shook her head.

"Do you have the journal with you?" Dugan asked.

"Yeah, I put it in my pouch." Marla patted the front of her hoodie.

"Good. Give it to me. I'll turn that over to them when they ask for evidence. I wish I had time to read it, but you did a great job getting what we needed to know from it."

"Thanks." Marla extracted the journal from the pouch and handed it to Dugan.

"Now listen. Let me do the talking. They don't know squat about the killing in Nags Head. At this juncture in the investigation I *do not* want to turn the serum and formula over to them. I know you're worried about that, but I'm going on my gut. That's why I don't want you to say anything."

Dugan's apprehension made her feel uncomfortable. "I didn't plan on saying anything."

"Once we sort things out and get a better angle on our options, I'll let them know about Hans Metzger. Besides, I want to see who's in charge here. The last special agents I dealt with had superiority complexes."

They turned the corner and climbed the back steps. Marla spied two men through the kitchen widow, one very tall, maybe six-four, and the other about six feet. They wore blue jackets with the FBI logo on the left breast. The dark-haired tall one stood on the opposite side of the kitchen table with his hands on his hips, staring down at the coagulated blood where Doctor Hopkins's head had once rested. His partner paced around the table, his shaved head reflecting the light above them.

Dugan halted a few feet from the door and motioned Marla to stand back from the window. "Let's listen for a minute," He whispered.

She slid to the side, out of sight, and heard one of the agents say, "Do you think it's still here? Maybe in the lab?"

"It's possible, but I doubt it. If it's here, we'll find it."

"If it's not?"

"Then our job gets more challenging. We need to find out who took it."

"The Russian?"

"That would be my guess, but he's only a hired gun. Someone else had to get the party started, someone who knew that Hopkins hit pay dirt."

"There're a lot of dead presidents on the line here. The Methuselah Triumvirate has more money than God Almighty himself. Rich bastards."

"More stacks of Benjamins than you and I could haul to hell and back in a semi-trailer truck."

"That's serious money."

"More serious than a fat kid in the Hostess Twinkie aisle."

Marla heard footsteps approaching, and Dugan quickly knocked on the door and entered, holding up his badge. The tall one stopped in his tracks.

"I'm not in uniform today, gentleman, but I'm Dugan Walton, Dare County Sheriff."

Both agents straightened, eyes intense, startled, as if Dugan and Marla's arrival had been an intrusion. They glanced at each other, and then the tall one stepped forward. He had yellow-green eyes and thick black butch-cut hair like an athlete from the fifties. "How long have you been standing out there?"

"Not long at all," Dugan said, "a few seconds."

Marla stepped beside Dugan and met the tall agent's glare.

"This is Deputy Easton," Dugan said. "She's been working with me on this investigation."

"I'm Special Agent Fetters," the tall one said. He thumbed over his shoulder to the bald guy standing by the table. "That's Special Agent Reed." Reed had a large, crooked nose.

Marla bobbed her head once toward Reed.

Dugan cleared his throat. "This must be an important crime scene for you boys to make an appearance."

"Very important," Fetters said. "We're from the Washington office. Director Miller sent us down personally."

"Wow." Dugan glanced at Marla and then focused again on the agent. "Director Miller, huh? This *is* a big deal. Why all the interest?"

"I'm not at liberty to give details. Let's just say this isn't your typical small-town crime scene." Fetters waved his hand, zigzagging it through the air. "We're taking over here. We need all the evidence you collected."

"You don't want our help? We'd be happy to cooperate on this one."

"Out of the question. This investigation is a matter of national security."

"Really? Sounds serious."

"We do need any information you can give us. Your forensic team handed over their evidence. Do you have any?"

Dugan raised the journal. "Just this. We found it in Doc Hopkins's front office. Some kind of diary."

Reed, the bald agent, stepped forward and took the book from Dugan. "Did you read it?"

Dugan shook his head. "Didn't have the time."

"Can you tell us anything else?" Fetters asked. "What do you think happened here?"

"A murder, of course."

Fetters shifted his weight from one foot to the other. "You're sure it wasn't a suicide?"

"Positive."

"Any speculation as far as motive is concerned?"

"The perpetrator shot Hopkins because he wanted him dead."

"No kidding. Any guess as to why?"

Dugan shrugged. "To eliminate the only witness. When we arrived last night, the lab was in shambles. My guess is the killer was looking for drugs, maybe even designer drugs Doc Hopkins had developed to improve athletic performance."

Fetters crossed his arms and gazed at Reed. He raised his left eyebrow and nodded. "Very insightful hypothesis, Sheriff. The FBI is involved in this case because we believe Hopkins developed a very powerful new drug. Anything else you can tell us?"

"Yeah. There were probably two suspects. Our crime tech guys found shoe prints in the lab out back. I'm sure they handed that information over to you already."

"They did," Fetters said. "We haven't had time to examine it yet."

"Anything else?" Reed asked.

"That's all I've got for you," Dugan said.

Fetters turned to Marla. "How about you, Deputy? Can you think of anything you've seen or noticed in the last couple days that might help us with this investigation?"

"Well . . . uh . . . uh . . . " *Why did they ask me?* Marla lowered her head and focused on the tile floor. The hotel scene in Nags Head flashed on the screen of her mind—the blood, the corpse, the thermos. *Now I'm tangled in this. Should I lie?*

11

Think, girl, think. I got it. Marla lifted her head, met Fetters's gaze, and said, "I believe that journal could be a critical piece of evidence. If you'd like, I'll take it home and read it and then report back to you."

Fetters took a half step backwards. "Thanks, but no thanks. Like I mentioned before, we have specific orders to clear the crime scene and carry out an exclusive investigation." He shifted his gaze to Dugan. "No offense to you or your department, Sheriff."

"None taken. If you need us, you know where to find us."

"Right," Fetters said. "We'll certainly contact you if we have any more questions."

"Good enough." Dugan motioned toward the door. "Deputy Easton, you ready to head on home?"

"Yes sir." More than ready, Marla thought. *Get me out of here before they ask a question I can't duck, dodge, or dance around.*

Back on the road to Buxton, Marla tried to relax. She stretched her legs as far as they would extend under the dash of the car, rested her arms in her lap, and leaned her head back against the headrest. She could still feel her heart beating in her ears.

"That was quick thinking back there," Dugan said.

Marla blew out a long breath and inhaled slowly. "Felt like I was playing a shell game with the facts. I didn't want to outright lie to a federal agent."

"So you turned the table on him."

"That's one way to put it." Marla shook her head. "I wanted him to retreat."

"It worked like magic. As soon as you brought up the journal, he went on the defense. Nice move."

"I'm not sure it was a nice move. I hope your instincts are right."

"Trust me."

Looks like I have to whether I want to or not, Marla thought. She sat silently, thinking about the trouble she may have gotten herself into. The face of the man in the black sports car kept invading her thoughts, his white scar like a lightning streak down his cheek, the short black hair and uni-brow. That sense of peril he'd instilled rose up again, and she quashed it by thinking of home and Gabe. She couldn't wait to get home. Then it hit her—she had a date tonight with Roger Stern. Did she really want to go out with him? Yes, but not tonight. She wanted to go home and decompress. She wanted to laugh with Gabe and talk about his week.

After quite a few miles went by, Dugan asked, "Are you okay?"

Marla stretched her arms. "I'm fine. Just zoned out for a bit."

"I wanted to get your opinion on what we overheard."

"Overheard? When we were on the back porch?"

"Yeah. Didn't their conversation sound a little . . . suspicious?"

"Well, they definitely knew about the Methuselah Triumvirate—the Medical Mafia, as we call them."

"Right. And they knew someone got away with what he referred to as a 'powerful new drug'."

"Sounded like Special Agent Fetters was determined to get his man."

"Maybe so," Dugan said, "but he's no Dudley Do-Right. Don't you think they seemed a little obsessed with the money the crook would make if he managed to transact the deal?"

Marla remembered the words they used—Benjamins and dead presidents and hauling a load of cash to hell and back in a semi-trailer truck. Dugan had a point. But who wouldn't be blown away by that kind of money? Nevertheless, they did give Marla the impression something wasn't on the level. "You might be right. However, I didn't hear them say anything incriminating."

"True, but if you were Eliot Ness, would they make your team of Untouchables?"

Marla had to admit it. "No."

"For now, we'll hold on to the serum and formula."

"Where are you going to keep it?"

Dugan gave her a quick sideways glance. "At your house."

"My house?"

"Yeah. Corky Seevers is staying with me. Remember? I told you about Corky."

Marla recalled Dugan had informed her earlier in the week about their old friend from the Ohio Valley. He'd lost his job when the Martins Ferry steel plant shut down. He came to the Outer Banks to hang out with Dugan for a while and check on job possibilities in the region. Corky was a fun-loving guy but at times irresponsible. "You don't trust Corky?"

"It's not that I don't trust him. I figure the fewer people who know about this the better. So far it's you, me, and Mee Mee Roberts. Besides, we need to keep the thermos out of sight, and I don't have any good hiding places at my house. Didn't you tell me you had a great hiding place in your bedroom where you keep your gun?"

"Yes." A section of the wooden floor under the bed could be removed providing a secret storage area. She also kept all of her important papers and jewelry there. Gabe knew she kept a gun in the house, but she didn't want him to know where to find it. He asked once, and she told him he didn't need to know. The gun was off limits. "How long will we have to keep the thermos there?"

"Hopefully, not long. I want to make sure I place it into the right hands. Fetters and Reed seem a little suspect to me."

"Who would qualify? This is big. We're talking youth serum here—eternal life. Who *could* you trust?" Dugan smiled. "Maybe the Pope."

"Very funny."

Gabe sat on the floor in the Buxton Village Bookstore near the window. Before him lay a large picture book filled with different kinds of sharks. He could hear Mee Mee in the back of the store opening boxes and stacking books. He had turned through the pages of the book three times. Now he was studying his favorite pages, dreaming about reeling in a shark. He'd been ocean fishing a few times with his buddy Ryan and Ryan's dad. He had caught three fish—two Spanish mackerels and a sea trout. On one trip they'd driven to the Cape Hatteras Lighthouse and fished on the Point. There he had watched Ryan's dad pull in a skate, which was a small ray. That was really cool. But wouldn't it be awesome to hook a shark? Maybe not a big one. He'd settle for a baby.

He stared at the picture of the great white in the book. It was taken by a diver under water. The shark came straight at him, grinning with a mouthful of sharp teeth. White streaks from the sun shining through the water crisscrossed the top of its body and zigzagged down the side of its head. *What would I do if I sunk my hook into one that big?*

He heard the door open and glanced up to see his mother and Dugan enter the store. "Dugan!" He sprang to his feet. "Are we going fishing tonight?"

"You bet."

His mother spread her hands. "What am I? Chopped liver?"

"What?" Gabe asked.

"In other words, am I invisible?"

"Invisible?" Gabe twisted his mouth and closed an eye, trying to figure out what she had meant.

"Never mind," his mom muttered. "Just come and give your mother a hug." She knelt and spread her arms.

Gabe leapt towards her, almost knocking her backwards. Somehow she caught him and managed to stay upright.

"Easy, Sport."

Gabe hugged her, kissed her cheek, and then pried himself loose and scrambled back towards the large book on the floor near the window. "Come look at this, Dugan."

Carrying the thermos, Dugan walked over and crouched next to Gabe. "That's a monster of a fish."

"I know. Did you ever catch a shark?"

Dugan shook his head. "Can't say I have, although I've seen people catch little ones from shore."

"I want to try to catch one tonight."

Dugan pointed at the picture. "A big one like that might pull you right into the ocean."

Gabe lifted his head and narrowed his eyes, meeting Dugan's gaze. "If I hooked a big one, would you help me reel it in?"

Dugan chuckled. "Sure thing, Sport. Me and you, buddy, we'll land it." Dugan raised his hand and Gabe slapped it.

"Did you hear that, Mom?" When Gabe faced his mother, he noticed Mee Mee had arrived with a box of books.

Mee Mee set the books on the counter and pointed to Dugan. "Did you bring me some coffee?"

Dugan lifted the thermos. "Evidence from the crime scene."

"What kind of evidence? Someone put some arsenic in the Maxwell House?"

"No." Dugan walked over and set the thermos on the counter next to the cash register. "Remember what we were talking about at lunch today?"

"The Fountain of Youth serum?"

Dugan nodded.

Mee Mee pointed at the thermos. "I drink a cup of that with my scrambled eggs tomorrow morning and I'm thirty again?"

"Seems like science fiction," Gabe's mom said, "but we're convinced it's true. Course you don't drink it; you inject it."

Gabe stared at the thermos. Lately he'd been watching *The Three Stooges* on the Retro Channel. They made him laugh really hard, especially Curly. On the show he watched yesterday they had invented a Fountain of Youth vitamin. A friend of theirs, a nice old lady, took it and became young and beautiful. Then a mean old man got a hold of it and gobbled down too much. He turned into a gorilla. Gabe laughed until he almost peed himself.

Mee Mee slapped Dugan on the shoulder. "Did you bring that serum in here to tempt me? I'd love to windsurf again, or run a marathon, or bike across the country."

"Sorry, Mee Mee," Dugan said. "It's evidence. No one touches this stuff. I intend to keep it safe until I can place it into the hands of the right people."

Gabe's mom said, "Dugan thinks he's on a mission from God."

"Like the angel in the Garden of Eden," Mee Mee said.

"That's right," Dugan said. "Weren't there two angels who guarded the Garden of Eden? Or was it two trees that God said not to eat the fruit thereof?"

"I think there was one tree and one angel," Gabe's mom said.

Mee Mee shook her head. "I'm sure there were two forbidden trees. The religion section is right here." Mee Mee pointed to a row of bookshelves. "Let me grab a Bible."

Mee Mee disappeared between the rows of books but returned quickly with a red Bible. Gabe's mom and Dugan crowded around her. Gabe looked over his shoulder at the green thermos. He wondered what the Fountain of Youth stuff looked like. On *The Three Stooges* it was like black goo. He walked to the counter. Behind him he could hear Mee Mee reading the Bible while Dugan and his mom listened. It was the story about Adam and Eve getting kicked out of the garden. Gabe had learned that one in Sunday school.

The green thermos sat on the counter right in front of his eyes. Something inside him told him to pick it up. He did. It wasn't too heavy. He wanted to sit down, open it, and look inside. Mee Mee was still reading the story. He decided to walk onto the front porch, sit down on the steps, and open it there. He took a quick peek at the adults again.

Mee Mee was reading: "And the Lord God said, 'Behold, the man is become as one of us, to know good and evil. And now, lest he put forth his hand, and take also of the tree of life, and eat, and live forever.' So he drove out the man and placed at the east of the Garden of Eden Cherubims and a flaming sword, which turned every way to keep the way of the tree of life."

"That's what I thought," Dugan said. "Cherubims—that's plural. There was more than one angel."

The adults kept talking about the story. That gave Gabe some time to check out the thermos. Mee Mee's bookstore was more like a little house with a small front porch. Gabe walked out the door and sat down on the wooden steps. It was cooler outside, but sunny. The breeze blew in his face. It would be a great night for fishing. Gabe stared at the black cup on top of the thermos. He grabbed it, squeezed hard, and turned it. The cup came loose, and he kept spinning it until it came off. That wasn't too hard. Now to get off the cap.

He glanced up at the patch of woods across the street. To the left he saw a black car parked on the side of the road leading to the Cape Woods Campground. That was weird. Cars usually didn't park there. Through the windshield he could make out a man wearing sunglasses and a big hat, the kind people wore on the beach. Was the man staring at him?

Pugach couldn't believe it. A young boy, maybe six or seven years old, sat on the stoop of the bookstore across the street holding the thermos. His heart thudded like a hammer against his ribcage. He wanted to jump out, sprint across the street, and snatch the thermos from the boy's hands. He eyed the sheriff's car parked on the right side of the gravel lot in front of the store sign. This didn't make sense. If the thermos contained the Methuselah serum, why would the sheriff let it out of his sight? *Shit.* Had Pugach assumed too much? Was the serum and formula back at the crime scene? Too late to second guess now. He gripped the door handle. *Don't think about it. Just do it and get out of there. Ready . . .go.*

As he pulled on the handle he noticed the screen door open. He quickly stopped the car door from swinging open and listened.

"Gabriel Michael Easton!" a woman's voice said. "What are you doing out there with that thermos!"

The boy looked over his shoulder. "I wanted to see what the Fountain of Youth vitamins look like."

"You get in here right now! You are in trouble."

The boy stood. "Aw, Mom. I wasn't gonna spill any."

The woman, the same hot babe from the hotel parking lot, stepped onto the small porch and extended her hand. "Give me that thermos."

The boy handed it to her and entered the store. She followed him and closed the door.

Good, she didn't notice the car, and the boy confirmed the serum was in the thermos. He thought about his choices. Option one—he could enter the store in broad daylight, kill all three of them and hightail it out of there with the serum. Pugach shook his head. Too risky. The sheriff may be armed. The store may have some kind of hidden alarm and video surveillance. Then there's the store owner and other possible customers. It would end up being a massacre. Besides that, he'd never killed a kid in cold blood. Could he do it? Yes, but only if he had to. Option two—continue to follow them to wherever the thermos ends up. Stake out the place. Break in at night and swipe the thermos. And if need be, kill any witnesses. That sounded more reasonable.

Pugach decided to back his car down the camping access road so it could not be seen from the front of the bookstore. He'd noticed very little traffic came down that road. Not many people camped on the Outer Banks in October. He started the engine, shifted the car into reverse, and backed up about forty yards, angling the car off to the side of the road. Then he walked back towards the bookstore and slipped into the patch of woods across the street. From the cover of live oaks, loblolly pines, and overgrown shrubs, he could watch without being seen. Ten minutes later the boy, woman, and sheriff exited the bookstore. They climbed into the sheriff's car and headed north on Route 12 towards Nags Head.

Pugach hustled to the Viper, although he wasn't worried. Route 12 traversed the spine of the Outer Banks all the way up to Corolla. Because the barrier islands weren't very wide, few roads ran parallel with it. He knew they would stay on Route 12 until they reached their destination. Then they would turn off a short side street and probably pull into the driveway of a private residence. He would patiently follow, keeping his distance. It wouldn't be hard to keep track of them.

Twenty-five minutes later in the town of Rodanthe, the sheriff's car turned left off of Route 12. Pugach, about 150 yards behind, slowed the Viper. A large green sign on two posts identified the neighborhood as Island Pines. As he made the left turn, he glanced at the street sign on the corner—Island Pine Drive. It looked secluded—a narrow lane lined by tall pines. Pugach glanced at his watch. Almost six. It would be dark in less than an hour. Slowly, he drove down the road which curved back and forth like a snake toward the Pamlico Sound. Patches of woods alternated with beach houses about every fifty yards. About two hundred yards in he spotted the sheriff's car parked on a cement driveway in front of a blue beach house supported by pilings.

He glanced to his right as he slowly passed but didn't see anyone. *Good. They were inside.* He made quick mental notes: A section of woods consisting mostly of pine trees stood to the right of the house. Wooden steps led up to the front door and divided the driveway. Cars could pull under the deck on either side of the steps. He could not see into the shadows under the house but guessed there would be an entry door with a laundry room and perhaps a game room on that level. The deck wrapped around the second floor. If it was like most other beach houses, each bedroom would have a door opening onto the deck.

The road went on for another 150 yards ending at a cul de sac where he turned around. About halfway back to the blue house he pulled off on the right side of the road and parked in the shadows of tall pines. From there he walked past the house and, making sure nobody was watching him, slipped into the woods. In the shadows of the trees he felt less skittish. His eyes quickly adjusted to the darkness. Pine straw covered the ground along with a multitude of large pinecones. He made his way to the edge of the woods facing the house and crouched behind a jumble of red bay shrubs. From there he could see anyone coming or going through the front entrance. To the right he noticed a sliding glass door giving deck access to a bedroom on the second floor. A light came on, and he spied the boy crossing the bedroom and opening a closet door. Must be the kid's bedroom, he thought. The boy came to the sliding glass door, fidgeted with the handle, opened it, stepped out onto the deck and picked up what looked to be a fishing pole. He re-entered the house and slid the door shut. Pugach bobbed his head slowly, taking in the details.

Patience. No need to make any hasty moves now. He reached his hand inside his jacket and felt the cold surface of his Glock 21. Hopefully, in a few hours the lights would go out and he would enter the house. While they slept, he'd retrieve the thermos from the kitchen table or maybe some closet in the hallway. He'd make his escape without anyone noticing and drive all night until he got to Washington D.C. to make the exchange. However, most of the time things never went that smoothly. In that case, he thought, sliding his finger along the barrel of the Glock, I'll have to leave a few more dead bodies behind.

12

Marla carried the thermos into her bedroom and turned on the light. She noticed the mess she'd left that morning—the pink-and-white bedspread twisted into a heap in the middle of the queen-size bed, four or five pairs of shoes scattered around the floor, a pile of dirty clothes. No time to worry about it now. Roger Stern would arrive in less than an hour to pick her up. Dinner and a movie. The last few days seemed like a marathon. It wouldn't surprise her if she fell asleep during the movie.

The photograph of her late husband hanging above the bed caught her eye. He was handsome with black wavy hair, a disarming smile, green eyes, and a thin yet muscular build. It had been seven years since he had been murdered. Seven difficult years. She missed him dearly. She thought about her date with Roger and felt a pang of guilt. She shook her head, casting off the sensation, knowing Gabriel would want the best for her and Gabe.

Was Roger the best? He was a likable guy, good at his job and dependable. His goofy sayings made him a little quirky, but Lordy he was good looking—lustfully good looking. It'd been so long since she'd made love to a man. Not that she wanted to jump into bed with Roger Stern. That part of life seemed distant and unfamiliar. Gabriel was such a great lover. If she ever did find the right man, she wondered if it could even come close to what she knew with Gabriel. She doubted it. What about Dugan, though? She couldn't believe she was actually considering him as a potential mate. This week had changed her perspective on Dugan. She knew he'd had a crush on her for a long time but had never acted on his feelings. Not enough self-confidence, perhaps. Maybe that would change as they worked together. Funny how ironic life can be—Dugan's willingness to watch Gabe made the date with Roger possible. Marla smiled. Relationships can definitely be complex.

Marla felt the weight of the thermos in her hand. Hiding it beneath the floorboard under her bed distressed her. She probably had nothing to worry about, but still, who knows what could happen? What if the FBI came looking for it? Or the killer? She lowered herself to her knees and set the thermos on the floor. She dipped her head and spotted her slippers just under the bed. The slippers marked the spot. With one hand on top of the bed she supported herself and used the other hand to slide the slippers out of the way. Using her fingernails she caught the edge of the floorboard and lifted, quickly scooted her hand beneath the board, and moved it to the side—not an easy task, but repetition had made her quite adept at it. She grasped the thermos and lowered it into the hole, nestling it next to her Magnum pistol. Quickly, she slid the board back into place and the moved the slippers on top of it.

She wanted to take a quick shower but knew she didn't have time. At least she could take fifteen minutes to freshen up before Roger arrived. First, though, she had to check on Gabe to make sure he could find everything he needed for the fishing trip. He was so excited. Marla knew how important it was for Gabe to spend time with a good man. She couldn't ask for a better male role model than Dugan. She exited her room and crossed the hall to Gabe's room. The sounds of objects being tossed here and there emanated from his closet.

"You finding everything you need, Sport?"

"I can't find my fishing hat, Mom. The one Mee Mee gave me for my birthday."

"I put it on the top shelf." Marla walked to the closet and lifted the hat, a khaki cotton hat with a nice brim for shade. She placed it on his head a little crookedly, and he lifted his chin, blinked a couple times and smiled at her. Her heart melted, and she took a moment to thank God for her boy. Then she knelt and hugged him.

"Why are you hugging me?" Gabe complained.

"Because I need to." She fought back tears and wondered why these floods of emotion came at the most inconvenient times.

Gabe struggled loose and scrambled to the side of his bed. "I'm taking my big flashlight, just in case we need to shine it into the water."

"Good idea." Marla stood, reached into the closet, and lifted a red, nylon jacket from the hanger. "Come here. I don't want you leaving this house without a jacket on." Gabe returned and stuck out his hand. She funneled the sleeve onto his arm, waited until he switched the flashlight to the other hand and then completed the task. "There, now you look like a real fisherman."

"I am a real fisherman. You wait and see what we catch tonight."

"I can't wait."

"Will you be home before I go to bed?"

"I doubt it." Marla sensed the sudden disappointment in Gabe's eyes. Was this date a mistake? Wouldn't it be great to go fishing with Gabe and Dugan? Too late. Roger might even be on his way by now. She had made a commitment and needed to stick to it. "Sorry, Sport. I'll come in and kiss you goodnight. If you're awake, you can tell me all about it."

"Mom?"

"Yes."

"Wake me, please? I just know I'm gonna catch a big fish tonight."

Marla smiled. "I will."

"Promise?"

"Promise."

At the front door Marla went over her mental list of everything Gabe could possibly need for his outing. Dugan stood patiently tapping his foot. Gabe fiddled with his reel, a monstrous thing designed for ocean fishing. Finally, Marla bent down and gave her boy a hug and big kiss on the cheek. He wiped the kiss away, screwing his face into that awww-Mom-that's-enough look.

A thought suddenly struck her. She stood and faced Dugan. "What about bait?"

Dugan raised his hand. "Not to worry. We can buy bait at the pier's tackle shop."

"Let me get my purse. I'll help pay for it."

"No way," Dugan said firmly. "This is on me. It's about time Gabe and I spent an evening together doing guy stuff. We'll stop and get burgers and fries at a fast-food joint, fish a few hours, and be back home before 9:30."

"You don't mind sticking around until I get back?"

"Not at all. I'll watch an old movie on TV."

"You're a good man, Dugan." Marla stepped up, gave Dugan a quick hug, and planted a kiss on his cheek. Once she did it, she realized how impulsive the act was. Clearly, her move shocked Dugan. He stood there, eyes wide, not knowing what to say.

Gabe reached up and tugged on Dugan's sleeve. "Aren't you gonna wipe it off?"

Dugan glanced down at him. "Wipe what off?"

"Mom's kiss."

Dugan met Marla's gaze and smiled. "No. I think I'll keep it on there for a couple hours anyway."

Marla felt her face heat up. She knew she was turning red. Now *she* didn't know what to say.

Dugan placed his hand on Gabe's shoulder. "Okay, Sport, time to head out." He opened the door, nodded at Marla, and followed Gabe onto the front deck.

"Catch me a big fish!" Marla called after them. "I love you!"

"You too, Mom," Gabe said.

Marla watched them climb into the sheriff's car. The colors had faded in the twilight. Everything had become mixed with shades of gray. Dugan started the engine and backed the car out of the drive. She glanced at her watch—6:30. Not much time to get ready. She hurried to the bathroom.

From behind the trunk of a loblolly pine, Pugach observed the sheriff and boy depart with the fishing pole. The woman was alone. How convenient. He could enter the house now, kill her, and take off with the serum. Or he could wait who knows how many hours until she was sound asleep. But by then the sheriff may return with the boy, and Pugach would have to deal with three people, one of them a lawman. No. The decision was easy: Ice the girl. Toss the body in the woods. Get the hell out of there with the thermos. Law enforcement would take days trying to figure out what happened to the woman before they came looking for him. By then he'd be a billionaire, on his way to some exotic island where assassins become faces in the crowd. Anonymous. Forgotten.

Pugach focused on the sky through the breaks in the trees above him. It was getting darker by the minute. Perfect timing. He waited another ten minutes as stars blinked on against the dark blue ceiling. He checked the windows to make sure she wasn't looking out. Then he scanned the surroundings. No houses or people in sight. He stepped out of the woods, cut across the yard, and entered the shadows under the deck at the back of the house.

First he checked the lower entrance. Locked. *Shit*. Of course, it wouldn't be that easy. Trying not to make a sound, he crept up the back steps and onto the deck. He headed to the side of the house in hopes the boy left the sliding glass door unlocked. When he reached the window, he ducked and crawled under. Then he stood with his back against the wall next to the sliding glass door. He edged to the pane and peeked. The light was still on, but no one was in the room. So far so good. He darted to the other side and checked the handle. Unlocked. Nice. He didn't count on luck in his business. His brains and the cold blood in his veins got the job done, but a little luck never hurt. He slid the door open just enough to squeeze through and then closed it silently.

He heard water running from a room across the hallway. Was she taking a shower? Washing her hands in the sink? He reached into his jacket and pulled out his Glock. He didn't want to make a big mess. If he shot her in the shower, clean up would be easier. First he'd ask her where the thermos was and threaten to blow her brains out if she didn't tell him. She'd chirp like a canary. Then he'd plug her right in the chest. The sooner the heart quit beating the better. Less blood. Hopefully, the bullet wouldn't go clean through her into the wall. Then he'd clean things up, find the thermos, haul the body into the woods and dump it. He could smell the bread baking already. By this time tomorrow Boris Pugach would be a rich man. Ungodly rich.

He left the boy's bedroom, stood in the hallway, and listened. The sound of running water came from the next room down. He edged to the doorway and peered into the room. It had light green walls and a vaulted ceiling of knotty pine. An unmade bed sat in the middle with clothes scattered here and there. On the other side of the room he spotted the door to the master bath ajar. *She's in there. Do it now. He who hesitates is too damned late.* He aimed the gun at the bathroom doorway and stepped inside the room. The phone rang—the one on the nightstand next to the bed. He hesitated, his momentum stalling. It rang again. He backed out of the room. The running water stopped.

"Who could that be?" the woman said.

He heard footsteps cross the room. Pugach leaned closer to the doorway to listen to the conversation. Could be important.

"Hello . . . Hi, Roger," she said. "Ten or fifteen minutes? . . . That's fine. I should be ready by then . . . Doesn't matter to me. You pick the movie . . . Okay, see you in a little bit."

Pugach stood in the hallway, gun ready in case she appeared. She didn't. After about thirty seconds he heard the water running again. Now what? He thought about the phone conversation. Was she getting ready for a date? Who was Roger?—the sheriff? Did he drop the boy off at a friend's house? Was he picking up a DVD at the local video store? Maybe Roger was a different guy altogether. Maybe they had a movie date. That would be much better. He'd show up in ten minutes, pick up the chick, and leave. Pugach would have the house to himself. Then the challenge would be to find the thermos. But if Roger was the sheriff, he'd return and they'd probably watch a movie together in the family room. Confusing. This could be a long night.

The best move now was to wait. Pugach headed back to the boy's bedroom and unlocked the window just in case the woman came back to make sure the sliding glass door was locked before she left. Then he slipped out the door onto the deck. The evening was cool and breezy. He needed a smoke to relax. Why not? No one could see him out there. He lit up a cigarette, took a long drag and blew a jet of smoke toward the stars, the points of light blurring until the cloud dissipated. Already he felt the calming effects of the nicotine.

Above him he saw Orion. He focused on the three stars in the hunter's belt—Mintaka, Alnilam, and Alnitak. As a boy in Russia he had searched for that constellation whenever he was outside on a clear night. His mother, a devout Russian Orthodox Christian, had taught him how to find it—three bright stars in a row. She had told him that death takes you beyond the stars to God's heaven. Seeing the constellation always comforted him. He chose the middle star, Alnilam, as his mother's star. She had died when he was ten from head trauma suffered after falling down steps. Like the stars, she was no longer of this corrupted world. She belonged to the heavens.

That was back in the eighties before things went to hell. When the Soviet Union fell, the economy crumbled, and his father lost his job. Things got tough. Being a former military man, his father was recruited by the mafia as a collector. Seemed like all military veterans worked for the mafia. Organized crime controlled everything—banks, businesses, prostitution, drugs, gambling.

Pugach dropped out of high school at the age of sixteen and began working for his father collecting protection money from local businesses. When he didn't put enough pressure on his clients, his father kicked his ass. When his father got drunk, which seemed like most every night, his father pounded on him for the least infraction. He often wondered if his mother's death was an accident. He doubted it. He guessed his father got drunk one night and knocked her down those steps. When he turned eighteen, Pugach got tired of working for the old man and looked into a new line of work—contract killing. Murder for hire was almost an industry in post-communist Russia. It didn't agree with him at first, but the money was good. Most of the men he killed were from rival organizations. He got used to it, took a pragmatic approach, and became numb to the violence. Eventually he progressed to the point where he could take a man's life without flinching—a true professional. Now that he was a killer, he no longer allowed his father to push him around. One night after gazing at Orion's belt for the longest time, he entered the house, pulled out his Glock, and shot his father between the eyes. It was the first time he actually enjoyed killing someone.

At that point he knew he had to get out of Russia. He kept hearing America was the land of opportunity. His connections paved the way to Brighton Beach in Brooklyn. The Russian mob had their hand in everything in New York City and had no qualms about murder—you cross the wrong people, you die. With his reputation from the Old Country, contracts came easy. After years of working for the crime bosses, he started freelancing in hopes he could make enough to get out of the business. If you live by the sword, eventually, you die by the sword. A couple of rogue federal agents tipped him off about this latest contract. This was it—the big one. He didn't know it until Metzger made the mistake of saying too much. Big mistake. *Those agents will be surprised when I show up instead of Metzger.* He chuckled to himself. *They won't care. They just want the serum and formula.* Pugach wanted the billion.

He smoked down the cigarette, crushed it out on the wooden railing, and flicked it into the yard. Crossing his arms, he glanced at his watch. Almost seven. He heard a car coming and saw headlights breaking through the black silhouettes of trees along the road to the east.

He crouched behind a gas grill. The car slowed and turned into the driveway. Must be Roger. Pugach backed against the wall and edged to the corner of the house. A broad-shouldered, tall guy got out of the car, wearing a white long-sleeved shirt and jeans. Pugach's luck was still holding out. The sheriff must have taken the boy out fishing for the night. Roger showed up to take the woman to the movies. Pugach rubbed his hands together. He couldn't wait to get a hold of that thermos.

To his left he heard a jostling noise at the door. His heart jumped and he reached for his gun. He could see the woman's shadow on the deck. Was she looking at something in the yard? Looking for an intruder? If she stepped out onto the deck, he'd have to shoot her, then go through the house, open the front door, and greet Roger with a .45 caliber hollow point. What a mess that would be. Faintly, he heard the doorbell ring—five or six distant chimes. The shadow withdrew, leaving a square of pale light on the brown deck, and then the light went out. He wondered if the woman suspected anything. He scoured his mind to recall if he had disturbed anything in the house. Did she notice the unlocked window? All he could do was wait and see what happens.

A minute later he heard the front door open and the woman's greeting. Five minutes after that he heard the front door open again and the nervous laughter and banter of a couple, probably on their first date. Good sign. She didn't ask Roger to check the deck or look around the property. The car doors opened and closed, the engine started, and, within thirty seconds, they were gone.

Pugach quickly tried the sliding glass door—locked. *Dammit.* Now he knew what she had been doing. Did she lock the window too? He stepped over to the window and removed the screen. He placed his fingers under the sash and lifted. The window edged upwards. This must be my lucky day, he thought. It was a tight squeeze, but he crawled through onto a dresser and managed to get to the floor without knocking anything over.

Where would they hide the thermos? Certainly not in the boy's room. He decided to go through every room starting at the back of the house. In the kitchen he worked quickly and methodically, looking through all drawers, closets, and cupboards. In one drawer he found a flashlight and used it to inspect under the sink and in the closets. After fifteen minutes he gave up on the kitchen. He worked his way through the dining room and great room. Nothing. What happened to his good luck?

It had to be in her bedroom. She had turned the lights out, so he used the flashlight to work his way around the room. On the wall above the bed he noticed a picture of a dark-haired man, not the sheriff or Roger. This chick got around, he thought. Three guys after her? He brushed the perverted notions out of his mind and focused on the hunt. He dropped to his hands and knees and panned the light under the bed. Just a pair of pink slippers. After twenty minutes of thorough searching, he gave up on her bedroom. No way could it be in there.

Now he was getting frustrated. Keep your cool, he told himself. You have plenty of time. He continued from room to room, turning over every possible leaf but finding nothing. *What in the hell did they do with it?* Finally, he entered the boy's room with little hope of finding it there. Nevertheless, he combed through everything as thoroughly as the other rooms. In the top drawer of a dresser he found an iPhone. *Kids get everything nowadays.* He glanced at his watch—8:55. He didn't count on much more time. The sheriff and boy might return at any minute. Then what? Confront the sheriff? Stick a gun in his face and demand he reveal the hiding place or die? Pugach shook his head. Not a good idea. If the sheriff had any brains, he'd know Pugach would off him whether he told or not. The sheriff had nothing to lose, which made him dangerous. What about the boy? They would never tell a kid the location of the serum and formula, would they? No way. *Wait a minute.* Pugach smiled as he formulated a new angle to solving the problem. *Of course—the boy.* He went to the dresser, opened the drawer, and picked up the iPhone.

An image of duct tape and clothesline appeared in his mind. Where did he see them? *The kitchen. One of the cabinet drawers.* He marched out of the boy's bedroom and straight into the kitchen. It didn't take him long. He found the tape and cord in the fourth drawer he opened. He carried them into the great room and peered out the large window at the driveway. The lights were out in the room, but a spotlight lit the driveway. No one could see him in the darkness from the outside. He'd wait patiently for the sheriff and boy to return. He bounced the clothesline and duct tape in his hands. As soon as they pulled into the driveway he'd head to the boy's bedroom and hide in the closet.

13

Gabe stood against the railing to watch Dugan cast his line into the sea. Dugan took three steps back, held the pole over his shoulder, charged forward, and flung the line far out into the water.

"That's a good one!" Gabe yelled. He couldn't see it splash into the ocean because it was so dark but knew it was way out there. The spotlights along the pier provided plenty of light to bait their hooks and see the end of the poles. They had walked clear out to the end of the pier where the platform widened and became a cross. Only two other people were fishing. It was so cool to be high above the ocean but a little spooky with the darkness and the wind blowing and waves crashing against the posts below. But Gabe felt safe with Dugan next to him, their poles side by side, leaning against the rail. In two hours they had caught only three fish—Dugan pulled in a flounder and Gabe caught two small croakers.

Hoping to catch bigger fish, Dugan had baited their lines with the small croakers. He had put the hook through the top near their fins to keep them alive. Now Gabe felt jiggly inside. He imagined sharks swimming around the little croakers, licking their chops. Gabe kept his eyes on the top of his pole, knowing at any minute he might get a bite.

"What do you think, Sport? Maybe a drum or a big blue out there ready to take that croaker?"

Gabe shrugged. "How about a shark?"

"Very possible. Lots of sharks in these waters. They'll bite on about anything."

"That's what I want to catch. Did you ever see the movie *Jaws*?"

"Sure. That's a classic. Did you?"

"I watched it at Ryan's house last week."

"Did it scare you?"

Gabe thought about the scenes in the movie—the girl swimming at night and the little boy on the raft, all the blood and screaming. He nodded. "Yeah, but I liked it. I could tell whenever something scary was gonna happen."

"How could you tell?"

"Dun . . . dun dun . . . dun dun dun . . .dun dun dun . . . dun dun dun."

Dugan laughed. "The *Jaws* theme song!"

"Whenever something bad is gonna happen in scary movies, the music lets you know."

"That's what you call setting the mood."

"What's your favorite scary movie?"

"Well . . ." Dugan rubbed his chin. "I like the old ones from back in the 30s and 40s like *Dracula*, *Frankenstein*, and *The Wolfman*."

"I've never seen any of those movies. Are they like *The Three Stooges*?"

"What do you mean?"

"No colors."

"Yeah, but I think they looked better in black and white. No computer-generated scenes either. They counted on the skill of the makeup artists. And the actors back then were the best—Lon Chaney played the Wolfman, Boris Karloff was Frankenstein, and my favorite was Bela Lugosi—the original Dracula. Those guys were born to play monsters."

The top of Gabe's pole dipped violently. "Did you see that?"

"Grab your reel. A big fish could pull it right into the ocean."

Gabe crouched, picked up his reel and held it tightly, keeping his eyes fixed on the top of the pole. It jerked again, this time even harder.

He pulled back as quickly as he could just like Ryan's dad had taught him. He wound the reel and felt the weight of the fish on the end of the line. It was huge "I hooked it! I hooked it!"

"Are you sure?"

Gabe nodded his head toward the end of his pole. It was bending clear down to the rail.

"Careful now," Dugan said. "Don't try to bring it in too fast."

"I can't bring it in too fast! I can barely wind it."

"That's okay. Let the fish wear itself out. Pull in a little line at a time."

Gabe bent slightly to give himself more balance. "Woooohooo!" He wound the reel a couple times.

Dugan, using a very low voice, sang, "Dun . . . dun, dun . . . dun, dun, dun . . . dun, dun, dun."

Gabe wound the reel again. "Do you think it's a shark?"

A high and crackly voice said, "Moight be, Sonnyboy." Gabe glanced over his shoulder to see an old lady standing next to him wearing overalls and a red ball cap. White hair sprang out from beneath the cap, and her face had a thousand wrinkles. She must have been a hundred years old. "Oi've caught many a shark off this pier. Nothing big, moind you, but plenty of two and three footers."

"Wow." Gabe liked the way the old lady talked. He turned the crank a few more times. "I really wanna catch one."

"Maybe today's your lucky day," the old woman said. "Don't get in a hurry. In twenty minutes or so the fish'll be ready to give up."

"He better," Gabe said, "'cause I'm not giving up."

Dugan said, "You sound like a Hoi Toider."

The old lady nodded. "Born and roised here. Oi'm a Hatteras Oiland gal. Grew up in a fishing family. Now Oi do most of moi fishing off this pier. Saves me a few dollars at the grocery store."

The minutes passed like hours. Both Dugan and the old woman kept warning him to take his time. His arms got really tired, and his fingers hurt from holding onto the crank tightly. Sometimes he would have to pull back on the rod in order to wind in the line. He took some deep breaths. His toes felt numb from standing in one place so long. He wiggled them to bring feeling back. Even though it was a cool night, sweat dripped into his eyes.

"Do you need help, Sport?" Dugan asked. "I could take over for a while and give you a break."

Gabe gritted his teeth and shook his head. He didn't care how bad his arms hurt. He was gonna catch this fish by himself.

"He'll be foine," the old woman said. "Oi can see he's a tough little gouy. He'll win this foight."

Finally, Gabe reeled in enough line to lift the fish to the surface of the water.

Dugan grabbed the flashlight and directed the beam onto the fish. "It's a big one! I'd say two and a half feet long."

The old lady bent over the rail. "Looks loike a little sand toiger. You've got yourself a shark."

Gabe couldn't believe it. "Really! A shark!" The news gave him a burst of energy. He kept winding. He felt the fish flipping around on the end of the line, making it more difficult to haul it in.

The old lady turned around and picked the net up off the wooden deck.

Now Gabe was really huffing and puffing but kept winding. His fingers went numb and his wrist hurt. Every turn of the crank took longer and longer. His hand cramped and he couldn't wind any longer.

"Almost there," the old lady said.

Gabe wanted to cry. With all his might he turned the crank one more time.

The old lady bent over the railing. "Troiy to lift the pole as hoigh as you can."

Gabe took a deep breath and heaved the pole upwards using every ounce of muscle he had left.

The old lady dipped the net, one foot coming off the deck. "Oi got it!"

"Great job!" Dugan yelled.

The weight on the end of the line disappeared. Gabe's arms felt like they might fall off. He lowered the reel onto the deck and shook his hands.

The old woman lifted the net above the railing and lowered the fish right before Gabe's eyes. The shark had a white belly and a gray top. He could see its teeth—lots of little ones.

"I did it!" Gabe said. "I really did it!"

Dugan slapped his back. "You're a real battler, Sport. That shark wasn't going to whip you."

The old woman pulled a pair of pliers out of her overalls and clamped them onto the hook. With a twist and a turn she removed it in a flash. "There you go, Sonnyboy. A noice little sand toiger."

Gabe peered up at Dugan. "Can we take it home? I want to show Mom."

"Sure thing, Sport. We'll pick up some ice and a cooler." Dugan glanced at his watch. "It's almost nine. 'Bout time to head home."

"Oi'm calling it a noight too," the old lady said. "Oi'll walk to the end of the pier with you."

They took a few minutes to reel in lines, clean off hooks, and gather up their equipment. The old lady put the shark on a stringer to make it easier to tote. Gabe insisted on carrying it, even though he had to hold up his arm to keep the tail from dragging. Together they walked down the pier.

"How long has this pier been here?" Dugan asked.

"Oi'd say bout fifty years. Survoived many a hurricane. It's a little whopperjawed, but so am Oi." The old lady suddenly stopped and stared down the long walkway. "Did you see that?"

"See what?" Gabe asked.

"That dark figure up ahead."

"I didn't see anything," Dugan said.

"Must be me old oiyes. 'Course . . ." the old woman smiled, "It could've been a ghost. This pier's haunted, you know."

"Haunted!" Gabe almost dropped the shark. "What happened? Did someone die here?"

"Do ya remember Hurricane Floyd?"

"Sure," Dugan said. "That was a bad one back in 1999, wasn't it?"

"That's roight. A terrible storm it was. Young Johnny Austin was about your age, Sonnyboy. A noice kid, he was, full of loife and fun. But he had an enemy, a bully in the neighborhood by the name of Vladmir Koslov. The bully was older and bigger and meaner than a bull shark. Vlad did the usual things bullies did—took Johnny's lunch money, made fun of him, pushed him down on the playground, stole his hat—those sorta things."

"I hate those kinda kids," Gabe said.

"Bad eggs, they are. Anyway, a few days after Floyd blew through, Johnny was combing the beach. You can foind lots of neat stuff after a hurricane, and Johnny found an old copper box about the soize of a brick. Insoide was a single coin wrapped in oilcloth—a 1658 British Crown in mint condition. The copper box had preserved it perfectly—no aging whatsoever. Johnny got so excoited, he showed the kids in the neighborhood. That was a big mistake. Vlad got word of it and come after him. Johnny saw him coming and started to run. This toime, Vlad wasn't going to take it from him. After a couple of blocks, Johnny knew he was in trouble. Vlad was bigger and faster.

"Then Johnny saw the pier. The storm had battered it. Surely, Vladmir wouldn't follow him onto a rickety pier. He cloimbed the steps and raced down the walkway. It wasn't long before he came to a gap in the boards and stopped. Behoind him he could hear Vlad's footsteps. He peeked over his shoulder and saw the bully coming closer and closer. Fear can make you flounder or floy. It made Johnny floy. He leapt that gap in the boards and ran to the end of the pier, leaping gap after gap. Then he turned round, thinking Vladmir would never risk all those jumps. But greed can droive a body too. Vlad kept bounding over the gaps, shouting, 'Give me that coin!'

"That left Johnny with no choice. He peered over the railing into the swirling water below."

"Did he jump?" Gabe asked.

"No, Sunnyboy. He threw the copper box into the drink. Vlad skidded to a stop. He couldn't believe Johnny did it. He leaned over the railing, troying to spot it. Suddenly, the railing, weakened by the storm, gave way, and Vlad tumbled into the sea never to be seen again . . . except . . ."

". . . on this pier," Gabe said, eyes wide.

The old woman nodded. "That's right. Tis the ghost of Vladmir Koslov that haunts this pier."

On the way home Dugan stopped by the Island Convenient Store along Route 12 to pick up a bag of ice and a Styrofoam cooler. To fit the shark in the cooler he had to flop the tail over. Then he poured the cubes over it to keep it from smelling. Hopefully, within the next few days he'd find time to haul the fish to the taxidermy shop in Elizabeth City. Wouldn't it be great to surprise Gabe with the shark mounted and ready to hang on the wall? It could be an early Christmas present. He deserved it. What a battle he had fought tonight. Dugan was impressed. The boy had grit just like his mother. Dugan kept picturing the three of them together—a happy family. Then he'd shake the vision out of his mind and scold himself. Entertaining those thoughts would only lead to a headlong tumble down Lovelorn Mountain.

A little after 9:30 they arrived home and washed up. Gabe wanted to wait up for his mom, and Dugan granted permission. He figured

Marla would get home between eleven and midnight. If the boy fell asleep on the couch, Dugan could carry him to his room and tuck him in bed. Dugan wondered how he would make a graceful escape if Marla invited Roger Stern in for coffee or hot chocolate. No way would he sit there and watch those two flirt with each other. He'd think of something. He definitely needed to head home and get some sleep. Dugan shrugged. That was more than enough reason to make his exit.

He poured two big glasses of chocolate milk and carried them into the family room. Gabe had cycled through the channels to the classic movie network. In his high-collared black cape Bela Lugosi eyed them from the screen, holding a candlestick. With a raised eyebrow and sinister smile he said, "I bid you welcome." Then he turned and climbed cobweb covered steps.

"This is it," Dugan handed one of the glasses of chocolate milk to Gabe. "The original *Dracula*."

"Can I stay up and watch it with you?"

"Promise me you won't get nightmares?"

"No way. This can't be as scary as *Jaws*." Gabe took a big gulp of milk.

Dugan scoured his memory but couldn't think of any gory scenes. Back in the thirties and forties the censors wouldn't allow explicit violence or sex. Everything was suggested, left to the imagination. Compared to today's horror flicks, *Dracula* seemed pretty tame. "Okay. You can watch for a little while. If you can whip a real shark, Bela Lugosi shouldn't scare you much."

Gabe puffed out his chest. "He don't scare me at all."

Dugan hadn't seen the flick for a long time. Now that he was in his mid-thirties, he wondered if his perception had changed. His experiences as a lawman had acquainted him with plenty of human depravity. As Dracula went from victim to victim, fulfilling his lusts, attempting to live forever by taking the lives of innocent people, Dugan recognized how clearly the film presented the dark side of human nature. The criminals he dealt with daily were out for themselves, lacking compassion for others and the ability to empathize. Of course, everyone had a dark side. Fortunately, most people kept their wicked desires in check. But why did some embrace evil, thrive on it? Tough question to answer, Dugan thought.

About halfway through the movie, after Dracula's attempt to control the beautiful Mina by feeding her his own blood, Gabe said, "Dracula's a lot like the bully in the old lady's story."

Dugan glanced at Gabe. "How's that, Sport?"

"He doesn't care if he hurts people as long as he gets what he wants."

Dugan nodded. *Good insight for a seven year old.* "I believe you're right. Why do you think he acts that way?"

Gabe knotted his brow. "Must be the black spot."

"What black spot?"

Gabe pointed to his chest. "In Sunday school we learned there's a black spot on our hearts called sin. It makes us do bad things. Without God's love to take it away, it grows and grows."

"I see. So the bully and Dracula had big black spots on their hearts."

Gabe clasped his hands behind his head and leaned against the pillow at the end of the couch. "Yeah. Kinda like a banana."

"A banana?"

"When it turns black it's no good."

"Hmmmm. You must pay attention in Sunday school."

"It's fun. You should come to church with us sometime. Mom wouldn't mind."

"I'd like that. Your mother and I went to the same church when we were kids."

"Really?"

Dugan nodded. Ten minutes later he looked over and noticed Gabe had fallen asleep. He cradled and lifted him, carried him to his room, and laid him gently on the unmade bed. The blanket, patterned with Transformers, lay bunched up at the bottom. Quietly, Dugan picked it up by the two corners and spread it over the boy. The light shining in from the doorway lit Gabe's smooth face. He resembled a cherub, one who had battled a sea monster and won, an angel who feared no evil. Dugan gently patted Gabe's head and tiptoed toward the door.

"Dugan?"

Dugan stopped in his tracks and peered over his shoulder. "Did you wake up, Sport?"

"Yeah. I need Blackie."

"Blackie? Who's Blackie?"

"My pirate bear. He's right there." Gabe pointed to the chest of drawers on the right side of the room.

Dugan turned and stepped toward the dresser. On top he could make out a plump teddy bear wearing a black pirate's hat with white skull and crossbones. A black scraggly beard rimmed the bear's jaw line. A patch covered one eye, and a golden hoop hung from the opposite ear. The bear wore a red vest which half covered a zipper that extended vertically to the bottom of the bear's belly.

Dugan picked the bear up by the arm. "Is this Blackie?"

Gabe nodded.

Dugan handed the bear to the boy, and Gabe clamped it across his chest. "I'll be fine, now."

"Does Blackie help you fall asleep?"

"Yep. He's got a part of my daddy in him."

"What?"

"Look." Gabe reached under the vest and pulled down the zipper. He reached inside of the bear's tummy and pulled out a yellow towel. "This belonged to Daddy."

"Let me see." Dugan took the towel and held it up in the sparse light coming from the hallway. *Terrible Towel* was printed in black stenciled lettering. He chuckled to himself, remembering Gabriel Easton's passion for the Pittsburgh Steelers. "Your dad was a big Black and Gold fan."

"So am I."

Dugan gave the towel back to Gabe, and the boy stuffed it into the bear and re-zipped the belly. Seven years before Dugan had been a part of Gabriel's murder investigation. The assailant had brutally beaten him with a tire iron outside his and Marla's apartment in Buxton. He languished in a brain-dead coma for months before life support was finally removed. Marla had just conceived Gabe before the attack.

"Good night, Sport."

"Dugan?"

"What?"

"Don't forget to tell my mom to come in and see me. I want to tell her about the shark."

"Will do. Now go to sleep."

From behind the louvered closet doors, Pugach had observed the lawman carry the boy into the room and place him in the bed. Then he listened to their conversation. The whole time he stood like a statue, barely breathing. In his hands he could feel the weight of the clothesline and duct tape. If the boy would fall back to sleep, it would be better to carry him out the deck-access door and then gag and bind him somewhere away from the house, perhaps in the woods. He would wait until the woman got home before he made the phone call. He'd use the iPhone he'd found on the boy's dresser. A mother would do anything to get her only son back safe and sound. She wouldn't think twice about exchanging the serum and formula for the kid.

Pugach waited ten minutes before gently shoving open the bi-fold closet door. He glanced at the bedroom door. The lawman had closed it. Good. He looped the cord around his neck, tucked the tape into his jacket, and softly stepped toward the sliding glass door, trying not to make a sound despite the hard soles of his boots. Unlocking the dead bolt, he glanced at the boy. Still sound asleep. He slid open the door, edged to the bed, and leaned over him. The boy's face glowed in contrast to the framing of his dark hair. His appearance disconcerted Pugach, causing him to take a step back. He chided himself for such an unreasonable reaction, although he couldn't deny the weird sensation that had charged through him. The boy's appearance seemed almost otherworldly in the blue shades and shadows of the room.

He steadied himself and leaned over to carefully slide his arms under the boy's body. His face almost touched the kid's neck. He tried not to breathe too heavily. With slow and deliberate movement, he lifted the body and stepped toward the open door. The blanket fell away, but the boy kept hold of the teddy bear. Once outside, immersed in darkness, Pugach relaxed. He hurried down the steps and toward the woods.

The boy stirred and clasped the teddy bear tightly to his body. "Dugan, is that you?"

"Keep your mouth shut, kid . . ." Pugach said, ". . . if you want to stay alive."

14

Dracula ended shortly before Dugan heard a car pull into the driveway. He checked his watch—11:05. Not too late. He collapsed the footrest on the recliner and rose, guessing the car belonged to Stern. He couldn't help drifting into the front hall to a spot where he could peek out the window onto the front deck. The room was dark, insuring he could observe undetected. The porch light brightened the exterior. Marla appeared first, pausing at the top of the steps, glancing behind her. Then she turned toward the front door, and Dugan glimpsed her profile—the long, dark brown hair, a fine nose, slightly flared nostrils, full lips and those blue eyes. Dugan wished her beauty didn't enthrall him. He disliked that discontented feeling it engendered like a thirst that couldn't be quenched.

Roger Stern rose up behind her, tall, blond hair and brown eyes, a flash of white teeth. Marla turned and faced him. He said something to her, but Dugan couldn't make it out—probably some off-the-wall comment that didn't make sense. Women didn't seem to mind his goofy sayings. His looks more than made up for them. They probably thought they added to his charm or quirkiness. Marla and Stern talked for a couple of minutes, and then he rested his hands on her shoulders. Oh no, Dugan thought. Here it comes—the goodnight kiss. Dugan felt a little guilty for spying, but he couldn't pull himself away. Would Marla kiss him on their first date? Stern leaned forward and planted one on her lips. She didn't protest. *Crap.* Dugan about-faced, walked back into the family room, sunk down in the recliner, and stared at a rain-cloud patterned weather map on the television screen.

A minute later he heard the front door open. Here they come, Dugan thought. Get ready to bow out gracefully. They don't need my stormy mood to drizzle on their romantic flames. The door closed and footsteps drew near.

"Hey, Dugan," Marla said, "How was the fishing trip?"

Dugan glanced up. Marla was alone. That didn't make sense. "We had fun. Where's Roger?"

"Oh, I . . . I told him I was exhausted. He understood."

"I see. Well . . . I better get going and let you get some rest."

"No need to rush out."

Was she serious or just being nice? "But you just said you're exhausted."

"I know, but I need to sit down and unwind a little before I go to bed. Why don't you hang out a while and have a cup of hot chocolate with me?"

Dugan wasn't expecting that response. Shouldn't Roger be the preferred bachelor in this circumstance? No reason to argue. "Sure. Hot chocolate sounds good."

Marla reached and touched his shoulder. "Come on out to the kitchen."

Dugan rose from the recliner, the storm clouds parting, and followed her. He sat on the stool at the counter as Marla filled two cups with water and placed them in the microwave.

"Hope you don't mind instant."

"The only kind I ever drink. Single guys are used to instant everything."

Marla smiled. "So tell me about the fishing trip. Did Gabe catch anything?"

"I think I'll let him tell you."

"Really? He must have hooked a big one."

Dugan couldn't keep a smile from breaking out.

"How big was it?"

Dugan raised his hand. "I'm not going to say a word. Don't want to steal Gabe's thunder."

"Okay. I'll pop into his room after we drink our hot chocolates." The microwave dinged, and Marla retrieved the cups of hot water. She set them on the counter, pulled a couple packets from a nearby box, and handed one to Dugan. "How exciting! My little boy caught a big fish tonight."

Dugan tore open his packet and dumped the brown powder into his cup. "Yeah, Gabe's a real angler. You should have seen him."

Marla handed him a spoon. "I wish I would have been there."

"Can't be two places at once. How'd your date with Roger go?"

Marla shrugged. "Fine. Roger's a good guy."

Dugan smiled. "Most women think he's pretty hot."

"Well . . . he is a hunk . . . but . . ."

"But what?"

"But nothing. I'm not sure if we're right for each other."

Dugan decided to take the objective observer approach. "Not sure? Most of the time it takes more than one date to be sure."

"Right. He wants to take me parasailing next weekend."

"Sounds exciting."

"We'll see." Marla took a sip of hot chocolate. "Anyone call tonight?"

"Your phone hasn't rung."

"I don't mean for me. Did the FBI call about the second crime scene or did the office call with any updates?"

Dugan shook his head. "I think my cell phone died. It's been a long couple of days and I haven't recharged."

"Aren't you worried you might miss something?"

"If the Feds want to talk to me about that second crime scene, they can wait 'til tomorrow. We've got plenty of deputies to handle whatever happens in this county."

"I guess you can't be two places at once either."

"I don't want to be. You'll find out soon enough—down time is important. If you don't set work aside and relax a few hours every day, you'll end up in a rubber room at Looney Bin Acres."

Marla fingered the rim of her cup. "I'll try to remember that."

They talked for a few minutes about the fishing trip. Dugan mentioned the old lady and the story about the bully. He disclosed how impressed he was with Gabe's spiritual insights concerning good and evil. Marla beamed as she talked about Gabe's love for God at such a young age—how he hated to miss Sunday school and always said his prayers at night.

Dugan glanced at his watch. "It's getting pretty late, and we're both on duty tomorrow. I wanted to show you the fish before I left."

Marla downed the rest of her hot chocolate and slipped off the stool. "Let me see if I can get Gabe to wake up and tell me about it first. I'll only be a couple minutes."

"Sure." Dugan watched her head into the family room and then turn left down the hallway toward the bedrooms. Did she walk that way on purpose? It was difficult for Dugan not to think about her sexually. When he caught himself doing it, he felt guilty, but sometimes he just couldn't help it. He was human. She'd never think about him in that way. Well . . . he didn't think so anyway.

"Dugan! Come here!" Marla shrieked.

He almost fell off the stool. What could be wrong? His mind whirled as he charged through the family room and angled toward the hallway.

He skidded to a stop in the boy's bedroom. The light was on, the bed empty, the Transformer blanket draped across the floor. A breeze blew through the open sliding glass door. "Where is he?"

Marla stood by the open door, her hair tousled by the wind. "I don't know. He's gone."

"Does he sleep walk?"

"Never."

"Could he have wondered outside?"

She shook her head, eyes straining. "I don't know."

Dugan rushed out the door onto the deck. "Gabe!" He stared into the darkness. "Gabe! Are you out here!"

Marla stepped up beside him. "Gabriel Michael Easton!" She leaned on the railing. "Gabe! Answer me!"

"Maybe he went to the bathroom," Dugan said. "Maybe he's somewhere else in the house."

"Yes. Yes. Let's check the house."

They reentered the house and hurried into the hallway to the bathroom. Marla flipped on the light. No Gabe. They quickly raced from room to room, yelling his name but seeing no signs of him. After working their way through the upstairs, Marla led the way downstairs to the laundry room and lower entry. Gabe had disappeared.

"He's got to be outside somewhere," Marla said.

"I've got a flashlight in the Impala." Dugan turned to open the lower entry door. The sound of someone playing blues on a piano tinkled from somewhere upstairs.

Marla grabbed his arm. "That's my cell phone. It's on the counter in the kitchen."

They raced up the steps, but by the time Marla reached her iPhone, voice mail had picked up. She checked the display. "Gabe! Gabe tried to call me." She held the phone so Dugan could see the alert message.

"That doesn't make sense. Why would he grab his phone and leave the house?"

"I have no idea. I'll call him back." Marla tapped the call button on the surface of the display. She pressed the phone to her ear, eyes intensifying.

"Gabe?" She shook her head. "Who is this?"

"What's wrong?"

"It's not Gabe."

"Who is it?"

"I-I-I d-don't know. He wants to talk to you." She handed Dugan the phone.

"This is Sheriff Walton."

"I've got the boy." The man's voice was gruff with a strong accent. Russian?

"Who is this?"

"Shut up and listen. I want the serum and formula. I know you have it."

"Okay. I'm listening. Go on."

"I'll exchange the boy for it."

"Whatever you say." Dugan's thoughts tumbled. The Methuselah serum meant little with Gabe's life on the line. But how could he insure the boy's safety. "How do you want to do this?"

"It's got to happen now. Have you made a copy of the formula?"

"No."

"Don't think twice about it. I'm giving you two minutes to set the thermos on the end of the driveway and return to the house. Then you'll receive further instruction. If you don't do exactly as I say, the boy dies."

The connection ended before Dugan had a chance to speak. He held out the phone and met Marla's gaze. "Gabe's been kidnapped."

The color drained from Marla's face. "Is he okay?"

Dugan nodded. "The thug wants to exchange Gabe for the serum and formula. We've got less than two minutes. Go get the thermos."

Marla hesitated as if she couldn't comprehend his words.

"Go!"

She blinked, turned, and sprinted toward her bedroom. Dugan's heart beat like a jackhammer in his chest. He stared at the iPhone and tried to calm himself. What were the kidnapper's words? Set the thermos on the end of the driveway and return to the house for further instructions. Dugan knew the guy wasn't playing games. He'd follow his orders exactly and hope the creep would hold to what he said.

For about thirty seconds the house became silent. *Hurry, Marla, hurry.* He turned and eyed the top of the steps. Footfalls padded somewhere behind him, getting louder. Marla entered the kitchen with the thermos. Dugan grabbed it and charged toward the steps. He descended so fast his feet became a jumbled blur. He stopped at the lower entry door and peered out to where the spotlight faded into the darkness at the end of the driveway. No headlights. No car.

He shot through the door to the end of the driveway and placed the thermos on the edge where the asphalt met the cement. He quickly glanced both ways down the road but saw only the black silhouettes of trees and distant houses. With adrenaline charging his muscles he pivoted and sprinted back to the house. Once inside, he closed the door and peered out.

Marla stepped next to him. "What do we do now?"

Dugan noticed the distress in her voice. He placed his arm around her shoulders and pulled her closer. "Wait and pray."

15

It didn't take long. The sound of an engine approached, and the dark shape of a car appeared coming from the direction of the cul de sac. The car skidded to a stop and the interior light flashed on as the door swung open. Dugan got a glimpse of the driver before the door closed. He wore a straw beach hat and had thick, dark eyebrows. Other than that he couldn't see much more. The engine revved, and the car sped away, the thermos gone.

"It's him," Marla gasped.

"Who?"

"The guy in the hotel parking lot. The one who drove the black sports car."

"Are you sure?"

"Yes. Positive. I saw the scar on his cheek."

Dugan pictured the silhouette of the car. "That could have been a Viper."

Marla faced Dugan. "What do we do? Follow?"

Dugan shook his head. "We better wait for his call. This guy's homicidal. We've already seen his handiwork."

Marla burst into tears and planted her forehead against his chest. Dugan slipped his arms around her, trying to calm her. Her body quaked as she tried to control her sobbing. Dugan held her closer, which seemed to help. Suddenly the phone vibrated in his hand, and blues piano notes sputtered out. Marla stepped back, eyes wide, tears streaking her face.

Dugan touched the screen of the iPhone and held it to his ear. "Sheriff Walton."

"Listen carefully. I will kill this boy if you contact the authorities. Do what I say and he will live."

"Whatever you say, we'll do."

"I'll call you back in fifteen minutes. Stay right where you are. Do not follow me, or I will kill the boy."

"All right. We'll stay put."

The line went dead, and Dugan lowered the phone.

Marla stepped forward. "What did he say?"

"He's going to call back and tell us what to do."

"Should we call the dispatcher and put out an alert?"

Dugan shook his head. "The stakes are too high. Right now we sit tight and play his game."

Marla leaned her head on Dugan's chest. "God, please help us."

Dugan embraced her. Good, idea, he thought, prayer is our best option.

To Marla, every minute that passed felt like a lifetime. The most important person in her life had been kidnapped—in the hands of a brutal murderer, a man obsessed with fortune but impervious to the value of human life. She had never felt so helpless. If Dugan hadn't had his arms around her, she would have crumpled to the floor. She knew she had to be strong. Something deep within her rose up, solidifying the trembling nerves and muscles. She stood straight and pushed herself away from Dugan. "There's got to be something we can do. We just can't let him take complete control."

"Well . . ." Dugan rubbed his chin. "We can't do much until he calls."

"We hope he calls. What if he doesn't?"

"Then we contact headquarters, the FBI, and every law enforcement office between here and Washington, D.C."

"How long do we wait?"

Dugan glanced at his watch. "He said fifteen minutes. It's been five."

"Ten more minutes. What can we do to get ready? We need to think."

"I'm guessing he's going to name a drop-off point. Then we'll drive to that place and hope Gabe is there."

"But what if he isn't?"

"Then we put out an all-points bulletin."

"What car should we take?"

Dugan shrugged. "He's expecting us to be in the sheriff's vehicle."

"We ought to take my car. What if we spot him? That would give us an advantage. We could follow him if need be."

"That's true. Do you have binoculars?"

Marla glanced up the steps. "I don't have binoculars, but I just bought Gabe a spyglass—a small telescope. It really works."

"Where is it?"

"Up in his room."

"Go get it." Dugan lifted the iPhone. "I'll wait for the call."

Marla charged up the steps. She refused to turn into a quivering mass of Jell-O. She'd do everything in her power to fight back. She had lost Gabriel. No way would she lose Gabe, even if it meant sacrificing her own life. She sped down the hallway and darted into Gabe's room. There it was, thank God, on the dresser. Sometimes Gabe left his toys in the strangest places. She scooped it up and raced out to the kitchen. On the counter she spied her keys, snatched them, and jammed them into her pocket. Then she hurried back downstairs.

When she reached the bottom, she asked, "Did he call?"

Dugan shook his head. "Let me see the telescope."

Marla handed it to him. It was about eighteen inches long, made of metal and painted cobalt blue.

Dugan stepped outside and walked to the middle of the driveway. Marla followed. He scanned the sky and then raised the spyglass to look at the stars. "Pretty powerful for a small telescope. You never know. It may come in handy."

Marla clasped her arms to her chest, shivering slightly. "Not that many stars out tonight."

"It's starting to cloud up, but there's still a few patches of open sky."

The blues piano erupted again, and Dugan handed Marla the spyglass and stuck the iPhone to his ear. "Sheriff Walton." Dugan bobbed his head slowly and then met Marla's gaze, lowering the phone. "Do you have your keys?"

Marla dug them out of her jeans pocket. "Right here." She tossed them to him.

"Let's go. Manteo. He said he'd call back in twenty minutes."

Marla owned a blue Ford Focus, a small car that got good gas mileage. Unfortunately, it didn't have much muscle but could get up over eighty if need be. They rushed under the left side of the deck where the car was parked and jumped in. Dugan started the engine, shifted into drive, and floored the pedal. To Marla's surprise, the tires actually peeled out and squealed around the turn onto Island Pine Drive. Within a minute they were flying north on Route 12.

"Why does he want us to drive to Manteo?" Marla asked.

"He has more options in Manteo to get back to the mainland. If he wanted to go west off the island, there's the Manns Harbor Bridge or the Virginia Dare Memorial Bridge. Or he could head east on Route 64 back to the Outer Banks and take 12 north to Kitty Hawk and cross on the Wright Memorial Bridge."

"Do you think he'll just let Gabe off on some street in Manteo and then let us know where to find him?"

Dugan nodded. "I hope it's that easy."

"What do you mean? What else might he do?"

"I don't know." Dugan shrugged. "He might complicate things to make sure of a clean getaway."

Marla didn't like the sound of that. She hated the idea of Gabe being used by a killer to ensure his escape. Then she remembered that a large part of Roanoke Island consisted of woods and marshland. "You don't think he would . . . dump Gabe in the woods, do you? He could end up tramping into the middle of a marsh, maybe even quicksand."

"That's a possibility. The longer it takes for us to find Gabe, the more time he has to get away."

"I don't care if he gets away as long as we find Gabe."

"Yeah . . . that's what's important."

Marla eyed Dugan. She sensed disappointment in his voice. "You're upset about losing the serum and formula, aren't you?"

"I'm upset about losing Gabe. He was my responsibility. Losing the serum and formula is just more baggage piled onto the cart of my ineptitude."

"It's not your fault. How could you have known the killer's plan?"

"It *is* my fault. I insisted you hide the thermos at your house. I put you and Gabe in jeopardy. I'm sorry this happened."

"I don't blame you. It's as much my fault as yours. If I would have done my job at the hotel parking lot, we could have arrested the guy at the shopping plaza."

"That's doubtful. The guy's a pro. We were trying to track him down, but he was watching us—keeping a step ahead."

Marla knew Dugan was right. That bothered her. This guy was intelligent. Would he give up his hostage knowing he would have to contend with a five-state manhunt? With Gabe safely recovered, how could he keep them from spreading a dragnet? Marla shuddered, trying to block out the darker side of the killer's options. She had to hold on to hope. Succumbing to gloom didn't help the situation.

Marla held out her hand toward Dugan. "Let's make a deal."

Dugan glanced at her hand and then refocused on the road. "What kind of deal?"

"No more playing the blame game. We can't get down on ourselves. We need to stay up for Gabe."

"Agreed." Dugan reached out, clasped Marla's hand, and shook it.

The iPhone rang as they were crossing the bridge to Manteo. Dugan slid his finger across the bottom of the face of the phone. "Sheriff Walton here."

"Drive to Festival Park," the gruff voice said before the line went dead.

Dugan slid the cell phone into his front shirt pocket. "That's odd."

"What's odd?"

"He wants us to drive to Festival Park."

"That's where the race ended."

"It would be deserted this time of night." Dugan strained his brain to figure some other reason the kidnapper would pick the park as a drop-off point. It was located on a small island with one way on or off—a bridge that crossed a fifty yard channel of water. What was on that island that provided an advantage to the killer?

Route 64 traversed through the middle of Manteo. About halfway through town Dugan turned right on Route 400 which led directly to the bridge. It didn't take long to cross the bridge onto the island. Dugan drove past the main buildings, which housed the museum and store, and parked along the side of the road near the path that led to the Pavilion Outdoor Theater. Two days before, Doc Hopkins had broken the tape at the finish chute set up on the lush Bermuda grass near the theater stage. Dugan turned off the engine.

"Why doesn't he call?" Marla said. "He must know we're here by now."

Dugan pulled Marla's iPhone out of his shirt pocket. "If we don't hear from him in the next five minutes, I'll put out an A.P.B."

"I don't understand. Why here?"

"I have a good idea." The phone vibrated in Dugan's hand and the blues piano played. Dugan slid his finger across the screen and stuck the phone to his ear. "Walton here."

"You'll find the boy somewhere on the island. Somewhere you've already been." The connection ended.

Dugan lowered the phone.

"What did he say?"

"Not what I wanted to hear."

Marla's mouth dropped open, her eyes pleading.

Dugan raised his hand. "It's not bad news. Just not what I wanted to hear."

"Tell me what he said."

"We'll find Gabe somewhere on the island. Somewhere we've already been."

"We walked all over this island the other day. Gabe could be anywhere."

"The killer needs time to get away. He figures the longer it takes us, the better his chances."

"Should we contact the office at least?"

Dugan shook his head. "My gut tells me no. He's made a puzzle out of this thing for a reason. As soon as we find Gabe, I'll call headquarters."

"His reason is obvious," Marla said. "Anything to give him more time to get off the Outer Banks. Like you said, he's got three bridges within twenty miles he could cross to the mainland. As long as he keeps us guessing, he doesn't have to worry about a police blockade."

"Right. He knows we won't call the law down on him until we find Gabe. To jump the gun would be too risky."

Marla spread her hands, palms up. "Where do we start looking?"

"Remember the clue. He said we've already been there. The other day we walked through the Settlement Site and the Indian Town."

"But how would he know where we walked two days ago?"

Dugan scratched his chin. "You're right. He couldn't have been tracking us Saturday morning unless he's psychic."

Marla reached out and grabbed Dugan's arm. "Wait a minute! Gabe must have said something."

"What do you mean?"

"A month ago Gabe and I came to the park. We toured the ship—the *Elizabeth II*. Gabe loved it. He wanted to climb the mast to the crow's nest, but I persuaded him to go below deck to see the cannons and brig."

"That's our best shot. Get the flashlight."

Marla popped open the glove compartment and snatched the light. "Let's go!"

They leapt from the car, and Marla took the lead, running down the asphalt walkway that skirted around the lawn of the amphitheater, the swath of light bouncing in front of her. She turned right between two buildings and followed a path through some overhanging trees that led to a dock. Dugan struggled to keep up in the dark, thinking he may trip on some obstacle hidden by the blackness at his feet.

Marla bounded up the steps of the dock, turned at the top, and beamed the light down on Dugan. "Hurry!"

He squinted up at the bright circle as he grasped the hand railing and mounted the steps. "I'm okay. Keep going. Right behind you."

Marla turned and hurried down the wooden walkway. Dugan could see the silhouette of the ship about thirty yards ahead.

At the end of the dock a tall gate blocked the passageway to the ship. A chain lay at their feet in front of the gate. Dugan lifted the handle on the gate and swung it open. "He cut the chain. They were here."

Marla stepped aboard. "Gabe! Gabriel Michael Easton!" No response.

The ship looked to be about seventy feet long with three masts, a great replica of a late 1500s sailing vessel. They quickly inspected the deck and quarterdeck, circling the masts, riggings, and cabin. No Gabe.

"He's got to be below. Follow me." Marla headed toward an opening in the middle of the deck. Wooden steps led into the dark bowels of the ship. "The crew quarters, galley, and brig are down here." At the bottom Marla panned the light around the inner hull. Posts, bunk brackets, and cannons cast shifting shadows across the wooden walls and floor. "This way! He must have put Gabe in the brig." She headed toward the stern, edging around the handles of the anchor-raising capstan.

Near the back Dugan caught sight of a row of bars. Marla skidded to a stop and directed the light into a small cell. Her eyes widened. Dugan peered over her shoulder and spotted a yellow cloth hanging from the ceiling. As he focused more intently, he recognized the black-stenciled lettering on the cloth—TERRIBLE TOWEL

Marla shined the light up, down, and across the small room. "He's not in here."

Dugan pointed through the bars. "What's that pinned to the bottom of the towel?"

"Some kind of note." Marla tugged on the barred door. "It's locked. Where's the key?"

"Step aside." Dugan stuck his arm between the bars, extending it as far as he could. His finger brushed the note, causing it to swing slightly. He flicked it several times to increase the arc of the swing motion. Within a few seconds he snagged the note and pulled it toward him. With his other hand he reached between the bars and grabbed the towel. He pulled on the towel, breaking it free from a line that had attached it to a hook on the ceiling.

Marla tore the note from a safety pin that had attached it to the towel. She spread the paper and read: "I'm taking the boy with me. Tomorrow I will let him go. Be smart. I will call you. Do not contact any law enforcement agencies or he will die." She looked up and met Dugan's gaze. "Gabe wrote something below the kidnapper's words."

"Let me see." Dugan took the note. The last two sentences were printed in a child's awkward handwriting: MOMMY. I AM STILL ALIVE. PLEASE DO WHAT THE MAN SAYS. I LOVE YOU. GABE. Dugan held the note in front of Marla. "Is that Gabe's handwriting?"

"Yes."

16

Dugan didn't worry about speeding through stoplights as they flew along Route 158 through Nags Head. After midnight in mid-October, very few cars traveled the highways along the Outer Banks. Unlike more commercialized resort towns with their bars and nightclubs, the Outer Banks catered to families. That's one reason Dugan enjoyed his job—he didn't have to put up with a lot of drunk college kids.

Marla braced her hands on the dashboard as they passed under another red light. "I hope you're right about this."

"I'm pretty sure. We know Metzger was from the D.C. area. He had the connection to the Medical Mafia. The killer has stepped into his shoes. It's my hunch he'll exchange the formula and serum for the money somewhere in Washington, D.C. The Wright Memorial Bridge is by far the fastest route."

"That's true. If you take the Manns Harbor Bridge or the Virginia Dare Memorial Bridge, you have to head fifty miles west just to get past the Croatan Sound."

"Hopefully, he'll stop at the red lights. No way does he want to risk a run-in with the law. I think we can catch him between here and Interstate 95."

Marla sat back and lowered her hands into her lap. On the left she spotted the high dunes of Jockey Ridge State Park. They wouldn't hit the next traffic light until they reached Kill Devil Hills. "Good thing we took my car. He shouldn't recognize it."

"I don't plan on getting too close. Where's the telescope?"

"Right beside me." Marla lifted the spyglass to her right eye. "Works great."

Dugan pushed the pedal to the floor, taking the car up to eighty-five miles per hour. Peering down the highway, he tried to detect any tail lights but saw none. If they caught up to the kidnapper, he wanted to keep his distance. Gabe's life was on the line. No way did Dugan want the killer to suspect he was being tailed. Who knows what the creep would do? Maybe he'd kill the boy or perhaps severely injure him and dump him onto the road. That would force Dugan and Marla off his trail and to the nearest hospital.

As they approached Kill Devil Hills, Dugan caught sight of tail lights several hundred yards ahead. He glanced to his left and spotted the Wright Memorial, a towering sixty-foot granite monument perched high atop Big Kill Devil Hill, the largest dune around. He slowed, knowing a stoplight awaited a couple hundred yards ahead. If they had caught up with the killer already, Dugan didn't want to stop directly behind him at the light. He'd make sure it turned green before he got there, allowing the kidnapper to put some distance between them.

"There's a car ahead," Dugan said.

Marla looked through the spyglass. "I see it. It's dark gray. An SUV, a Chevy, I think."

"Too bad. I was hoping we caught him."

The light turned green before they got there, and the gray Traverse turned right onto Prospect Avenue. Dugan hit the gas and sped through the intersection. He guessed there were eight to ten traffic lights between there and the bridge. If the killer got caught at three or four of them, that would help. Then again, the guy may not be as cautious as Dugan assumed. If a deputy pulled him over, the killer might just shoot him without thinking twice.

The first three lights in Kitty Hawk were red. Dugan flew through them. By the time they reached the middle of town, they had caught up with another car. Dugan hit the brake, keeping a couple hundred yards between the two vehicles. "Take a look with the telescope."

Marla raised the spyglass. "It's a black car, a sports car."

"That could be him. We've been making good time. Let's see if he turns right onto Route 12 or stays on 158." Route 12 headed north along the Outer Banks through the small towns of Duck and Corolla, but Route 158 cut west across the Wright Memorial Bridge. The span, about a mile long, carried traffic over the Albemarle Sound. "Does it look like the back of the vehicle you saw in the hotel parking lot?"

"I can't tell for sure. Could you get a little closer?"

Dugan picked up speed and closed within a hundred yards. "How about now?"

Marla adjusted the focus on the spyglass. "Yes. That's the same kind of car."

"There's not too many Vipers on the road nowadays. Chances are we've already caught him." Dugan let off the gas and drifted back. The black sports car turned left toward the bridge.

"Do you think he suspects anything?"

"No. I don't see how he could. He never expected us to find his note so quickly, and he shouldn't recognize this car. There's just one major problem."

"What?"

Dugan shook his head in disgust. "I left my magnum in the sheriff's car."

"I forgot to get mine, too." Marla leaned back against the seat and took a deep breath. "Maybe it's better we're unarmed."

"Why do you say that?"

"I don't want Gabe in the middle of a gun fight."

"Yeah, but if Gabe wasn't near, and I could get a bead on that guy, I'd put him down without hesitation."

Marla nodded. "Me, too."

After crossing the Wright Memorial Bridge, Route 158 headed north along a peninsula of the North Carolina mainland, passing through towns with names like Powell's Point, Jarvisburg, and Coinjock. Dugan kept his distance. As he predicted, the black car continued up 158 which turned into 168—the fastest route toward Washington, D.C. Dugan knew things would get tricky when they crossed into Virginia and, eventually, merged onto the interstate. Then they'd have to contend with more traffic and several possible route variations of bypasses around the bigger cities. He didn't want to lose the kidnapper, but if he did, he knew the killer's destination would take him to 95 North, a highly traveled major thoroughfare that led right into Washington, D.C.

In Chesapeake they took I-64 to I-664 across the Hampton Roads Beltway into Newport News. Dugan checked his watch—almost 3:30 A.M. A few early morning commuters were merging onto the interstate. Dugan knew he had to close the gap or he'd lose him. With a few more cars on the road, he felt fairly sure the kidnapper hadn't spotted them. He'd keep a car or two behind to make it more difficult for the killer to notice. In all likelihood the creep figured he'd gotten away without a hitch. Dugan feared the killer would hang on to Gabe as long as he needed him and then dispose of him. So many kids disappear and are never found. They had to make sure they kept on his tail.

"Can you see him?" Dugan asked.

Marla held the spyglass to her eye. "He's three cars ahead."

"Make sure you watch the exits."

"It's getting more difficult to track him."

"I know. Do the best you can. If I'm right, he'll take 64 to Richmond and then north on 295. We need to make sure he doesn't dart off in a direction we don't expect."

"When he gets to Washington, do you think he'll call us?"

Dugan doubted it but didn't want Marla to lose hope. "There's a chance, but I plan to keep on his ass just in case he has other plans." Dugan glanced at Marla and noticed she had closed her eyes.

"Dear Lord, don't let that murderer harm my boy."

Dugan reached and patted her hand. "Amen."

By the time they reached Interstate 95 the number of vehicles on the road had doubled. Dugan didn't mind because the traffic gave him more cover. During the day 95 could be congested despite the four northbound lanes. But now, at 4:15 in the morning it wasn't bad at all.

Marla leaned forward, the telescope pressed to her eye. "He's getting off."

"You sure?"

"Yes!"

Dugan checked the exit sign—REST STOP. Dugan's heart leapt in his chest. This could be dangerous. The killer probably had to take a crap. Would he lock Gabe in the car while he went to the restroom? If he did, Dugan could attempt a rescue. But how would he get the car door open? Gabe could open it. But what if Gabe were tied up or asleep? Would it be worth the risk? Yes. Definitely. Dugan would park a few cars down and then rush to the car as soon as the kidnapper entered the visitor center. That would give him at least two minutes.

Think. Think. If Gabe couldn't get the door open, then what? The killer probably carried his gun with him. A frontal attack would be suicide. Dugan could crouch at the rear of the car and ambush him. *That's the plan. No more time to think.* Dugan pulled into a parking space about six cars down from the Viper. He put the car in park but left the engine running.

"What are you going to do?" Marla asked.

Dugan kept his eyes on the Viper. "As soon as he heads to the restroom, I'll go after Gabe."

"What if he takes Gabe with him?"

"Then I'll ambush him when he gets back to the car."

"Dugan, no. It's too risky."

"It might be our best chance."

"What if he shoots you or turns the gun on Gabe?"

"I'll have to play it by ear. I won't put Gabe in more danger than necessary."

Marla let out a sigh. "I don't know about this . . ."

"What's he doing? Sleeping?"

Marla leaned forward to get a better look. "Why isn't he leaving the car?"

"Stay here. I'm going to edge around to the back of the Viper."

"Why?"

"I need to know if Gabe is in the vehicle."

"Dugan, please don't take chances."

"I'll be careful."

Dugan opened the car door, slipped out quickly, shut it, and crouched between Marla's Ford and a white Honda Civic parked next to it. He kept down and scrambled to the back of the Honda and then crawled across the asphalt until he reached the back of the Viper. The killer had cut the engine, and Dugan heard movement in the car. Was he tying up Gabe before he hit the restroom?

Dugan edged to the corner of the passenger's side back bumper. He rose up slightly and noticed smoke drifting from the driver's side window into the blackness of the sky. *He's smoking a cigarette,* Dugan thought. The inside light came on. Dugan froze. He hadn't heard a car door open. *Must be looking for something in the car.* Dugan leaned to the right to get a better view and rose up a few inches. With the interior light on he caught a glimpse of the top of Gabe's head leaning against the passenger side window. The boy looked to be asleep. If the killer would just head to the restroom, Dugan could grab Gabe and get out of there.

Dugan focused on the kidnapper. He had removed his straw hat, his head sprouting a few days growth of black hair. The interior light carved a deep shadow across his cheek down to his chin, the ragged groove of a scar. He lifted something into the light—a hypodermic needle and bottle of yellow-green liquid. That's why he stopped, Dugan thought, to inject himself with the serum. Dugan watched as he lowered the needle, but the back of the seat blocked his view of the killer injecting himself.

"Ooowwww. Shit. Damn, I hate needles." The man's voice was low and gruff. With the driver's side window open, Dugan heard him, but barely.

Dugan withdrew to the back of the Viper as the killer fumbled with something—a latch? A briefcase? *Must be putting the needle and serum back into some kind of container.* Then Dugan heard the faint sound of the tones of a cell phone. *He's calling somebody. Maybe his contact in Washington.* Dugan held his breath to listen as acutely as possible.

"Is this Hinkle?"

Dugan moved to the other side of the back of the car, a better position to hear the conversation.

"Pugach here. I've got the serum. You want to live forever?"

Dugan couldn't believe it. This could be crucial—names, times, places—information that could break the case. Dugan focused on his words.

"Does it work? Hell, yes. I'm already feeling ten years younger."

Dugan wondered who this Hinkle could be. A part of the Methuselah Triumvirate?

"It'll cost a cool million—cash. Hundred dollar bills. I'll meet you at the Days Inn in Fredericksburg, the one on the south side of town. I'll be there in forty-five minutes. Look for a Dodge Viper. The light in my room will be on."

Dugan repeated the information in his mind—Pugach, Hinkle, Days Inn, Fredericksburg, a million dollars. Certainly he wasn't handing over the serum and formula for a million dollars?

"No, Metzger isn't with me." The killer chuckled. "You could say I dissolved my relationship with him."

Now Dugan wondered if the kidnapper would even get out of the car. Perhaps he only stopped to inject himself with the serum and make this phone call.

"If you're not there in an hour, forget it. I'm not staying at the hotel for long. I've got an appointment to keep. Listen, I'm doing you a favor. Right now I'm the only man in the world who's getting younger by the minute. Bring me a million bucks if you want to join the club."

The conversation appeared to be over. Dugan heard rustling coming from the front seat. The engine thundered on, hot exhaust spewing out beside him. Fear shot through him. The killer was about to throw the Viper into reverse, and Dugan crouched there like a raccoon about to be road kill.

17

Dugan whirled and leapt. He skidded onto his belly, his hands scraping the asphalt. The Viper's back tire clipped his toes as he retracted his legs and rolled under the bumper of the adjacent vehicle. He prayed the killer didn't notice him. Glancing up, he caught sight of the passenger-side window and the top of Gabe's head. The Viper sped away, and Dugan crawled out from under a small pickup truck. He scrabbled across the ground, keeping low until he got to Marla's car. He opened the door, jumped in, and jerked the car into reverse.

"Did you see Gabe?" Marla asked, anxiety edging her voice.

"Yes." Dugan backed out, shifted into drive, and took off. "He was asleep in the front seat."

"What happened?"

"The guy stopped to inject himself with the serum and make a phone call. We need to catch up." Dugan floored the pedal, and the Ford Focus accelerated down the onramp and merged onto the highway.

"Who'd he call?"

"Somebody with lots of money, a man named Hinkle. He offered him a dose of the serum for a million dollars."

"Do you think Hinkle is a member of the Medical Mafia?"

"No. He's a customer. This Pugach may be a killer, but he's also a business man."

"Pugach?"

"That's what he called himself."

"Where're we headed?"

"To a Days Inn in Fredericksburg. Use the telescope. See if you can spot him."

Marla raised the spyglass and adjusted the focus. "I see several cars ahead. I don't know. One of them must be the Viper."

The adrenaline that had charged through Dugan's system made it difficult to organize his thoughts. He needed to calm down and reason things out. Taking a deep breath, he tried to relax.

"At least we know where he's headed," Marla said. "Do you think he'll get a room there?"

Dugan nodded. "For a couple hours anyway. He wants privacy to make this transaction. He'll inject this Hinkle guy with the serum and then count up the cash. Hinkle must have some kind of connection to Hopkins and Metzger. It wouldn't surprise me if he's a former colleague, a medical researcher. He knows Pugach was Metzger's hired gun and understands the significance of the serum."

"What's our next move?"

"We have to stay with him. All we need is an opening—an opportunity to grab Gabe when he's not paying attention."

Marla gazed through the spyglass again. "Slow down. We're catching him."

Dugan hit the brakes and drifted behind a minivan. "Fredericksburg isn't far from here—half hour or so."

"I hope this nightmare ends there. God help us."

Dugan sensed the desperation in Marla's voice. This was entirely his fault. Why had he become so obsessed with this Fountain of Youth concoction? He should have followed regulations, documented the evidence, filed it away at the office, and contacted the FBI. A mission from God? Where'd he get that idea? The angel, that's where. The image of the bronze statue in Doc Hopkins's front yard materialized in his mind—the wings and their detailed feathers, the folds of the robe, the sword, and the eyes gazing into heaven. The figure had given him such a startling first impression that it moved him spiritually. Shook him up. Made him think God had spoken directly to him like Moses at the burning bush.

When Dugan was a kid he let his imagination carry him away from the misery of his broken home. He often blended his fantasy with reality, boasting to neighborhood kids about heroic deeds he had accomplished in his make-believe world. His neglectful father became a high-level government agent spending most of his time on assignments around the world. Of course, his classmates saw through Dugan's fabrications. He became the brunt of their mean-spirited derisions and target of practical jokes. Everyone, that is, except Marla and Gabriel. They seemed to understand his circumstances and afforded him some creative leeway.

Now the one person left in this world who had accepted his peculiarity had become its casualty. The serum and formula no longer held Dugan's fascination. Gabe had to be rescued. The mission of defending the Tree of Life seemed foolish compared to the life of the boy. But the odds were against them. That was reality at its most dreadful certainty. Courage wasn't a problem. He'd do anything to get Gabe back. Opportunity, so random and rare, would be the major factor.

Marla felt sick in the pit of her stomach—not carsick or nauseated or feverish, but rather sick with dread, knowing the circumstances facing them. Dugan hadn't said much in the last thirty minutes. He seemed lost in his own world. She feared he was sinking into the mire of self-blame and guilt. Deep down she knew this wasn't his fault. Something dark, something evil had crossed their paths and disrupted their lives—something that enters the souls of men like an insidious virus.

She had kept the spyglass focused on the Viper for the last half hour. In the dark it wasn't easy to track it, but the car's sporty profile and airfoil helped. Finally, in Fredericksburg the killer took the Jefferson Davis Highway exit. Dugan followed a couple hundred yards behind. They passed a Friendly's, a Hooters, and a Waffle House before they reached the Days Inn on the right. Dugan drove by the entrance.

"Where are you going?"

"I don't want to pull in right behind him." Dugan glanced at his watch. "It's four in the morning. He'd know something was up. We'll go around the block. Give him time to register."

The block seemed extraordinarily long to Marla. They turned down Business Drive, made a right on Spotsylvania Avenue and then another on Market Street which led back to Jefferson Davis Highway. When they finally turned onto the hotel entrance road, the Viper was gone.

Marla's heart hammered in her chest. "He took off."

"I don't think so. Once you register, you drive around the perimeter of the building to your room. It didn't take him long to check in." Dugan circled the small front parking lot and headed to the left side of the building, a two-story yellow structure with three sections.

As Dugan proceeded cautiously along the first section, Marla eyed every vehicle, trying to identify the Viper. "I don't see the car on this side."

"Maybe they're on the back side." Dugan turned the corner just as a man and a boy entered a room about midway on the lower level.

"That's them," Marla gasped. "And there's the Viper."

The light beamed on through the window, a lone square of yellow against a wall of black. Dugan slowed the car. "Room one-thirty. We'll try to get one-thirty-one."

The curtain was wide open, and Marla spotted Pugach pacing around the room. Then Gabe's face appeared, gazing out the window. Pugach rushed to him and pulled the curtains together, leaving only a sliver of light. "Let me out. You get the room. I'll keep watch here."

Dugan hit the brakes and the car jolted to a stop. "Okay. Be careful. Don't take any unnecessary risks."

"I'll be fine." Marla thrust the door open. "Hurry back."

Dugan sped away, and Marla darted to the building and pressed her back against the wall next to the window. She edged toward the small opening of light, about a two-inch gap. She wanted to see Gabe. Stepping out from the wall, she peered in and spied Pugach sitting on the bed with cell phone in hand. *He's calling someone.* With her limited view she couldn't see Gabe. She focused on Pugach's mouth, knowing her lip-reading ability could come in handy.

Pugach raised the phone to his ear and waited. Then his lips moved: *This is Pugach . . . I have the serum and formula . . . That's right. Metzger's dead . . . Now you deal with me . . . the price hasn't changed—one billion.*

There was a long pause, Pugach's face remaining motionless like an ancient Roman bust, pitted and scarred. Then his lips moved again: *I want guarantees. I'll use my cell phone to make sure the funds have been transferred to the account . . . I want a million in cash, hundred dollar bills, and the rest placed into the account . . . That's right, I'll be leaving the states. No one will find me . . . Nothing has changed. Same time, same place—noon at the World War Two Memorial near the wall with the Eisenhower quote . . . I'll be there. Guaranteed.*

Pugach ended the call and tossed the phone on the bed. Then he lay back, cupping his hands behind his head against the pillow. Marla tried moving to her right to get another angle into the room but still couldn't see Gabe. She slipped back against the wall and closed her eyes, allowing the information she had just acquired to soak in. *Noon at the World War Two Memorial near the wall with the Eisenhower quote.*

The minutes passed excruciatingly slowly. Marla took a couple more peeks in the window but didn't see much. Finally, Dugan arrived and parked about six rooms down next to large SUV. He slipped out of the car and trotted toward her. Within seconds he had the door open to room one-thirty-one, and they entered.

"Don't turn on the light," Dugan whispered. "No one needs to know we're here."

Marla headed to the window and pulled the curtain closed, leaving only a few inches to see out. A swath of light brightened the parking lot, and a midsized sedan came into view and parked next to Pugach's Viper. "Dugan, the customer is here."

Dugan rushed to her side and hovered over her to see through the small opening. Marla felt his hand resting on her back. His nearness helped to steady her nerves.

"It's an Audi. The guy's got money," Dugan said.

Both doors opened at once and the interior light revealed an older man in the passenger seat and a large bearded guy on the driver's side. They stepped out of the vehicle, and the driver, the size of a professional wrestler, headed to the back of the car. He lifted the trunk, pulled out a suitcase, shut the trunk, and then joined the older man. The big guy wore black trousers and a black nylon jacket. Marla assumed he was the rich guy's bodyguard.

The older gentleman had thick white hair, combed back in the style of the fifties pop stars. His yellow dress shirt was decorated with black scrolling lines around the pockets and sleeves. Suspenders held up faded jeans on his thin frame.

The old guy glanced up and said something to the big man. Marla caught part of it as she watched his lips—something about a present. The bodyguard slipped his big paw inside his jacket. His smile revealed a gold front tooth. To Marla he resembled a mountain man with his brown beard and scruffy long hair. Slowly, he pulled out a gun and held it in front of the old man. It looked similar to Marla's weapon—a Magnum pistol. He slid the gun back inside his jacket, and the two men walked toward Pugach's room out of Marla's field of vision.

Faintly, Marla heard a knock and then the sound of a door opening.

"What do we do now?" Marla asked.

"Try to hear what they're saying." Dugan moved to the adjoining wall and pressed his ear against it.

After about a minute Marla said, "Hear anything?"

"No. The words are muffled."

Marla rushed to the sink at the back of the room. In the dark she struggled to identify the items on the counter. *There's got to be a cup here somewhere.* Using her hands to feel the objects, she managed to find a cup wrapped in cellophane. She tore off the thin plastic and rushed to the wall. "Let me try." She placed the opening of the cup against the wall and pressed her ear to the bottom.

Their words were definitely muffled, but she could make most of them out:

"I didn't say you could bring anyone with you," a gruff voice said.

"I didn't know I needed your permission. This is my insurance man, Bobo Barr."

"Insurance man?"

"Yeah. Life insurance. Who's the kid? Boris Junior?"

"That's right. He's my son. We're spending some quality time together."

"Bullshit. You abducted that boy."

"That' right. He's *my* insurance guy."

"You are lower than a lizard's belly. What're you gonna do with him when this is over?"

"Why? You interested in little boys?"

"Maybe. There's a big market for little boys."

"That makes you lower than a snake's belly."

"Like Popeye said, I yam what I yam. You're gonna kill him anyway. Why not sell him to me?"

Marla felt nauseous. She withdrew from the wall and handed the cup to Dugan. "I can't listen anymore."

Dugan took the cup, stuck it to the wall, and listened.

Marla tried to calm herself, but their words kept echoing in her mind. An impulse charged through her. *Go outside and bang on that door. Do something. Save your son.*

Gabe lay on the hotel bed. With his eyes barely cracked open he could see the man with the scar counting money, lots of money. He had prayed and prayed before the other two men got there, begging God to help Mommy and Dugan find him. Once the two men showed up, though, he couldn't concentrate on praying. He pretended to sleep and listened to what they were saying. The skinny old man had said something about buying Gabe. Is that why the man with the scar was counting the money? *Why would that old man want to buy me? You can't sell people, can you?*

Gabe didn't like what was happening at all. He felt like crying but held it in. Mommy would want him to be brave. He tried to have faith. In Sunday school Miss Shirley told him you have to believe God will answer your prayers. *Please, God, please, get Mommy and Dugan here as fast as possible.*

"You don't trust me much, do you, Pugach?" the old man said.

"As much as I would trust a mad dog."

"You're the mad dog. I'm just tossing you a few bones."

The man with the scar smiled and put the last bundle of money into the suitcase. "Then be very careful. Mad dogs don't mind biting the hand that feeds them."

"What's that mean?" the big man with the beard said.

The skinny guy laughed. "Mr. Pugach is a very dangerous man. A little crazy. But we're not frightened, are we, Bobo?"

The big man put his hands on his hips. "Not at all."

The old man pointed at the suitcase. "All there?"

The man with the scar nodded. "The bones are in order."

"All right." The old man held out his arm. "Shoot me up."

The man with the scar opened a little suitcase on the stand next to the bed. He lifted out the plastic thing with the needle—the same thing the doctor used to give Gabe his shots. It had green stuff in it. Then he pulled out a long strip that looked like a big broken rubber band. He went over to the old man, tied it around his arm, and pulled it tight.

"Are you good with needles?" the old man asked.

"I'm no junkie, but I can handle a needle. You don't trust me much, do you, Mr. Hinkle?"

"As much as I would trust a mad dog."

The man with the scar stuck the needle in the old man's arm and pushed the top, making the green liquid disappear. The old man took a deep breath. "Is it my imagination, or do I feel younger already?"

"Welcome to the Methuselah Club." The man with the scar turned toward the little suitcase.

The old man held up his hand. "Don't put the needle away yet."

The man with the scar stopped and turned. "What?"

"I said don't put the needle away yet. My friend Bobo here wants to join the club, too."

The big man stepped forward and smiled. Gabe saw one of his teeth sparkle like a shiny penny. He pointed to his chest and said, "That's right. I'm in my prime and want to stay that way."

"Fine," the ugly man said. "Give me another million bucks."

The old man shook his head. "No. We want the first-cousin deal—two for one."

"Right." The ugly man laughed and turned to put the needle away.

"Not so fast." The big man reached into his jacket and pulled out a gun. "Put your hands up, or I'll blow a hole through your skull."

The man with the scar slowly raised his hands, and the big man walked over and reached inside the ugly man's shirt and pulled out another gun.

Gabe could feel his heart beating in his chest. He knew guns were bad. They kill people. His mommy always hid her gun somewhere in her bedroom so Gabe couldn't find it. He felt really scared. His eyes filled with tears and spilled over. He couldn't stop himself from crying. When he tried to keep his mouth closed, he only cried louder.

"Now look what you've done," the man with the scar said. "You've upset my boy. Let's put the weapons away."

The big man raised both guns and pointed them at the ugly man. "Make him shut up."

The ugly man pointed to the dresser. "He probably wants his teddy bear."

"Give it to him," the old man said.

The ugly man walked across the room, picked up Gabe's pirate bear, and handed it to him. "Here you go, kid. Shut your mouth and take good care of that bear."

Gabe hugged Blackie. He closed his eyes and prayed God would make him brave. It helped. He took a couple of long breaths and stopped crying. With one hand holding onto Blackie he used the other hand to wipe the tears from his face and then opened his eyes.

"Back to business," the old man said. "Where's the rest of the serum?"

"It's not here."

"Right."

"Go ahead and search the room."

The old man looked around the room. "Then it must be out in the car."

"That's right," the ugly man said. "It's in the trunk."

"What about the formula?" the old man asked.

"The formula? What're you talking about?"

The old man stood up from the bed. "Now that I'm feeling younger, I need a long-term financial plan. That formula has got to be worth a lot of greenbacks, at least twenty or thirty million."

"Come on now. I did the dirty work to get the formula. I'm willing to give Boo Boo here a shot of the serum, but you can forget about getting your hands on the formula."

The big man stepped closer. "Then you can forget about becoming the oldest man on earth. We'll be planting you in the ground tonight."

The ugly man waved his hands. "Okay. Okay. You guys turned out to be a couple of real bastards. Follow me out to the car. I'll give you what you want."

The old man pointed to Gabe. "You stay on that bed, little boy, and hang on to your bear."

The man with the scar walked to the door, opened it, and went out. The other two followed him, the old man shutting the door behind him.

Somehow Marla had controlled herself. She realized charging into that room would only endanger Gabe's life. She had to be patient.

Dugan backed away from the wall, lowered the cup, and pointed to the window. "They went outside."

Marla hurried to the window and peeked out. She saw Pugach leading the way, the bodyguard and old man trailing close behind. The Audi had been backed into the parking space, and Pugach stopped, dug his keys out of his pocket, and popped open the trunk. A spotlight somewhere farther down along the building gave Marla a good view of the scene. Pugach bent over, his head disappearing into the shadow of the trunk. The bearded man stood right behind him, holding a gun. The old man stood a few feet back.

Pugach whirled, and light flashed from his hand. A gun? No. She didn't hear a shot. The big man dropped his gun and grasped his chest. When he turned around, Marla could see a large knife embedded in his chest, the spotlight reflecting off the blade. The bodyguard's eyes widened. He stumbled two or three steps toward the hotel and fell. The old man bolted around the car toward the dark end of the parking lot. Pugach dropped to his knees.

"He's looking for the gun," Marla whispered.

"Get ready," Dugan said. "Now's our chance.

Pugach sprung to his feet and took off after the old man.

18

"Gabe!" Marla shouted. "Open up! It's your mom!" She pounded on the door.

Dugan peered through the two-inch gap in the curtain and beat on the window. "Gabe, it's me! Dugan!"

In the darkness from beyond the hotel's parking lot lights, several shots erupted.

"Hurry, Gabe, hurry!" Marla called.

The door swung open, and Gabe stood there, wide-eyed, tear-streaked cheeks, his teddy bear clasped to his chest. Marla dipped and swooped him up in her arms. "Let's go!"

Dugan sprinted down the sidewalk toward the Ford Focus, and Marla tried to keep up. Skidding to a stop, Dugan yanked the passenger-side door open. Marla leapt in with Gabe tightly clamped against her. Dugan hurdled the hood of the car to the other side, slid off the front fore panel, and jerked the door open. He plopped down onto the seat and speared his hand into his pants pocket for the keys. After jangling them for a few seconds, he jammed one into the ignition and started the engine, revved it and threw it into reverse, the tires squealing.

Marla watched through the windshield as the world whooshed backwards. Dugan swerved to a stop in the middle of the perimeter road. Rain droplets splattered against the glass. The headlights cut through the darkness, a sudden shower slicing through the beam. Dugan threw it into drive and punched the accelerator. A figure stepped into the beam of the headlights and raised his hands—the old man. Blood soaked his yellow shirt near his shoulder. Dugan slammed on the brakes and managed to stop before hitting him. The old man fell forward, catching himself on the front of the car.

Horror filled his eyes. "Help me!" he screamed.

A shot fired and the old man's forehead burst. He slumped onto the hood. Red and white matter seeped out of the crater in his head. Pugach bounded from the blackness onto the hood of the car. Dugan hit the gas, throwing the old man forward and thudding over his body. Pugach slid into the windshield and planted a hand against the glass. His other hand waved a gun. Dugan hit the brakes. The car skidded to a stop. Pugach flew off the hood, rolling several times on the asphalt. Dugan hit the gas again. Marla couldn't watch. She knew Dugan was going to try to flatten him. She closed her eyes, held tightly to Gabe, but didn't feel any sudden jouncing. She twisted, craning her neck, and peered out the back window. Pugach stood up empty handed and scoured the ground. He had rolled out of the way to avoid the car but had dropped the gun. Just before Dugan made the turn, Marla caught sight of Pugach picking something off the ground.

"He found the gun!" Marla cried. "You've got to step on it. He'll come after us."

"He might," Dugan said. "But why? We don't have the serum or formula."

"It was the look on his face. I just know he's coming after us. Maybe he's crazy."

"He's definitely crazy. Gabe, are you all right?"

Gabe had buried his head into Marla's chest.

Marla rubbed his back. "Are you okay, Sport?"

Gabe lifted his head. "I kept praying, Mommy. I kept praying you and Dugan would come."

Dugan flew out of the hotel parking lot and swerved right onto Jefferson Davis Highway.

"Where are we going?" Marla asked.

"I want to find a country road. That's our best chance of losing him."

Marla twisted in her seat and focused out the back window. "He just pulled out of the parking lot about a hundred yards behind us."

As they sped by a Wendy's, Dugan said, "There's a sign ahead—Mine Road. That's got to lead out into the country." Dugan made a hard right at the next intersection, the back of the car sliding around the turn. He floored the pedal, and the motor strained, picking up speed. They shot through a red light and entered a residential area.

Marla glanced back. "He's still behind us. He's closing."

"I'm going almost eighty."

They went around a slight turn, and Dugan hit the brakes and made a hard left onto Landsdowne Road. After a couple hundred yards he turned right onto Lee Drive. The road cut through a forest, and a sign declared they had entered the Spotsylvania National Military Park. The name struck a chord of memory with Marla—this was the location of a famous Civil War battle.

"I can't lose him," Dugan said.

They passed between thousands of tall trees, as if they were speeding their way through a deep groove in the earth.

Marla looked back again. "Fifty yards and gaining. We're in trouble."

"Please, God, please," Gabe prayed, "make the bad man wreck."

Headlights flashed in Marla's eyes.

"A car is heading this way," Dugan said.

Marla couldn't believe it. She saw a rack of lights on top of the vehicle. "It's a cop car. Flash your high beams."

Dugan flipped the brights on and off just before the car sped by. "It's a state trooper."

Marla whipped her head around and focused out the rear window. A siren blared in the distance and blue and red lights flashed on. Then they vanished behind trees as the little Ford rounded a turn. The Viper kept coming on. The patrolman didn't scare him.

"Faster! He's going to ram us!"

"I've got it floored."

A sudden jolt thrust Marla backward. She squeezed Gabe with all her might. Another collision sent the rear end of the Ford Focus sliding. The world twirled, and Marla caught sight of the front of the car clipping the Viper. The car did several 180s before it slammed into a tree. The airbags inflated and then hissed. Marla heard another crash across the road.

"Is everyone okay?" Dugan asked.

"Mommy, you're hurting me."

Marla realized she still had Gabe so tightly clasped that he was in pain from the pressure. She loosened her arms. "Are you all right, Sport?"

"I think so."

"We need to get out of here." Dugan shifted into reverse. "He'll come after us." He hit the gas, and the engine roared, but the car wouldn't budge. "Crap! The transmission's damaged. We've got to go on foot. I'm against the tree. We'll have to get out your side."

Marla tried the door, but it was locked. She hit the unlock button on the armrest and flung the door open. Headlights brightened the road beside her, and a siren blasted and faded. The vehicle skidded to a stop, red and blue lights flashing. "It's the state trooper."

"Wait!" Dugan shouted. "Don't make any fast moves. The officer has no idea who we are."

"We've got to warn him about Pugach." Marla leaned out the open door. "Sir! Be careful. There's a man with a gun out there!"

"Where?" the officer called.

Marla peered into the darkness and made out the Viper, upside-down and off the other side of the road. She pointed to the overturned car. "Over there!"

"Stay where you are! I'll check it out!" The trooper's voice boomed.

A flashlight cut through the raindrops and illuminated the upside-down Viper. Marla watched the officer approach the vehicle, her heart thudding in her chest.

He stopped, directed the light into the driver's side window, and raised his pistol. "I am a state patrolman! Drop your weapon and come out of the car!"

Marla didn't hear any rustling noises, only silence. The broken glass on the ground glittered in the light like a thousand diamonds.

The patrolman crouched, getting a better angle to view the inside of the Viper. "Anyone in there? Are you hurt?" He edged closer. Finally, he moved to where he could shine his flashlight into the interior of the car. "He's gone."

"Can you find his gun?" Dugan hollered.

The officer placed his hand on the ground, lowered his shoulders and stuck his head inside the car. After about a minute he withdrew and stood. Holding the light near his shoulder, he panned the woods, the circle of light gliding over tree trunks and low boughs half-filled with fall leaves.

"Don't see him or his gun." The officer shifted the light toward Marla. "Are you all right?"

"I think so," Marla said.

He walked toward them. "How about the boy?"

Gabe squinted into the bright glare. "I'm okay."

The patrolman directed the light to each of their faces and then turned his back to them and scanned the woods again. "Are you sure the other driver has a gun?"

"Positive," Dugan said. "The guy's a killer. We just saw him blow the top of some guy's head off."

The officer faced them again. He looked to be about forty, well built, with chiseled features and dark eyes. "Where?"

"The back parking lot of the Days Inn," Dugan said.

"Is that why he was chasing you?"

Marla shook her head. "It's a long story."

The officer turned and panned the light again. "He may be out there watching us, but I don't see him."

Dugan leaned forward. "I wouldn't go after him in the dark."

"I don't plan on leaving you here unprotected." The officer put his hand on the top of the car door. "I'll call for back up. Come on out of there and head over to the patrol car."

Gabe slid off of Marla's lap and onto the road. He stood there, clutching his pirate teddy bear to his side. Marla sent up a quick prayer, thanking God that Gabe was alive and well and safe. Then she wondered just how safe. Pugach could be hiding in the shadows of the woods with his gun trained on them. The thought made her shudder and she grabbed Gabe's hand and hurried to the patrol car.

The officer ordered them to sit in the back seat while he entered information into the onboard computer. Gabe sat between them, hugging his bear. She felt safer in the car but kept checking the perimeter of the woods just in case Pugach appeared.

Marla tousled Gabe's dark brown hair. "You were very brave, Sport. I'm proud of you."

"No doubt about that," Dugan said. "I'm going to make you an honorary Dare County deputy."

Gabe lifted his head and eyed Dugan. "Really?"

"Sure thing."

The patrolman turned around, planted his elbow on the back of the seat, and looked at Marla. "You're Marla Easton, the owner of the Ford Focus?"

"Yes sir."

He shifted in his seat and stared at Dugan. "And you must be Dugan Walton, Dare County sheriff?"

"That's right."

"I need to see some I.D."

Dugan pulled his wallet from his back pocket, fished out his driver's license, and handed it to the patrolman.

In the excitement Marla had left her purse at home. "I don't have mine with me. How about my cell phone?" She extracted the iPhone from her jeans pocket and navigated to the owner's info screen. "Here." She held up the phone so the officer could examine the screen.

"Well isn't that a shot in the dark—finding you two out in the middle of the Spotsylvania Military Park." The patrolman nodded slowly, his features hard to distinguish in the dim glow of the lights from the instrument panel. "There's an A.P.B. out for you."

"An A.P.B.?" Dugan said. "Why?"

"From what I can gather from my info," he thumbed over his shoulder toward the computer screen on the dashboard, "finding you two is a high priority."

"Who wants us?" Dugan asked.

"I don't know, but I'll definitely make a call and find out."

Marla met Dugan's gaze, and he raised his eyebrows. She figured it had to do with the murder scene in Nags Head. Those two Federal agents probably wanted to know what Dugan and Marla had found in the hotel room and had issued a high priority alert to find them. Marla wondered if they were in big trouble because they had removed evidence from a crime scene without proper documentation—not to mention losing possession of that evidence.

The patrolman dialed a number on the car phone and held it to his ear. "Patrolman MacFarland here. I'm at the scene of an accident near Fredericksburg and have received a report of a possible gunman and murder . . . Supposedly there's a body in the parking lot of the Days Inn about two miles from here . . . Really? Well then, my source must be reliable." After a long pause he reported their location coordinates and then said, "The alleged gunman is on foot. No description as yet, but I'll try to get one. We'll need a search team here as soon as possible . . . That's not all. I've got a couple in my back seat who are listed on the high priority sheet . . . Marla Easton and Sheriff Dugan Walton."

"Mommy," Gabe said, his big eyes gazing up at her, "are you in trouble?"

"I don't know, Sport. I don't think so." Marla knew Dugan would have to bear most of the responsibility. She understood protocol had been broken, but as a rookie deputy she lacked experience in these circumstances. Poor Dugan. She feared he may be called out on this. Could he be in big trouble? She glanced over at him and noticed his stare fixed on the officer.

"Is that right?" the officer continued. "Hmmmph. Are you sure about that? . . . Okay, if that's what they want. We'll head up there right now." The officer returned the phone to its holder on the dash.

Dugan leaned forward. "Up where?"

"Washington, D.C. They don't even want me to hang out until the local cops get here. What have you two been up to?"

"Is it that bad?" Dugan's voice wavered. "Who wants to talk to us? The FBI?"

"You guessed it. But not just a field agent."

"Who?" Marla asked.

"The director himself, Robert J. Miller."

19

Pugach stood in the shadows of the forest next to the thick trunk of a pine tree. He glared at the state trooper's vehicle, a silver Crown Victoria, its headlights slashing through the pouring rain. The couple and boy were safe in the back seat for now. But they had something he wanted, something he had already killed several men to get. He would eliminate them too, if necessary. Now he waited for the patrolman to come looking for him. That would be the best-case scenario. He'd shoot the officer and then go after the couple. Patience. Patience . . . and then at the right time—swift and lethal action.

Blood dripped down his face from the gash on his forehead. It mingled with the rain and flowed, thinning and channeling down the scar on his cheek and grooves in his face. He swiped his hand across his mug and glanced at his palm but couldn't see much in the darkness. I must look like a red-faced monster, he thought, a monster waiting in the dark to slay his next victim.

The idea that he had become a monster bothered him. He wasn't always like this. It took time and the right conditions to reach this state—that of a cold-blooded killer who suffered little remorse. It didn't happen overnight. He could blame a thousand things—his father, the death of his mother, the mob, his neighborhood, but what was the use? Eventually you have to own up to who you are. He accepted himself.

Yet he often longed to be a normal human being, a respected man with a wife and family. That's why the money was so important. It meant a new start. With it he could escape to a place where no one knew the monster ever existed. He would become a new person. Grace on his own terms, not on his suffering mother's terms—that would require forgiveness. She had always told him that God forgives and gives new life. Could God forgive someone like him? He doubted it. Mercy and grace had become foreign to him. If God offered grace would he even accept it? Tough question. That would demand repentance, and repentance meant turning from the deeds of darkness. Pugach chuckled to himself. That would require giving up the billion and facing the electric chair. No way. Wasn't that ironic? The very thing that offered him a new start would have to be sacrificed to partake of grace. And grace would be his demise—in this world anyway.

The patrol car backed up and turned, its back tires dropping off the road onto the shoulder. Then it took off toward town. Pugach couldn't believe it. "What the hell?" Something was up. Why didn't the officer at least wait until more cops got there? The F.B.I. had to be involved. The patrolman must be taking them to the nearest field office or maybe even headquarters in Washington, D.C. Now what?

He had to find a vehicle. After sliding his pistol into his jacket pocket, he reached down and picked up the briefcase. The federal agents wouldn't be happy with him, but he'd still meet with them at the World War II Memorial at noon. There was enough serum left in the second vial he had filled to offer at least two people eternal life. That was his ace in the hole. Who doesn't want to live forever? Somehow he had to convince them he would retrieve the original vial and formula. That damn couple and boy.

Pugach turned and marched deeper into the woods. Sooner or later he'd find a house and steal a car. He knew the forest couldn't be more than a mile wide. He checked his watch: 5:15. If he could swipe a vehicle within the next two hours, he'd be fine. From Fredericksburg it took only an hour to get to Washington, D.C., two or three hours if he ran into heavy traffic. Plenty of time. His biggest challenge would be finding the couple and getting back the serum and formula. Perhaps the corrupt agents could be of help. The F.B.I. had the technology to track down anybody. If not, the Methuselah Triumvirate had plenty of means at their disposal—lots of money could provide access to the right technology.

After trudging through woods for half an hour, Pugach emerged onto a two-lane highway. He saw plenty of houses on the other side of the road but wanted to find one off by itself. He passed a sign identifying the road as Mine Road—the same road on which he had chased the couple. He had come full circle and now could easily find his way back to town and Interstate 95. Farther down he saw a street called Lee's Crossing Lane that led back into a subdivision. Too many houses. Walking another quarter mile, he spotted a long driveway with a huge house sitting on an open tract of land. Not good, he thought, no trees, no cover. The next driveway was tree-lined. Four or five large shade trees grew in the yard, partially blocking the view of the house from the road. This one would do. It would have to. He didn't want to waste any more time.

He glanced up and down Mine Road to make sure no traffic was coming. Then he hurried down the driveway, sticking close to the tree line. The white house had a large covered front porch, a modern version of a southern farmhouse. He climbed the few steps and passed a couple of rocking chairs and a glider. The front door, situated at the middle of the porch, had a leaded glass design with diamonds and rectangles. Rich son of a bitch, Pugach thought. Good. He should have a nice car.

He reached and pressed the doorbell and faintly heard the chimes. After about thirty seconds he did it again. The porch light came on. An elderly lady, probably in her seventies, opened the door. She had short, curly white hair and wore a pink robe over her thin frame. Her eyes widened when she saw Pugach's face, and she gasped.

"Ma'am, I wrecked my car down the road a little ways. Could I use your phone?"

"Of course. Are you okay?" Her voice trembled.

"I think so. Probably need some stitches."

"Wait here. I'll bring the phone out to you."

Before she could close the door, he jammed his foot between it and the frame.

Her eyes riveted on his foot and then peered up at him, wide and alarmed.

He thrust the door open sending her flying backwards onto the tile floor. He stepped into the house, slammed the door behind him, reached into his jacket pocket, and pulled out his pistol. "Don't make a sound. Do exactly what I say, and I'll let you live."

She grimaced in pain, her bony legs spread, with the robe drooped over them. "I think I'm hurt." She rubbed her hip.

"You're fine. Now get up."

Slowly, unsteadily, she rose to her feet.

"Is there anyone else in the house?"

"Yes. My husband is upstairs asleep."

Damn, Pugach thought, the body count just keeps rising.

The trip to Washington, D.C. didn't take long, maybe an hour. FBI headquarters was located on Pennsylvania Avenue between Ninth and Tenth Streets. Its rhythmic architecture repeated a series of columns on the first level and five floors of square windows above. Dugan had never been to the J. Edgar Hoover Building but had to confess he had dreamed of working there as a youngster. He'd never imagined his first visit would be under these circumstances. They passed through several security checks, and then a female agent, a well-built blonde, directed them to separate rooms for a strip search. The blonde went into the other room with Marla, and a heavyset, moonfaced guy accompanied Dugan. Just my luck, Dugan thought. He figured they were hoping to find the formula. After the strip search, the lady agent led them to Director Miller's office.

The surroundings seemed more utilitarian than luxurious. Through the windows the cloudy dawn cast a gray sheen on the furniture. An American flag stood behind a medium-sized oak desk stacked with papers. A computer monitor sat on top of the left extension of the desk with an empty chair facing the monitor. Five high-back, black leather chairs surrounded the desk. Another security officer, a tall black man, probably in his thirties, motioned toward the five chairs and instructed them to have a seat and wait for Director Miller, who would arrive shortly. Gabe climbed up onto Marla's lap. Clearly, he didn't want to sit alone in the big chair. He clutched his pirate teddy bear to his chest. One of its legs hung loosely by tattered threads and its fur was matted and scuffed.

The officer stood at the door and crossed his arms. Dugan met Marla's gaze. She appeared tired, strained, yet, under the circumstances, quite beautiful. What had he gotten her and Gabe into? Sheepishly, he shifted his focus to the floor. Dugan was ready to take the blame for everything. He would confess to removing the evidence from the scene without properly cataloging it. Then there was his failure to report the second crime scene to Fetters and Reed, the agents at the Manteo crime scene. It was his fault the serum and formula had been lost. Over the years he had learned to take ownership of his mistakes. Embracing the truth had transformed him from a kid with a poor self-image to a man entrusted with the responsibility of protecting and serving the people of Dare County. The truth may hurt his career for now, but in the long run he knew he'd become a better man by accepting the consequences of his actions. If only he hadn't involved Marla and Gabe.

Feeling tired and low, he looked up at the white-tiled ceiling above him. A soft hand suddenly covered the top of his hand and squeezed. It was Marla's. His eyes met hers, and she smiled.

"Everything'll be fine," she said.

He nodded. "Sooner or later. It's out of our hands now." He turned his hand over and clasped hers, their fingers intertwining. It felt right. Warmth, like drinking a good cup of hot chocolate on a cold day, spread through him. Gabe reached and put his hand on top of theirs. Now Dugan felt even more complete. He wondered if Marla felt the same way.

Director Miller entered the office. A man of medium height and build, he wore a dark blue suit and red tie. His hair was silver with a few darker streaks, neatly parted on the left. His strong jaw line and deep set eyes made him appear to be a man of great determination. Dugan released Marla's hand, and they stood, Gabe sliding off Marla's lap.

Director Miller held out his hand. "Robert Miller. You must be Sheriff Walton?"

Dugan shook his hand. Miller had a firm grip. "Yes. Dugan Walton, Dare County sheriff."

Miller turned to Marla and offered his hand. "And you are Deputy Easton?"

"Yes, sir." Marla shook his hand as Gabe gazed up at him. "This is Gabriel, my son."

The director crouched to meet Gabe at eye level. A smile broke his stern demeanor as he extended his hand to Gabe. "You certainly are a brave young fellow."

Gabe placed his small hand in Miller's. "Do you own this place?"

Miller laughed. "No, I just work here."

The sound of footsteps echoed in the hallway. Two agents entered the office, their familiar faces catching Dugan's attention—Fetters and Reed. They both wore black Polo shirts with yellow FBI lettering on the left breast.

Director Miller turned and nodded toward the two men. "You've already met Special Agent Fetters and Special Agent Reed."

"Yes," Dugan said, making eye contact with Fetters, the tall one with the butch-cut black hair. "We met at the Manteo crime scene."

Reed shook his head, his large crooked nose casting an odd shadow across his lips. "We did meet, but unfortunately, Sheriff Walton must not have understood the gravity of our investigation."

Director Miller's lips tightened. "Let's sit down before we get into this." He pointed to the five black chairs in front of his desk. "I'm sure Sheriff Walton has a good explanation for what happened." Miller circled his desk, spun his chair away from the monitor on the desk's side extension, sat down, and glided up to his desk to face the five chairs. Dugan and Marla sat in the two far left chairs, and Gabe climbed onto Marla's lap and clutched his teddy bear. The agents sat in the chairs on the right, leaving an empty one in the middle.

Miller cleared his throat. "Okay, Agent Reed, what kind of interaction did you have with Sheriff Walton and Deputy Easton at the Manteo crime scene?"

"We informed them that we would be conducting an exclusive investigation. We needed all evidence and information they had collected."

Miller eyed Dugan. "Would you agree to Agent Reed's summary of your conversation?"

Dugan nodded. "We handed over all evidence we had found at the Manteo crime scene and left the premises."

Fetters leaned forward and stared at Dugan. "But you investigated another crime scene in Nags Head that morning, one clearly connected to the Manteo murder."

"That's true, but I considered the Nags Head crime scene our responsibility until otherwise notified."

Reed scratched the side of his bald head. "But how can we notify you if you don't report it to us?"

"That's right," Fetters said. "You knew the crime scenes were related. When you arrived at Manteo, you should have informed us."

"Let me ask you this, Sheriff Walton," Director Miller said. "Did you, in fact, realize the crime scenes were connected?"

"Yes."

"How did you know it?"

Dugan glanced at Marla. "We found evidence at Nags Head taken from the Manteo crime scene."

Fetters sat up in his chair. "What kind of evidence?"

Dugan met Fetters's glare. "A thermos that contained a vial of yellow-green liquid and a formula."

"Anything else?" Director Miller asked.

Dugan nodded. "Instructions concerning the Methuselah serum—how to inject it with a hypodermic needle."

Miller nodded. "The Methuselah serum." Then he took a long breath and blew it out slowly.

"Yes. We realized Dr. Hopkins had concocted some kind of youth drug. After watching him win the Colony Lost and Found 5K, we knew he had used it on himself. Obviously the killer wanted the serum and formula."

Reed asked, "What did you do with the serum and formula?"

"I didn't want to leave it in the hotel room. I figured the killer may come back for it, so I told Deputy Easton to take it to the squad car. That's when she spotted the suspect."

"I see." Miller folded his hands on top of the desk. "And you pursued him?"

"That's right," Dugan said.

"Why was he so suspicious?"

Marla cleared her throat. "When I was in the squad car, the suspect sat at the wheel of a Dodge Viper next to me. When I called Sheriff Walton, the suspect took off. He must have seen me make the call."

Fetters shook his head. "Obviously, he knew you called for backup."

"I got down to the parking lot as fast as I could," Dugan said. "He had a head start, and we lost him. Then we got the call from headquarters to report to you guys at the Manteo crime scene."

Fetters said, "So when you arrived at Manteo, the serum and formula were still in your possession?"

"That's right," Dugan said. "The killer must have followed us back to Rodanthe where Deputy Easton lives. That night he kidnapped Gabe and then demanded we hand over the formula and serum in exchange for the boy. Apparently, you know the rest of the story."

Director Miller rubbed his chin. "You made the exchange, but then went after him. In Fredericksburg you caught up with him and somehow rescued the boy."

"Right," Dugan said. "We were lucky. At the Days Inn the killer scheduled a transaction with a customer. It went badly. To me it appeared to be a double-cross. When the killer went after the customer out in the parking lot, we grabbed Gabe and took off."

"Then he came after you," Miller said.

"Right. He rear-ended us in the middle of that military park and both cars bit the dust. That's when the state trooper showed up."

Fetters scooted his chair forward and faced Dugan. "Sheriff Walton, there's a very important question that needs to be answered. What happened to the Methuselah serum and formula?"

"Did you search the suspect's car?"

"Of course," Reed said. "We checked his car and your car."

Marla said, "You strip searched us, so obviously we don't have it."

Fetters crossed his arms. "Hmmmph."

Reed said, "You might have hid it somewhere, maybe in the woods."

"Come on, now," Dugan said. "Did you interview the trooper? He'll tell you we were in the car when he arrived, pinned against a tree. We had no opportunity to hide the serum and formula."

Director Miller raised his hand. "Sheriff Walton is right. We searched the woods near the vehicles. The suspect must have taken the Methuselah serum and formula with him." Miller directed his gaze to the agents. "You two need to get back out there and find the suspect. That's where you'll find the formula."

Fetters gritted his teeth and then said, "Whatever you say, sir. We're on our way."

The two agents stood, Reed giving Dugan a final perturbed glance, and left the office.

Director Miller waved toward the door. "Don't mind them. They're under a lot of stress. As you can see, this has become a high priority case. I believe your story. Unfortunately, you got caught up in something much bigger than anyone imagined. That serum and formula has become a matter of national security. Do you know much about it?"

Dugan nodded, "A little."

"Did you know it could possibly hold a cure for some types of cancer?"

"Yes," Marla said. "I read Dr. Hopkins's journal before I turned it over to Reed and Fetters. Apparently, the serum cured the doctor's prostate cancer."

Miller nodded. "Then you also know the serum's effects on aging."

Dugan wondered how much he should reveal, but Miller's apparent confidence in his story increased his comfort level. "Yes. We examined Dr. Hopkins's distance running stats on the computer in his office. He injected himself with the Methuselah serum about a year ago. His times dropped steadily as the months went by. This past Saturday he posted a world-class time for his age group at the Manteo race—the same time he ran as a thirty-five-year old. The journal entries plus his running records made it clear he had succeeded in discovering the Fountain of Youth."

Miller nodded. "That's why we're involved. Do you understand the implications of a serum that could cure cancer and offer another forty or fifty years of life?"

"That might be a conservative estimate," Marla said. "According to his journal entries, Dr. Hopkins's believed he could live forever."

"Well . . ." Miller shook his head. "That didn't happen, did it? Apparently, the serum doesn't stop bullets."

"No, it doesn't," Dugan said. "But it would create a whole new set of problems for society."

"You're right," Miller said. "Overpopulation, lack of resources, business and government monopolized by those who control access to the serum. It could create more problems than it would solve. But there's another reason we're involved at such a high priority level."

"International complications?" Dugan asked.

Miller shrugged. "That's a definite possibility, but there's something else . . . something I'm not at liberty to reveal at this point in time."

20

Director Miller assigned Division Chief Ronald Clooney the responsibility of conducting a more in-depth interview with Dugan and Marla and then accommodating them in regards to transportation. Miller explained that Clooney was deeply involved in the Methuselah case. Both Fetters and Reed reported to him. Division Chief Clooney, a short, squat man with a bad comb-over and hair sprouting out of his ears, took them into another office to question them further. His demeanor reminded Marla of her Uncle Willy, a jovial, good-natured fellow.

The interview began about 9:30 A.M. and took an hour as Division Chief Clooney extracted more details about the last three days. Marla tried to answer the questions directed to her with clarity and accuracy. She told him about the killer's rendezvous with the Medical Mafia contact at noon at the World War II Memorial. After receiving that information, he called Special Agent Fetters and told him and Reed to report back to headquarters. She wanted to help as much as possible and then be done with it. The sooner she and Gabe returned to the comfort of their home in Rodanthe the better.

When Dugan revealed the killer's name to be Pugach, Clooney appeared slightly rattled, as if the name meant big trouble. Clooney rubbed his large jowls. "We were afraid he might be involved. He's a bad egg, that's for sure. A Russian mobster. Intelligent and callous—a deadly combination."

"I was surprised he came after us," Dugan said. "He had possession of the serum and formula. Why take the risk of a high-speed chase through the streets of Fredericksburg? It could only increase the chances of attracting the attention of law enforcement."

Clooney chuckled. "Lucky for you those odds paid off. Patrolman MacFarland saved your assss . . . I mean skin." Clooney glanced at Gabe, a wry smile breaking out.

"Patrolman MacFarland was a Godsend," Marla said.

Dugan tousled Gabe's hair. "A child's prayer and a dependable officer—that's a lifesaving combination."

Clooney closed his notebook. "We're done here. I've got all the information from you I need. Unfortunately, your car isn't drivable. Might take a week to get it fixed." He handed Marla a small white business card. "You can call that number to make arrangements for repairs. Where're you headed? I can give you a ride."

Marla glanced at Dugan. He had that look of great relief in his eyes. Clearly the feds weren't going to press any charges or even reprimand him for carelessness in conducting an investigation. Dugan could leave here without worry of repercussions impacting his professional status as Dare County's sheriff. Things were looking up. Now they could head home and put this behind them.

"What about the crime scene in Fredericksburg?" Dugan asked. "Do I need to report to law enforcement there to answer questions?"

Clooney shook his head. "That's all taken care of. We're in charge of all three crime scenes. You've answered my questions. I'll need both of your cell phone numbers in case anything else comes up."

"Sure thing," Dugan said.

Marla and Dugan gave the agent their numbers, and he entered them into the contact list of his cell phone. Then he insisted they enter his number on their contact lists just in case they needed to get in touch with him.

"So, where to?" Clooney asked.

"We're headed home," Dugan said.

Marla glanced at the ceiling. "Thank God."

Dugan said, "If you could give us a ride to the nearest car rental agency, we'd appreciate it."

"Sure thing . . . Oh, I forgot." Clooney reached down, lifted a plastic bag and set it on the desk. "These items were found in your car. Figured you might want to take them with you." He slid the bag in Marla's direction.

She opened it and saw Gabe's Transformer toy, an umbrella, collapsed and folded into a neat nylon cover, a charger for her iPhone, and the spyglass. "Thanks."

She pulled out the toy and Gabe said, "Optimus Prime!" He took it from her and quickly shape-shifted the robot warrior into a semi truck. "He's ready to roll now."

Clooney raised his eyebrows. "Wow! Presto chango. That boy is quick with his hands and smart too. He'd make a good G-man one of these days."

"No thanks," Gabe said. "I want to be a Dare County sheriff like Dugan."

A smile broke across Dugan's face. He reached and patted Gabe's head. "You are a smart boy."

Clooney drove them to a Hertz Rent-a-Car around the corner and a few blocks down 7th Street. Older buildings lined the street: an AT & T office, a Fuddruckers, a Radio Shack, a few sandwich shops, an Urban Outfitters. This section of town reminded Dugan of Wheeling, West Virginia, across the Ohio River from his hometown of Martins Ferry, Ohio, making him a little homesick. The buildings weren't very tall, and they had that familiar look of the architecture of the early 1900s, the kind that characterized so many small towns in the Ohio Valley.

Dugan thanked Clooney for the ride and assured him they'd be fine from here, but Clooney insisted on escorting them into the car rental office and informed the counterperson the government was footing the bill for the rental. After signing papers for a Chevy Malibu, Clooney shook their hands and departed.

"I can't wait to get home," Marla said as they drove down 7th Street and stopped at a light.

"Aren't you curious?" Dugan asked.

"Curious about what?"

"About the meeting between Pugach and his contact."

Marla sat silently until the light turned green. "Yes. I guess I am curious. I'd feel safer if I knew Pugach had been captured. Then we wouldn't be looking over our shoulders on the drive back to the Outer Banks."

"I say we take a stroll around the grounds of the World War II Memorial. Should be lots of people there. We can keep our distance from the wall with the Eisenhower quote. Clooney gave us back the spyglass. We'll find a secluded spot and witness the arrest."

Marla pointed to a Salvation Army store on the right. "Stop here!"

"Why?"

"We need jackets and hats—anything to keep Pugach from recognizing us."

Dugan hit the brakes and pulled along the curb next to a parking meter.

They spent ten minutes in the thrift store finding hats and jackets. All three picked out toboggans. Dugan found an extra long black one that he could pull down to his eyebrows. Gabe wanted one just like it. Marla picked out a crimson toboggan with earflaps and a fluffy ball on top. There were lots of nylon Washington Redskin jackets in the coat section. Dugan suggested they find similar jackets and buy them a size or two too large to further disguise their body shapes. With a ton of Redskin fans in the D.C. area, Dugan figured they would blend better with the crowd.

They left the store at about 11:30. Dugan knew the World War II Memorial wasn't far away—west on Constitution Avenue and south on 17th Street. A few years ago he had visited the memorial and most of the other famous landmarks in the area. To the right Dugan saw the long Reflecting Pool with the familiar Lincoln Memorial on the far side. The World War II Memorial, located at this end of the Reflecting Pool, reminded Dugan of a modern Stonehenge with its granite pillars in a circular pattern. He passed the memorial and turned right into the parking area off of 17th Street and drove along a row of cars to the end and pulled into an empty spot facing the back of the Pacific Arch. He glanced at his watch—11:35, plenty of time.

"The Eisenhower quote is on the Atlantic side of the memorial," Dugan said. "Let's head to the back of the Pacific side. We should find a safe spot to watch from there."

Marla scanned her surroundings, turning in her seat, peering out the back and side windows. "I don't see Pugach or the agents."

Dugan tugged on the sides of his toboggan. "Everybody pull your hats down."

"Mommy," Gabe said from the back seat. "Can I take Blackie with me?"

"No. You leave that teddy bear in the car."

"Right," Dugan eyed the raggedy bear sitting next to Gabe, its arm dangling and crumpled pirate hat. "Pugach might recognize it, even from a distance."

They got out of the vehicle and walked through a stand of half-bare trees, the remaining leaves all yellow and brown. The rain had stopped, and the sun broke through an opening in the clouds brightening the back of the granite pillars before them. They stopped in the shade of an oak tree, standing close to its wide trunk.

The pillars stood along the rim of the oval-shaped memorial. Dugan pointed to the tower in the middle of the pillars on this end, more than forty feet tall with arched openings on each side. "That's the Pacific arch. They'll meet across the plaza at the Atlantic arch where the Eisenhower quote is located. Let me see the telescope."

Dugan closed his left eye, peered through the spyglass, and adjusted the focus. "Can't see the quote from here. Let's move behind that pillar just to the right of the Pacific arch." Dugan clasped the spyglass to his side and led the way, quickly moving across the grass between the trees and pillars.

They stood against the back of the tall, rectangular pillar. Dugan checked his watch—11:45. Won't be long now, he thought. He leaned to his right and looked across an oval pond circled with spouting fountains. Now it was much easier to see the Atlantic arch. He raised the telescope and focused on the Eisenhower quote to the right of the arch. "You are about to embark upon the great crusade toward which we have striven these many months. The eyes of the world are upon you . . . Have full confidence in your courage, devotion to duty, and skill in battle."

"Is that the quote?" Marla asked.

"That's it."

"Let me see."

Dugan handed her the telescope, and she leaned to the right of the pillar and looked through it. She adjusted the focus. "I can see it very clearly."

"We've got a great view from here."

Gabe tugged on Marla's sleeve. "Can I see?"

"No, Sport, you stay behind the pillar."

"Aw, Mom."

Marla stiffened. "Dugan." She adjusted the focus. "Pugach just showed up." Marla pulled back behind the pillar.

Dugan took the telescope, leaned slightly beyond the pillar and looked through the spyglass. Pugach stood in front of Eisenhower's words, glancing around the plaza. Then he straightened and focused intently on something to his left. Dugan lowered the spyglass and scanned the area. Two men wearing black pants and gray hooded jackets walked toward Pugach from that direction. One carried a large black briefcase. With their hoods on, Dugan couldn't see their faces clearly.

Dugan raised the spyglass and focused on them. "It's Fetters and Reed."

Marla pressed her hand against Dugan's shoulder. "Fetters and Reed? That doesn't make sense."

"Yes it does."

"But shouldn't they wait until the contact arrives before they make the arrest."

Dugan pulled back from the edge of the pillar and met Marla's gaze. "They are the contacts."

"You think this is a sting?"

"No." Dugan peeked around the pillar. "Pugach knows they're federal agents."

"So they want a slice of the pie too."

"Exactly. They're talking to Pugach. I wish I knew what they were saying."

"Let me see the spyglass."

Dugan withdrew from the edge of the pillar and handed Marla the telescope.

Marla crouched and scooted to where she could get a good view. She adjusted the focus. "Reed's talking. He said, 'What do you mean you don't have the serum or formula?' Pugach said, 'The couple has it.' Fetters is talking now. 'You're lying. We searched their car and the woods around the vehicles. We even strip searched all three of them.' Fetters is reaching into his jacket pocket. I think he's got a gun. He's pointing it through his jacket. Now he's talking again. 'You've got the formula and serum, Pugach.' Pugach is shaking his head. 'I don't have it. I swear. You just don't know where to look. I know exactly where it is.' 'Tell us or you die,' Reed says."

Dugan leaned closer to Marla to peek over her shoulder. If they shot Pugach on the spot, he wanted to witness it. He may be called upon to testify in court against a couple of rogue agents.

"I wanna see," Gabe said.

Marla shooshed him. "You stay behind the pillar. Pugach just told them he has two doses of the serum left. He's willing to give them the doses for free if they work with him to get the formula back."

Dugan didn't understand. The agents were standing right there with a briefcase full of money. Why was Pugach lying? Why didn't he hand over the formula for the money? Unless . . . unless he really didn't have it. Where was it?

"They're leaving together," Marla said.

Dugan pulled away and pressed his back against the granite. "Oh no."

Marla slipped behind the pillar and faced Dugan. "What's wrong?"

"Pugach isn't lying about the serum and formula."

"But he said we had it."

Dugan nodded. "We do."

21

Marla clenched Gabe's hand and rushed to the car, pulling Gabe along behind her. As she clasped and yanked on the handle, she quickly scanned the area in all directions. No Pugach or federal agents in sight. Now what?

Dugan opened the driver's side door of the Malibu. "We can't go back to the Outer Banks."

Gabe scrambled into the back seat, and Marla shut the door behind him. "Why not?"

"I told Clooney we were heading home. I'm sure he told Fetters and Reed. Hurry, get in the car."

Marla climbed in and shut her door. "Do you think Clooney is in on it?"

Dugan shrugged. "I don't know." He turned in his seat and reached toward Gabe. "Let me see Blackie, Sport."

Gabe picked up the teddy bear. "Why?"

"Just let me see him." Dugan took the bear, found the hidden zipper, and unzipped it. He reached into the bear's belly and pulled out a white towel, carefully unraveling it. A piece of wrinkled paper slipped out and landed on the armrest between them.

Marla picked it up. "The formula."

Dugan reached into the bear's belly and pulled out a vial, half-filled with yellow-green liquid. "And here's what's left of the serum."

"They're coming after us, aren't they?"

Dugan bobbed his head.

"All three of them?"

"That would be my guess. That's why Pugach chased us. He knew we had the teddy bear."

"Why does he want to team up with Fetters and Reed?"

"They're the connection to the Medical Mafia. They've been hired to exchange the formula and serum for the money and then deliver the goods."

It made sense to Marla. Because Pugach knew exactly where the formula and serum could be found, he had the upper hand. Fetters and Reed would have to depend on him. Marla felt a sinking feeling in her stomach. Her cozy family room in Rodanthe seemed so far away. This was far from over.

Dugan started the engine. "Let's get out of here."

"Where're we headed?"

"To the Ohio Valley. Maybe we can hide out at Pastor Byron's house."

Good idea, Marla thought. It had been a while since she had talked to Byron and Lila Butler. Both Marla and Dugan had attended the Scotch Ridge Presbyterian Church during their teen years and had gone through confirmation class together. Byron and Lila had always been there for them. They were solid rocks in a shifting world.

The drive from Washington, D.C. to Martins Ferry took about five hours. Gabe fell asleep in the back seat. Most of the time Marla stared out the windshield, not saying much. Dugan knew she was tired, irritable, and scared. Who wouldn't be? He struggled with this turn of events. Why had they been drawn back into this maelstrom? He felt terrible about Marla's and Gabe's involvement and the danger they now faced, but what could he do? At least they had rescued Gabe. Keeping him safe wouldn't be easy.

He pondered the significance of the formula and serum falling back into their hands. Everything happened for a reason. Life wasn't random. God must have orchestrated these circumstances. Dugan had placed the formula in his wallet and serum in his jacket pocket. Were Gabe, Marla, and he angels appointed by God to guard the Tree of Life? It seemed fantastic, something a religious fanatic would believe, but too many things had happened in the last three days to pass it off as coincidence.

Marla stirred from her trance and placed her hand on Dugan's forearm. "I guess it was a good thing we witnessed what went down at the World War II Memorial."

Her hand felt warm and comforting. "Now we know what's going on. They can't catch us off guard."

Marla took a deep breath. "Pugach would have hunted us down on the way back to the Outer Banks and murdered us."

"That was a definite possibility. Now we've got to worry about Fetters and Reed, too."

"At least we know who our enemies are."

Good point, Dugan thought. Fetters and Reed must be expecting a big payday, too. Were they as coldblooded as Pugach? Dugan doubted it, but who knows? The desire for riches had corrupted people and nations throughout history, turning so-called moral men into ruthless killers and respected countries into opportunistic oppressors. For millions of dollars Fetters and Reed may cross those lines of conscience without hesitation. Now the question was who do you trust?

"What was your impression of Division Chief Clooney?" Dugan asked.

"He reminded me of my Uncle Willy—short, fat, and jolly. He was very accommodating."

Dugan agreed. He liked Clooney. "Yeah, but was it an act?"

Marla shrugged. "I don't know. He may be as rotten as the other two. What about Chief Director Miller?"

"Hard to say." Dugan recalled J. Edgar Hoover's long reign as Chief Director and the downward spiral of corruption he spawned. Even with incontrovertible evidence of his dirty dealings, the government overlooked his missteps and still named the FBI building after him. "This serum and formula has a strange power over people. It offers eternal health and unlimited wealth. Miller could take advantage of his position to pick the fruit for himself and take a bite."

"So you're saying we can't trust anyone?"

Dugan glanced at Marla. "I trust you."

Marla raised her eyebrows. "You think I'm incorruptible?"

"I'm willing to bet my life on it. Do you trust me?"

Marla squeezed his arm. "You know I do."

"That makes two people we can trust."

Marla shook her head no. "There's three." She thumbed toward the back seat.

Dugan eyed the rearview mirror. Gabe lay slumped over the seatbelt, head resting on Blackie the pirate teddy bear, sleeping peacefully.

Harold Fetters had never injected a drug into his body in his entire life. He hated dopers. He'd arrested dozens of users and dealers during his eighteen-year law enforcement career. Today he'd make an exception. He had in his possession a dose of the most highly valued serum in the world—the Methuselah serum. At thirty-nine years old, he faced middle age. He didn't want to become old, fat, and absentminded like Division Chief Clooney. What a stooge. The guy had no idea what was going on.

They had pulled off Interstate 64 in Newport News, Virginia to get gas at a BP station along Route 143. Reed pumped the gas. Fetters sat at the wheel, scanning the surroundings to make sure no one was watching. The tinted windows made it difficult to see into the Crown Vic. He wasn't too worried, but, still, why take the chance? He pinched the skin on his forearm and inserted the needle. Easy enough. He pressed the plunger. His forearm felt suddenly cool, as if someone had poured water over it. The sensation spread up into his shoulder and chest. The feeling was exhilarating.

Reed opened the passenger door. "Couldn't wait, huh?"

"Now is as good as time as any."

Reed got in and shut the door. "Give me the needle."

Fetters handed it over.

"You don't have AIDS or syphilis do you?"

"Screw you."

Reed uncapped the small vial and drew 10 milliliters of the yellow-green liquid into the chamber. He pinched the skin on his forearm, inserted the needle, and injected the serum. "Hot damn! I felt it instantly. What a charge."

"You did that like an old pro. Didn't know you were a junkie."

Reed chuckled. "I shot up a time or two during my wild and crazy days. I'm straight as an arrow now, though." He winked.

"Right. You and me, we're incorruptible G-men."

Fetters's cell phone rang, an AC/DC tune, "Highway to Hell." He fished the phone out of his pants pocket.

"Who is it?" Reed asked.

Fetters checked the incoming call on the face of his Droid Bionic. "Clooney. Wonder what he wants?" He pressed the answer icon. "Fetters here."

"Sorry boys, but you're going the wrong direction." Clooney's squeaky voice never failed to irritate him.

"What? You told us they were headed back to the Outer Banks."

"I know. I assumed they were. Then I got to thinking maybe they changed their minds."

"Why would they do that?"

"You reported that Pugach told his contact that he didn't have the formula or serum. He guaranteed the contact he would get it back from the couple."

"Right. Our surveillance equipment picked up their conversation."

"If the couple has the serum and formula stashed somewhere, then they know Pugach would come after them again. That got me thinking. No way would they want to head back to the Outer Banks if Pugach is waiting for them there. I did a location search on Sheriff Walton's cell phone. Fortunately, he left it on. They're driving north on Interstate 79 halfway between Morgantown and Pittsburgh."

"Dammit!" Fetters felt like throwing his phone.

"Now relax. As long as Walton keeps his phone on, we'll be able to track them. You're only a few hours behind them."

More than a few, Fetters thought. "All right. We'll turn around and head northwest. Keep us updated on their location."

"Another thing, Agent Fetters . . ."

"Yes sir?"

"Maybe that couple lied to us, maybe they didn't. Pugach could be the one lying for all we know. Either way you need to find them first. If Pugach gets there before you, they're dead meat."

What a fool, Fetters thought. "Of course, sir, we'll make it a priority to protect that couple and the boy. And if they have the formula and serum, we'll get it."

Fetters ended the call and stared at Reed.

"What the hell's going on?" Reed asked.

Fetters started the car. "We're off track. Pinhead Clooney just realized he could track Walton's cell phone. They're in West Virginia heading for Pennsylvania."

Reed slammed his fist against the door. "You've got to be kidding me."

Fetters yanked the Crown Vic into drive and zoomed back out onto Route 143.

"Are you going to inform Pugach?" Reed asked. "He said he'd meet us in Manteo."

"I will in an hour or two. Maybe we won't need him."

"Come on, Harold. We searched the couple and the boy. We checked the woods in Fredericksburg. They hid it somewhere. Pugach is the only one who knows how to get it from them."

Fetters floored the accelerator and sped east, merging onto Interstate 64. "There're other methods, my friend. Methods I am willing to apply in special circumstances like this. We'll get a head start on Pugach and then call him. If I can persuade the couple to hand over the serum and formula, we won't need him."

"How'll you do that? Got a bottle of sodium pentothal with you?"

He reached inside his gray jacket and patted his pistol. "I can be very persuasive when a billion smackaroos are on the line."

Dugan drove north on Interstate 79 into Washington, Pennsylvania, and then took 70 west to the panhandle of West Virginia. As the car sailed down a long hill into Elm Grove, the familiar landscape comforted him. They were back in the Ohio Valley, his old stomping grounds. After going through the Wheeling Tunnel, they exited the interstate onto Wheeling Island and crossed the Purple Heart Bridge over the Ohio River into Bridgeport, Ohio. It was almost six o'clock. The Butlers lived about three and a half miles farther north along Route 7 in a neighborhood known as Floral Valley.

Dugan turned off Route 7 into the subdivision, a quaint collection of modest homes nestled at the base of an Allegheny foothill not far from the river. The thirty-five or so ranch-style dwellings were constructed back in the early sixties when the steel mills flourished and blue-collar workers could afford to build new houses. Dugan decided to pull into the driveway which led to the back of the house. The Malibu would be out of sight there. He turned off the motor, glanced at Marla, and then peered into the back seat at Gabe. Dugan felt secure and at peace for the first time in two days.

"Finally, we made it," Marla said.

Gabe rubbed his eyes. "Where are we?"

"Pastor Byron's house," Dugan said.

"But I want to go home," Gabe said.

Marla opened the car door. "We'll be safe here, Sport. Don't worry, sooner or later we'll get home."

Dugan removed the charger out of his iPhone and slid the phone into his pants pocket. He got out of the car and drew the crisp air deeply into his lungs. Feeling somewhat revived, he scanned the neighborhood. The sun had recently set, dousing the flaming colors of the multitude of fall trees on the hillside. The hills to the west and across the river to the east offered a sense of protection. He'd forgotten how insulated life had been in this small Ohio town. Now it seemed like a place of refuge, a place to reconnect with a man who had been a source of encouragement and guidance throughout his life. Byron Butler would know what to do with the serum and formula. A deeply spiritual man, Pastor Byron reminded Dugan of Moses—a prophet of God committed to the long road of ministry.

They mounted the back steps to the deck, and Dugan knocked on the kitchen door. An older man with a week's growth of gray beard entered the kitchen. Byron? At first it didn't look like him. The man's hair was silver-gray and long, combed straight back and receded more than Dugan remembered. Deep shadows darkened his eyes and wrinkles creased his cheeks and forehead. His mustache, untrimmed and gray, covered his upper lip. He approached the door wearing a dingy white sweatshirt and gray sweatpants cut off at the knees.

His eyes widened when he saw them, and he threw open the door. "Dugan! Marla! What a surprise!"

"Pastor Byron!" Marla stepped forward and hugged him. When they released each other and stood back, Marla motioned to Gabe. "Do you remember my son?"

"Of course, Gabriel." The preacher knelt and held out his hand. "You've grown about a foot since the last time I saw you."

Gabe shook Pastor Byron's hand. "I don't remember you."

"That doesn't surprise me. I've grown old in the last couple of years." He arose and embraced Dugan. "How're you doing, Sheriff Walton?—top lawman of Dare County, North Carolina. I'm so proud of you."

Dugan hugged him, squeezing tightly, patted his back, and stepped away. "I'm okay, I guess. Considering . . ."

Byron put his hands on Dugan's shoulders, a puzzled aspect entering the preacher's eyes. "Considering what?"

"It's a long story. I hope you have time to listen."

The preacher nodded slowly. "I have plenty of time. Come on in, and I'll put on a pot of coffee and break out some leftovers. We've got a lot of catching up to do."

In the kitchen Marla, Dugan, and Gabe plopped down on oak chairs that surrounded an oval pedestal table. Byron rushed back and forth, gathering the necessary items to make coffee. Once he got the coffee brewing, he threw some fried chicken and potato wedges in the microwave. Then he retrieved half a pumpkin pie from the refrigerator and set it in front of them.

"Where's Lila?" Dugan asked.

Byron paused, his face blanching. "In bed."

Marla sat up. "Is everything okay?"

Byron delivered coffee mugs and plates to the table. "I'm afraid not."

"What's wrong?" Dugan asked.

Byron blinked, his dark eyes watery. "Pancreatic cancer."

Marla gasped. "I'm so sorry, Byron. We had no idea . . ."

Bryon raised his hand. "I know. I should have called. It's been difficult. We've only known for a couple months."

"How is she holding up?" Marla asked.

"Not good."

Dugan tried to remember what he had heard about that type of cancer. Wasn't it one of the most difficult cancers to cure? Byron had to be devastated over his wife's condition. No wonder he looked so bad. "What do the doctors say?"

The microwave dinged and Byron brought the food to the table. He shook his head. "They give her a month or two. This kind of cancer is hard to diagnose. They caught it late. At this stage there's only a ten percent survival rate."

Marla brushed a tear from her cheek.

"Why are you crying, Mommy?" Gabe asked.

"I'm sad because Pastor Byron's wife is very sick." Marla filled a plate with a couple pieces of chicken, potatoes, and a slice of pie and slid it in front of Gabe. "Here. Eat. You've got to be starved." Gabe dug in.

Dugan realized they had arrived at a bad time. How could he expect Byron to focus on their problem when Byron had his own battles to fight? He didn't know what to say or even if he should bring up their circumstances.

Byron sat down across from Dugan. "I've been a man of faith for most of my life. I've served God with all my heart. And now this." He took a deep breath and let it out audibly. "Some reward, huh?"

Dugan glanced around the room, struggling to find something to say. Then he remembered what Byron had always told him. "Everything happens for a reason. We might not understand now, but one day we will."

"You're right. I know it, but I don't understand why God would let this happen now. The nest is empty. It's just me and Lila. I planned on retiring next year. We wanted to travel, see the country, and spend time with our grandkids."

"There's still hope," Marla said. "Didn't you say there's a ten percent survival rate."

Byron rubbed his grizzled jowls. "Yeah, but that's a one-year survival rate. Beyond that the percentage drops down to nothing. Believe me, the doctors don't give much hope. I know God could heal Lila, but for some reason it doesn't seem to be God's will. Maybe it's my lack of faith."

"No way," Dugan said. "That can't be it. You're the most spiritual man I know."

Byron shrugged. "Thanks, but I don't think God is too impressed."

Marla stood, walked around the table, and put her arm around the preacher. "We're so sorry, Byron. Is there anything we can do?"

Byron hung his head. "Not much . . . unless . . ."

"Unless what?" Dugan said.

"Unless you've got a miracle in your pocket."

Dugan and Marla's eyes met. He reached into his jacket pocket and cradled the vial of serum.

22

Lila Butler appeared in the doorway leading to the dining room. "I didn't know we had visitors, Byron. Why didn't you wake me?" She wore a white terrycloth robe. It hung on her thin frame like an old shirt on a scarecrow. Her brown hair had thinned, her green eyes dark and sunken.

Marla tried to subdue her dismay at Lila's appearance. She stood, walked to her, and embraced her gently. "I've missed you so much, Lila. Come, sit down, and talk to us."

Lila gripped Marla's elbow as Marla ushered her to a chair. Byron arose and assisted, gently helping to lower Lila to the seat.

"I can do it myself," Lila said. "I'm not dead yet."

Byron and Marla let go, and Lila steadied herself by placing her hands on the table before sitting.

Marla tried to smile at Lila's comment but knew her expression must have belied her uneasiness. She glanced at Gabe. His eyes, filled with distress, were fixed on the dying woman. "Gabe, do you remember Lila?"

Gabe shook his head no and clasped Blackie more tightly to his chest.

Lila smiled at the boy. "I must look a fright."

"You look fine," Byron said.

Lila eyed Dugan. "What a pleasant surprise. What's the sheriff of Dare County and his newest deputy doing in our neck of the woods?"

Dugan scanned their faces, reached into his jacket pocket, extracted the vial, and placed it in the middle of the table. "We're here because of this."

"What is it?" Byron asked.

"It's called the Methuselah serum," Dugan said.

Byron picked up the small bottle. "It looks toxic."

"Looks can be deceiving. Some would call this serum miraculous."

"Miraculous?" Byron set the bottle back on the table. "You haven't become a snake oil salesman have you, Dugan?"

Dugan reached into his back pocket, pulled out his wallet, and extracted a folded piece of notebook paper. He slid it across the table toward Byron. "Check this out."

Byron picked up the notebook paper, unfolded it, and examined the complex equations. "My algebra is a little rusty. It's been several decades since my last chemistry class. I have no idea what I'm looking at here."

Lila held out a bony hand. "Let me see it." Byron handed it to her and the paper trembled slightly between her fingers.

Dugan pointed at the paper. "That's the formula used to create the Methuselah serum."

Byron scratched the whiskers along his jaw line. "I know Methuselah was the oldest man in the Bible, but I didn't know he created a serum. What's it good for?"

Marla scooted closer to the table. "We have strong evidence that the serum can reverse the aging process in human cells. It may also cure certain types of cancer."

Byron raised his eyebrows. "Are you serious?"

Dugan nodded. "Dead serious."

Lila placed the formula next to the bottle. "What types of cancer can it cure?"

"We know for sure it has cured prostate cancer," Dugan said.

"Has it been tested on anything else?" Byron asked.

"No," Dugan said. "About a year ago a medical researcher, an old doctor, injected himself with the serum."

"What happened?" Lila asked.

"Like I said, it cured his prostate cancer, but that's not all. It also reversed aging in his cells. He reverted back to mid-adult state."

Byron picked up the vial again. "That's amazing. Are you saying this could be the Fountain of Youth?"

Dugan nodded.

"How's the doctor doing now?" Lila asked.

"He's dead," Marla said. "Murdered."

"That doesn't surprise me," Lila said.

Byron eyed his wife, concern etching his face. Then he turned to Dugan. "How did you get your hands on this?"

"I took it from a second crime scene, another murder."

"It was left behind?"

"The victim hid it. We found it."

"Then we lost it," Marla said, "but got it back at a third murder scene."

"That's quite a trail of bodies," Lila said.

Dugan nodded. "Unfortunately, that seems to be the pattern."

Lila folded her hands in front of her on the table. "And now you're in danger."

"Right," Marla said. "We're being pursued by several people—the killer and a couple rogue FBI agents."

Byron straightened and placed his hands on the table. "Corrupted agents are after you? Why don't you inform their superiors?"

Dugan held out his hands. "We don't know who to trust."

"What are you going to do?" Byron asked.

"I feel responsible. It's as if God has dropped this into our laps and appointed us as guardians."

An odd smile crossed Lila's face. "You're guarding the Tree of Life."

Byron glanced at his wife. "Huh?"

She patted her husband's hand. "Like in the Garden of Eden, dear. God didn't want mankind to have access to eternal life so he placed cherubim around the tree to keep man from eating its fruit."

"Exactly," Dugan said. "We've talked about that particular reference. It seems like God has placed us in front of that tree."

Yeah, Marla thought, whether we want to be there or not. "Pastor Byron, we've come here to get your advice. We don't know what to do with this stuff."

Byron stared at the bottle, transfixed.

"Byron?" Lila said. "Are you still with us?"

Byron shook his head, breaking the trance. He eyed Dugan. "If this cured prostate cancer by reversing the effects of aging in cells, it may cure other cancers."

Dugan nodded. "Maybe all cancers. No one knows."

"Don't get any ideas," Lila said.

Byron glanced at her. "What do you mean?"

"I know what you're thinking. Give me a dose and see what happens."

"Why not? What have we got to lose?"

"You must not have been paying attention," Lila said. "These angels here have been called upon to guard the fruit, not give it away."

Byron's eyebrows tensed. "But . . . but" He shifted his gaze to Dugan. "Would you be willing to give Lila a dose?"

"Well . . ." Dugan stared at the bottle.

"Of course we would," Marla said.

Dugan flicked his eyes to Marla. "We would?"

Marla lifted the bottle from the table. "If this serum holds any hope of healing Lila's cancer, we should offer it to her."

Dugan nodded. "You're right. Lila, if you want a dose, it's yours."

Lila shook her head. "I wouldn't touch the stuff."

"Why not?" Byron asked.

"Let's say you inject me with the serum, and it works. Wooohooo, I'm healed. In time I become young again. Do you think I'd want to hang out with an old guy like you?"

"Please, Lila," Byron said. "Be serious."

"I am serious." Lila eyed Marla. "Do you believe this serum really works?"

Marla bobbed her head.

"Then I don't want to be forever young by myself. Is there enough for all of us?"

Marla held up the bottle. "Each dose requires 10 milliliters. I think there would be enough for all of us."

That odd smile lit Lila's face again. "Well then, let's do it."

Byron placed his hands flat on the table and leaned forward. "But we're not dying. You are."

"We're all dying, my dear. It's just a matter of time." Lila shifted her gaze to Dugan. "You first."

Dugan shook his head. "Not me. If you all want to, go ahead. But I'm not convinced God wants us to be young forever."

Lila chuckled and held up a finger. "That's why you were chosen." She scooted her chair out and stood on her own. "I love you all very much, but I'm tired. I'm going back to bed." She placed her hand on the table and leaned forward. "But before I say good night, listen carefully to my words. I've settled my accounts on this earth. When my time comes to leave, I'm not afraid to die. It's not the worst that could happen. Maybe . . . just maybe, it's the best thing. Maybe this dark and suffering world will crumble away and I'll be engulfed in infinite light." She stood, walked to the doorway, and faced them again. "And don't feel sorry for me. In the scope of eternity, you're only a step or two behind me." Lila turned and hobbled through the dining room out of view.

"She's given up hope," Byron said.

"I don't think so," Dugan said. "She's just transferred her account."

After considering Lila's words, Dugan felt more convinced than ever God had called them to guard the serum. But what should they do with it? Destroy it? Deliver it to some trustworthy saint? Hand it over to the Federation of American Scientists? Byron didn't have any answers. Every few minutes Dugan noticed him staring at the serum like some miser distracted by a stack of golden coins.

After Dugan placed the serum back in his jacket pocket and the formula in his wallet, Byron came out from under the spell. They began to talk about old times—youth group trips to Kennywood Park, Christmas Eve services at the church, a vacation they took together on the Outer Banks when Dugan was twelve years old. Laughter broke out now and again, and the tension eased. Byron put on a new pot of coffee and dug a half gallon of chocolate ice cream out of the freezer. They feasted on the treat, Gabe eating three bowls. Then Byron pulled a coloring book and box of crayons from a corner closet and handed them to Gabe. With determined focus, Gabe worked on a picture of Bugs Bunny nonchalantly chomping on a carrot while Elmer Fudd aimed a shotgun at the rabbit's heart.

Later that evening the conversation reverted back to the serum and formula, Byron struggled with Lila's stubbornness. They talked about death and how devastating her loss would be to him. Marla agreed with Byron. She knew firsthand the empty hole left behind by her husband's death. She admitted that the passing of time helped but never completely filled the hole.

"I understand what you're saying," Dugan said, "but we see death from this side of the curtain. It's always the villain. It steals our loved ones from us. But when you look at it from the other side, isn't death a doorway?"

Byron glanced at the ceiling. "You're right. I've proclaimed that hope at more than a hundred funerals." He leveled his vision at Dugan. "It's much tougher, though, when it hits you personally. You want to fight it tooth and nail until the very end. I guess I don't want to let go."

"I don't blame you," Marla said. "How can you give up as long as there's a chance?"

Byron met Marla's gaze, his head moving up and down. "Yes. That's how I feel. Maybe that's why God sent you here. It's a chance. Lila could die in a month or two. The serum might be the one chance God has sent our way."

"Are you going to force it on her?" Dugan asked. "I don't think she'll cooperate."

Byron rubbed his whiskers. "I don't know if I'll be able to talk sense into her, but there's another way. Right now, while she's sleeping soundly, I could take a dose and inject her. She wouldn't even know it."

Dugan's head wagged slowly. "You would secretly shoot this into your wife's body against her will? Pastor Byron, do you really think this is what God wants, or is it what you want? "

Byron banged his hand on the table making Gabe look up from the coloring book. "I don't know. At least give me the chance. Just one dose. It'll be on my head, not yours."

Dugan reached into his pocket and held up the bottle. The yellow-green liquid swirled and leveled. "I just don't feel right about this."

Marla grasped Dugan's arm, making the liquid slosh back and forth. "This is a matter a life or death, Dugan. How do you know what God wants? You might hold the key to Lila's life in your hands. Give him enough for a dose."

"No!" Gabe's voice rang out. The three adults turned and riveted their eyes on the boy. "Those bad men at the hotel . . ."

"What about those men?" Marla asked.

Gabe pointed at the bottle. "They wanted it, but they died. God doesn't want people to have it."

The doorbell rang, chimes reminiscent of church bells.

Dugan shifted his focus to Byron. "Are you expecting company?"

"No."

Dugan shot up from his chair and held out his hand. "Don't answer it. Let me check out the window first."

The doorbell rang again. Dugan hurried through the dining room and into the darkened living room. Marla followed him to the edge of the living room doorway and stopped, her heart thumping against her ribs. How could the agents or Pugach have found them? No way.

Dugan edged along the wall to the window and peeked out. The porch light reflected off the bald head of Special Agent Reed. Fetters stood next to him. Dugan pulled back and pressed himself against the wall, and mouthed, *it's them*.

We're in trouble, Marla thought, big trouble. Where's Gabe? She rushed back into the kitchen, Dugan trailing her.

Dugan skidded to a stop. "We've got to get outta here."

Pastor Byron stood near the sink. "Who is it?"

"Those rogue agents, Fetters and Reed. Stall them for us. Keep them here as long as you can."

"I'll do my best."

Marla reached her hand toward Gabe. "Come on, Sport, we've got to go."

"Where's Blackie?" Gabe spouted. He dropped to his knees. "There he is." Gabe crawled under the table and emerged on the other side, clutching one of the teddy bear's legs.

Marla bolted around the table and latched on to Gabe's arm. "Let's go!"

Dugan shot across the kitchen to the back door and yanked it open. They rushed to the Malibu and jerked the doors open. Dugan raised a finger to his lips. Gabe climbed in, and Marla shut the door gently behind him.

After Dugan and Marla slid into their seats, Dugan paused before inserting the key. "We've got to give Byron time to answer the door and let them into the house."

"Right." Marla focused on the kitchen windows. "How long should we wait?"

"I don't know, maybe thirty seconds." Dugan dug into his pocket and pulled out the bottle. He handed it to Marla. "Here, stick this back in the teddy bear just in case they catch us." He leaned forward, took out his wallet and removed the formula. "This too."

Marla turned and reached toward Gabe. "Give me Blackie, Sport."

Gabe handed over the bear, and Marla found the hidden zipper, stuffed the serum and formula in the folds of the towel, and zipped it back up.

"Can I hold Blackie?" Gabe asked.

Dugan's eyes met Marla's. "It's up to you."

Marla hesitated and then passed the bear back to Gabe. The boy clasped Blackie to his chest. Marla looked at Dugan. "The bear gives him comfort."

"Don't worry, Dugan," Gabe said. "I know what to do."

Dugan peered into the rearview mirror and caught the determined expression on Gabe's face. He really does, Dugan thought. What a trooper. Dugan started the car and shifted into reverse. He backed out, eased it into drive and crept along the side of the house. Marla watched the windows as they passed.

As they neared the end of the driveway, Marla turned in her seat to peer into the front porch window—the living room window. "Oh no."

Dugan turned left onto the street. "What's wrong?"

"Reed spotted us! I saw him in the living room, pointing out the window at us."

"Crap!"

Marla grasped Dugan's shoulder. "Go! Get out of here! They're coming after us!"

23

Dugan stomped on the gas pedal and peeled around the turn onto Glenns Run Road . He hoped traffic wouldn't be bad just ahead on Route 7, a four-lane highway. Slowing down as he approached the stop sign, he glanced to his left and saw an old pickup truck about a hundred yards down the road coming at them. Not hesitating, he punched the gas and zoomed onto the highway. The pickup's horn blared as its lights, two blazing circles, filled the rearview mirror. The Malibu sped away, climbing to over sixty miles an hour within seconds. Dugan took it up to almost ninety.

A traffic light awaited about a mile away at the Hanover Street intersection. At just after eight in the evening traffic could still be a problem. Dugan weaved around a couple cars and glanced in his rearview mirror to see if Reed and Fetters were catching up. He couldn't tell, seeing only a few headlights trailing away. He focused on the highway and spotted green lights ahead in the distance. He knew it would come down to timing, but right now his timing didn't look good. About a quarter mile from the intersection the light turned yellow. *Oh hell. I've got to get through this light.* Dugan hit the brakes as the light turned red. Five cars were stopping for the light, two in the left lane and three in the right. He checked the rearview mirror again, seeing headlights coming on. Fetters and Reed?

How could he get around this traffic? To the left he noticed room between the cars and the medium strip. He slowed down enough to make sure no vehicles coming up Hanover Street would collide with them.

"Careful!" Marla braced her hands against the dashboard.

"Hold on." Dugan swerved to the left, cut through the small opening and sailed across the intersection. Some horns blasted but no one came close to hitting them. "Check behind us. See if they're on our tail."

Marla twisted in her seat and peered out the back window. "I see them. They made it through the red light. Dugan, they're catching us!"

Dugan knew if they stayed on Route 7 they didn't have a chance. The Crown Vic was too fast. He had to find an area where they could lose them. A half mile away he spotted the green light at the Aetna Street intersection. Should he turn off there and try to shake them on the back streets of Martins Ferry? No. He had another idea. He'd cross over to Wheeling Island, lose them in the neighborhoods on the south end, and then cut across the Wheeling Suspension Bridge into Wheeling, West Virginia. From there he'd have more options. He glanced at his rearview mirror. The Crown Vic bore down, less than a hundred and fifty yards behind. Dugan checked his speed—85 mph. He prayed the light would stay green at Aetna Street.

No such luck. The light flashed yellow and then red. "Hold on tight! I'm going through." Dugan gripped the wheel and leaned forward.

Marla braced herself on the dash. "We're going to crash!"

Dugan shot through the intersection and swerved to miss a car. Another vehicle, a minivan, squealed to a stop just in time. The back of the Malibu wagged back and forth as Dugan regained control.

Marla whipped around and peered out the back window. "I don't see them. Wait. There they are. They had to slow down but now they're through."

Dugan floored the gas pedal. He hoped to maintain the gap as long as possible. He'd take the Bridgeport exit a half mile ahead and hope for green lights and very little traffic.

By the time they turned off the highway onto the exit ramp, the Crown Vic had closed to within fifty yards. Dugan immediately realized taking the exit had been a mistake. The lights at the Route 40 intersection were red, and traffic had backed up to Wilson's Furniture on the corner of Route 250. They were trapped. Dugan slowed to a stop behind a red Cadillac Escalade in the left lane. The Crown Vic pulled up beside them, and the driver's window lowered. Fetters sat at the wheel pointing a large handgun at Marla.

Fetters's mouth moved but Dugan couldn't hear him.

Marla reached and grasped Dugan's arm. "He said pull over."

Dugan glanced to his left and saw the onramp back onto Route 7 North on the other side of the overpass. He reached for the top of Marla's head. "Get down!" He whipped the wheel to the left and hit the gas. The car bounded over the curb and rumbled across the grass and under the overpass toward the onramp. Instead of turning left back onto Route 7, Dugan jerked the wheel to the right and headed down the one-way ramp in the wrong direction. Cars blasted their horns and pulled to the side. A gunshot blasted, and the back window shattered.

Gabe screamed.

Dugan veered left and then right, avoiding oncoming cars. "Stay down, Gabe!"

"Are you all right, Sport?" Marla yelled.

"I'm scared, Mommy!"

Dugan managed to weave through the oncoming cars and turned left across the railroad tracks and onto the Purple Heart Bridge. He anticipated another gunshot but didn't hear any. He hoped the agents got jumbled up in the traffic on the ramp. Dugan floored the pedal and flew across the bridge that arched over the Ohio River onto Wheeling Island. He knew the island well. During his junior and senior years in high school he worked as a litter getter at the Wheeling Downs dog track. As they crested the arch and descended, another gun blast made him flinch.

"Stay down!" Dugan saw the red traffic light ahead. Cars waited in the left lane to turn into the parking lot next to Abbey's, a popular restaurant. Only one car blocked the right lane. Dugan steered the Malibu toward the sidewalk on the right, jolted onto it, skirted around the car and drove back onto the street. He turned right and raced down Huron Street, made a left through a stop-and-go light and a right at the next corner. Gabe whimpered in the back seat, and Marla kept her head low. Dugan checked the rearview mirror and spotted a car rounding the turn. He assumed it was them.

He made a quick left on Orchard Lane and a right on Broadway. The dog track and casino were only a few blocks ahead, occupying the south end of the island. Now Dugan wanted to backtrack to the Wheeling Suspension Bridge. He checked the mirror again and didn't see any cars. He swerved left onto Fink Street and immediately turned left again to head north. He guessed the bridge to be six or eight blocks from there. He needed to work his way over to Front Street. He made a right on Florida Street, heading toward the river and quickly covered the three blocks to Front Street. He slowed for the stop sign and glanced at the rearview mirror. No cars. Had he lost them? *Please God, let it be true.*

He checked both ways and turned left on Front Street. The bridge wasn't far, maybe three or four blocks. Dugan kept eyeing the rearview mirror but saw no cars. Then the Crown Vic appeared, emerging from a side street. Dugan flew by the agents, that sinking feeling in his stomach. Fetters roared after them, the Crown Vic closing fast. *Two blocks to the bridge. Lord, do something. Help us.*

A gunshot exploded, and the front window shattered. Dugan weaved back and forth to make the Malibu a harder target. The Crown Vic rammed the back bumper, and Dugan struggled to control the vehicle as the road turned slightly left. Another shot blasted off the side mirror. Ahead on the right, Dugan could see the ramp leading to the bridge. They were going too fast. He sent up another prayer and whipped the steering wheel to the right. The car skidded into the turn, heading for the sandstone abutment wall. A white van coming off the bridge squealed its brakes. The Malibu spun, a 180, its rear end crashing into the sandstone blocks.

As he flew backwards against the seat, Dugan glimpsed the van slamming into the Crown Vic. The airbags deployed and cushioned his rebound. Dugan looked to his right. Marla pushed herself away from the dash, the airbags deflating.

"Are you okay?" Dugan asked.

"I don't know. I think so." Marla turned and peered into the back seat. "Gabe!"

The boy leaned forward, his arms clasped over his head. "Mommy, tell them to stop shooting."

Dugan pressed the accelerator, but the Malibu wouldn't budge. "I smell gasoline." He turned off the engine. "Let's get out of here." He shoved his door open, stepped out of the car, and yanked open the back door. Dugan reached out his hand. "Gabe, come on."

The boy, tears streaking his face, unbuckled his seatbelt, grabbed the teddy bear by the arm and scooted out of the car. Dugan grasped Gabe's hand.

Marla rounded the front bumper. "Where to?"

Dugan pointed to his left. "Across the bridge."

As they scurried toward the sidewalk Dugan peered over his shoulder at the collision. The white van had plowed into the Crown Vic on the front passenger side. The impact had thrust Special Agent Reed through the windshield. Reed lay on the hood of the car, his bald head split open, brains exposed. *The fool should have put on his seat belt.* Dugan couldn't see what happened to Fetters. He caught sight of the sign on the side of the van: *Friends of Wheeling New Life Methodist Church.* He prayed the van occupants had survived. Feeling responsible, he stopped in the middle of the street.

"What're you doing?" Marla called from the sidewalk.

Dugan let go of Gabe's hand. "Go to your mother." He met Marla's gaze. "I need to check on the people in the van."

Marla shifted her focus to the mangled vehicles. "No! We've gotta run!"

Dugan whipped around to see Fetters step out of the Crown Vic, turn, and duck his head back into the car. *He's looking for his gun.* Dugan charged toward Marla and Gabe. "Let's go!"

They sprinted up the sidewalk toward the bridge. Huge steel cables rose up to two towers on each side of a tall sandstone arch looming on the edge of the river. From the top of the towers the cables drooped down to the middle of the span and then up again to the towers on the other side. A myriad of steel cords linked the bridge to the large cables.

When they reached the towers, the cement sidewalk became an open grating. The wind picked up and raindrops sliced through the lights shining from lamps mounted along the cables. Dugan could see the dark river forty feet below through the steel mesh. He glanced over his shoulder and spied Fetters running toward them. *Crap! Did he find his gun?*

"Stop!" Fetters hollered. "I'll shoot!"

They kept running, Marla and Gabe leading the way.

A shot fired.

He found the gun, Dugan thought.

"I swear I'll shoot you right in the back!"

"Stop!" Dugan yelled. "He'll kill us for sure."

Marla and Gabe slowed and halted about a third of the way across the bridge.

Dugan slid to a stop on the wet grate. "Quick, Sport, give me Blackie."

Gabe handed Dugan the teddy bear. With a quick flip of his hand Dugan tossed it about ten feet into the air. It landed on top of the thick cable slanting down toward the middle of the bridge. Dugan raised his finger to his lips, and Gabe nodded.

Dugan turned to see Fetters charging up the steel mesh walkway.

Fetters slowed, breathing heavily, stopped, and raised his pistol. "Okay, hand it over."

Dugan held out his hands. "Hand what over?"

"I'm done playing games. Where's the serum and formula?"

"I swear we don't have it. It's in the car."

Fetters stepped forward and planted the muzzle of his pistol against Dugan's chest. "No way you'd leave it in the car. I'm giving you five seconds. If you don't tell me, I will blow a hole clean through your heart. Then I'll shoot your pretty deputy here between the eyes and toss her boy in the river. One . . . two . . . three . . . four"

"All right. I'll tell you. I threw it into the river."

Fetters eyes narrowed with rage. "No one would throw a billion dollars into the river. I've changed my mind." He pivoted and aimed the gun at Marla's head. "She will die first, then the boy, then you." His finger tightened on the trigger.

"Hold on," Dugan said. "It's right there." He pointed above Fetters's head. "It landed on top of the cable."

Fetters lowered the gun, stepped back, and focused on the stuffed animal. "What is that?"

"Gabe's teddy bear. You guys didn't think to check inside of it."

"Damn." Fetters shook his head. "Department ineptitude." He eyed the bear again and then faced them, waving the gun in front of him. "You three stay right where you are. I think I can reach it if I stand on the railing."

Go for it, Dugan thought.

The agent placed his free hand on the railing and swung his leg and hopped up like a man climbing into a saddle. Sitting on the railing, he reached up and clasped a steel suspension cord. He placed his foot on the railing and lifted himself to his feet.

In the distance Dugan heard a siren. Someone had called for an E-squad, probably one of the church people in the van. Then he heard the hum of tires rolling across the mesh decking of the bridge. Should he try to get their attention?

Fetters raised his gun. "Don't move or say a word."

Headlights brightened the roadway and a white SUV passed without even noticing them.

Fetters gazed up at the bear and extended his hand. The bear's leg dangled just out of reach, maybe four inches. He eyed Dugan again and waved his gun at all three of them. "Don't move." He centered his feet directly under the bear, re-gripped the suspension cord, and stood on his toes, using the cord to pull himself upward. He raised his gun and nudged the bear's foot with it several times.

Now's my chance, Dugan thought. He lunged forward and plowed into the agent's knees. The gun discharged into the sky. Fetters fell backwards, his arms flailing. He screamed as he dropped into the darkness.

On the cable above, the teddy bear slowly slid. A loud splash sounded from the river below.

"Blackie's falling!" Gabe shouted.

Dugan held out his hands and caught the soggy toy. Blackie smiled up at him.

Music exploded from Dugan's pocket—Lady Antebellum's "Need You Now."

Dugan handed the bear to Marla and fished his cell phone out of his jeans pocket.

Marla cradled the bear in her arms. "Who could that be?"

Dugan checked the face of his iPhone. "Division Chief Ronald Clooney."

"Should you answer it?"

The song played on.

24

Dugan closed his eyes, seeking some kind of instinctual guidance. He remembered the interview with Clooney. The division chief seemed like a good guy. Dugan opened his eyes, touched the face of the phone, and held it to his ear. "Sheriff Walton here."

"This is Division Chief Clooney. Listen. We think you might be in danger."

Dugan glanced at the railing where Fetters had stood a minute ago. "Really?"

"Yes. We haven't heard from Agent Fetters or Reed for a couple hours. Something's wrong. They should have reported in."

"What do you think happened?"

"We've been tracking you by your cell phone. I wanted Fetters and Reed to find you before Pugach got to you. He may have the means to track you, too. I gave them specific orders to protect you."

Dugan chuckled to himself. Clooney is clueless, he thought. "I appreciate your concern, but . . ."

"Listen," Clooney interrupted, "we know you still have the formula and serum. Either you hid it somewhere or you have it with you."

"How do you know that?"

"Fetters and Reed set up surveillance at the World War II Memorial. They witnessed Pugach meeting with his contact. Pugach swore to the contact that you still possessed the serum and formula. He vowed to come after you and get it."

"Pugach might be lying."

"Is he?"

Dugan hesitated. Clooney seemed trustworthy, but Dugan still had doubts. "I'm sorry. You're starting to break up. Must be this cell phone."

"Listen to me. We've dealt with Pugach before. Fetters and Reed arrested him last year for a contract killing but the charges didn't stick. If he has the means to track your cell phone, then you're in big trouble. We don't know what happened to Fetters and Reed. They may have crossed paths with Pugach. Who knows? He may have killed them. If so, you have no protection."

Dugan felt tempted to spill the beans about the rogue agents but tussled with that nagging issue of trust. "What do you want us to do?"

"If you have the serum and formula, Pugach *will* come after you. As soon as you get off the phone with me, turn off your cell phone. Find a secluded place to hang out for a couple of hours. We'll send help."

"Okay. We can do that. Anything else?"

"Keep your eyes open. Pugach might be near. Where're you heading?"

Dugan thought about it. He didn't want to give out too much information. "I've got a place to hide out not too far from here. I'll call you when we get there. Don't worry. I won't use my cell phone."

"Good enough. Take care now."

Dugan ended the call, turned off his phone, and met Marla's gaze. "Clooney thinks Pugach killed Fetters and Reed."

Marla combed her fingers through her wet hair, raindrops tracing streaks down her face. "Is Clooney an idiot?"

"He has no idea what's going on. However, he believes Pugach may be tracking us, too. You better turn off your cell phone."

Marla extracted the phone from her pocket and pressed the off button. She swiveled her head, scanning the length of the bridge. "Let's get out of here." They hurried across the walkway toward Wheeling. Sirens wailed in the distance from the other side of the bridge. When they reached Main Street, a police cruiser, lights whirling, turned onto the bridge diagonally and stopped, blocking both lanes. The officers didn't seem to notice them as they waited for the pedestrian light to flash its signal to cross.

As they crossed the street Dugan pointed to a restaurant on the opposite corner, the Bridge Tavern and Grill. "Let's head over there and figure out our next step."

"Good idea. I'm about to collapse. I need a strong cup of coffee. How about you, Sport?" Marla tousled Gabe's hair. "A glass of milk?"

Gabe looked up at his mom. "Could I get a chocolate milkshake?"

"More ice cream?"

"I love ice cream."

"After what he's gone through tonight, he deserves it," Dugan said.

Inside the restaurant no hostess greeted them, so Dugan led them to a booth in the back, one that couldn't be seen by someone passing on the street. The place wasn't busy. An older couple sat a table nearby, and three patrons occupied the seats at the counter. The waiter, a thin guy in his early twenties with a faint mustache and dark brown hair, showed up within a minute, handed them menus, and took their drink orders.

After the waiter walked away, Marla folded her hands on the table. Her hair was wet and tangled, and dark circles had formed under her eyes. "Okay, Sheriff Dugan Walton, what's our next step?"

"We need a vehicle."

"I agree. How do we get one?"

Dugan reached into his pocket for his cell phone. "I'll call Pastor Byron. Maybe he'll lend us his car."

"He probably will, but . . ." Marla pointed at the phone. ". . . don't use that phone to call him."

"Right. Pugach might be tracking us. Sorry, it slipped my mind." Dugan slid the phone back into his pocket and glanced around the restaurant.

Marla raised her finger. "That could be a fatal slip."

When the waiter returned with their drinks, Dugan asked, "Is there a payphone nearby?"

The waiter smiled. "What's a payphone?"

Dugan chuckled. "They are just about extinct, aren't they?"

"Here." The waiter dug into his pants pocket. "Use my cell." He handed Dugan a Nokia, similar to Dugan's iPhone.

"Thanks." Dugan dialed the preacher's number and clasped the phone to his ear. When Byron answered, Dugan said, "Guess who?"

"Dugan, is that you?" Byron's voice crackled with stress.

"It's me."

"Are you safe?"

"Barely. We need some help."

"Whatever I can do. You know you can count on me."

"We had an accident, but everyone's fine. Could we borrow your car?"

"No problem. Where are you?"

"At the Bridge Tavern and Grill on Main Street in Wheeling."

"I'll be there in ten minutes."

"Don't come across the suspension bridge. It's blocked off to traffic."

"I always take the I-70 bridge. It's quicker. Are you sure everyone's okay."

"Positive."

"Dugan, I'm just curious. Do you still have the serum?"

Dugan eyed Gabe. The boy clutched the pirate bear to his side. "Yeah, we still have it."

"Okay. I'll be there in ten minutes."

Dugan ended the call and handed the phone back to the waiter. "Thanks again."

"No problem." He slid the phone back into his pocket and pulled a pen and order pad from his apron. "Do you all want something to eat?"

Dugan eyes met Marla's. "This place is famous for their burgers and cheese fries—fattening but delicious."

A faint smile crossed Marla's face. "Sounds great. After what I've gone through tonight, I deserve it."

Harold Fetters crawled out of the Ohio River onto a muddy bank. His stomach and legs still stung from his less than perfect entry into the water. Dripping wet and chilled to the marrow of his bones, he stood in tall weeds, shivered, and gazed across the river at the red, blue, and yellow lights of the emergency vehicles gathered at the other end of the suspension bridge. He smelled the muck of the river, the odor of dead fish. He emerged from the water about a hundred yards downstream from the bridge. Somehow he had survived the impact and managed to tread water until he got his bearings. Then he had contemplated an important decision: Does he swim back to Wheeling Island, the shorter distance to shore, or does he swim to the other side, downtown Wheeling. He made an educated guess and swam toward the city, figuring the couple would head in the opposite direction from the accident.

What damn bad luck. His partner for the last six years, Rory Reed, lay dead on the hood of the Crown Vic, his head split open and brains oozing out. Too bad. Good old Rory thought he would live forever. Killed by a church van, of all things. Hard to believe. What a waste of the Methuselah serum. Losing his partner didn't help, but losing his gun really sucked. Somewhere on the bottom of the Ohio River lay his trusty Glock 22. He loved that gun. He couldn't even remember letting it go. All he could remember was that son of a bitch sheriff pushing him and the hard smack of the river. He guessed the jolt of the water must have dislodged the gun from his hand.

No sense in crying about it, he thought. He tried to look on the sunny side. With Reed dead, his profits would double. That's only if he could retrieve the serum and formula. Now he had to refocus. Where did the couple and boy go? Probably to some establishment in Wheeling where they could hang out until they got help. He needed to hustle up the bank and start looking for them. Gotta get moving, he thought. That's the only way to keep from freezing.

Joe C. Ellis

Fetters climbed the steep bank by grasping weeds and the trunks of small trees. When he crested the top, he took a few steps and eyed his surroundings. He stood on an asphalt path, maybe eight feet wide, probably a walking trail. A tall retaining wall blocked his progress toward town, and a building, eight or nine stories high, loomed above the wall. He turned to his right and peered down the trail. A couple hundred yards away lights brightened what looked to be some kind of riverside amphitheater. He didn't see any people, so he jogged in the direction of the lights. As he came to within fifty yards or so of the stage area, he noticed a large circular building beyond the amphitheater. That had to be some kind of arena or civic center. *How big is this town?* He hoped not too big. They could be anywhere.

He examined his surroundings to his left to find the nearest alley or side street to lead him to a main thoroughfare. He trotted past a playground and made a left on a deserted street that wound up a hill. At the top, lights brightened a downtown area with lots of stores on each side of the street. *This is more like it.* He turned left toward the bridge and walked past an appliance store and a pawn shop. He checked his watch—just after nine. Most businesses were closed at this time of night. He scanned both sides for some kind of restaurant or bar. Farther up across the street he saw the Wheeling Business College building and next to it a bar, Yesterday's Draught House and Stage.

They could have wandered in there, he thought. He crossed the street and peered in the window. The stage at the back of the large room was empty. Not much happening on a Monday night. Twenty or so college-age kids were scattered around at small tables and drinking brews. A few stood at the bar. He stepped in and looked around but didn't see the couple. The place smelled like draft beer, that stale smell of his party days when he was twenty-one years old and loved to get drunk. Rap music blared from several speakers mounted on the walls. He hated rap music.

He spread his feet and put his hands on his hips. "Could I have your attention!"

Several patrons glanced up, and the bartender, a fat guy with long greasy hair, turned in his direction.

"I'm looking for a couple and a boy. The boy is six or seven years old. Anyone see them?"

Heads shook sideways, and the bartender said, "Ain't seen no kid." He waved his hand toward the occupied tables. "But there are some couples here."

Fetters scanned the room again to make sure. The few couples were in their early twenties. He pointed to the back corner. "What's up those stairs over there?"

The bartender glanced over his shoulder and then eyed Fetters. "That's our second story party room. There's another stage up there, but it's only open on the weekends."

"Anyone up there?"

"No."

Shit. Fetters turned and walked out of the bar. He headed up a block and noticed the Capitol Music Hall across the street. He had heard of the place. Years ago it had been famous for the country music stars who regularly performed there. What was it called? The Jamboree USA? Country music—that was more like it, something he could understand. To hell with that rap crap. He grew up in Poteet, Texas, hometown of George Strait. Now there's a man who could belt out a country song.

To his right he noticed a small, one-story yellow and brown building with a large sign mounted on the roof—The Sesame Café. He peered in the window. An old bearded guy wearing a red ball cap sat at the counter drinking a cup of coffee and talking to the waitress. No one else was in the place. *Dammit. Where did they go?*

About forty yards down the street he spotted a police car blocking the entrance to the suspension bridge. It wouldn't be long before the local authorities figured out he was missing. Agents from the Wheeling FBI office would be on the scene in no time. He hadn't reported in to Clooney for several hours. Did Clooney suspect anything? *Probably not. He's denser than a sack of wet oatmeal.*

A compact SUV, one of those Honda CRVs, passed by, and Fetters caught sight of the driver. The face was familiar. Who was it? He scoured his mind. Of course—the preacher! Walton's friend from across the river. Fetters remembered his name from the brief introductions earlier that evening—the Reverend Byron Butler. What luck! The CRV crossed into the left lane and parked at the meter in front of the Sesame Café. *He's come to their rescue.*

Fetters slipped into the nearest storefront doorway. The sign on the window identified the building as the Children's Museum of the Ohio Valley. He edged to the corner of the large display widow and peered down the street. The preacher walked in his direction. Fetters turned and faced the other way, pretending to examine the exhibit on the other side of the pane of glass. He heard Butler's footsteps go by. Fetters leaned to his left and watched the preacher walk to the curb. Butler crossed the street and entered a restaurant on the corner of the next block—the Bridge Tavern and Grill.

"Dugan, you know he's going to ask for a dose." Marla didn't understand why Dugan was so adamant about withholding the Methuselah serum from Pastor Byron. Couldn't Dugan understand the depth of love Byron had for his wife? After losing her husband, Marla empathized much more deeply with people who suffered the loss of a loved one.

Dugan held up his hand. "I know. Believe me, this decision isn't easy."

"Think of all he's done for you."

"Please, Marla, I feel bad enough. I admit he's been like a father to me. You've got to understand my position. If God has placed this serum and formula into my hands, then I'm accountable to a higher power."

"I thought God placed it into *our* hands."

"He did."

"Then it should be a joint decision." After the words slipped out, Marla regretted it. She knew her emotional attachment to the Butlers increased the pressure she applied to Dugan to compromise his values.

Dugan's eyes seemed laden with disappointment. "You heard what Lila said. She wanted no part of the serum. She didn't want to live forever in this world. Would you?"

Marla had to confess she hated aging. She knew she was an attractive woman, but in the last couple years the telltale signs of new wrinkles and an occasional gray hair confronted her with the cold truth that her beauty was fading. When Lila raised the prospect of all of them injecting a dose of the serum, she didn't discount it. The possibility hung there like an apple to be picked from a tree. Wouldn't it be great to maintain her looks for years to come? Indefinitely? But wasn't that a foolish dream? Inner beauty was so much more important than outer beauty. Right now she didn't feel beautiful inside or out.

Marla shrugged. "I don't know what I want out of this world. Right now I just want to be safe at home with my boy." Over Dugan's shoulder Marla noticed a familiar figure coming their way. "Byron's here."

Byron hurried to their booth and slid into the seat next to Dugan. "Thank God you're safe. Those agents took off after you like a couple of lions chasing a family of gazelles."

"Thanks for helping us," Dugan said.

"Let's just say you owe me one."

"Sorry, but we don't have much time to talk. We need to get out of here before the wrong people find us."

"I understand. Well . . . here's the keys." Byron dropped them into Dugan's hand. "I'm parked right down the street. I've already called a taxi to pick me up here."

"I do owe you one. Let's head out. We can talk on the way to the car." Dugan pointed to the teddy bear. "Gabe, let me carry Blackie"

Gabe handed the stuffed animal across the table, and Dugan tucked it into his jacket and pulled up the zipper.

When they exited the restaurant, Marla checked the area. Two policemen leaned on the cop car across the street, still blocking the bridge. She wondered about the unfortunate people in the van. How badly were they hurt? She sent up a prayer for them as she inspected the dark doorways of the storefronts along Main Street. Could Fetters have survived the fall into the river? In all probability he did. What about Pugach? Did he have the technology to track her cell phone? Both of those creeps could be somewhere in Wheeling looking for them. She noticed a man walking in their direction. Her heart raced. When he walked under the street light, the glow brightened the figure, and she noticed he was an older man wearing a red ball cap. *Stay calm, girl. If we can just get to the car and get out of here, we'll be fine.*

As they crossed the street, Byron placed his hand on Dugan's shoulder. "Dugan, I'm going to ask you this once, and then I'll keep my mouth shut about it. Before you answer, remember you owe me one. Are you willing to give me a dose of the serum for Lila?"

"I'm sorry, I can't. My mind's made up."

Byron's hand slipped off of Dugan's shoulder.

They walked in silence. Marla wanted to make one last appeal to Dugan but decided she better keep her mouth shut.

A half block down Byron stopped in front of a green, compact SUV. "Well, here we are. By the way . . ." He turned and motioned toward the bridge. "I noticed that police car over there. Anything to do with your accident?"

"Yeah. We crashed the car on the other side of the bridge. Two other vehicles collided." Dugan shook his head. "It wasn't pretty. At least one person died."

"God have mercy. I didn't realize how bad it was."

"Listen, the authorities will be looking for us. We don't know who to trust. Please don't tell anyone you saw us."

Byron ran his finger across his lips. "Won't tell a soul."

"I want you to know where we're heading just in case something happens to us. No one can know but you. I'll call you tomorrow morning to let you know what's going on. If you don't hear from me, you'll know we're in trouble."

"Where're you heading?"

"My Uncle Elwood owns a cabin near Black Water Falls. He gave me the key a few years back. We're going to hide out there a day or two until I can figure out what to do next."

Fetters couldn't believe what he had just heard. He knelt behind a Jeep Grand Cherokee parked next the preacher's CRV. For two minutes he had suppressed the impulse to ambush them, grab the boy, and demand they hand over the serum and formula. If he hadn't dropped his gun in the river, he would have acted on that impulse. That would have been a mistake. There were too many risks: he didn't have a vehicle; two policemen stood within shouting distance; Walton and the preacher might have double teamed him. Now it didn't matter. He knew exactly where they were heading—to Uncle Elwood's cabin near Black Water Falls. They even planned to hide out there a day or two. Perfect. That gave him time to formulate a better plan. Fetters leaned against the bumper of the Jeep and tilted his head to more clearly hear their conversation.

"What do I do if you don't call me tomorrow morning?" the preacher asked.

"Contact the sheriff's office in Davis, West Virginia. Tell them to check Elwood Walton's cabin. They'll know where to find the place."

"I don't like the sound of this. Your lives are in danger."

"I think we'll be safe. Remember what you always told your congregation."

"What's that?" the preacher asked.

"Tomorrow isn't guaranteed to anyone."

25

After the CRV pulled away, Harold Fetters watched the preacher head back down the sidewalk, cross the street, and enter the restaurant. *I've got to get moving. Where can I get a car and a gun?* He stood, shivering, and eyed the tall buildings on each side of the street. *Not around here. There's got to be a residential area not far from here.* He walked briskly along Main Street for several blocks and then turned left on 14th Street. After jogging a couple minutes, his body warmed up. Eventually, parking meters disappeared, and houses, two-story dwellings that had seen better days, lined the street.

He slowed to a walk and turned left on McColloch Street. There he began inspecting the cars parked along the sidewalk. A sticker with the word "Cabela's" on the bumper of a Subaru Outback caught his attention. *Jackpot.* Cabela's was a major hunting and fishing outfitter. He peered into the back seat and spied a hooded sweatshirt with brown and tan camouflage. The car was parked in front of a modest two-story house with a brick front porch. Fetters knew he had to be careful. West

Virginians took their home security seriously. By law, the Castle Doctrine, they could shoot dead any intruder who broke into their premises without worry of legal repercussions or civil lawsuits.

Fetters proceeded down the brick walkway, mounted the few steps to the front porch, and gazed in the window to the right of the door. The entry hall was dark, but in the next room the glow of a television lit a pair of white stockinged feet on the extended footrest of a recliner. Fetters retreated down the steps to the walkway and pried a brick out of the wet ground. He set the brick aside, pulled his soaked wallet from his back pocket and extracted his ID. After taking a deep breath, he focused on the door. This could get ugly, he thought, and bloody.

He climbed the steps and rang the doorbell. The porch light came on, and Fetters blinked against its glare. The door swung open, and he held up his ID. A squat man with a thick, dark beard and receding hairline stood in the doorway wearing a gray sweatshirt and red athletic shorts that came down to his knees. He held a can of Bud Light in his hand as he scowled at Fetters.

"Sorry to bother you." Fetters held up his ID "My name is Special Agent William Hoffman with the FBI, Wheeling Bureau. We are facing an emergency situation in this neighborhood. Is there anyone else in the house?"

"No. What's the emergency?"

"Does that Subaru parked out front belong to you?"

"Yeah. What about it?" the man grunted.

"I need to commandeer it."

"Like hell you do." The man gulped down the rest of his beer and crushed the can in his hand. "Let me see that ID again."

Fetters held out the plastic card. When the man leaned to look, Fetters whipped the brick around from behind his back and cracked the guy's skull. The man stumbled forward and thudded to the ground. Blood poured from a deep gash on his temple. *Lucky strike.* He grabbed the guy's feet and dragged him back into the entry hall. *He'll be out for awhile. Maybe for good. Now, where does he keep his guns and car keys? Best guess would be the bedroom.*

Fetters entered the living room, the light from the television casting its weak glow onto shabby furniture—an old brown recliner and threadbare couch. To the left he found a stairway. He bounded up the steps, entered the closest bedroom, and flipped on the light. On the dresser he immediately spotted car keys, snagged them, and stuffed them into his pants pocket. He rifled through the top drawers, and in the third one under a pair of raggedy BVDs, he uncovered a pistol. He picked the gun up and inspected it. A Colt 45. *Am I a lucky bastard or what? This thing can shoot through a tree.* He checked the clip—fully loaded.

All the way down Interstate 79 Dugan battled the guilt of his decision. Was he being too idealistic? Had he become some kind of religious fanatic, one of those guys who thinks he hears the voice of God but fails to hear the voice of reason? Lila Butler will probably die within the next couple months. Was he to blame? Marla didn't help. She stared out the windshield like a zombie. Gabe had conked out in the back seat.

Finally, Dugan said, "Maybe I made a mistake. Maybe I should've given Byron the serum."

His words snapped Marla out of her trance. "I don't know, Dugan. Sometimes my emotions overpower my reason. I love Lila. She had a great influence on my life. Losing the people I love bothers me deeply."

"I'm willing to turn around and head back, but Lila has to make the decision, not Byron. It's her life."

"You're right. It is her life, but are you making the offer to turn back because you know she won't have anything to do with the serum?"

Dugan thought about it. Of course that's why he offered to turn around. He knew Lila wanted no part of the serum. "Yeah, that's probably true. Sorry. I guess I don't want you to be mad at me."

Marla reached and placed her hand over his as it rested on the console between the seats. Her warm touch caused a tingling that went up his arm and into his chest. To regain focus on the road he gripped the steering wheel more tightly with his left hand.

"I'm not mad at you." She intertwined her fingers between his. "You're my best bud. I love you whether you agree with me or not, so don't worry about making me mad."

Dugan took a few seconds to process her words. *Did she just say she loved me? Of course she loves me. We've been friends for years. Get a hold of yourself, Walton.* Dugan glanced at Marla's hand on top of his. *But she's never been this affectionate with me before. Could she be falling in love with me? Don't go there. She's just being a good friend.* Dugan wanted to slap himself into rationality but that would require separating his hand from hers. He didn't want to do that quite yet.

After another minute she pulled her arm away. "I don't know about this world anymore. I can't blame Lila for not wanting to remain here much longer."

The withdrawal of her hand gave him a sense of rejection. He figured she didn't want to give him any wrong ideas. "Yeah, this world can be a cold, dark place." Quit being such a lovesick pup, he told himself.

Marla twisted and peered into the back seat. "Gabe's out like a tired little soldier."

"He's been through a lot."

"And he's only seven years old. Don't you think this world is a terrible place to grow up nowadays? With all the crime and drugs and sexual perversion everywhere you turn?"

Dugan bobbed his head. "Can't disagree with you there. Seems like it gets worse every day, but we can't give up on this world."

"Why not?"

"It's the only one we got, for now anyway. Someone's got to step up and make a difference. Isn't that why you became a deputy?"

"I guess so. Do you think we really make that big of a difference?"

"Yes I do. Ever since I was a kid I wanted to be that kind of person, you know, someone to look up to. Not Batman or Spiderman or some kind of superhero, just a guy who stood up for what was right. Someone who didn't back down when the bad guys showed up. I always wanted to protect those who couldn't defend themselves."

"Why was that so important to you?"

Dugan knew why but didn't like talking about it. With Marla, though, he felt less guarded. "Because . . . because there were times when no one was there when I needed protection."

Marla placed her hand on top of his again. "Your father wasn't around much, was he?"

"After the divorce, hardly ever. I remember one time he took me on a camping trip down to New River Gorge in southern West Virginia. He dropped me off to set up camp and went to pick up supplies at some nearby town. He never came back."

"You're kidding me."

"No. I put up the tent, tried to collect some wood for the fire, and waited. After a while I went looking for him. Thought maybe he'd wrecked. When it got dark, I found my way back to the campsite. I wasn't able to find any matches so I couldn't start a fire. It was the longest night of my life."

"What did you do?"

"Sat in the dark all night. You'd be surprised how loud wilderness noises can be when you're nine years old. I could have sworn bears, mountain lions, and rattlesnakes had surrounded that tent."

"What happened to your father?"

"He stopped at a bar on the way back, got drunk, and passed out. The cops hauled him off to jail to sleep it off. In the morning they discovered he'd left me out in the woods. 'Course, they arrested him. They found me in the morning walking along the road again, hunting for my father."

"Did you hate him after that?"

Dugan shook his head. "Not really. I guess that's when I started to feel sorry for him. In my mind he died that night. I turned him into somebody I wanted to be—a good man, a responsible man, someone who would lay his life down for his family. I guess I had a vivid imagination."

Marla squeezed his hand. "I know. I remember the stories you told about him—that he was a government agent working undercover and that he knew President Bush."

"Yeah. The kids at school saw right through my stories. They made fun of me, everyone that is except for you and Gabriel. You two always treated me kindly."

"I saw through to your heart. I knew you wanted to grow up to be a good man. And guess what?"

Dugan glanced at Marla and caught a gleam in her eye. "What?"

Marla patted his hand. "You *are* a good man, one of the best."

"Thanks. That means a lot to me coming from you." Dugan looked up in time to see the sign for Grafton Road. "Here's our exit." He turned off the interstate and headed east on Route 310. "Mostly country roads from here, maybe another forty or fifty miles."

Marla sat back, clasping her hands behind her head. "That's another hour of driving. I just want to fall into a comfortable bed and sleep."

At about quarter 'til midnight, Dugan pulled into a Gomart in Grafton, West Virginia to get gas. When he went inside to pay the cashier, he noticed a food section in the back of the store and hurried over to pick up some eggs, bacon, bread, milk, butter, orange juice and cereal. The next morning he planned on cooking them a good breakfast. The cashier, a thin, older lady with short silver hair, yawned as she took his money.

"Long day?" Dugan asked.

She nodded and placed the items in a plastic bag. "Longer than an old Presbyterian preacher's sermon." She glanced up and smiled. "And almost as boring."

"Not much happens around here, I would guess."

"Not much." She handed Dugan the bag.

Good, Dugan thought. Let's keep it that way.

From Grafton, Dugan took 50 east and then 219 south, which led to the Appalachian Highway right into Davis, West Virginia. He hadn't vacationed at Uncle Elwood's cabin for several years but had no problem remembering the way. Just outside of Davis he took a right on Public Road 13 and then located the gravel road that wound its way about a mile up the mountain to the small log cabin. He drove up to the front steps, the headlights illuminating the covered porch where two rocking chairs sat on each side of the door.

Gabe stirred in the back seat.

"I'll get the door open and the lights on," Dugan said. "Then I'll come back and carry Gabe in."

The clouds had blackened the sky like a thick quilt. Dugan killed the engine but left the headlights on so he could see what he was doing. It didn't take long to get the door open and interior lights on. He noticed a stack of wood near the fireplace. Great, he thought, I'll get a warm fire going in no time. He rushed back out to turn off the headlights and help with Gabe, but the boy had woken up, rubbing his eyes.

"Where are we?" Gabe asked.

Marla reached back and tousled his hair. "At a cabin in West Virginia,"

"A cabin? Really?"

"That's right, Sport," Dugan said. "My uncle's cabin."

Gabe unsnapped his seatbelt, shoved the car door open, jumped out, and led the way to the cabin. Dugan grabbed the groceries from the back seat and hurried to catch up.

When they stepped inside, Gabe said, "This is really cool!"

"I agree." Marla clasped her arms against her chest. "Too cool. I'm freezing."

"I'll get a fire going," Dugan said. "It'll be toasty in here in no time."

The large room was a kitchen/living room combination. To the right two brown cushioned chairs and a matching love seat faced the fireplace. The kitchen area on the left offered a refrigerator, stove, and pine cabinets. A pine table and four wooden chairs took up the space by the cabinets. Knotty-pine paneling covered the walls and vaulted ceiling, and a few framed paintings of West Virginia landscapes added color to the wood-grained surroundings. Above the fireplace hung the mounted head of a twelve-point buck.

Dugan walked to the kitchen area and placed the groceries on the table. Then he turned and pointed to a door on the right side of the fireplace. "That's the bathroom if you need it."

"I'm guessing that's a bedroom," Marla said, waving toward to the door on the other side of the fireplace.

"Yeah," Dugan said, "the only bedroom."

Gabe tugged on Marla's sleeve. "Mommy, I've gotta pee."

"Go ahead, Sport. I'll go after you."

Gabe disappeared into the bathroom, and Marla collapsed into the well-cushioned armchair in front of the fireplace. "Do you need help with the fire?"

"No. Just relax."

Dugan found matches on the mantel and kindling in a box by the stack of wood. As he fiddled with the kindling, he tried to figure out the best sleeping arrangements. If Marla and Gabe slept on the queen-size bed in the bedroom, he'd have to scrunch up on the love seat or sleep on the floor. The loveseat, only about five feet wide, would definitely be uncomfortable. The floor would be better. He could lay the cushions from the couch and chairs on the floor and then stretch out on them. Hopefully, there were extra blankets in the bedroom. The kindling flared up, and he arranged several smaller pieces of wood over the flames. Then he selected a couple of medium-sized logs to stack over the burning wood.

Gabe stepped out of the bathroom and crawled up on the loveseat. "Your turn, Mommy."

Marla struggled to her feet. "I don't think I've ever felt this tired."

"I know the feeling," Dugan said.

By the time Marla finished in the bathroom, the fire blazed, warming the cabin, and Gabe had fallen asleep on the small couch

Dugan pointed to the bedroom door. "You and Gabe can sleep on the bed in there."

Marla walked to the fire and stood next to him. "Where will you sleep? Certainly not on that little couch?"

"No. I'll be fine on the floor."

"The floor? Are you kidding?"

"I'll use the cushions from the couch and chairs."

Marla turned and gazed at her boy. "That couch is just the right size for him. You and I can share the bed. We both need a good night's sleep."

"You . . . uh . . . and me . . uh . . ."

"Listen, Dugan, if I can trust anybody in this world, it's you. Haven't you ever seen that old movie, *It Happened One Night?*"

Dugan had seen it several times. In the screwball comedy Clark Gable and Claudette Colbert, an unmarried couple, spent a night in a motel room. Gable hung a blanket on a rope to separate them and called it the "Walls of Jericho."

"Sure, I've seen it. Do you want me to hang a blanket between us?"

"You didn't bring a trumpet with you, did you?"

"A trumpet?"

Marla giggled. "That's how the walls fell at Jericho. Anyway, we'll need all the blankets we find just to keep warm."

In the bedroom closet Marla found a thick quilt and an extra pillow and took them out to Gabe. Dugan eyed the queen-size bed. It was neatly made with a brown comforter and several pillows. He wondered how this arrangement would work out. Could he even sleep lying next to her?

Marla entered the room and rummaged through the drawers of the pine dresser. "Looky here! Boxer shorts." She held up white shorts with red polka dots. "Thank God. I hate to sleep in my jeans. There's another pair in here. Do you want them?"

"Sure." Dugan had been wearing his pants for two days. The boxer shorts would definitely be more comfortable. Marla tossed the shorts to him, and he snagged them from the air. They were red and green plaid and about his size. "I'm hitting the bathroom. Be back in a few minutes."

Marla smiled. "I'll be here."

After relieving himself, Dugan decided to take a quick shower. Two days of traveling made him feel like a slime ball. As the warm water poured over him he fought off fantasies about Marla, holding her in that bed, kissing her passionately, making love to her. Most guys would sacrifice their pinky finger or at least their small toe to be in his place tonight. Dugan knew better. He didn't want his mind to travel to places where reality denied him access. It only led to frustration. Besides, he wanted to be an upright man, although he was flesh and blood, and like most men could not always control his lustful thoughts.

After toweling off, he slipped into his underwear, boxer shorts and t-shirt. He stared at himself in the mirror. His jaws sported two days growth of reddish-brown beard, giving him a lumberjack appearance. He rubbed the whiskers on his chin. Not a bad look for me, he thought. He took a deep breath, let it out, and faced the doorway. *Now to get a good night's sleep. Yeah, like that's going to happen.*

When he entered the bedroom, the light was still on. Marla lay on the right edge of the bed sound asleep, wrapped in the brown comforter. He walked to the closet and pulled a patchwork quilt off the top shelf. With his own blanket he wouldn't have to unravel and retrieve part of the comforter from her. He eased onto the bed, stretched out on his back near the edge, and stared at the ceiling, leaving at least two feet between them. He heard her gentle breathing and knew this could be a long night battling his human urges. But the bed felt cozy, and the sounds of the fire crackling in the other room soothed him. He closed his eyes, and the world, even thoughts of Marla, faded away. Within minutes he drifted off to sleep.

26

Dugan felt pressure on his chest, something warm and ticklish. He opened his eyes to a dark pine ceiling and slowly turned his head to the left. Marla had rolled over and draped her arm across him. Her head nudged against his shoulder, and he could smell the fragrance of her hair—vanilla and wildflowers. The fire must have died, chilling the cabin. Marla, still asleep, had snuggled next to Dugan for warmth. He could feel the slight movement of her body as she breathed.

He didn't know what to do. Just lie still and enjoy the moment, he told himself. Let her sleep. He couldn't help imagining they were married and cuddling on a cold fall morning. After several minutes he began to feel guilty. If she were awake, she wouldn't be doing this. Was he taking advantage of her unconscious state? But he hadn't done anything wrong. He closed his eyes and tried to fall back to sleep but couldn't. Marla snuggled closer. He could feel her breath on his neck. His insides melted and his stomach felt like he had just leapt off a cliff. Is this what love does to a person?

He hated this loss of control over his emotions. He didn't want to fall in love with someone who wouldn't love him in return. That's why he'd never married. At thirty-five years old he knew his youth was slipping away but didn't want to end up in a relationship like his mother and father. On the seesaw of love he had been either up or down, never finding a woman who loved him equally. But could falling in love be prevented? Was love something his will couldn't refuse even if it meant avoiding the wounds of rejection? It didn't seem fair.

Dugan steeled his faltering resolve. He wasn't going to allow this to happen. "Marla," he whispered. "Marla, wake up." He bounced his rear slightly on the bed, and she stirred.

She removed her hand from his chest, wiped her eyes, blinked, and focused on him. "Dugan?" She reached and brushed the two-day growth on his jaw.

"Surprise, it's me."

"You need a shave." She giggled and rolled onto her back. "I'm sorry. I didn't mean to crowd you."

"I know. I'm a warm body on a cold night. I just didn't want you to think that I . . . you know . . . that I would . . ."

Marla turned onto her side and faced him, lifting herself slightly on her elbow. "That you would enjoy being so close to me?"

"No. I mean . . ." What did he mean? This wasn't going well. "I didn't want you to get the wrong impression of me. I would never take advantage of you in circumstances like this."

"Take advantage of me? Hmmmm. Interesting. So you didn't mind me snuggling up next to you, but because I was asleep you didn't feel right about it."

"Well . . . I know you wouldn't snuggle up to me if you were awake."

Marla's brow tensed, one eye slightly closing. "Why do you say that, Dugan?"

"Would you?"

Marla edged toward Dugan, laid her arm across his chest, and nuzzled her head against his ribs. "Put your arm around me."

Here we go again, Dugan thought. He placed his arm over her shoulder.

"Pull me closer."

Dugan's insides turned to Jell-O as he drew her closer. She rested her head on his chest and pulled the cover over them, her legs against his, her belly pressed on his thigh.

She gazed up at him. "This isn't so bad, is it?"

To Dugan it felt like heaven, but he said, "No, it's . . . it's nice, but . . ."

"But what?"

"But . . . but I don't know what this means."

"Don't be so dense, Dugan Walton." She thrummed her fingers on his chest. "It means you and I are taking a step in a new direction."

"We are?"

"Yes, we are."

Suddenly Dugan felt bold. "If that's the case then . . . may I kiss you?"

Marla lifted her head and gazed at him. "What are you waiting for?"

Dugan focused on her lips and turned his head slightly. How many times in his life had he dreamed of this? A thousand?

"Mommy!" Gabe's voice trumpeted from the other room.

Dugan jerked forward, thrusting Marla off him. He scooted up to get off the bed but lost his balance on the edge of the mattress and slid off, hitting the floor with a loud thump. Cringing from the pain of the fall, he sat up, drew his legs to himself, and leaned forward to rise. He could hear Marla giggling under the covers. When he stood, he glanced up to see Gabe standing in the doorway.

"Are you okay, Dugan?" Gabe asked.

"I'm fine." Dugan coughed once into his hand. "Just slipped," he motioned to the ground, "and fell onto the floor there."

Gabe tilted his head. "What were you two doing?"

Marla stopped giggling and lowered the blanket, uncovering a red face. "Not much."

"Just . . . talking," Dugan said.

"Oh . . ." Gabe scratched his head. "Do we have anything to eat? I'm hungry."

Dugan marched toward the door, raising his finger. "Give me fifteen minutes, and I'll serve up the best country breakfast you've tasted in years."

The smell of bacon and eggs caused Marla's mouth to water. Her stomach growled as she sat at the table, sipped coffee, and watched Dugan orchestrate breakfast like a maestro shifting his focus from one section to another—the eggs, the toast, the bacon, the coffee. He appeared comfortable in front of a stove, a seasoned bachelor who regularly cooked himself a hearty breakfast. The fire blazed in the hearth, warming the cabin, and Gabe sat across from her, gobbling Cheerios.

With a spatula Dugan shoveled a heap of scrambled eggs from the frying pan and ladled them onto a plate. He speared several strips of bacon with a fork and draped them next to the eggs, reached and popped the toast, snatched the slices, and leaned them on the eggs and bacon.

Dugan pivoted and slid the plate in front of Marla. "Bet you didn't know I worked as a short-order cook at Denny's for a couple summers during college."

"I'm not surprised." Marla picked up her fork. "You look like a real pro."

"How 'bout me? I want some eggs." Gabe tilted his bowl and gulped down the remaining milk from his cereal.

Dugan held the spatula like a baton. "Golly, Sport, you are one hungry monkey. Yours'll be ready in three minutes."

Gabe leapt off his chair and did his best chimpanzee impression, screeching, scratching, and scrambling around the room on all fours.

Marla laughed. Wasn't it odd that in the midst of danger she felt suddenly happy? Gabe appeared oblivious to what he'd been through the last two days. Was it because of Dugan? They almost seemed like a young family on vacation, delighting in each other's company. Dugan beamed like a boy on his birthday. Marla wondered if she had fallen in love with him. She wasn't quite sure. If so, it wasn't a sudden drop, more like a leisurely tumble down a grassy knoll. Falling hard for someone wasn't so great, anyway. Rarely did the intensity of emotion last. But still she wondered, would Dugan's kiss have sent her to the moon? She had to admit, cuddling with him felt good.

Dugan finished up the cooking and joined them at the table, delivering his and Gabe's plates. As the fellows dug in, Marla watched them. Dear God, she thought, this feels so right. Maybe she didn't need to fall head over heels for someone to really love them. Hollywood did its best to make people think love was some kind of emotional zenith, some explosion of hormones and desires which resulted in a blissful consummation. Wasn't love more about character, commitment, and caring? By far, she cared more for Dugan than any other man and had always admired his character. As far as commitment was concerned, Dugan was more faithful than a Marine on the battlefield. I must be growing older and wiser, Marla thought. Right now Dugan Walton looks better to me than Brad Pitt.

After breakfast Marla and Dugan carried the dishes to the sink, and Gabe stationed himself at the window looking out at the early dawn. The sun hovered above the hills to the east, streaming rays through the window onto the hardwood floor. Marla glanced over her shoulder to see Gabe's silhouette against the light. With the outer glow he reminded her of a little cherub. The rain and clouds had departed. A new day, a beautiful day had begun. Perhaps the three of them could hike through the woods later that morning.

Marla took on the washing duties while Dugan stood ready with the dish towel. She purposely brushed against him whenever she handed him a plate or cup. He didn't seem to mind. In fact, he leaned closer than necessary to receive the dishes. Funny, she thought, how much you can tell about a man's feelings toward you by his reactions when you stand close to him. They laughed and talked about the most insignificant things—the best way to clean a glass, how strong they liked their coffee, ingredients they preferred in their omelets.

Marla felt a sudden tug on the back of her t-shirt. She turned to see Gabe smiling up at her.

"Mommy, can I go outside?"

"No, you better wait until we're ready to go out with you, Sport."

"Please, just on the porch. I want to watch the birds."

Marla glanced at Dugan.

Dugan shrugged. "I think we're safe here."

Marla knelt and put her hands on Gabe's shoulders. "You do not take one step off that porch. Do you understand me?"

Gabe's noggin bounced like a bobble-head toy.

"Dugan and I will be out as soon as we finish up the dishes."

"Okay, Mom. I promise to stay on the porch." Gabe twirled and sprinted for the door. It took him only a few seconds to unlock the knob and deadbolt, throw open the door, and then bound out onto the porch.

Marla turned and faced Dugan. "That kid . . . sometimes . . ."

Dugan placed his hands on her shoulders. "He's a great kid."

Marla eyes locked onto his. "He thinks you're something special, too."

"Do you?"

Marla reached up, clasped his cheeks and drew his face to her. The two-day growth on his jaws felt rough on her palms, but his lips were soft, wet, and warm. He pulled her tightly against him, and her heart soared . . . to the moon.

Harold Fetters had arrived in Davis about one o'clock in the morning but had no idea where Uncle Elwood's cabin could be. There had been no great hurry. No one knew the couple and boy had arrived in central West Virginia except for the preacher and him. After clubbing the redneck back in Wheeling, Fetters knew his career as a special agent for the FBI was over. How could he explain his circumstances—the assault and battery, the stolen car, the preacher's knowledge of his illegal actions? If he had any hope of keeping his job, not only would he have to eliminate the couple and boy, but then he'd have to go after the preacher, and hope the redneck had died from head trauma. Somehow he'd have to explain it all. Nope. His best chance was retrieving the serum and formula, connecting with the Methuselah Triumvirate, and collecting the billion buckos. Then he'd have to leave the country. All my eggs are in one basket, he thought. He chuckled to himself and patted the Colt 45 in his jacket pocket. *I've put all my bullets in one gun. I've got to make this work.*

He had driven down William Avenue and parked in front of Hellbender Burritos. Across the street he'd spotted a place called Sirianni's Café. Reclining the seat, he had stretched out in the Subaru to catch some Zs. He had slept uneasily, waking several times during the night only to see the deserted street. About six in the morning the lights in the café had come on. He had strolled across the street, entered the establishment, and ordered the Big Blackwater Breakfast, which consisted of a three-egg omelet with all the fixings, grits, biscuits, orange juice, ham, and plenty of coffee. As he ate the meal, he had sparked up a conversation with the waitress, asking her where his buddy Elwood Walton's cabin was located. He had explained that good ol' Elwood had invited him to stop by for a few days, but he'd forgotten what road led up to the cabin.

The chubby blonde knew Uncle Elwood and had served him often when he would stop in during his stays at the cabin during hunting season. Without hesitation she had given Fetters specific directions and offered to stop by that evening if he needed some company. Fetters had smiled, winked at her, and left a big tip. By the time he left the café, the sun had peeked over the eastern hills, giving him ample light to locate the gravel road to the cabin.

Now, as he drove cautiously up the road, he put his mind into black op mode—that emotionally detached, focused state his job often required. He understood that the task at hand involved coldblooded machinations. When the cabin came into view, he stopped and backed up to keep the car out of sight. He knew exactly how he wanted to handle this. He pulled the Subaru into the weeds on the side of the road and exited the vehicle as quietly as possible. His heartbeat intensified as he crept along the edge of the woods until he came to a vantage point where he could see the cabin. He couldn't believe it. There on the porch, leaning on the railing, the boy stood, gazing into the sky. What a lucky bastard I am, he thought. Can't waste time. He cut into the woods to circle to the side of the cabin without being seen.

The foliage had begun to turn colors, oranges and yellows, and the trees had lost about a third of their leaves. Still, he had plenty of cover as he made his way through the underbrush. Luckily, there weren't many thickets, vines, and thorn bushes to impede his progress. The fallen leaves crunched under his feet as he followed a deer path to a position where he could spot the side of the cabin through the branches. He pulled the Colt 45 from his jacket pocket, emerged from the woods, and scurried across the opening to the side of the cabin. Pressing his back against the log wall, he took a deep breath and tried to relax. He needed to be as coolheaded as possible to pull this off.

The faint sounds of conversation wafted on the air. He couldn't make out the words but knew the sheriff and deputy must be near a window or door. Fetters crept to the corner of the cabin. The boy had stepped up on the porch railing, his feet between the posts as he gripped the top rail. Now was the time. He needed to act fast before the adults came outside. The deck was about three feet off the ground. Fetters raised his foot and placed it on the deck. He thrust upward, leapt over the railing, shot across the porch, and grabbed the boy.

The kid let out a wail, but Fetters already had the barrel of the gun against the boy's head. He twirled and faced the front door with the boy clenched against him. The woman appeared first in the doorway, her face contorted with dread. From behind her, Sheriff Walton shoved open the screen door, and they both burst onto the porch towards him and the boy.

"Stay right where you are," Fetters warned.

Walton stopped in his tracks and raised his hands. "Okay. Take it easy. He's just a kid."

"And I'm a desperate man. I have nothing to lose. This Colt 45 will blow this boy's head clean off."

"Mommy!" Gabe cried. "Help me!"

Marla stepped forward and reached her hand toward them.

"Don't do it," Fetters ordered. "Not another step."

Marla froze. "Please, please don't point the gun at his head."

"Shut up!"

"Okay," Walton said. "Whatever you say, we'll do it."

"Where's the serum and formula?"

Walton thumbed over his shoulder. "In the house."

"Everybody inside."

Dugan backed to the screen door and opened it. The woman entered first, followed by the sheriff, Fetters and the boy trailing behind them. Once inside, Fetters made Walton and his deputy stand against the counter.

Fetters, still gripping Gabe around the chest, pointed the gun at Walton. "Where is it?"

Dugan pointed to the kitchen chair closest to Fetters where the teddy bear sat. "Inside the bear."

Fetters released Gabe, and the boy rushed into his mother's arms. He picked up the stuffed animal, located the zipper, and unzipped it. He stuck his hand inside the bear's belly and pulled out a white towel.

He waved the gun toward the sheriff and deputy. "Don't move."

"We won't budge," Dugan said. "Just take it and go."

"Yeah, right. It's not going to be that easy for you."

Fetters set the towel on the table and unrolled it to uncover the small bottle with the yellow-green liquid and the notepaper containing the complicated formula. He rolled the items back into the towel and inserted it back into the teddy bear.

"Hope you brought your hiking shoes," Fetters said. "The four of us are about to take a long walk through the woods."

27

This would be the worst part. Fetters wondered if he had the guts to pull it off. Cold-blooded murder. He had no choice. If he let them live, Walton would alert the authorities, and a nationwide manhunt would ensue. The FBI and all other powers at the president's disposal would track him down before he had a chance to make the transaction and get out of the country. He needed at least two days. He had killed three men in the line of duty—a drug dealer, a psycho, and a desperate armed robber, but never the innocent. To keep from getting soft, he kept thinking about the money, the life of luxury and pleasure that awaited him for years and years and years. An unending life of bliss was worth it.

With the teddy bear clutched in his left hand and the Colt 45 in his right, he marched the three of them outside and around to the back of the cabin where he quickly found a deer trail into the woods. He made Walton lead the way, followed by the woman and the boy. Fetters brought up the rear, keeping the kid near him in case Walton tried to make a foolish move. They followed the path for about fifteen minutes up the mountain and about halfway down the other side. He figured they had trekked about a mile through the tall pines, oaks, birches, and maples. Luckily, the deer path helped to keep their progress steady through the thickets and underbrush with very few obstacles except for an occasional fallen branch.

He ordered Walton to stop in front of a huge oak tree. The woman and boy halted beside him. They stood in the deep shadows of the forest in a spot where ferns hovered above the ground like a floating green carpet. In the distance he could hear falling water, some mountain stream spilling over a crag onto rocks below. Good, he thought, a waterfall would help to drown out gunshots.

Fetters waved the Colt 45 at the ground in front of them. "Everyone, on your knees."

"Please, don't do this," the woman said.

The boy peered up into his mother's face. "What's he going to do, Mommy?"

"Shut up! On your knees!"

"You better think twice about this, Fetters," the sheriff said.

Fetters lifted the teddy bear. "I don't have to think twice about it. I hold the elixir of youth and wealth. Not much else matters to me now."

"Listen to me," Walton insisted. "You're not like Pugach. He's a monster. It's not too late. You don't have to live the rest of your life with this on your conscience. For God's sake, Fetters, think of the years of guilt and regret."

Fetters tried to block out Walton's words. There was no turning back. He had crossed the line. He possessed what the world wanted and wasn't giving it back for nothing. "Shut your damn face and get down on your knees!" He pointed the gun at the boy. "Do it now or the kid goes first!"

The sheriff raised his hands. "Okay! Take it easy. We'll get on our knees."

"Why do we have to get on our knees?" Gabe asked. "To pray?"

"Yes, Sport." The woman sniffled and wiped tears from her cheek, "Pray that God will help us."

The boy dropped to his knees and folded his hands. His mouth moved, forming silent words.

Fetters eyed the boy. *Don't get soft now, you bastard.* "Stop praying!" He pointed the pistol toward the woman and Walton. "You two, on your knees and then lean forward with your heads down."

The sheriff and woman lowered themselves to their knees.

Fetters decided to shoot the sheriff first. He was the biggest threat. He stepped to his right, stood in front of the lawman, and raised the gun. Walton glared up at him. "Lower your damn head."

"Mommy, look." The boy pointed into the woods. "A little bear."

Fetters heard an odd whining behind him. *A little bear?* He glanced to his right and caught sight of a bear cub. Then he heard the growl. He twirled and faced the sound of underbrush rustling. A large mother black bear charged through the forest from thirty yards away. Fetters fired twice but hit the thick branches of trees. His third shot caught the bear on the shoulder. The beast rose up and swatted the gun before Fetters could fire again. The other claw swiped across his cheek, ripping through the skin, shattering his jaw. He hit the ground and rolled into a tree.

The bear stood on its hind legs, towering above him. Excruciating pain jolted through the right side of his face, and blood gushed from the gaping slices across his cheek. He struggled to his feet, but the bear clubbed his back, smashing him to the ground. He managed to scrabble around a tree in hopes of getting something solid between the bear and him. *Where's my gun? I dropped everything.* He shuffled back and forth as the bear dipped and angled around the tree. *I've got to run for it.* He glanced over his shoulder and saw a deer path cutting through the woods. He pivoted and sprang toward the path. He'd try to weave around trees as much as possible to keep the beast off balance.

Behind him he could hear the bear thrashing through the low branches. *The falling water. Get to the stream.* As he charged like a fullback, slicing back and forth through tackling dummies, he focused on the sounds of water splashing. The deer path headed in the direction of the waterfall. If he could jump into the stream, maybe the bear wouldn't follow. He slashed behind tree after tree, zigzagging on and off the path. The bear rumbled only a few steps behind him, skidding and changing directions in and out of the trees in an attempt to overtake him. Fetters gained ground. The large bear struggled to manage the quickly altering angles and the narrow gaps between trees. Luckily, Fetters had kept in shape, running and lifting regularly. He had plenty of endurance, but the bear was faster. He had to keep ducking and darting.

After several minutes he had gained maybe twenty yards on the bear. The sound of the falling water increased in volume, becoming a roar. Not good, he thought. How big could the falls be? He broke through the trees onto the banks of the stream. To his right he spied the edge of the water rushing over a crag of boulders. The rain of the last few days had gorged the stream, causing the water to churn and roil over the edge, thundering onto the rocks below. He spun and faced the bear. The beast barreled toward him, eyes wide with rage. Fetters backed up, and his foot slipped off the bank, tumbling him into the water. The rushing current tugged him toward the falls. He lunged and clasped at the saplings and weeds on the bank. His feet tried to dig into the unstable streambed.

When he looked up, the large, round face of the bear hovered over him. The beast growled, its hot breath shooting through its nostrils and teeth. Fetters blinked against the foulness of the smell and drips of saliva. The bear rose up and pounced on top of Fetters's head. The weeds and saplings ripped away as Fetters went under. The current tumbled him toward the falls. He managed to surface and gasp for air. The undertow submerged him again like a burly wrestler going for the pin. At the crest of the falls his head broke the surface. He spotted several people about forty feet below along the shoreline, their faces aghast with horror. The water spewed him into the air. He plummeted head first toward a large boulder at the base of the falls. The descent felt like a slow motion dream. But then it ended abruptly with blackness.

The agent's pistol ended up next to a pine tree. It went flying when the bear swatted his hand. Thank God for the prayers of a child, Dugan thought. He picked up the Colt 45 and shooed the bear cub away. It scurried off in the direction its mother had chased Fetters.

"Can't we take him home with us?" Gabe asked.

"No!" Marla said.

Dugan scoured the ground, looking for the stuffed animal. Did Fetters drop it? Dugan tried to remember, but everything happened so fast. "Do you see the teddy bear anywhere?"

Gabe leaned over and lifted the leaf of a large fern. "I found Blackie!"

Marla picked up the raggedy bear. "We've got to get out of here before Momma Bear gets back."

"This way." Dugan pointed to the deer path by the large oak. The mother bear didn't worry Dugan nearly as much as other threats. Clearly, Uncle Elwood's cabin no longer provided a safe refuge. Now what? Should he call Division Chief Clooney? Even if Clooney could be trusted, he didn't know who his reliable agents were. Now Dugan had to worry about Pugach. If Fetters found them, certainly Pugach could find them. At least Dugan had a gun. Kneeling before Fetters, he had felt defenseless and doomed, ready to accept his fate. *If not for the faith of a child.* Dugan could think of no other explanation except for divine intervention. Dumb luck? A random encounter with an enraged black bear? What were the odds? One in a billion? But not if God intervened.

On the way back to the cabin Dugan didn't say much. He focused on the path, making sure they didn't take a wrong turn. Time was of the essence. They had to get out of there before some other cut-throat tracked them down. Almost running at times, he checked over his shoulder regularly to make sure Marla and Gabe kept up. When they broke through the edge of the woods at the back of the cabin, Dugan held his hand up to stop Marla and Gabe from advancing farther. He wanted to check out the cabin and road first to make sure they wouldn't be ambushed.

"Wait here," he whispered. "Keep quiet. I'll be back in a minute if it's clear."

Dugan rushed to the back of the cabin and peered in the nearest window. No sign of any intruder. He edged around the side of the house, his back to the wall, until he got to the corner. Scanning the front of the property, he saw the CRV but didn't notice any other vehicle. He climbed onto the front porch and hurried to the door. Inside he checked the few rooms. No one. He slid the pistol into his jacket pocket and gathered their few belongings. In the bedroom he opened the window and hollered for Marla and Gabe to meet him at the car. On the way out he glanced at the bed and remembered those incredible moments with Marla. The thought of her so close, their bodies pressing against each other, legs and arms intertwined, sent a jolt of joy through him. He actually had a chance at love with her. One day they could be married. What were the odds? If asked yesterday, he would have said one in a billion. But now it seemed like all things were possible if . . . if they survived.

Dugan stepped onto the front porch, yanked the door shut, and locked it. Marla and Gabe waited at the CRV. Dugan scooped the key from his jacket pocket and pressed the unlock button as he hurried to the car. They opened the doors and climbed into the vehicle. Dugan started the engine, shifted into reverse, backed out, and then flew down the gravel road. He slowed the CRV as they passed a station wagon parked in the weeds. Dugan noticed the Subaru logo on the front grill. Fetters assailed some poor son of a bitch, Dugan thought. He wondered if the guy survived. Dugan reached down and pressed his hand against the Colt 45 in his jacket pocket, realizing the gun in all likelihood belonged to the victim. The trail of bodies in the wake of the Methuselah serum were definitely mounting.

"Do you have the teddy bear?" Dugan asked.

"Yes. Right here next to me." Marla held up Blackie. "Where're we headed?"

"Back to the Outer Banks. We'll hole up at the detention center in Manteo. The only people I trust in this world are you and my deputies. We'll figure out our next step from there."

Pugach stood at a gas pump of a Citgo in Thomas, West Virginia, filling the tank of a Lexus IS F. It had been a long night of driving, and he had been running on fumes the last few miles. Hugh Simmons, a member of the Methuselah Triumvirate, had provided the vehicle for him back in Washington, D.C. Pugach had managed to convince the three pharmaceutical kingpins that Fetters and Reed would never retrieve the serum and formula on their own. Bottom line—the Medical Mafia didn't care who delivered the goods, whether it be a team, a partnership, or the devil himself. The money would go to the persons or person who placed the Fountain of Youth into their hands. Pugach hoped he wasn't too late.

Those double-crossing sons of bitches, Pugach thought. He had waited in Manteo for several hours before he'd concluded that Fetters and Reed had cut him out of the loop. Luckily, the Medical Mafia had the means to track Fetters's personal cell phone. The tracking device led to a cabin in the mountains near Davis, West Virginia, only a few miles away. Then the agents must have taken the sheriff, woman, and boy deeper into the forest to execute them. Pugach chuckled to himself. He didn't think they'd have the balls to do it. *What did my mother used to say? The love of money is the root of all evil. Must be true if those boys were willing to slaughter the innocent for a billion bucks.*

About thirty minutes ago Fetters had gotten wise and turned off his cell phone somewhere in the woods near Black Water Falls. That was the last location update. Pugach believed his odds of finding the agents were good. He figured they needed time to bury the bodies and clean up any evidence at the cabin. That's where he hoped to ambush them. He'd follow the road up the mountain and park a couple hundred yards away. Then he'd play it by ear. If they were inside, he'd shoot them like monkeys in a barrel. Revenge would be a barrel of fun, he thought. If he ran into them coming down the mountain road, things could get ugly—possibly a shootout. Hopefully, he'd have the advantage of surprise.

Pugach withdrew the gas nozzle from the vehicle and hung it back on the pump. He needed to hurry. After screwing the gas cap back on, he turned to open the car door. At that moment a little green SUV drove past. Pugach recognized the woman on the passenger side. I'll be damned, he thought.

28

Division Chief Clooney stood on the bank staring at the body of Special Agent Harold Fetters. Local authorities had strung crime scene tape along the shore to keep onlookers back. Several tourists had reported that the agent had sailed over the falls and slammed head first against the large boulder at the base before flopping into the water. The strong current had washed the body downstream about fifty yards before it lodged against a rock near shore. Fetters's skull had been crushed and both forearms snapped by the impact. How in the world did this happen?

Two young men had pulled him out of the water and laid him on the grass. They had found his ID and called the number on the card, which put them through to an office at the Washington Bureau. Director Miller immediately dispatched Clooney to the scene via helicopter. An evidence response team of local agents had just arrived, and Clooney instructed them to stand by until he was ready to proceed.

Clooney ordered his assistant, Special Agent Melvin Hobbs, to thoroughly check through Fetters's pockets, to loosen and, if need be, remove the clothing. He doubted they would find anything. Obviously, Fetters was a corrupt agent. He had gone after the couple and boy because he had been convinced they still possessed the serum and formula. Did they? Fetters wouldn't have risked everything that mattered in life—his reputation, his career, his future—unless he believed he could get his hands on the prize.

What about Pugach? Was he out of the picture? Probably not. Fetters and Reed must have had a reluctant relationship with the thug. Somehow they had acquired information from him with hollow promises and then left him hanging on the line. Pugach would show up again, madder than hell. Clooney was sure of it.

Fetters had become a desperate man after the collision near the Wheeling Suspension Bridge. With Reed dead, he went after the couple and boy with reckless abandon. Clooney figured Fetters had bashed in the head of the Wheeling resident in order to steal his car. The Subaru Outback would probably be found nearby sooner or later. How in the world did Fetters track the couple and boy to Davis, West Virginia? Did he find them? Did he kill them? Some questions he couldn't answer right now. If the couple and boy managed to escape Fetters, they probably still possessed the serum and formula.

Special Agent Hobbs, a thin man with a bulbous nose, peered up at Clooney. Hobbs wore the standard blue nylon jacket with the yellow FBI lettering on the black and white latex gloves. Fetters's half-naked corpse, his clothes strewn here and there, lay beside him. "There's nothing here sir but this cell phone." He held up a Droid Bionic, its face shattered in the pattern of a spider web.

"You checked every nook and cranny?"

"Yes sir." The agent pointed at some items on the ground beside the body. "His wallet, some change, and a cartridge. That's about it."

"Doesn't surprise me. I'll order the team to start searching the shoreline and stream, but I doubt if they'll find anything." Clooney's cell phone erupted in his pocket, an old fashioned ringtone, the way phones sounded back in the sixties. He checked the caller ID—Director Miller. "Clooney here."

"Was it Fetters?"

"Yes sir. Couldn't find anything on him, though."

"Too bad . . . What's your next step?"

"We'll search the area. Who knows? We may find something."

There was a long pause, and then Miller said, "Give me your best guess. Where's the serum and formula?"

"There's a good chance the couple still has it, if they're alive."

"We need to find out. What about their cell phones?"

Clooney shook his head. "For their own safety, I instructed them to turn off their cell phones, but there's another possibility."

"What's that?"

"If we can figure out whose car they're driving, there may be a tracking device pre-installed in the vehicle, a theft prevention chip."

"We need to get on that now."

"I've already contacted a couple of agents in Wheeling. They're checking the rental agencies and other possible connections with old friends."

"What about the Russian? Is he still at large?"

"We haven't accounted for Pugach. I'm sure he's trying to find the couple, too."

Miller took an audible breath and blew it out. "If they're still alive, we need to locate them before he does . . . for their own good."

"Yes sir. Pugach is a fiend, and who knows who else might be in on this."

"Put someone in charge there and get back here as soon as possible. I have a briefing in two hours at the White House. I want you to be there."

"Will do, sir." Clooney ended the call and turned to Hobbs. "We need to get back to the helicopter. Supervisory Agent Straub and his crew can take care of the things on this end."

"What's the hurry?"

"I've got a meeting, and I don't want to be late."

"Who with?"

"I'm not sure, but it's at the White House."

Dugan had decided to head north on Route 219 for about ten miles to catch George Washington Highway, which had taken them east to Interstate 81. After going south on 81, they had crossed into Virginia and had taken Interstate 66 south. Dugan figured this was the fastest route, about an eight-hour drive. He'd only have to stop once for gas, probably somewhere in northern North Carolina. The sooner they got there, the better.

He was tempted to call headquarters to let them know they were alive and well. The staff had to be wondering what happened to them. He decided against the call, knowing the possibility of an adversary tracking their location. At the detention center in Manteo they would be safe. With manpower, weapons, and even jail cells, they could set up camp and wait until Pugach or any other threat to their well being was eliminated. Then, before the Feds got there, Dugan could document what they had in their possession: take photographs, make copies of the formula, gather witnesses, create a detailed timeline of the events leading up to his decision to circle the wagons.

If the Feds forced him to hand over the serum and formula, he wanted to make sure he had plenty of evidence and witnesses. No way would he allow some government agency to whisk away the golden goose and then claim it never existed. Someone needed to be held accountable. God had called him to guard the serum and formula, and he had committed life and limb to fulfill the mission.

Marla stirred beside him as they sped down Interstate 66. She stretched her arms. "What are we going to do when we get to the detention center?"

"I'll call in all my deputies and let them know the truth. We can't allow a cover up. We'll document everything."

"Hmmm. Then you plan on handing over the serum and formula?"

"Only if they force me to."

"Why don't you just destroy it?"

Dugan considered the question for a minute. "That's always a possibility, but think about the story from Genesis. The angels didn't destroy the Tree of Life, they only guarded it. It's not my decision to destroy it. If God wants the serum wiped from the face of this earth, he'll take care of it."

Marla reached and placed her hand on Dugan's thigh. "Back in that cabin, when we were in bed together . . . when we ate breakfast like a family on vacation . . ."

"What about it."

"It felt like the Garden of Eden. Everything seemed perfect, if only for a few hours."

Dugan clasped her hand and intertwined their fingers. "Are you saying that you and I were . . . you know . . . like . . . Adam and Eve?"

Marla squeezed his hand. "Yes. In a way. Of course, we weren't naked. And we never . . . consummated the relationship."

"Of course not, but . . . maybe . . . maybe some day?" Dugan stole a quick glance.

Marla smiled and nodded. "That's always a possibility."

Division Chief Clooney had met with the president on two other occasions but never in the Oval Office. Director Miller led the way down the corridor of the West Wing to where a security guard stood in front of the door. The guard immediately recognized Miller, stepped aside, and opened the door, nodding at them as they entered. The oblong office wasn't as big as Clooney imagined, maybe twenty-five feet wide. To the right President Denzel Jackson sat at the famed Resolute Desk, a large, ornately carved, reddish brown desk made from the timbers of a British ship. President Jackson appeared haggard, hollow-cheeked, his once close-cropped black hair now mostly gray. Behind him three large windows offered a view of trees and shrubbery on the White House lawn. Clooney quickly glanced around the room and noticed a grandfather clock to his left, a portrait of George Washington above the fireplace behind them, and another portrait of Abraham Lincoln on the wall to the left of the door they had entered.

President Jackson, lean and tall, stood and spread his hands. "Have a seat, gentlemen."

Two wooden chairs sat on each side of the desk. Clooney crossed the carpet, trying not to step on the large presidential seal in the middle. He felt like his heart had climbed into his throat, the same way he felt as a kid when Mickey Mantel had signed his baseball after a Yankees game. He sat on the left side of the desk, facing an American flag. Miller sat on the right, facing a blue flag with the presidential seal.

The President sat down and folded his hands in front of him. "Do you have an update for me, Director Miller?"

Miller shook his head. "Sorry, Mr. President, but we don't have much more to tell you. The evidence investigation team hasn't found anything yet at the Black Water Falls scene—at the cabin or along the stream. We did discover the stolen vehicle near the cabin. It was thoroughly searched but the items weren't found."

The President's lips tightened, and he shifted his focus to Clooney. "Did your suspicions about the two agents prove correct?"

Clooney cleared his throat. "Yes sir, I believe they had connections to the Medical Mafia. They were looking for a big payday."

President Jackson templed his fingers. "And the Medical Mafia is the organization putting up the money for the Methuselah formula."

"That is correct, sir," Clooney said.

"And we have no idea who they are?"

Director Miller nodded. "Only that they exist. It's not a big organization."

"Hmmmm." The President placed his hands flat on the desk. "Perhaps this is good news. If the agents never got their hands on the serum and formula, then the couple must still have it."

Miller sat straight up. "That's very possible. We found tire tracks leading away from the cabin. The couple must have escaped. We believe if we find the couple, we'll find the formula and serum."

"How well do we know this couple? Do they understand the possibilities and potential of the formula?"

Clooney bobbed his head. "I interviewed them. They've seen all the evidence. They knew Dr. Hopkins personally. I think they get it."

"Maybe they want to cash in, too," the president said.

Clooney rubbed his chin. "I don't think so, but you never know. They're human. The possibility of riches and long life can get to you, if you let it."

President Jackson slid his chair back. "Ironic, isn't it? This serum offers wealth and long life, but those who possess it end up dead." He stood, pivoted, and ambled to the tall windows directly behind his desk. He gazed at the White House lawn. The sun's rays bathed him in light, contrasting with his dark blue suit. The room became strangely silent except for the president's long inhale and exhale. Then he faced them. "Gentlemen, I must confess I have an ulterior motive for wanting to acquire the Methuselah formula. I understand the impact and ramifications of this discovery on mankind. No doubt, it will change the world as we know it. The people who . . . control access to its life-giving powers must be noble and wise in their management and dispensation of the serum." He lowered his eyes and shook his head. "From what I understand the serum could possibly be a cure for certain types of cancer. Correct?"

Director Miller said, "We have evidence that it cured advanced prostate cancer. Our experts attribute the cure to its ability to reverse aging in the human cell."

The president leaned on his desk. "Then it's possible the serum may have the same effect on other types of cancer."

Miller nodded. "It's definitely possible."

President Jackson straightened and walked back to the window. He squinted into the sun's rays. "Last week my wife and I . . . received very bad news." He turned and faced them. "My eighteen year old daughter, Maria Ann, has been diagnosed with acute myeloid leukemia. The five year survival rate is less than twenty-five percent."

Clooney didn't know what to say. He couldn't imagine one of his own children afflicted by such a devastating disease.

"I'm sorry to hear that," Miller said.

The president's dark brown eyes watered. "Now you know why I called you here. I don't believe God gave us such a beautiful and intelligent child in vain—to be sacrificed to this disease. She wants to be a teacher. She wants to make a difference in this world."

Clooney's cell phone rang, making him jump. He pulled it from his pants pocket and checked the caller ID—Supervisory Agent Straub. "Excuse me, Mr. President, but I need to take this call."

"Go right ahead."

He pressed the answer icon. "Clooney here."

"Good news, sir. We identified the tire tracks from the road to the cabin. They are newer tires, commonly used on a Honda CRV."

"Great. Did you coordinate this information with our people in Wheeling?"

"Yes sir. A close friend of the couple, a Reverend Byron Butler, owns a new CRV. There's even better news. The car has a theft prevention tracking chip, and we just pinpointed its location—heading south on 168 just south of Chesapeake, Virginia."

29

When Marla spotted the "Welcome to North Carolina" sign along Route 168, she felt a great sense of relief. She knew they weren't out of danger, but at least they weren't far from home, less than two hours. Now they would pass through a series of small towns along the Currituck Sound until they reached the Wright Memorial Bridge which crossed the Albemarle Sound over to Kitty Hawk. Gabe had fallen asleep in the back seat. She tried to stay awake to keep Dugan company. Occasionally he yawned, rubbed his eyes, took deep breaths, and leaned forward to keep alert. It had been a long three days. Her stomach growled. They had made a quick rest stop to go to the bathroom but hadn't eaten since breakfast.

"How's our gas?" Marla asked.

Dugan glanced at the gauge. "We need to stop soon."

"I'm starved."

"There's a Seven-Eleven not far down the road in Barco. We'll get gas there and grab a sandwich. I don't want to stop for more than a couple of minutes. No sense in taking any chances. We're almost home."

"Amen to that." Those words sounded so good. She was anxious to get to the detention center and be rid of the formula and serum. Then once things settled down, she and Gabe could head home. What would home be like now? Her relationship with Dugan had catapulted to a new level. Things would definitely be different. Had she fallen in love with her boss and best friend, a person she had known since grade school? What an unexpected turn of fate. A month ago she never would have guessed it. Spending a week with him riding around in the sheriff's car and then the pandemonium of the last three days had swirled her emotions like a strawberry and banana daiquiri in a blender. It felt like love. She was ninety-nine percent sure. Could anyone be one-hundred percent sure?

"Did you hear that?" Dugan asked.

"What?"

"On the radio just now."

Marla hadn't been paying attention. "No. What's up?"

"There's a tropical storm in the Atlantic heading our way."

"That's all we need. How bad is it?"

"Not a hurricane yet, but the potential is there."

Marla hated to hear that. The Outer Banks was a perilous place to be during a hurricane. "When will it hit?"

"Two to three days."

"Hopefully they won't order an evacuation."

"You never know." Dugan pointed to his right. "There's the Seven-Eleven." He turned off the highway and pulled up to the gas pump. "What do you want to eat?"

"A ham-and-cheese sandwich and some Cheetos sound great, and a coffee with cream."

Gabe came to life. "I'm hungry, too, Mommy."

Marla twisted her torso to peer into the back seat. "Do you want a ham-and-cheese sandwich too, Sport?"

Gabe nodded "And Oreos and milk."

Dugan opened the car door. "Three ham-and-cheese sandwiches, a package of Oreo cookies, Cheetos, milk, and two coffees. Got ya." He stepped out of the car, stretched his arms to the sky, arched his back, and then strode to the store entrance.

"Are we almost home, Mommy?"

"Won't be long now. Maybe an hour and a half."

"I'm tired of riding in a car."

"Me, too."

"Mommy, can I see Blackie?"

Marla had placed the bear between her feet. The stuffed toy had been a source of comfort to Gabe for years. She didn't see any harm in him holding it for a while. She reached down, picked up the bear, and handed it to him. "You can hold Blackie until Dugan gets back. Then I have to keep him up front with me."

Gabe hugged the tattered bear. "Because of what's inside of him, right?"

"That's right, Sport."

Gabe glanced to his right, his eyes growing wide.

A shadow crossed over Marla, and she shifted in her seat to look out her window. The door flew open, and someone stuck a pistol in front of her face. Her heart thrummed like the wings of a humming bird. She focused beyond the barrel to see the scarred face of Boris Pugach.

His voice was low and rough. "Where's the serum and formula?"

"I . . . I . . . don't . . ."

Pugach clasped his hand around her neck, squeezed, and pointed the gun into the back seat. "Tell me now or the boy dies."

"It's . . . it's inside the bear."

Pugach let go of Marla, yanked open the back door, and wrenched Blackie from Gabe's arms. He unzipped it and checked to make sure the formula and serum were inside.

"Please, take it and go," Marla pleaded. "It's all yours. Just leave us alone."

Pugach leaned and unbuckled Gabe. "You think I'm stupid?" He grabbed Gabe by the arm and pulled him out of the car.

"Help me, Mommy!"

Pugach slammed the back door and stepped toward Marla. He lowered his head to within inches of her face. "Listen carefully. I am a very desperate man. If the law comes down on me, your boy dies. I will put a bullet through his head. I swear on my mother's grave. Do you understand me?"

Marla's head jerked up and down almost uncontrollably.

"You make sure your sheriff friend understands. No one follows me. Got it?"

Again Marla nodded.

"I will call you in three days to let you know where to find your boy. If no one comes after me, he'll be alive. You have my guarantee."

"Please don't take my boy." Marla couldn't keep the words from slipping out.

Pugach raised the pistol and stuck the barrel against her forehead. "Didn't you hear anything I just told you? I meant every word I said. Don't make me kill you. Now close your eyes."

Marla closed her eyes. "Okay. I'll wait for your call."

"Count to sixty before you open your eyes. Understand?"

"Yes." The cold circle of the gun barrel lifted from her forehead. After about twenty seconds she opened her eyes. Pugach and Gabe had disappeared. She spun in her seat to see which direction they went.

Behind her a golden car peeled out of the parking lot and onto Route 168 heading south. Marla tried to identify the make but didn't recognize the logo—a circle with an L. She leapt out of the CRV, dashed to the store entrance, and flung open the glass door. Dugan stood in the back at the deli. Marla didn't want to alarm anyone in the store. She had to keep the kidnapping under wraps to prevent any news from spreading. If it went public, and Pugach found out, he may panic and kill Gabe. She marched toward Dugan, trying to calm herself.

"Dugan," Marla said. Her voice sounded strained.

Dugan pivoted and met her gaze. "What's wrong?"

"We need to leave now."

A flash of alarm lit Dugan's eyes. He glanced over his shoulder and told the deli clerk, a large brunette with meaty arms, he had to cancel his order. The woman, in the middle of wrapping a sandwich in plastic wrap, knotted her brow.

They rushed to the front of the store, Marla leading the way, and exited.

Just outside the door Marla spun and faced Dugan. "Pugach . . . " Tears flooded her eyes and streamed down her cheeks.

"Did he take the serum and formula?"

Marla swallowed and nodded, trying to get control of her emotions.

"What happened? Where's Gabe?"

"Pugach took him."

Dugan's eyes flamed. "Which way did they go?"

"We can't follow them. We can't tell anybody. He swore he'd kill Gabe if he suspects he's being pursued."

Dugan's eyes flitted around the parking lot, his face muscles tightening. He placed his hands on Marla's shoulders. "We have to go after them."

Marla shook her head. "He promised he'd call in three days. He said he'd let me know where to find Gabe. Pugach is desperate. He has nothing to lose."

Dugan glanced at the CRV. "He'll recognize the car. We need a different vehicle. I could commandeer another one."

Dugan turned toward the store entrance, but Marla reached and grabbed his arm. "No! Don't you understand? He will put a bullet through Gabe's head if he suspects he's being followed."

"We have to do something."

"Listen to me, Dugan. Until we have a good plan, we sit tight and keep our mouths shut."

A shadow crossed over them, and Marla heard the thrum of helicopter blades. The droning grew louder, and they peered into the sky. A large helicopter, the bottom half green and the top half white, descended. A strong gust of wind swirled the parking lot, raising dust and blowing debris in all directions. Marla and Dugan raised their arms and lowered their heads against the blast of air. The copter lowered into a tight space between the gas pumps and far end of the parking lot. Above the four windows were the words UNITED STATES OF AMERICA. It had two doors, a front and a back, with an American flag decal above the front door. The back door popped open. An older man wearing a black suit and sunglasses appeared in the doorway. Marla immediately recognized his face—Division Chief Ronald Clooney. The roar of the engine faded, and Clooney planted his foot on a metal step and then lowered the other foot to the ground.

Marla couldn't believe it. How did the FBI track them down? She pictured Gabe in the golden car with Pugach. She recalled the cold round barrel of the pistol against her forehead. If the FBI pursued Pugach in a helicopter, then he would take that gun and put it against Gabe's head and pull the trigger. She forced the image out of her mind.

She reached and grasped Dugan's forearm, pulling him near. "Don't say a word. Do you hear me?"

Dugan's lips tightened as his head slowly bobbed.

When Marla focused on the helicopter door, she recognized the second man descending the step to the ground—Director Robert Miller, the head of the FBI. Then a third and a forth man appeared, descended, and waited on each side of the step. Wearing black suits and ties, and dark sunglasses, they panned the area, glanced up at the opening, and nodded. A light-skinned black man dressed in a blue suit and red tie emerged from the copter. The two men in black suits extended their arms to give him a hand. He met Marla's gaze and her mouth dropped open. Denzel Jackson, the President of the United States, stepped down from the helicopter.

30

The five men approached them, the president leading the way flanked by the two men in black, Clooney on the far right and Miller on the far left. Marla had to pull herself together. She wiped her cheeks and wondered if tracks of tears still streaked her face. She straightened and took a deep breath. What would they do if she told them Gabe had been kidnapped, if she gave them the description of the car and divulged the direction Pugach went? No doubt, they would go after him, and Gabe would probably die.

The president extended his hand to Dugan. "You must be Sheriff Walton. I'm Denzel Jackson."

Dugan shook his hand. "I know who you are, Mr. President. It's an honor to meet you."

The president turned and offered Marla his hand. "And you are Deputy Easton?"

"Yes, Mr. President." Marla shook his hand.

Division Chief Clooney stepped forward. "You two weren't easy to find."

"Somehow you managed," Dugan said.

"Your friend's CRV has a theft-prevention chip in it," Director Miller said.

Clooney faced Marla. "Where's your boy?"

Think. Think. Think. "We . . . we dropped him off at a relative back in Virginia."

Director Miller wagged his head. "The only stop you made in Virginia was at a rest stop."

Marla met the director's gaze. "That's where the relative met us."

"What relative?" Clooney asked.

"None of your business."

The three men exchanged glances.

The president cleared his throat. "Listen, we're on your side. You can trust us. We've come to help. Don't you realize you are in great danger?"

"Mr. President," Director Miller said, "we might be too late. The boy is missing. Obviously, Deputy Easton has been crying. Pugach may have gotten to them first."

The president turned to Miller. "But why would she lie?"

Miller shrugged. "To protect her son."

The president put his hand on Marla's shoulder. "Are we too late?"

Marla thought she might fall apart at any second but somehow held it together. "I told you, we left Gabe with a relative."

"Then you still have the Methuselah serum?" the president asked.

"No, we do not," Dugan said. "You can check us and search the vehicle. We don't have it."

"But did you have it in your possession earlier today?" Clooney asked.

Dugan lowered his eyes and shifted his feet. Marla crossed her arms.

The president's hand slipped from Marla's shoulder. "Please, if you know where it is, tell us. I am here in person because circumstances in my life have reached a crisis point. My daughter . . . my daughter . . ." The president's voice trailed off, and he stared at the ground.

"What about your daughter?" Marla asked.

The president inhaled through his nostrils and raised his head, his watery eyes blinking. "My daughter, Maria Ann, is dying of acute myeloid leukemia."

Marla sensed the pain in his voice. "And you're willing to go to extremes to save her life?"

"Yes," the president said. "The serum may be our only hope."

Marla reached and took the president's hand. "Then you must understand my predicament. My son is in great danger, and I'm willing to go to extremes to save his life."

"Listen," Clooney said. "You have a much better chance of seeing your son rescued if you let us help you."

Marla shook her head. "I'm not convinced of that. Don't ask me any more questions because I'm not saying another word."

Clooney turned to Dugan. "Sheriff Walton, you're a man of reason. Please cooperate with us."

"I'm sorry, but lately, my encounters with the FBI haven't been pleasant." Dugan put his arm around Marla's shoulder and pulled her close. "We're sticking together."

Director Miller crossed his arms. "Chances are Pugach will kill your boy whether we go after him or not. We have people who specialize in hostage rescue. At least there's an outside chance if you work with us."

"We'll keep that in mind," Dugan said. "Gentlemen, it's been a long three days. We're going home."

Most of the day Tuesday Mee Mee Roberts had kept her ear to the radio, hoping to keep abreast of the developing storm in the Atlantic. Several tourists had visited her bookstore that morning and wondered if they would have to cut their vacations short if the tropical storm became a hurricane. Mee Mee had given them her opinion without hesitation: *Go home. You do not want to be on the Outer Banks when a hurricane hits, even if only a category one storm.*

Mee Mee knew from experience. She'd opened the bookstore in 1984, the same year Diana hit. Gloria followed in '85, which passed right over Hatteras Island. Those two would have scared most new business owners off, but Mee Mee didn't scare easily. She picked up the pieces and started again. Hugo arrived in '89 but had spent most of its fury in the mountains before brushing the coast. In 1993 Emily showed up, her eye just thirteen miles off the shore of Hatteras Island, causing tremendous flooding and property damage. Then two hit in one year—Bertha and Fran in 1996. Things got worse in '99 when Dennis,

Floyd, and Irene battered the North Carolina coast in succession. The new millennium brought Isabel in 2003 and Irene in 2011 and a score of others in between. No doubt about it, living on the Outer Banks was a perilous proposition, especially during hurricane season.

At five in the afternoon, Mee Mee closed up shop. The weather reports weren't promising. Tropical storm Nadine would probably become a category one hurricane by the time it reached the island late Wednesday night. She stepped out of the front door onto the store's small porch and eyed the eastern sky. Cumulus clouds piled up over the horizon, but directly above, the sky remained clear blue. The breeze had picked up slightly but not anything out of the ordinary. Tomorrow at this time the outer bands of the storm would arrive, the wind velocity would increase, and rain would pour down. In the morning she would nail plywood to the windows, get gas for the generator, and stock up on emergency supplies.

She shook her head. Was she crazy for pitching her life's tent in the path of yearly whirlwinds? Most people would think so. To Mee Mee, though, it was worth it. Nothing compared to an early morning walk along the beach, the salt air, the roar of the waves, the surprises washed up on shore, the sunrises. Living on the Outer Banks gave her that sense of living on the edge: the edge of adventure, the edge of incredible beauty, the edge of the world, the edge of danger. The storm would blast through tomorrow night, and she would endure, pick up the pieces, put them back together, and reopen the bookstore, probably within a week. Mee Mee considered herself a tried and true Hatteras gal—tough, determined, unflappable.

She turned to head back into the store just as a golden Lexus zipped by. Was that Gabe in the passenger seat? The license plate was white with blue numbers and letters between two red horizontal lines. She couldn't see the name of the state, but obviously, the car wasn't local. *Couldn't have been Gabe.* The flash of the kid's face and dark brown, medium length hair just reminded her of the boy. Gabe and Marla had been on her mind all day. She hadn't seen them since Sunday afternoon at Lisa's Pizzeria in Rodanthe. She made a mental note to call Marla when she got home. With the hurricane coming, Mee Mee wanted to make sure they were well prepared.

On the way back to Washington, D.C., President Denzel Jackson stared down at the tops of trees as the helicopter passed over acres of Virginia forest. Hope for Maria Ann slowly drained away. How ironic, he thought. He was the candidate who had based his presidency on hope. Director Miller had promised him the FBI would do everything they could to locate the serum. They would tap phones, use highly sensitive listening devices, set up round-the-clock surveillance of Sheriff Walton and Deputy Easton in case the kidnapper contacted them, and begin an extensive manhunt.

President Jackson had ordered them to hold off on the dragnet. They had wanted to move now before it was too late, but he had insisted they wait, believing the kidnapper would kill the boy if he suspected any kind of pursuit. Maybe he would give his approval in the next hour or two, but it didn't feel right. Morally, he had always tried to take the high road, although his position as the most powerful man in the world made it tempting to cross those lines, especially when they became blurred by personal concerns. His hesitation to order the manhunt could cost his daughter's life.

Why had they arrived on the scene a few minutes too late? *Why, God, why?* Now a Russian gangster held the elixir of life in his hands, the panacea that could change the fate of the world. Some lowlife thug had seized the best hope of eradicating cancer from his daughter's body.

As the trees blurred below him, his mother's oft-repeated words echoed in his mind: *Denzel, honey, you can't see the forest for the trees.* He never understood what she meant when he was a kid. She had always seen his potential and worried about him wasting his God-given gifts like so many other young people who grew up on the wrong side of town. Unfortunately, his lack of insight and poor judgment as a teenager had resulted in several moral failures—alcohol and marijuana use, even some experimentation with cocaine and heroin.

His mother never gave up on him. She kept preaching the gospel of rising above his circumstances instead of floundering in them. Her prayers must have gotten through. During his senior year in high school he woke up. After several buddies went to jail for drug trafficking and a best friend died from an overdose, he began to understand the principle of reaping what you sow. Tragedy served as his teacher. It shocked him and frightened him and shook him and shattered him. But then it raised him up and opened his eyes to his own potential.

If bad decisions brought on destruction, then good decisions would build one upon another toward a successful future. That lesson he embraced with a passion. He envisioned himself rising above his surroundings to become a man of accomplishment and power. His love for the written and spoken word would clear his path. That was his gift—communication. At first he never imagined how far that gift would take him. With time, though, it became evident: he had that unique ability to connect with the common man and offer hope. In these financially and socially unstable times, people needed hope.

When the doctors had met with him and his wife to disclose the diagnosis of his daughter's illness, he struggled to maintain hope. He knew he had to be strong for his family and country. Then came news of the Methuselah serum. The reports seemed fantastic, the stuff of science fiction, but the more he researched the details, the higher his hopes climbed.

Now he faced reality. The odds were against retrieving the serum and formula. Maria Ann would probably die within the next year. He had prayed God's will be done many times. Was this God's will? How could it be? Then again, the serum reportedly reversed aging in the human cell. Perhaps God didn't want his design to be altered. *There is a time for every season, a time to be born and a time to die.* Clearly, the Creator didn't intend the temporary to be eternal. President Jackson sat back in his seat and crossed his arms. The forest abruptly ended as the copter flew over the gray-blue waters of the Chesapeake Bay. Soon they would pass over the grid of streets and highways of Washington, D.C. *The dragnet? What should I do about the dragnet?* He slipped his cell phone out of his breast pocket and scrolled to Director Miller's name on the contact list. *A simple phone call. This could be the hardest decision of my presidency.*

Marla feared Dugan would want to head home or to department headquarters to take care of any duties that had been neglected these last few days. However, when she asked him to stay at her house, he didn't hesitate. He said he wanted to be with her and do everything he could to offer his support. He'd call the office to check in but was sure everything was running smoothly without him. They drove to her house in Rodanthe and parked in the driveway.

Before she stepped out of the car, Marla fought off a strong impulse to tell Dugan she loved him. She had told him she loved him before, but that was as a friend. This was different. Somehow she kept her mouth shut. In the back of her mind she realized the stress and difficulties of the last few days may have sent her emotions into overdrive. She would wait until life settled down again before mentioning the "L" word. Maybe by then she would view those feelings from a different perspective.

Inside the house, Marla put on a pot of coffee, rummaged through the freezer, and found a frozen pizza. Dugan stood at the back window, staring at the sky. Marla turned on the oven and faced him. "Do you want some pizza?"

"I never say no to pizza."

"What're you looking at?"

"Just checking out the eastern horizon. We've got some hellacious weather coming our way tomorrow."

Marla crossed the room and stood beside him. "Do you think Gabe is somewhere on the Outer Banks?"

Dugan met her gaze, draped his arm around her shoulders, and pulled her close. "That's a good possibility. From Barco Pugach headed south. He may have turned west on 158 a half mile down the road. That would have been his last opportunity to avoid crossing over to the Outer Banks. Think about it, though. With the right contacts he could easily escape from here. A boat could pick him up on the sound side and then head out one of the inlets into the ocean. If he has enough money, the world becomes his oyster."

"And he'll find some country where no one cares who he is or what he's done."

"That's what he's hoping for anyway."

Marla took a long breath and swallowed in an effort to stifle the urge to cry. When she gained control, she said, "I don't care if he gets away with a boatload of money and lives to be a thousand, just so he doesn't harm Gabe and leaves him behind."

"There's no need for him to harm Gabe. What would be the point? Pugach is a hired gun. He kills for a reason not for pleasure."

"He told me he would keep his word."

"Sometimes even evil men take pride in their word."

"But . . . but . . ." Marla sniffed and wiped a tear from her eye. "He also promised he'd put a bullet through Gabe's head if the law came after him."

"I know . . . I know. Let's hope and pray President Jackson doesn't order a dragnet of the area."

The phone rang, making Marla jump. "I'm tenser than a turkey in November. Wonder who that could be."

"Remember. They probably tapped the line."

"Right."

She crossed the dining room, picked up the phone, and checked the caller ID. "It's Mee Mee." She pressed the talk button. "Hello."

"It's me. Haven't talked to you in a couple days. What's going on?"

Marla tried to make herself sound as calm and collected as possible. "Not much. Just hanging out at home."

"How are the investigations going?"

"They're coming along fine."

"I haven't seen much in the paper."

"Not much to report yet." Marla wondered how convincing she sounded. Mee Mee would be hard to fool.

"So you and Gabe are just hanging out at home?"

"Yep. Just chillin'."

"Could I talk to Gabe? I wanted to tell him about a new shark book that came in today."

"Uh . . ." Marla glanced around the room. *Think, think, think.* "He headed to the bathroom a few seconds ago. I'm not sure how long he'll be in there."

"That's okay. I can talk to him later. Are you ready for the storm?"

"We'll be ready."

"It's still a tropical storm, but it's gathering strength, probably a category one by the time it gets here tomorrow night. I could drop off some plywood and supplies tomorrow morning if you need anything."

"No. We'll be fine. You make sure you get the bookstore hurricane-ready."

"Is Gabe out of the bathroom yet?"

Marla paused and then said, "Not yet."

"Don't tell him about the book. I'll call back later."

"Okay. See ya."

"Bye."

Marla ended the call and placed the phone back onto the holder. Her eyes met Dugan's. "Mee Mee suspects something."

31

Gabe stared out the large glass door on the top floor of the big yellow house. He could see over the dunes to the ocean. To his left a long ramp led up to the top of a dune where a small building sat on posts. On the ocean side of the building a fishing pier reached a long way out into the sea. It reminded him of the pier in Rodanthe. The ugly man had driven through Rodanthe and Buxton right past Mee Mee's bookstore. Gabe had seen Mee Mee outside the store and wondered if she had spotted him. He tried to remember the name of the next little town where the ugly man parked in the driveway of the big yellow house. Was it Frisco?

The ugly man had told him that if he was a good boy nothing bad would happen. Gabe didn't believe him. He knew the ugly man killed people. If Gabe could figure out a way to escape, he'd go for it. He looked at the third-floor deck and saw the steps that led to the ground. He thought about opening the door and running for the steps. He jiggled the door handle, but it was locked. Glancing over his shoulder, he saw the ugly man sitting in the big chair and watching the weather channel on the big screen TV that hung above the fireplace. The weather guys kept talking about a bad storm. On the other side of the big room was the kitchen and dining area. Gabe thought about sneaking past him down the steps to the second floor and out the front door. If only he would fall asleep in the chair.

The ugly man stood and faced Gabe. "Boy, it's time for you to go in the bathroom."

"I don't have to pee," Gabe said.

He pointed to the bathroom door near the steps. "I don't care if you have to take a piss or not. Get in there!"

Gabe hurried across the shiny wooden floor and entered the bathroom.

The ugly man brought two cushions from the couch and dropped them unto the bathroom floor. "I'll let you out in the morning if you don't cause me any trouble." He closed the door.

Gabe heard the sound of something being slid across the floor. It sounded heavy. The couch? Then something bumped against the door and it moved slightly. I'm trapped in here, Gabe thought. He glanced around the room and saw the toilet, tub, and sink. On the wall opposite the door he noticed a window shaped like a stop sign. He walked to the window and looked up. The sky grew darker. He felt like crying. *Help me, God. Please send someone to save me.*

Dugan unfolded the sleeper sofa in the family room. Marla had suggested he sleep in Gabe's bed, but he wanted to keep his eye on the local news, and Gabe's room lacked a television. With the hurricane approaching, WITN, a local station, gave regular updates. They were predicting eighty-to-ninety-mile-per-hour winds—not the worst-case scenario but definitely strong enough to cause widespread damage. With debris flying, they would probably lose power sometime during the night. The biggest worry was flooding. Most of the houses on the Outer Banks were suspended above the ground on posts. However, with the storm surge, the streets may flood. This could cause complications if they went after Gabe.

That was a big "if." Dugan did his best to keep Marla hopeful, but he knew the grim reality: Pugach didn't care whether the boy lived or died. Gabe's fate would be dictated by the circumstances. Pugach wouldn't take any chances. If eliminating Gabe improved his odds of escape, he wouldn't hesitate doing the dirty deed. A rescue attempt offered better odds than trusting the word of a coldblooded murderer. Without thinking twice about it, Dugan would go after the boy, if only he knew where to find him.

Lying on the sofa bed, Dugan drifted in and out of sleep. The weather reports repeated themselves—the tropical storm edged closer gathering strength as it approached. Predicted arrival time—late tomorrow evening. A little after midnight he heard Marla's bedroom door open. He glanced over his shoulder to see her plodding toward him in red-and-white-striped pajamas. Tears streaked her face.

"Are you all right?" he asked.

She climbed onto the sofa bed next to him and leaned her head on his shoulder. "I just had a dream about Gabe."

Dugan clasped her hand. "Do you want to talk about it?"

Marla drew in a shaky breath. "I dreamed he was in a dark place crying for help, but I couldn't get to him."

"It was just a dream"

"I know but . . . I'm afraid . . . I'm afraid he won't make it out alive unless . . . unless someone rescues him."

The next morning Mee Mee Roberts decided to drive down to the little shopping center in Frisco to stock up on food and fill her tank at the Shell station before the storm arrived that evening. Then she'd stop at Dare Building and Supply in Buxton to pick up any supplies she needed to secure her house and store. Driving her Jeep Liberty 4 x 4 south along Highway 12, she couldn't help replaying her phone conversation with Marla over and over again in her mind. Something wasn't right. She could sense it in Marla's voice. Perhaps Gabe was in the bathroom and couldn't come to the phone, but she doubted it. The glimpse of that boy's face in the window of the golden Lexus as it flew by crystallized on the screen of her memory. What if the kid was Gabe? Why would he be in that car? Why wouldn't Marla tell the truth?

Mee Mee turned right off the main road into the small plaza and pulled up next to the gas pump. A stiff breeze greeted her when she climbed out of the car. The sky, a leaden gray, threatened rain. Three other customers tended their vehicles with nozzles in hand, and she nodded at Bob Bowman, a local banker who stopped in the bookstore occasionally. His comb-over fluttered in the wind, revealing his bald crown. With a lot of people fearing the worst, the flow of traffic heading north toward the bridges had increased. Overly cautious? Mee Mee wondered. Probably not. She slid her MasterCard through the pay slot, uncapped the tank, lifted the nozzle, and inserted it into the line. The smell of gasoline assaulted her nostrils.

When the feed kicked off, she capped the tank and replaced the nozzle. She eyed the lot for a parking space near the market. *Great, one space open by the entrance.* A golden flash zoomed by, and she glanced up to see a car, a Lexus, shoot into the empty space. *That's the one.* A man stepped out of the vehicle wearing a straw hat, sunglasses, and a black leather jacket. A white scar zigzagged down his cheek. He looked her way, and she averted her gaze, focusing on her car door. Glancing up again, she watched him enter the store. She opened her door, jumped in, started the engine, and drove slowly past the market. She didn't see a kid in the car but could read the license plate—CV-S001. She squinted to make out the words under the red horizontal rule: *Washington, D.C.* She stopped in front of the next store, Frisco Rod and Gun, and backed into an empty space. Her heart pounded into her throat. She took a deep breath. *What do I do now?*

Of course, she had to follow him, at least find out where he and the boy were staying. Then what? Call Marla again and try to figure out what's going on. Could this man have kidnapped Gabe? With the Methuselah investigation ongoing, anything was possible. But why would Marla not tell her. There had to be a reason. *Settle yourself down. This might not be anything at all.*

Behind her she heard the rap of a hammer. Glancing over her shoulder, she spied a man nailing plywood to the gun shop window. Smart thing to do. To her left, she noticed a clerk from the market applying duct tape to their front windows. Mee Mee preferred plywood. She'd been through enough of these storms to know better. Later on that afternoon she'd make sure her store windows were covered. Better safe than sorry.

Ten minutes later the man with the scar exited the store holding two bags of groceries. He placed one on the roof of the car and opened the back door. After putting the groceries onto the seat, he climbed in, started the vehicle, and backed out of the parking space. Mee Mee turned the ignition, and the Jeep's engine roared to life. She waited until he turned south on Highway 12 before pulling out. Keeping her distance, she leaned forward and concentrated on the back of the Lexus.

He drove about a mile and turned left on Cape Hatteras Pier Drive. By the time Mee Mee got to the turn, she noticed the car had disappeared. She spotted the Frisco Pier tackle shop suspended on large posts above the dunes with the long ramp leading up to it. She stopped and glanced to her right. He must have made a quick turn onto Sandpiper Drive. She spun the wheel and headed south along the residential street. Two houses down she spied the golden car parked in the driveway of a three-story yellow beach house. The man with the straw hat and scar mounted the steps to the second floor. Mee Mee drove on past at a normal rate of speed, hoping the guy didn't notice her. *Mission accomplished. Now to get home and call Marla.*

Gabe liked Honey Nut Cheerios but wanted something different. He had eaten two bowls for breakfast and two for lunch. That's the only kind of food the ugly man would give him. The smell of fried fish from the kitchen made his mouth water. Maybe the man would offer him fish for supper. He hoped so, but more than that he hoped and prayed someone would rescue him. The ugly man had a strange look in his eyes that scared him. The holster and pistol strapped across his shoulder and chest didn't help. Gabe wondered how many people he had killed. Would Gabe be next?

On the counter by the refrigerator sat Blackie. The ugly man had told Gabe not to touch the pirate teddy bear. Gabe knew why. He had seen the ugly man pour some of the green liquid into another bottle. Then he had taken the first bottle, which was about half full, and wrapped it along with the important paper into a white towel. He had stuffed the towel back into Blackie's belly and zipped him up. The ugly man must have thought that Blackie made a great hiding place. Gabe wished he could take Blackie with him when the ugly man shut him in the bathroom. He didn't feel so nervous with Blackie by his side.

Gabe heard noises downstairs, a door opening.

"Anybody home?" a deep voice yelled.

The ugly man pulled the pistol out of his holster and walked to the top of the steps. "I'm up here!"

"There's three of us. We're coming up. We've got your money so don't do anything stupid."

Gabe heard footsteps getting louder and then they stopped. Someone said, "Whoa! Why the gun?"

"Just making sure you didn't bring some trigger-happy goon with you."

"We're not the Capone gang from Chicago. We're here to do business. Deal straight with us, and we'll deal straight with you."

The ugly man stuck the gun back into his holster. "Come on up. Supper's almost ready."

"Fresh fish. Smells good."

The ugly man backed away, and three guys wearing suits appeared at the top of the steps. One was fat with short gray hair. He had big lips and a red face and carried a black suitcase. Next to him stood a short guy with brown hair and muscular arms. He had lots of small dents on his face. The other man was really old, tall, skinny, and bald.

The fat man pointed at Gabe. "Who's this, your son?"

The ugly man shook his head. "He's my insurance policy."

The old, tall man raised his hand. "We agreed there would be no other witnesses. Just us four. Why the kid?"

"He's the reason no one knows where we are," the ugly man said. "Trust me."

"Looks like we have to trust you whether we like it or not," the old man said.

"Now, now, Pemberton," the fat one said, "I'm sure Mr. Pugach has a plan in place to keep this young one quiet."

"Yeah," the ugly man said. "I'm good at keeping people quiet. Where's the money?"

The fat man lifted the suitcase. "One million bucks in one hundred dollar bills. Traveling money. Once we get on the boat tomorrow we'll head out one of the inlets and make our way to Welles Island."

"Welles Island?" the ugly man said.

"It belonged to my father. Now it's mine. It's about fifty miles south of here. Very private. There we'll work out the details for the rest of the funds."

"I'll take the money." The ugly man reached and grabbed the suitcase from the fat man. He crossed the dining room and headed down the steps.

"Must not trust us," the fat man said.

"I don't trust him," the old man whispered.

A couple of minutes later the ugly man appeared at the top of the steps. "The food's about ready. Grab yourself something to drink out of the fridge and have a seat."

The three men walked to the refrigerator. The fat man opened it, and they took turns reaching in to get their drinks. After they sat down at the table, the ugly man brought a big plate of fish from the stove. Gabe noticed a bowl of corn and another bowl of green beans on the table. His stomach growled. It had been a long time since he had eaten his last bowl of Cheerios.

"Tell me, Welles," the brown-haired man said, "can this house withstand a hurricane? It'll be here in an hour or two."

The fat man laughed. "It's been through ten hurricanes. A little damage here or there but nothing major. Besides, last I heard it was still a tropical storm. We might get eighty or ninety mile an hour winds. This house has seen a lot worse."

The old man swallowed and wiped his mouth with a napkin. "Too bad we have to spend the night here."

The fat man stabbed a piece of fish with his fork. "You definitely don't want to go back out on that boat tonight."

"Hmmmph." The old man raised a beer bottle and took a drink. "Let's just hope the boat's still there in the morning."

"You worry too much, Pemberton." The fat man slapped the old man's back. "The boat'll be safe on the sound side. If not, I'll make a phone call. In two hours we'll have another boat."

As the four men ate, the fat man did most of the talking. The ugly man hardly said a word. The fat man liked to talk about money and cars and houses. The old man didn't seem very happy. He reminded Gabe of a neighbor who always yelled whenever a baseball or football bounced onto his property. The brown-haired man bragged about how big his company had grown. He claimed it was due to hard work and good decisions—lessons he had learned in high school when he was a halfback on the football team. Small but Mighty they had called him.

After they ate, the fat man reached inside his suit jacket and pulled out a cigar. "I brought some Cubans for the occasion. Anybody care for one? Simmons?"

"No thanks," the brown-haired man said.

"I'll take one," the old man said.

The ugly man reached into his shirt pocket. "I prefer Camels." He took a cigarette out of the pack.

The fat man reached in the direction of the ugly man, flicked a lighter, and lit his cigarette. Then the fat man lit the old man's cigar and his own. They puffed, causing smoke to gather above the table.

The brown-haired man coughed. "I thought we came here to get younger and healthier."

The fat man blew out a smoke ring. "And richer."

"Why the hell are you smoking then?"

"I've smoked all my life," the old man said. "It hasn't killed me."

"Yet," the brown-haired man said.

The old man shook the ash off his cigar. "Only if the serum doesn't work."

"It works," the ugly man said.

"What are we waiting for then." The old man held the cigar like a nurse holds a needle and pointed it toward his arm. "Let's put it into our veins."

"Any time you're ready," the ugly man said.

"We're ready," the fat man said. "Go get the needles."

The old man raised his hand. "Wait a minute. I don't want the boy watching this."

The ugly man shifted his eyes to where Gabe sat on the big chair across the room. "Hey, boy, it's time for you to go into the bathroom."

Gabe climbed off the chair. "Can I have something to eat?"

"Not right now." The ugly man thumbed toward the bathroom. "Get in there."

Gabe hung his head and walked into the bathroom. The ugly man walked over and shut the door. Then Gabe heard the sound of the couch being shoved against the wall. He was trapped inside again. He walked over and looked up through the window on the opposite wall. The sky was very dark and he could hear the wind howling like a wolf. Rain splattered against the glass. He closed his eyes and prayed that God would send help.

When the telephone rang, Marla snatched it from the charging base and checked the caller ID. "It's Clooney."

"Better answer it," Dugan said.

The FBI hadn't called them since they had arrived home. "Hello."

"This is Division Chief Clooney. Have you heard anything from the kidnapper?"

"You tell me. Haven't you tapped our phones and staked out my house?"

"We've taken some measures to help protect you, but still, we don't know everything. Maybe he found another way to contact you."

"Oh please. Anything you do places my son in greater danger."

"Ma'am, we're sorry about how all this went down. We're trying to do our best."

Marla felt like screaming. "Just stay out of our lives until we pick up my boy."

"That's one reason I called. Until now the president has postponed the manhunt. He didn't want our movements to alarm Pugach and risk the boy's life. But it's been two days."

One day and a few hours, Marla thought. "So the president is ordering a dragnet?"

"Once the storm passes, probably early tomorrow morning, we'll begin. That's why I need to know if Pugach contacted you or not."

"Damn all of you." Marla hung up the phone. She felt like an air mattress that had been snagged on a nail. Her eyes met Dugan's. "President Jackson ordered a manhunt to begin after the storm."

"There's got to be something we can do." The phone rang again. "He's calling back."

Marla checked the ID. "No. It's Mee Mee." She had called earlier that day, but they decided not to answer. Marla didn't want to have to lie about Gabe again. Mee Mee had left a message—*Please call me back. It's very important.* Of course, Marla didn't call back, although the strain in Mee Mee's voice made her wonder what was up. The phone rang three more times before the message recorder picked up.

"It's me again. Hey, I just wanted to let you know about that used car you asked about last week. Remember? That golden Lexus. I know where the owner lives. Give me a call if you're still interested. Anyway, keep safe. Hopefully the storm won't do too much damage. Talk to you later."

Dugan tilted his head. "The golden Lexus?"

Marla shook her head. "That's the car Pugach was driving. She's spotted Gabe. She knows where he is."

"Don't jump to conclusions."

"What else could it be? I'm not interested in a used car. The manhunt starts in the morning. We've got to do something *now*. I'm calling her back."

"Wait. Be careful what you say. They're listening."

Marla closed her eyes and ran through a conversation in her mind, something that wouldn't sound suspicious. Then she picked up the phone and dialed Mee Mee's number.

Mee Mee answered after one ring.

"Hey, this is Marla. Just got your message. I'm still interested in that Lexus."

"Marla? Is that you? Your voice is breaking up. Must be the storm."

"Can you hear me? Listen, I'll stop by sometime soon and we can go see the guy."

"Hello? Hello?"

The line went dead. Outside, the wind velocity increased, and the house creaked and shuddered like an old man waking from a nightmare.

32

When the phone went dead, Mee Mee's mind whirled. Now what? She had made out enough of Marla's words to know the golden Lexus meant something. But what? If the man with the scar had kidnapped Gabe, then obviously Marla didn't want it mentioned over the phone. Why else would she lie and say Gabe was with her? Someone was listening in on her phone conversations. The FBI? Mee Mee remembered the discussion at Lisa's Pizzeria about the Medical Mafia mentioned in Sylvester's journal. Maybe they had something to do with this. Whoever it was, Marla didn't want them to know Gabe's location. But what could she do? She wasn't sure, but she had to do something.

Her Jeep Liberty 4 x 4 was parked under her house, which was elevated on pilings. She had driven the vehicle through a lot a bad weather but never through a hurricane. She worried about flooding. If the water from the storm surge rose above the road two or three feet, the car could stall out and maybe get washed into the Pamlico Sound. She lived halfway between Buxton and Frisco, about three miles from the

Frisco pier. The hurricane had just arrived. Certainly the roads hadn't flooded yet. If she could make it to Frisco, she could at least peek in the windows of the yellow beach house to see if she could spot Gabe. Then what? *I'll jump that hurdle if I get there.*

She rushed into the kitchen and opened the drawer where she kept her tools. *Might need to break a window.* She snatched a hammer and hurried to the coat closet. There she found her good jacket, one that was well-lined with a water-repellent outer fabric. *One more thing.* She hurried to the bedroom, opened the top drawer of the nightstand and pulled out her Smith and Wesson pistol. She checked to make sure it was loaded, slipped it into her jacket pocket, and then headed for the door.

When she stepped onto her little porch, the gale almost blew her over. Wiry and strong, she only weighed about a hundred and ten pounds. To counteract the force, she had to lean into the wind and hold tightly to the railing as she descended the steps. Leaves and twigs pelted her. At the bottom of the stairs she broke away from the railing and pressed toward the car. Under the house the wind eased slightly. She worked her way around the Jeep, opened the door, and climbed into the seat. Blinking her eyes, she wiped the rain droplets from her face, scooped the keys out of her jacket pocket, and started the car. *What am I getting myself into?* She shifted into drive and pulled onto the narrow lane.

The downpour blurred her windshield, making it difficult to see the road. She set the wipers on high. *That's better, thank God.* Traveling at about ten miles per hour, she focused intently ahead, trying to see through the deluge. She flicked on her brights, but that didn't help, creating too much glare against the sheets of rain. Large plastic trash cans tumbled across the lane. Branches came hurtling at her, slapping the windshield. Ahead she saw the stop sign where she would turn right onto Buccaneer Drive. A whoosh of green flailed before the headlights as a tree slammed to the ground. She hit the brakes. *Shoot!* She eyed the branches and trunk. *It's only a medium sized tree. I think we can get over it. Come on, ol' Liberty, show me what you got.* She engaged the four-wheel drive and crept forward. The tires rumbled over the smaller branches as the leaves folded under the car. But then the trunk halted the Jeep's progress. *Come on, now.* Mee Mee gave it more gas, and the vehicle jolted over the trunk. *Atta girl.*

She eyed the stop sign as she came to the end of her lane. It convulsed in the wind like a damaged kite. Must be blowing at seventy miles per hour at least, Mee Mee guessed. Buccaneer Drive headed east toward the ocean for about four hundred yards into the teeth of the wind. She could feel the vehicle bulling forward as if fighting off invisible linemen. The wind had ripped several large branches off nearby trees and scattered them across the road. As the Jeep rumbled over them, Mee Mee prayed nothing would puncture the tires. Street lights and porch lights flickered and went out. No more power. It took forever, but finally she reached Route 12, the main highway. She turned right and headed south toward Frisco.

Now the winds buffeted the left side of the vehicle, rocking it as Mee Mee forged ahead. Just past the miniature golf course and go-cart track the road dipped down near a large pond. The Jeep's lights cut through the slashing rain and illuminated the flooded roadway. The pond, fed by the surging ocean water, had overrun the highway. She hit her brakes. The water appeared to be rising and flowing toward the sound. *I've got to take the chance.* She edged forward, and the front tires entered the water. As she proceeded slowly, the dark water rose around her. She heard trickling and realized it was seeping into the interior through the door cracks. The engine sputtered and died. The water lifted the car and drifted it toward the Pamlico Sound.

Mee Mee felt helpless. She swiveled her head, trying to survey her surroundings, but the rain and darkness made it difficult to see the best direction to head for land. *I've got to get out of this car before it goes under.* She unbuckled her seat belt and rolled down the window. As water spilled in, she managed to climb through the opening. The shock of the cold water almost paralyzed her. The lining of her coat sopped up water like a sponge, becoming heavy. It dragged her toward the bottom. She needed air. Trying to fight off the panic that threatened to seize her, she unzipped the jacket and slipped out of it. She shot upward and broke the surface, gasping for breath. The strong current carried her away. Her only hope was to swim harder than she'd ever swum in her life.

She tried to swim but made little progress. The flow had carried her into the Pamlico Sound. She could make out the dark shapes of houses along the shore about a hundred yards away. Growing tired, she battled to keep her head above the surface. A tree trunk floated by, an old oak. She latched on to it and gasped for air, her lungs heaving. Swimming seemed like a waste of energy against the current. Branches and debris littered the surface of the water. As she held on for dear life to the tree, she noticed the shoreline receding. Her limbs shivered, and her teeth chattered. Something brushed against her arm. In the darkness she barely identified the serpentine form—a cottonmouth! She sucked in a quick breath and held it. The snake slid by her, propelling itself by swerving back and forth in an "S" pattern. *God help me. If I don't start swimming again, I'll end up on the North Carolina mainland.* She hugged the tree and started kicking her feet, like a swimmer who uses a float to practice his leg technique. No use. The unrelenting wind and swift current made progress impossible. Clearly, she was at the mercy of the current. At least the log helped her to stay afloat.

Dugan suggested they wait a couple hours before venturing into the storm. He didn't want to leave immediately after Mee Mee's phone call for fear their departure would raise the suspicions of the agents assigned to watch them. Marla agreed, believing Pugach would wait out the storm before making any moves concerning Gabe. If they could find the house sometime during the night, she would be willing to take a calculated risk and make a rescue attempt. No way did Marla want to jeopardize Gabe's life. If circumstances appeared too precarious, they would have to depend on Pugach's word and wait for his call.

Shortly after midnight they stepped out into the blast of air and pressed through the downpour toward the CRV. Dugan covered the interior lights as soon as he opened the door. He hoped the agents, wherever they may be stationed, weren't paying attention. He started the engine but kept the headlights off. As they left the driveway, Marla panned the surroundings to make sure no one followed them.

The plan was to drive to Mee Mee's house, thirty minutes away on the other side of Buxton. From there Mee Mee could lead them to where she'd spotted the golden Lexus, probably to some beach house in Frisco. Dugan had placed Marla's Magnum in his jacket pocket. Marla hoped he wouldn't have to use it. She had tried to convey to Mee Mee some semblance of a plan over the phone without giving away anything to the feds. Unfortunately, the line went dead before much could be said. Mee Mee was a sharp gal, though. Marla prayed she would be waiting at her house and ready to help them.

Driving through the hurricane proved horrendous. After two hours of weaving through fallen branches and debris and creeping along the partially flooded highway, they reached Buccaneer Drive.

"Not far now," Marla said. "She lives about a quarter mile from here."

"If Mee Mee could lead us to the house, I'm sure I could figure out a way to break in and find Gabe."

"We'll see," Marla said. "I'm afraid Pugach won't be asleep when we get there. How can anyone sleep through this storm? If he's up and walking around, I don't want to take the chance."

"You know how much I love your boy. I'll only do what you want me to do."

"I know you will. We just need to be careful."

"You can count on me."

"Dugan . . ."

"Yeah."

"I love you." Marla couldn't believe she said the words. They just spilled out.

Dugan glanced at her and then back at the road. "I love you, too."

Marla pointed to the left. "Turn here. That's Mee Mee's street."

Dugan didn't drive far before they encountered a fallen tree. He hit the brakes and skidded to a stop. "Look at those tire marks on the trunk. Someone drove over it once already. I think we can do it. This CRV has all-wheel drive."

As the little SUV clambered over the tree, a sinking fear settled like wet cement in Marla's stomach. Dugan drove to the end of the lane and turned into Mee Mee's driveway. Marla stared at the empty space under the house. *Those were Mee Mee's tire tracks. She took off on her own.*

Ogden Welles had never felt this good in decades. The Methuselah serum was fantastic, invigorating, empowering. He stretched out on the recliner in his bedroom and extracted a Cuban from his shirt pocket. What a night they had had. After injecting the serum everyone's attitude changed. Even old Pemberton came to life. They felt like they had joined an exclusive fraternity, one reserved for the rich, the powerful, and the eternally young. Very few members belonged to this elite club, and he wanted to keep it that way. His two partners, Pemberton and Simmons, were in agreement. The Methuselah Triumvirate now controlled the spigot on the Fountain of Youth. Access to its rejuvenating powers would not be cheap. Was eternal life worth a billion dollars a dose? He thought so.

He lit the cigar and puffed it, savoring its flavor, its aroma, its richness. A bottle of Jim Beam sat beside the chair. He gripped the neck of the bottle, raised it to his lips, and took a swig. The whiskey went down smoothly, and he returned the bottle to the floor and let out a satisfied sigh. After injecting the serum, they had decided to play some poker. Even Pugach joined in. The howling of the storm outside didn't faze them. Luckily, the generators supplied plenty of power after the lights went out. They had laughed, sung, drunk wine, and gambled until two in the morning. Welles had lost twenty thousand dollars, but he didn't care. Hell, with possession of the formula and control of production and dispensation of the serum he would become one of the wealthiest and most powerful men in the world. He pictured himself as a king on a golden throne, looking forward to a long reign.

Tomorrow they would head out on his yacht, slip through the Oregon Inlet, and sail to Welles Island. There they would finish up their dealings with Pugach. What a thug. Welles hoped Pugach would find some remote corner of the world and disappear, never to show his ugly face again. Pugach had informed them he wouldn't turn over the formula and serum until the transactions were completed and the funds secured in several accounts he had set up somewhere in Europe. Who cares if they had to pay him a cool billion. It would be worth it to be rid of him.

The boy was definitely a problem. Pugach told them not to worry, that he'd take care of the boy. Poor kid. Welles figured the heel would toss him into the ocean when no one was looking somewhere between here and Welles Island. Too bad. The kid wasn't his responsibility, though. If Pugach decided to x-out the boy, that would be another stain on the killer's soul, not his. However, it would eliminate a witness—a small but tragic sacrifice. Oh well, what could he do about it?

Welles puffed on the cigar and then folded his hands in his lap, being careful not to touch the lit end to his gray gabardine pants He stared at the ceiling and forced the boy's face out of his mind. He had other things to think about, dreams and fantasies once impossible but now within his grasp. When he regained his youth he would begin exercising again and chasing women. He had been impotent for years. Of course, he would carefully manage this new priceless commodity, but he wanted to have fun, too. He had worked hard all his life to build his pharmaceutical empire. Now he would finally have time to enjoy the spoils of his labor. His eyelids became heavy. He took a deep, relaxing breath and imagined himself in the arms of a young Elizabeth Taylor.

Mee Mee had floated with the current for about an hour. Flashes of lightning lit brief glimpses of the storm's fury—pine trees snapping and oaks uprooting, shingles and tin roofing whirling through the air like candy wrappers. Certainly, Nadine had whipped up beyond the predicted category one status. Mee Mee had no idea how far south she had drifted. After another half hour of watching the lightning show, she noticed land extending farther out into the sound. Could that be Sandy Bay? This was her chance. She released the log and swam toward the shoreline. After fifteen minutes of slicing through the water, her arms and legs felt like lead. She rested, dog paddling. Lightning split the black sky, illuminating the shoreline about a hundred yards away. *Progress!* With renewed determination she stroked and kicked for another ten minutes.

Exhausted, she reached the bank and crawled onto land. She lay in the marsh, lungs heaving. It smelled of peat and salt. She tried to rise up on her arms but her muscles wouldn't cooperate. She closed her eyes, shivering. *Rest a few minutes. Regain your strength.* The wind whipped over her as if she were speeding down the interstate in a convertible. She figured it must be two or three in the morning. How far had the current carried her away from Frisco? She had no idea. After about ten minutes she rose to her hands and knees. She rocked back and pushed with her arms in an effort to stand, but the blast caught her square in the chest and blew her backwards. Her foot slipped down the bank and she tumbled into the water. Survival adrenaline kicked in, and she scrambled, kicked, and clawed until she made it back to the spartina grass against the shoreline. Using her remaining strength, she crawled back up on the bank. Everything went black.

When Mee Mee regained consciousness, she had no idea how long she'd been lying there. I'm *going to have to crawl to get out of here.* She lifted her head and squinted against the wind. She scrabbled on her hands and knees for about two hundred yards through the muck and mire of a marshy section of ground, altering her course several times to avoid flooded areas. Finally she reached a road. The wind velocity had decreased slightly, the heart of the storm now moving across the Pamlico Sound to the mainland. She tried to stand again. This time she managed to stay erect, leaning into the gale. Ahead she spotted a house. There she could find a respite on the lee side and rest her weary body until she recovered enough to move on.

Inch by inch she plodded forward, slipping and falling a couple times on the wet grass. Each time she struggled to her feet and trudged on. Finally she made it to the darkened house. She stumbled onto the porch and beat on the door, but no one answered. Must be an empty rental, she thought. It felt so good to be out of the wind. Where was she? She spied an address placard next to the door: 56161 Austin Lane. She recognized the street name. She had landed on the north side of Hatteras, about two miles south of Frisco. That was a lonely stretch of road, one of the narrowest strips on the Outer Banks with very few houses. She plopped down on the deck and pressed her back against the wall of the house. Ten minutes of rest out of the wind, that's all she needed. She leaned her head against her hands, elbows on her knees, and closed her eyes. After a few minutes she caught herself falling asleep and jerked awake. She listened and noticed the volume of the storm had decreased. Everything felt numb, and her wet clothes didn't help.

She forced herself to stand, took a deep breath, and headed out into the wind. Austin Lane met with Austin Road, which led back out to Highway 12. The wind had died down to about forty or fifty miles per hour. Still, as fatigued as she felt, each step took a major effort. One step at a time, she kept telling herself—one step at a time.

33

For a mile and a half Mee Mee trudged up Route 12, leaning against the wind and slogging through deep puddles on the road. The rain slacked off to a drizzle, and the wind gradually decreased. Just before reaching Frisco a slight glimmer appeared on the eastern horizon. The sun would rise in another hour. The faint light enabled her to see the way ahead, but what appeared disheartened her—a wide swath of water covered the highway. The ocean waves thundered to her right and the Pamlico Sound stretched out to her left. She couldn't tell if the road had been washed out or just submerged. How deep was it? She didn't have the strength left to struggle against a strong current. If she got swept out into the sound or the ocean, she could easily drown.

The yellow beach house was about a half mile away. Was Gabe even there? She imagined him alone and crying, locked in a room. With the storm ending and dawn approaching, the kidnapper may be ready to move out. Mee Mee eyed the dark surface. *Everybody's gotta go toes up sooner or later.* She stepped into the water, and the shock of the cold stiffened her whole body. Her arm and leg muscles tensed so much she staggered forward like the Tin Man into the depths. Halfway across, the water rose to her chest. She felt the tug of the current toward the sound. *Keep going. Don't stop now.*

On her next step the ground disappeared. She went under, realizing the road bed had been washed away. With what energy she had left, she kicked and stroked, struggling to reach the surface. She broke through to air and gasped for breath. With her head above water she got her bearings. The current slowly drifted her toward the sound. Everything felt so heavy. She could barely sweep her arms through the water, but she kept trying. Her hamstrings cramped, but she kept kicking. She swam for about two minutes before her muscles refused to respond—total lactic acid build up. She sank. When she hit bottom, she pressed her hands on the smooth surface of asphalt. *The road! Stand up! Get up!* She managed to get her feet under her and rise. She needed air. Looking up, she could see the surface of the water above her. Her hand broke through. She jumped and fluttered her arms to get her head above the surface. She took two quick breaths and went down again. Under water, she couldn't see the road. *Walk straight.* She took three slow-motion steps, stood on tiptoes, and lifted her face to the sky. Her nose broke the surface, and she breathed in air and water. She coughed and held her breath for two more steps. Now her face cleared the surface, and she gulped air between coughs. She plodded on, and the water level lowered with every step until she reached the other side.

She stood dripping on the yellow line in the middle of the road, hands on her knees, heaving air. Her head spun. *God give me the strength.* After several minutes she stood, shivering. *One step at a time. One foot in front of the other.*

It took her ten minutes to walk the final half mile to the yellow beach house. She peered down the long concrete driveway lined with sea oats and spotted the golden Lexus. Next to the car, wide steps led up to the second-floor porch, the main entrance of the house. On the left side of the structure she noticed another staircase rising to a deck on the second floor that probably wrapped around to the back of the place, giving each bedroom outside deck access. She guessed there would be five or six bedrooms on that floor—good places to check for Gabe. The sun hadn't risen yet, but the glow in the eastern sky above the sea painted the surroundings with pale tones. She headed for the side stairway, hoping the kidnapper wouldn't spot her.

Mee Mee climbed the steps as quietly as possible and peeked in the first window. She spied an older man on a king-size bed, lying on his back with his arms and legs spread and mouth wide open, sleeping soundly. No Gabe. She couldn't see in the next two rooms because the blinds were closed. As she expected, the deck wrapped around the back of the house to the ocean side. An interior light glowed through the next window's half-open blinds. She glimpsed a man leaning over the bed and opening a black suitcase. Immediately, she drew back from the window. Was it the man with the scar? Was he packing?

She edged to the window again and peeked. The man with the scar hovered over the suitcase placing stacks of money into it. He wore a white tank-top with a holster and pistol strapped to his chest. His muscular arms were covered with tattoos. Mee Mee quickly scanned the room but didn't see Gabe. She dropped to her knees and crawled below the window.

She hurried to the next window, but the blinds were closed. She slipped by and headed to the last window on the back side. At the end near the railing, steps led up to the third floor deck. Maybe they kept Gabe on the top floor. The blinds were open on the last window by the steps. Mee Mee took a quick peek. Smoke clouded the room. Through the haze she spied a heavyset man stretched out on a recliner. On the floor a whiskey bottle had fallen over where flames shot up from the carpet. Something had caught the spilled alcohol on fire. The man didn't move as the flames licked at the leather recliner.

"Oh no! Where's Gabe?" she gasped. A new surge of adrenaline charged her weary body. She rushed to the steps and clambered up to the top deck. A sliding glass door looked in upon the great room. She pressed up to the glass. Scanning the room, she noticed a large couch had been pushed against a door on the other side of the dining area. *He's trapped in that room.* She reached for the handle and pulled but the door didn't budge. *I need something to break the window. Where's my hammer?* Then she remembered her hammer and pistol had gone down with her jacket.

She spun and spotted a huge ceramic flower pot with a fern sprouting from it. She grabbed the lip of the pot and pulled it onto its side. With her other hand she clasped the bottom. Crouching, she took a deep breath, lifted the pot, and then stood. Using every ounce of strength left in her arms, she thrust it toward the window. With a loud crash it shattered the glass and burst onto the great room floor, the dirt spilling and shards tumbling.

Mee Mee stepped through the jagged hole. From below, she heard the footfalls of someone charging up the steps. She halted, eyes wide, mind whirling. The man with the scar bounded up the last few steps and trained his pistol on her.

"Who are you?" he demanded.

"I'm your neighbor. Your house is on fire."

"Right." He stepped closer and raised the gun, aiming at her forehead. "I don't believe you."

A smoke alarm blared from the second floor. The man's dark eyes narrowed.

"Can't you smell it?" Mee Mee asked.

He sniffed the air, eyes widening with alarm. "My money!" He whirled and dashed down the stairs.

Mee Mee bolted to the couch, clamped her hands onto the back, and tugged with all her might. The couch inched away from the door. Using her legs, she thrust backwards, moving it farther.

The door popped open, and Gabe peeked out. "Mee Mee!"

"Come on, Sport." Mee Mee reached and grabbed Gabe's hand. "We need to hightail it out of here." She turned and led him to the sliding glass door. Quickly she flipped the dead bolt and slid the door open so they wouldn't have to duck through the broken glass.

"Wait a minute!" Gabe hollered. He broke free of Mee Mee's grip and charged across the great room into the kitchen.

Mee Mee couldn't believe it. "Gabe! We've got to get out of here!"

Gabe snagged a raggedy teddy bear off the counter next to the refrigerator. He turned and sprinted toward Mee Mee. "I've got Blackie!"

Mee Mee heard someone stomping up the steps. "Let's go!"

They shot out the door and unto the deck.

"Stop!" the man with the scar yelled.

"Down the steps, Gabe."

The boy descended, feet shuffling in a blur. Mee Mee glanced over her shoulder and saw the kidnapper lugging the big suitcase through the door. She didn't see the gun in his hand. Did he set it down? She couldn't keep up with Gabe. At the bottom, he turned left and cut across the yard around the pool toward the wooden fence. If he could just get to the neighbor's house.

Mee Mee had to do something to slow down the kidnapper. At the bottom of the steps she turned and faced him. He wasn't far behind.

"Get the hell out of my way!"

He swung the suitcase at her. She clamped her arms around it as it struck her, and she pulled it to the ground when she fell. The force of the fall helped break his grip. She lay on the ground, hugging the suitcase full of money. He kicked the suitcase, but she held on.

He reached into his jeans pocket and whipped out a switchblade. With a flick, the blade flashed open. "I will cut your throat."

"Hey you!" Gabe yelled. He stood on the other side of the wooden fence in the neighbor's yard and held up the teddy bear. "I've got Blackie!"

The man's mouth dropped open. "The serum!" He pivoted and sprinted after the boy.

Gabe ran to the gate, flipped the latch, and burst through onto the street. He glanced back and saw the ugly man jump over the first fence. Gabe turned toward the ocean and spotted the ramp that led up to the yellow building on top of the dunes. *The Frisco fishing pier.* He remembered the story about Johnny and the bully the old woman had told him the night he caught the shark at the Rodanthe pier. He sprinted toward the ramp.

Gabe was a good runner, but he knew the man was strong and probably fast. When he reached the ramp, he looked back. The ugly man had already jumped the second fence. He charged toward Gabe with the knife in his hand. Gabe gripped Blackie's arm as tightly as he could and dashed up the ramp. The doors to the little yellow building had been blown open by the storm. Gabe rushed through the room, leaping over fishing poles and racks of jackets and hats. The wind had turned the little fishing store upside-down. He flew out the doors on the other side. The hurricane had beat up the pier something awful. Some of the boards were buckled and the walkway drooped in places. Behind him, Gabe heard the man tromping through the building.

Gabe took off. He could feel the pier swaying as he ran, making it hard to keep his balance. He leapt over a gap in the walkway and tumbled to the wooden boards. Glancing up, he saw the man closing in on him. He scrambled to his feet and took off down the damaged walkway.

The second half of the pier looked like a rollercoaster. It went up and down with a bunch of the floorboards missing. Gabe could hear the roar of the ocean and see the swirling water forty feet below through the gaps, but he kept running up and down the walkway, stepping over the missing boards.

Near the end, the walkway had split apart. He skidded to a stop on the edge and stared down at the splintered wood and the space between him and the other side which had dropped down several feet. The waves crashed against the posts below, making the pier rock back and forth. Could he jump that far? He had to. The man was almost on top of him. He took three steps back. Just as the man lunged for him, he shot forward and leapt. His body thudded against the wooden planks, and he let go of Blackie. As he slid down, he dug his fingernails into the wood to stop from falling off the edge. His legs dangled toward the ocean.

The teddy bear lay above him out of reach.

"Give me your hand," the ugly man growled. "I'll pull you back over."

Gabe glanced over his shoulder. The ugly man hung on to the railing and leaned in Gabe's direction, his hand outstretched to him.

Gabe couldn't reach him and didn't trust him anyway. He clawed his way up the boards, grabbed Blackie, and turned over.

The ugly man stood above him on the other side. "Listen to me little boy. Throw me that teddy bear."

Gabe shook his head and crab-crawled backwards up the boards.

"Throw me the teddy bear, and I won't hurt you. If I have to jump across to get it, I swear I'll toss you in the ocean."

Gabe had climbed to where it was level enough to stand. The end of the pier wasn't far away. He sprang to his feet and bolted toward the end of the pier. Behind him he heard the loud clomp of the man landing on the wood. *He's coming after me.* Gabe skidded to a stop at the railing. Peering over, he saw the ocean churning below. He spun, faced the ugly man, and held up Blackie.

"Now you're getting smarter." The man reached toward Gabe. "Hand it over."

Gabe twirled and flung the bear into the ocean.

The ugly man rushed to the railing. "You stupid little bastard!"

Gabe backed away, watching the man. He kept looking for Blackie in the ocean.

"I see it!" The man pointed. "It's floating!" He lifted one leg then the other over the railing and jumped.

Gabe heard a splash. He stepped up to the railing and peered over. The man thrashed around in the water.

"I've got it! I've got it!" The ugly man held up Blackie.

A rip tide began to suck him out into the ocean. He kicked and splashed but couldn't break away from the strong current. Gabe watched as the man became smaller and smaller and then disappeared.

"Gabe!" a woman's voice called.

He turned to see Mee Mee standing on the edge of the fractured pier. Gabe walked to the edge of his side. "Should I try to jump?"

"No! That's at least a five feet gap, and you're a lot lower than me. I saw some rope along the railing back along the pier. Just wait there."

With the pier swaying, it seemed like it took Mee Mee forever to get the rope. Finally she made it back and tossed him one end of the rope.

"Tie it around your chest, just under your arms. Make a double knot."

Gabe did what Mee Mee told him. She wrapped the rope around her waist and then tied the end to a post. She yanked on it to make sure it would hold.

She spread her legs and held the rope with both hands. "Okay, Sport. I've got this end. Step off and I'll pull you up."

Gabe stared down at the ocean. The waves crashed against the pilings below. He glanced up at Mee Mee.

"Come on, Sport. You can do it. I got you."

His stomach filled with butterflies. He took a deep breath, gripped the rope tightly, stepped off the edge, and dropped toward the ocean. The rope jolted him, and he swung like a monkey on a vine. Mee Mee stood above him, gritting her teeth and holding the rope as he dangled there. The edge of the pier was about four or five feet above him. Mee Mee backed up and raised him until he could reach the splintered wood. Inch by inch she edged backwards, helping him to climb onto the walkway.

He stood and dusted himself off. Mee Mee untied the rope, and together they walked back along the rickety pier being careful to step over the gaps where the boards were missing. They made their way through the fishing tackle store and stood at the top of the ramp. Smoke poured into the sky from the yellow beach house, and flames shot out of the windows. Several neighbors stood on the street, making calls on their cell phones. Gabe watched the fire climb the side of the house and remembered being trapped in the bathroom.

"Mee Mee," Gabe said.

"Yeah, Sport."

"Why did you come rescue me?"

"I didn't want to lose my little angel, now did I? Something inside of me kept me going."

"Was it God?"

"I guess you could say God gave a job to do, and I did it." She patted the top of his head. "What made you throw the teddy bear into the ocean?"

"Same as you."

The top of the dunes suddenly brightened. Gabe and Mee Mee turned to see the sun rising over the ocean, blazing the blue-green water with a brilliant orange streak.

34

Dugan hadn't felt this unsure of himself in years. It had been two weeks since the hurricane. At times it seemed like it was all a dream—the investigation, the kidnapping, the rescue and flight to West Virginia, all that time spent with Marla. He had needed a couple weeks to get things back to normal. Now he faced new possibilities. He wondered if his life was about to be turned upside-down again. As he pulled into Marla's driveway, he noticed a brand new red Jeep Liberty 4 x 4. Dugan chuckled to himself. *Mee Mee must have picked up her new car.*

Dugan reached for the two gift bags, a small one and a bigger one, sitting on the passenger seat. He got out of the Impala, closed the door, and trotted up the front steps. His stomach didn't feel quite right. Was it the blueberry pancakes he scarfed down at T.L.'s Country Kitchen or was he just nervous? The pancakes were delicious. Had to be the nerves. Before he could reach the doorbell, the door flew open, and Gabe popped into view.

"Hey, Dugan! I've been waiting for you. Come on in."

"What's up, Sport?"

"Mee Mee's here. Follow me. They're in the kitchen."

Dugan trailed the boy, who hopped, skipped, and jumped his way toward the kitchen. Mee Mee, sitting across the table from Marla, glanced up from a newspaper. Dugan nodded at the women, and Marla smiled. Oh, that smile, Dugan thought. It gets me every time.

Gabe plopped onto a seat and opened a picture book. "Mee Mee brought me a new shark book. Looky here—a great white."

"Cool." Dugan noticed a large blue-gray shark on the page, mouth wide open and full of sharp teeth. "Maybe you'll catch a great white next time we go fishing."

"That would be awesome." Gabe lifted the book, spread open so they could see. "Dun . . . dun dun . . . dun dun dun . . .dun dun dun . . . dun dun dun."

"Listen to this," Mee Mee adjusted the newspaper. "The third victim of the Frisco beach house fire, Adam Pemberton, died on Friday morning at the Mount Sinai Medical Center in New York City. Pemberton, a billionaire, was the CEO of Medic-Ready Pharmaceuticals. Pemberton survived for twelve days after suffering third-degree burns over seventy-five percent of his body. Two other Pharmaceutical CEOs perished in the blaze which investigators believe was started by careless smoking." Mee Mee folded the newspaper and tossed it onto the table. "That's got to be one of the worst ways to die. I'd much rather drown."

Dugan rubbed his chin. "As far as I know that's everyone who injected the serum. They all died."

Marla sat back and clasped her hands behind her head. "Everyone that is except for Pugach. We don't know what happened to him."

Dugan said, "Chances are he found Davey Jones' locker unless he's one heck of a swimmer."

"He's dead, too. I'm sure of it," Mee Mee said.

"How do you know?" Marla asked.

"I overheard some fishermen talking while I was at Conner's Supermarket yesterday. Said they were out about two miles the day after the hurricane when they spotted someone thrashing in the water, yelling and screaming. They turned the boat and headed in that direction, but they were too late. A couple bull sharks had pulled the guy under and tore him apart. By the time they got there all that was left was an arm which they managed to scoop up in a net. It was covered with tattoos."

Marla scooted up to the table. "But lots of men have tattoos on their arms."

Mee Mee shook her head. "I interrupted the men and asked if one of the tattoos was a skull with a crown. They looked at me like I was psychic. One of them tapped the side of his bicep, nodded, and said, 'Right there—a skull with a crown, smoking a cigar.'"

Marla gasped and put her hand to her mouth. "I saw that tattoo on Pugach's arm."

"I did, too," Mee Mee said.

"Looky here." Gabe flipped through the pages of the book and planted his finger on a gray shark with a white belly. It had a huge dorsal fin and side fins. "This is a bull shark. Did the ugly man get eaten by these kinds of sharks?"

"I believe so," Mee Mee said.

Gabe's eyes narrowed, his forehead scrunching. "They must've been really hungry to eat *him*."

"He probably gave them indigestion," Marla said.

Dugan's eyes met Marla's, and he tried not to laugh but couldn't help it. He didn't want Gabe to think the death of a human being was a trivial thing, even if the person was evil.

Smiling, Mee Mee stood, stepped away from the table, and eyed Dugan. "Have a seat, Sheriff Walton. It looks like you have a couple fancy gift bags to pass out. I've got to be on my way. A bookseller's work is never done."

After saying their goodbyes, Mee Mee departed, and Dugan slid the two bags to the middle of the table.

"Is one for me?" Gabe asked.

Dugan bobbed his head. "The big bag."

"Awww, I was hoping for the big bag," Marla said.

Gabe snatched the bag, reached inside, and pulled out a teddy bear. It had a patch over its eye and a captain's hat. "It's just like Blackie!"

Dugan pointed at the bear's belly. "Check out what's inside."

Gabe hurriedly unzipped the bear's belly, inserted his hand, and tugged out a yellow towel. "A Terrible Towel! Thanks, Dugan." Gabe clutched the towel and bear with one arm, slid off his seat, rounded the table, and gave Dugan a big neck hug with his free arm.

"Where did you find those items?" Marla asked. "Not around here I would guess."

Dugan shook his head. "You can get about anything you want on the internet nowadays."

Marla raised her eyebrows. "That's true."

"I'm taking Blackie Number Two into my room," Gabe exclaimed. He bolted around the corner, his footsteps pattering down the hall.

Marla reached for the smaller bag, a purple one with lavender tissue paper sprouting from the top. She picked it up and shook it. "Let me guess. A new box of bullets for target practice?"

"Not quite."

"Pepper spray?"

"You have to open it and see for yourself."

Marla withdrew the tissue paper, reached in, and pulled out a small pirate teddy bear. "Awww, Dugan." She sat it on the table in front of her. "How cute."

"That's not all."

Marla picked up the bag and inspected it. "Nothing else in here." She eyed the little bear. "I get it." She picked up the bear and found the hidden zipper on its belly. With her fingers she wiggled out a small box. "What's this?"

Dugan took a deep breath. *Settle down, stomach.*

When Marla took the lid off the box, her eyes grew wide. "Dugan! It's . . . it's a diamond ring!"

Outer Banks Murder Series - Book 1:
Murder at Whalehead by Joe C. Ellis
Excerpt from Chapter 1
Now available on Nook and Kindle

Laura Redinger drew in a deep breath and let it out haltingly, trying not to cry. She listened—silence, except for the wash of water around the piers supporting the old boathouse. Her arms ached, but yanking the chains as hard as she could didn't budge the U-bolts that kept her spread eagled against the wooden plank wall. The cuffs on her ankles had dug into her skin, bloodying her feet.

"Somebody help me!" she yelled. No answer. A single light bulb dangled from a wire slung from the middle rafter, casting deep and distorted shadows from the objects around the room—the slats of crab cages, lengths of thick rope, floaters and netting hanging from the cavernous ceiling, the spokes of her wheels and handlebars against the opposite wall.

Why did he bring me here? He must be a psycho. "Oh God please, somebody help me," she whimpered. She took another breath and screamed. Her throat hurt from yelling. *He wants to kill me. I know it. I could see it in his eyes. But where'd he go?* Concentrating, she slowed her breathing and listened. Footsteps. Coming up the walkway from shore. "Help me! Somebody help me! Who's out there?"

The door creaked on its hinges.

She stared into the dark opening. "Whoever you are, please get me out of here."

Earlier that day Laura Redinger pedaled her blue mountain bike north along Route 12 into a strong headwind. The salty breeze winnowed her long auburn hair. She should have ponytailed it with a scrunchy, but that would have been too confining. Today, June second, she was truly free. Today she turned twenty-one.

A red Camaro zoomed by, and a longhaired teenage boy stuck his head out the passenger-side window and yelled, "Hey, sweet mama!"

She eyed him, smiled, but didn't wave. Too young. She was an adult now. If she wanted, she could stop in Grouper's Grill at the Timbuktu Plaza and chug down a Bud Lite without having to worry about a fake I.D. But she would rather keep riding. Biking toned her body for bikini season.

Outer Banks Murder Series - Book 2:
Murder at Hatteras by Joe C. Ellis
Excerpt from Chapter 1
Now available on Nook and Kindle

The nylon rope felt good in his grip. When he pulled it taut, it constricted his hands causing that pin-prickly feeling in his fingertips. He closed his eyes and imagined tying it around a slender wrist and lashing it to a bedpost. The vision excited him. He drew in a deep breath, the salty air filling his lungs, and exhaled slowly. The fantasy faded as the breeze from the ocean picked up and cooled his face. He opened his eyes and scanned the shoreline. The Cape Hatteras Lighthouse shot a beam above the waves out to sea. Night had arrived.

He let go of one end of the rope and reached on top of his head for the mask. His fingers brushed over the horns, grasped the forehead, and tugged slowly downward until he could see through the eyeholes. The papier-mâché felt rough against his cheeks. Sliding his hand over the jaw line, he sensed grape forms and the grooves of the beard. *Dionysus.* He had just downed a bottle of Mogan David. The smell of the sweet wine intensified as he breathed against the mask.

At his feet two ghost crabs scampered towards the surf. The full moon's glow lit the leading edge of the water as it rushed up the bank engulfing the crabs, then withdrawing, dragging them into the ocean. He turned away from the black and white striped tower and headed north along the shore towards the apartments. The stretch of beach before him was empty. *Good. No one to notice me. This could be the night I tie a few things up.* He snapped the rope like a whip. An ache of desire quivered through him. *I'm tired of watching someone else have all the fun. I'm ready to rope and ride.*

It was warm for early October, mid-sixties. The short walk up the beach caused beads of sweat to trickle down his forehead and cheeks. The black warm up suit didn't help. "It's like a sauna under this thing," he said. His voice sounded creepy, distorted by the electronic device he had inserted into the mouth opening. The oddness of its tone stirred his wicked frame of mind even more. He slid the mask up and wiped the sweat from his face. The sea breeze refreshed him. When he peered across the dunes he saw the four-unit apartment house, its walkway

3

zigzagging through the sea oats to the beach. He twirled the nylon towrope, allowing it to slap the sand at intervals as he approached the walkway.

At the steps he grabbed the wooden handrail then hesitated to peer down the narrow boardwalk that traversed the dunes. He focused on the downstairs apartment about forty yards away. The bedroom window glowed in the shadows under the second-story deck. The blinds were wide open. *She's stretched out on that bed. And he's gone.* For a moment he considered walking away, denying this dark craving that had been growing ever since the couple had arrived. He'd crossed that line only once before, but oh, what a charge it gave him. Was it too late now that he'd done the deed, forced himself on an unwilling woman? Lately, fantasizing about it consumed him, especially with her—a girl he wanted so badly but could never have. His hands trembled, so he wound the end of the rope around his free hand and yanked it tight. The nylon dug into the latex. The pain steeled him. After snapping the rope several times, he mounted the steps and headed down the walkway.

He descended the steps to a sandy path that cut through sea oats and ended at the lower section of the house, which served as a laundry room for all four apartments. No one had turned on outside spotlights yet; the darkness under the lower deck made it hard to see the laundry room entrance. *The darker the better.* The back decks didn't have stair access. To ascend he had to climb the two-by-six crossbeams that created X-es between the deck's supporting posts. Climbing wasn't his specialty, but he'd manage as quietly as possible. He hung the towrope around his neck and tied it with a simple knot to free his hands. Grabbing an upper crossbeam, he tested its soundness. *Should hold me.* He lifted his foot, placed it halfway up the board, pulled himself up, and secured his other foot where the boards crossed. *Halfway there.* Repeating the maneuver, he rose to deck level and scissored one leg over the railing. He shifted his weight, hearing a plank creak, and carefully pulled the other leg over.

The bedroom window was only three feet to his left. He pressed his back to the wall and edged to it, then craned his neck to take a peek. She sat on the bed, back propped on a pillow against the headboard. Her short, black negligee clung to her svelte body, red panties slightly exposed. In her hands she held a book, a thick paperback that rested against her knees. She wore blue-framed, chic glasses, and a tress of her dark brown hair had caught on the rim's corner and slashed across her cheek. Her beauty stalled his desperate lust the way light stuns unprepared eyes. He stared for many seconds without thinking.

When his hands began trembling again, he grasped the towrope and untied the knot. Wrapping it around one hand then the other and pulling tight sent a bite of pain across his knuckles and snapped him back to the task at hand. He eyed the space of the open window and the bottom of the frame where he could grasp and lift. But the screen still blocked his entrance. With the window open he could plow through the screen like a monster out of the darkness. *Get ready*. He slid his hand along the frame and lifted slightly. The window budged a fraction of an inch.

She glanced up from her book and yelled, "Gabe is that you!"

Ohio Valley Mystery Series - Book 1:
The Healing Place by Joe C. Ellis
Excerpt from Chapter 1
Now available on Nook and Kindle

Joshua Thompson and his buddy, Billy McGlumphy crouched at the edge of the woods and watched Elijah Mulligan walk along the path through the meadow and up the hill. White butterflies danced and flickered just above the tall yellow grass. They could hear him singing in a deep voice the song about the old rugged cross. He sang loudly like he did in church on Sunday mornings. Because the man was so huge and always wore bib overalls, Joshua thought he looked like Hillbilly Bubba, the professional wrestler. Billy had told Joshua that Mulligan had killed a man with his bare hands, claiming his father told him so. Joshua wondered if it was true. Billy made things up sometimes. When Mr. Mulligan reached the top of the hill, he pushed aside leafy branches and stepped between two tall trees, disappearing into the shadows of the woods.

"What's up there, Doc?" Billy asked.

"That must be the place he walks to every morning. We gotta check it out. I bet he's hiding something up there," Joshua said.

"How do you know?"

"I'm smarter than the average bear. Come on, Boo Boo." Joshua stood and bounded into the sunlight.

"Wait," Billy said. "What if he sees us in the open field?" But Joshua had already picked up his pace, trotting up the path toward the top of the hill. Billy jumped to his feet and ran to catch up. When they reached the top they dropped to their hands and knees and crawled through the grass to the edge of the woods. Joshua could hear Elijah talking to someone. To the left Joshua saw a patch of thick blackberry bushes. He nudged Billy's shoulder and motioned for him to follow. Like an army ranger, Joshua scooted silently across the ground on his belly until he entered the thick growth.

To see into the woods, Joshua reached up and pulled the branch away in front of him. His eyes widened and heart pounded when he saw Mr. Mulligan aglow in the rays. He stood in the middle of a circular opening, hands clasped just below his chin. Sunlight sifted down through the branches, a thousand beams splashing over the man like a rock star on stage. The light spots dotted his shoulders, chest, curly brown beard and long hair that rimmed the bald top. A sudden breeze blew, trembling the bushes around Joshua and scattering leaves across the clearing. He heard Billy's teeth chattering so he raised his finger to his lips, and Billy clamped his mouth shut. The wind calmed, and with the stillness came silence. A chipmunk near the bottom of a big tree froze, clutching an acorn.

"Now it's time to bring up that old subject again, Lord," Elijah Mulligan said. His eyes closed, and his head swiveled back and forth as he spoke. "Some days I hate to think about it, but I know there's something you want me to do. It's just . . . Oh, hell's fire. It's just that the man scares me a little. There. I admit it. That feller gives me the creeps. Forgive me for judging a man before I truly know him, but I just don't trust the rascal." His head lifted, but his eyes remained shut. The beams from the tops of the trees lit his face. "I need some guts, Lord. I know you want me to stop by his house and talk to him—invite him to church. I've put it off long enough. Since Easter." He lifted his arms, positioning his hands in front of his face, and the rays filtered though his fingers. "Years ago I did plenty of bad things. He can't be much worse than I was. I know you washed the black stain of sin away, but the scars are still there. They remind me of the second chance you gave me. That's why I gotta talk to that strange feller. Perhaps you want to give him another chance."

He lowered his hands and head. "Go before me, Lord, and open the door." Clenching his fists, he said, "Give me the courage to approach the gates of Hell and snatch a soul from Lucifer himself. In the good Lord's name I pray. Amen."

Ohio Valley Mystery Series - Book 2:
The First Shall Be Last by Joe C. Ellis
Excerpt from Chapter 1
Now available on Nook and Kindle

The bodies rotted for two days in the tropical heat. Judd Stone swiped sweat from his eyes. From the top of his shell hole he gazed across Horseshoe Valley. Coral ridges and mesas loomed on all sides. The stench sickened him. He could never get used to the smell of death. Twenty Marines lay scattered across the field, swarms of fat blowflies buzzing above the bloated corpses. The wild palms that once covered the hillsides were now splintered stumps, peels of white bark drooping from their trunks.

Stone's good buddy, Private Emery Snowfield, lay between two black stretcher-bearers, his exposed viscera crawling with maggots. *Sonovabitch.* Stone shook his head. *Thievin' sonovabitch.*

Glancing down, Stone spotted his canteen next to three empty ammunition cans. He snatched the container and shook it. *Not even a gulp left.* After screwing off the top, he drained the last drops into his mouth, tried to swallow, gagged and coughed.

A slight movement to his left startled him and he dropped the canteen. In an instant he whipped his M-1 to his shoulder and panned the barrel across the draw.

Eyes wide and ears attuned, he inspected the carnage for an infiltrating Jap. His heart thumped in his throat. When Josiah Jackson, one of the black stretcher-bearers, rolled over, Stone almost fired. Jackson opened his eyes and lifted his chin.

"What the hell?" Stone whispered.

The lanky Negro reached his hand toward him, his large brown eyes pleading.

"You're dead!" Stone yelled. "You thievin' sonovabitch. You're dead!"

Jackson stumbled to his feet, but before he could take a step, small arms fire erupted from the hillsides, the bullets snapping and popping into the coral around him. He staggered towards Stone, hands outstretched. Bullets ripped through his already tattered dungarees. One caught the side of his helmet, flipping it off his head. It clanked on the ground in front of Jackson, and he kicked it toward Stone.

Stone's eyes narrowed as he watched the bullets ripping through Jackson, tearing off chunks of flesh. "Go down," Stone said. "Go down, you bastard."

Five feet away Jackson tripped and crumpled onto the sharp coral. The firing stopped. He lay motionless. Stone took a deep breath and exhaled slowly. Jackson raised his head. "Help me, Stone," he groaned.

The dead can't talk. You can't be alive. No way.

Half of Jackson's left ear had been shot off. When the black man lifted his hand, Stone could see two fingers missing. Stone surveyed the hillsides, expecting more enemy fire to finish Jackson off. Instead he heard the agonizing scuffling of the wounded man inching across razor-edged coral. Their gazes met—Jackson' eyes glistening. Maggots infested the open wounds on his face.

"I'm going crazy," Stone said. "This can't be happening."
Jackson's words were barely audible: "I've got . . ." He crawled closer. " . . . a three-year-old son." His shoulders rose as he thrust with his legs and edged forward on his flayed forearms. "Why did you . . . why did . . ." Within two feet of Stone, Jackson collapsed, air hissing from his lungs like a tire going flat.

Stone swallowed and released his breath, his ribcage quivering. He dropped his rifle and leaned on the side of the crater. "Jackson," he whispered. "Jackson." He reached over the rim of the shell hole and touched Jackson's hand—the one with the gold watch. "Why'd you do it, Jackson?" Stone slid his fingers around the face of the watch and tugged until the band slid over the bloody hand. Stone drew it near his mouth and blew the coral dust from the glass cover. He turned the watch over and read the inscription: *First Marine Division Middle Weight Champion.*

Jackson's hands shot toward Stone as if propelled by rockets. They clamped around Stone's neck. His airway shut off, Stone dropped the watch and gripped Jackson's wrists but couldn't dislodge the chokehold. Blackness swallowed Stone's vision of Jackson's grimace. Twitching and jerking, Stone gave one last yank, ripping the hands away. He gulped air. Something to his right beeped rapidly. When he opened his eyes, he saw the heart monitor next to his bed, the digital readout flashing 155 bpm.

About the Author

Joe C. Ellis, a big fan of the North Carolina's Outer Banks, grew up in the Ohio Valley. A native of Martins Ferry, Ohio, he attended West Liberty State College in West Virginia and went on to earn his Master's Degree in education from Muskingum College in New Concord, Ohio. He has been employed by Martins Ferry City Schools for the last thirty-three years where he currently teaches art and computer graphics at Martins Ferry High School. He also has been lay preaching for the Presbyterian Church U.S.A. for the last twenty-one years. He pastors two churches in the Martins Ferry area, the Scotch Ridge Presbyterian Church and the Colerain Presbyterian Church.

His writing career began in 2001 with the publication of his first novel, *The Healing Place*. In 2007 he began the Outer Banks Murder Series with the publication of *Murder at Whalehead* and in 2010 *Murder at Hatteras*. The popularity of this series continues to grow with his 2012 installment, *Murder on the Outer Banks*.

Joe credits family vacations on the Outer Banks with the inspiration for these stories. Joe and his wife, Judy, have three children and three grandsons. Although the kids have flown the nest, they get together often and always make it a priority to vacation on the Outer Banks whenever possible. He comments, "It's a place on the edge of the world, a place of great beauty and sometimes danger—the ideal setting for murder mysteries."

One of Joe's passions is distance running. *Murder on the Outer Banks* opens with a 5K footrace in which an older man runs to victory against much younger competition. In the last year (2011) Joe has posted 5k times and half marathon times at the national class level for his age group. Because running definitely keeps him younger physically and mentally, he enjoyed writing a novel with these themes as important threads in the plot. Joe hopes to continue to write stories set on the Outer Banks and run along its beaches for many years to come.

Printed in the United States

ISBN 978-0-9796655-4-7

51595

9 780979 665547